The Tears of Monterini

The
Tears
of
Monterini

Amanda Weinberg

Red Door

Published by RedDoor
www.reddoorpress.co.uk

ISBN 978-1-913062-36-1

A CIP catalogue record for this book is available from the British
Library

Cover design: Clare Connie Shepherd
www.clareconnieshepherd.com

Typesetting: Jen Parker, Fuzzy Flamingo
www.fuzzyflamingo.co.uk

Printed and bound in Great Britain by Clays Ltd, Elcograf S.p.A.

For Natasha for believing in this book, and for Elena

In love is found the secret in divine unity.
It is love that unites the higher
and the lower stages of existence,
that raises the lower to the level of the higher –
where all become fused into one.

The Zohar

PART ONE

A Perfect Place: 1921-1929

CHAPTER 1

Monterini 1921

S ilence weighed as heavy as the heat.

It was the hour of siesta. Olive trees balancing on the parched earth provided shelter for sagging vines. Beyond the river, a golden mound of *tufo* burst heavenwards. From the seams of this limestone rock Monterini sprouted; hectic, unplanned, a mélange of rooftops and church spires.

The sun sliced through gaps between houses, toasting washing draped across poles in every *via* and *vicolo*. To remain outside in the sweltering afternoon was considered foolhardy, so the villagers escaped to the coolness of their homes, the comfort of their beds.

Except for two men.

In one of the cobbled streets that crisscrossed the village they waited, in silence. Unaware of the dust settling on his clothes, Jacobo Levi sat on a wooden stool, lower back pressed against a stone wall. His suit and shirt clung to his back. He loosened his tie and reached up to remove his hat. He used it to fan his face, then with the back of his hand, wiped away the garland of sweat moistening his forehead. He breathed deeply, staring ahead of him at the black shutters of his house. He replaced his hat on his head and from the inside of his jacket pocket, removed a small, leather-bound prayer book. He thumbed through the pages, lips moving silently. '*Eso Enei. Eso Enei.*'

Next to him, shuffling on a stool too small for his limbs sat his neighbour Angelo Ghione. He was gazing up at a house with grey shutters. The skin of Angelo's face was pockmarked and toughened by the sun. His hair, the colour and texture of sand, was covered with a cloth cap. His blue overalls were pinned up with string. He was a farm worker, one of the *contadini*.

From Angelo's left hand hung a rosary. It was his mother's. Jacobo knew Angelo had carried it with him since the day she'd died, hiding it in his pocket, so no one would notice this female ritual. Now his fingers shamelessly played with the tiny, black beads.

Angelo shook his head from side to side muttering, 'What a heat wave, I could do with a drink.' His eyes wandered up and down Via Meravigliosa as if hoping a door would open and a neighbour would spare a mouthful of pasta, a sip of espresso. Jacobo smiled, then returned his gaze to his prayer book. The streets remained silent save for the pattering of a dog's paws on the San Gianni path.

The houses were set back from the street, reached by a flight of uneven steps. Like a bridge across two continents a veranda stretched from the black to the grey door, uniting them. Terracotta pots of geraniums covered the chipped, tiled floor and sunflowers trailed over the iron railing supporting the steps.

Behind the grey door lived Angelo Ghione and his wife Santina. Behind the other lived the Levis. To escape from the sweltering heat, Jacobo and Angelo had moved their stools into the cool shade of the narrow street. Here, they waited as the hours mingled into the stillness of the afternoon.

A scream disturbed the tranquillity. Jacobo raised his gaze towards the black shutters of his wife's bedroom; they remained tightly closed. Angelo made the sign of the cross and peered at the shutters of his house. A hand appeared between them, wrinkled, covered with brown liver spots, and moved the shutters apart. They flew open and a face appeared, red with uncombed hair pressed against the forehead. It was Clara Todi, the village midwife.

'Angelo. *Un maschio. Vieni.*' Voice and face faded into the blackness of the room.

The two men turned their heads towards each other. Their eyes met. Angelo removed his cap and wiped the sweat gathering at his temples. His rosary slipped from his grasp, the beads cascading down the cobbled street in a ripple of coloured waves. He picked up and kissed the small, silver cross.

'Thank you, Virgin Mary, mother of God.'

Jacobo closed his Hebrew prayer book and placed it in his suit pocket. 'So, yours is first then,' he chanted as if still praying.

'A son? My son? And so soon!' A ladder of creases appeared at the corner of Angelo's eyes. He attempted to rise but sank back onto his stool. 'My legs are shaking; I can hardly stand.'

'*Vieni*, I'll help you.' Jacobo placed one hand under Angelo's elbow and the other behind his back. Resting his lips close to Angelo's ears, he whispered, '*auguri*' and guided him up the crooked steps, around the flowerpots and through the grey door into the kitchen. The stone floor was sprinkled with flour and, in the centre of the table, a bowl lay on its side; the ingredients for a *crostata* Santina had been baking smoothed the edges.

Jacobo and Angelo crossed into the sitting room and climbed the stairs up to the first floor. At the door of the bedroom Angelo shared with Santina, Clara Todi waited, a whimpering bundle nestled in her chubby arms. Face streaked with blotches, she greeted them.

'*Auguri* Angelino. You're a father now. Meet your son.' Passing the baby over to Angelo, she added, with a mixture of pride and pleasure, 'To think I delivered you both. And now your children!'

'And Santina? How is she?'

'*Benissimo*. She's a strong woman, that wife of yours. Go in and see her now, *vai*.' Turning to Jacobo, she patted his arm and said with a smile, 'Not long for you now, Jacobo Levi. No doubt your Bella's persuaded her baby to wait until I'm good and ready! She knows what she wants that one. He'll be out in no time, don't you worry.'

Jacobo and Angelo peered into the blanket nestling in Angelo's arms. Charcoal eyes gazed back at the two men. Angelo struggled to speak; words seemed to hang on his lips like invisible burdens.

'Enrico,' he whispered finally. 'Enrico... because now my life is richer.'

The sun sank low in the sky; an orange glow tinged the clouds. Via Meravigliosa throbbed with early evening energy; women happily sauntered in and out of Angelo's house to greet the new baby, carrying trays of *crostini* and *minestra* for Santina. Men clinked glasses of Chianti. From across the street, Pino Petri the blacksmith, cradling a donkey's hoof in one hand, nodded at Jacobo.

'It will be Bella's turn soon Jacobo, you'll see.' Pino plied off the old shoe, replacing it with gleaming new metal.

'Let's hope it's not too long.' Jacobo's voice barely rose above the clamour. He attempted a smile. The fragrance of sweet bread and braised beef mingled with the smelting of iron and the smell of cats' spray.

He returned his gaze to his prayer book, eyes darting from one psalm to the next. His heart continued to bang in his chest, the muscles around his throat tightened. If only prayer would take away the worry of waiting. He removed the round-rimmed spectacles from his nose and looked around him. An air of celebration drifted through the streets of the Fratta, the area on the west side of the village, where sunsets painted the skies. Palatial buildings bordered dilapidated hovels; rosy-cheeked statues of the Madonna adjoined houses with *mezuzahs* pinned to their doorposts.

It was a mélange of class and wealth.

And religion.

The news of the double pregnancy had spread around Monterini quicker than a fire in the vineyards. Every Monterinese was aware that the Levi-Ghione babies were due within the same month. The villagers from both sides of the religious divide were convinced that God in his mercy had blessed the families simultaneously. And about time for the Levi family, Jacobo heard them utter under their breath, what with the loss of Jacobo's two older brothers during the Great War. But for labour to arrive to Santina and Bella on the same day, was more religious intervention than the village could contain. The news drifted, not only through the gaps of every shutter in Monterini, but over the mountains to the villages of Montore and Favore, sliding through the slits of each doorway. *Contadini*, businessmen, children and housewives waited with bated breath for the arrival of baby Levi.

And they waited, amidst the chaos that was early evening.

The sun slid behind the hills, staining the sky pink. Angelo joined Jacobo on the veranda. They gazed up at the black shutters; they remained tightly closed. Around them a group of women, pinafores tied around their waists, swept the cobblestones. Signora Petri, the blacksmith's wife, unpegged the washing stretching across Via Meravigliosa, worn hands smoothing the fabric, folding it into neat piles. Men with shirtsleeves rolled up to their elbows, stretched out on metal chairs reading the evening paper. Spirals of cigarette smoke curled above the smart hats and cloth caps. Children still played in the street, some sat together drawing chalk circles on the stones, others collected pails of water from the stone fountains at either end of Via Meravigliosa.

Jacobo's prayer book lay unopened on his lap. He twiddled with the gold wedding band on the fourth finger of his left hand. He couldn't stop the thoughts from flitting through his prayers like irritating insects. He wondered whether his son would be blessed with the deep, inky eyes and strong Levi jaw that he had inherited. Would his son and Enrico pass the bonds of friendship from one generation of neighbours to the next, just as Jacobo and Angelo and their fathers had done? After six generations of sons there was no doubt in Jacobo's mind that Bella would give birth to a boy. But could he love him as much as he loved his Bella, his beautiful wife? The thought disturbed him, so he pushed it away.

The black door opened. Cosimo Levi, Jacobo's father, stepped on to the veranda. He wore the same round-rimmed spectacles and shared the long, straight nose and sculptured cheekbones that were the Levi trademark. But Cosimo's hair was white and his short beard was speckled with grey. His knuckles were swollen with arthritis and when he spoke, he breathed heavily into the night air.

'It won't be long, *mio figlio*.' Cosimo placed a wizened arm around Jacobo's shoulder and nodded towards the end of the street. 'Looks like you have some company.'

Jacobo squinted into the distance. Striding down Via Meravigliosa from the Ghetto district, Rabbi Coen led a procession of followers wearing skullcaps and holding prayer books.

'Jacobo!' the rabbi shouted as he approached. 'We thought a few extra souls might be helpful tonight. So, we'll perform *maariv* here in the street with you.'

Jacobo sighed. Coen had been the rabbi for as long as he

could remember, his beard like whisked egg whites and his smiling eyes never seemed to age as the years passed. Neither did his casual attempts to engage Jacobo in the service seem to tire. But that night relief flooded through Jacobo at the sight of the rabbi and his men.

The group came to a halt at the bottom of the stone steps leading to the veranda. Pulling their prayer shawls over their heads they faced east for the evening service. Backwards and forwards they shuffled, heads low as Hebrew prayers floated over the rooftops, fusing with church bells and the mating call of crickets.

Midnight crept into the early hours. The stream of supporters dwindled; only Jacobo and Angelo remained in the empty street. From behind the black shutters, screams pierced the night air. Jacobo raised his eyes to Monte Amiata shrouded in the black night and mouthed the words of the prayer *Eso Enei*:

'I raise my eyes to the hills from whence comes my strength. My strength comes from the Lord.'

But Bella's screams echoed wild and endless. Jacobo placed his hands over his ears.

'I can see her waving at me,' he said.

'Don't be silly!' Angelo's hand fumbled in his pocket for the rosary beads, but they sparkled like jewels in the cracks beneath his feet. He made the sign of the cross and stared up at the shuttered room. 'You're exhausted, that's all, it makes you see things.'

'Bella.' Jacobo pointed towards the mountains, dark and eerie in the quiet night. 'It's Bella. Can't you see her? She's over there.'

'Don't worry, Dottore Mazzola's there. And old Dottore Vetrulli. They'll look after her, you'll see.'

'But can't you see her?' Jacobo grasped Angelo's shirtsleeve and pointed beyond the two houses, where the valley full of

Etruscan tombs lay hidden in the darkness. 'Look, Angelo, in the moonlight. She's blowing kisses to me.'

'No Jacobo, you can hear screams. It's childbirth. Listen.' Angelo placed his finger to his lips.

'She's going, Angelo. I know it, I feel it.' Jacobo tapped his heart. He pointed into the distance. '*Eccola*. There she is.'

He sprung from his stool, knocking it against the wall of his house and ran across the veranda. Flinging open the front door, he crossed the kitchen where jars of rice and flour sat orderly on shelves, polished and clean. The tiled floor sparkled, chairs were placed neatly around the solid, oak table. He sprinted upstairs to the bedroom, pummelled at the locked door.

'Let me in.'

'You can't come in, Jacobo. The doctors are here.' There was the sound of clunking metal and Clara Todi appeared in front of him, her face the colour of slate, eyebrows knitted together.

'But I have to.' Jacobo jammed her against the open door as he fought past her. Her chubby hand grabbed his hair, his arm, his suit jacket. He shook himself free.

The screams faded as quickly as morning mist.

From the arms of Dottore Mazzola came a bleating sound, like lambs, Jacobo thought. He stared at the bed. Bella, nightgown ripped and bloodied, was draped across the sheets; layers of hair like autumn leaves tumbled around her pale face, with its arched eyebrows and soft, pink lips. Her body motionless, legs covered with blood. Shy, beautiful Bella with flashing, green eyes and hair that rippled like the Fiorina waterfall at sunset. His Bella, who barely one year ago promised to bear his children, love him forever.

Jacobo sank to his knees, arms reaching towards his dead wife. He opened his mouth to scream but there was no sound.

It was the twenty-first of June 1921, the day Jacobo became a widower. And a father.

The new day dawned like any other. Streaks of crimson chequered the rooftops and the village stirred. Smells of brewing coffee flickered on the nostrils of those still sleeping. As the sun's rays danced on the stained-glass window of the Beit Israel Synagogue, life began again.

But not for Jacobo.

He sat on the rocking chair in the sitting room overlooking the silvery leaves of the olive trees. All around him everything seemed the same; the vase of cornflowers he had collected with Bella on the San Gianni path two days earlier; the acres of books lining the shelves on every wall of the sitting room; the ticking of the clock on the mantelpiece. The day before he had been filled with love. Now all that remained of that love was air.

Angry bleats of sound punched the silent room. Jacobo flinched but his body remained rooted to the chair. The front door slammed. A chair screeched in the kitchen as it was pushed sideways, heavy footsteps crossed the stone floor. Angelo appeared in front of Jacobo, his eyes shadowed with half-moons, his straw hair tousled. Deep grooves littered his pockmarked skin.

'I've brought you coffee and some *cornetti*.' Angelo touched Jacobo's arm and unwrapped the pastries, still warm from the oven. 'They're from Signor Carlo. He heard the news this morning, in the bakery.'

Jacobo tightened his lips into a thin line. His fingers stroked a photograph of Bella on her wedding day. The angry bleats became louder, more forceful.

'Jacobo!' Angelo's eyes darted from nook to corner, resting finally on a wicker basket under the bookshelf. 'Your baby's crying. Can't you hear her?'

Angelo sank to his knees. He bent over the basket, reached out his thick arms, and gathered the baby into them. 'Why hasn't Dottore Mazzola sent a wet nurse?'

Jacobo's gaze focused on a point beyond the valley, where

Etruscan tombs glistened in the morning sunlight. He couldn't speak, couldn't think. Everything felt numb, deadened inside him.

Shaking his head, Angelo swept the screaming baby over his shoulder. He patted her with hands as large as vine leaves and smudged with purple stains. He walked back into the kitchen. The sound of water splattering onto porcelain mingled with the baby's cries.

Angelo reappeared in front of Jacobo. In one grape-stained hand he balanced the baby over his shoulder, in the other was a jug. Eyes blinking furiously he paused then threw the contents over Jacobo.

Jacobo sprang into the air.

Entangled sobs filled the room; father and child.

Footsteps creaked on the stairs. Cosimo stooped into the sitting room, rubbing his eyes. His hair had gathered more grey overnight, his skin hung loosely around his chin.

'What have you done?' Cosimo's wounded, tired eyes moved from Jacobo to Angelo, his mouth gaped open in shock. He stumbled towards Jacobo who was shaking the water from his clothes and hair, like one of the village dogs after a dip in the Piccolina river. Jacobo's fingers still clasped the gilt-framed photograph of Bella. Cosimo placed two hands on Jacobo's shoulders and smoothed back the wet locks of hair from Jacobo's forehead.

'*Mi dispiace, zio*.' Angelo gestured towards the floor. 'She's been crying, nobody heard her. I'm sorry, Jacobo, I just didn't know what to do.'

'I don't know what to do.' Jacobo spoke at last, hollow words, muffled with despair. His hand shook as he pointed to Angelo's shoulder. 'With her.'

'She's coming with me.' Angelo patted the baby's back. 'We'll find her a wet nurse, from here or Favore. For now, Santina will feed them both.'

Cosimo stepped in front of Angelo, chest heaving on his small frame, as if trying to keep his emotions at bay.

'Are you taking her away, Angelino?' he said.

'For a while. That's all.'

'Take her. I can't bear to look at her,' Jacobo whispered. He touched his face and felt the black stubble dotting his chin. He sensed that behind his round-rimmed spectacles, his eyes would appear vacant, lifeless, just like his Bella's.

With one hand clutching the baby, Angelo crossed himself. He gave Jacobo a long searching look, then turned. Stepping across the kitchen and out to the veranda, he returned to the house where life had triumphed.

⊚≫≪⊚

Upstairs, in the bedroom Angelo shared with Santina, light was just beginning to filter through the slits in the shutters, slicing the room with oblong patches of rose. Angelo stood at the door. Santina lay propped up against a pillow, dark hair loose around her pale neck. Her hair was usually hidden under a scarf, even when she slept. Her face beetroot red from the sun and working in the fields looked blotchy and blistered with purple shadows under her eyes. She was large limbed, much like his own mother, with heavy eyelids and an ample chest. But when she smiled, two hidden dimples appeared on her cheeks.

Now her eyes were shut, and long lashes brushed her cheekbones. A pinkish glow heightened her skin. How beautiful she looked, Angelo thought. He felt a stirring in his chest for this woman he'd married without giving it much thought. She'd been considered suitable by his father, and after a brief courtship they were united under the piercing eyes of Padre Giacomo at the cathedral in the village.

Soft gurgling sounds filled the room. Santina opened her

13

eyes and looked up at Angelo. In her arms lay Enrico, plump fingers clasping his mother's thumb.

'You both look so peaceful.' Angelo smiled.

As if to deliberately disturb the calm, the baby, wrapped in a yellow blanket in Angelo's arms, began to holler. Deep, stricken cries pulsated around them. Angelo pressed her against his shoulder and rubbed her back with wide, sweeping movements.

'I'm sorry, Santina, but here's another mouth to feed.' He placed the baby girl with flashing green eyes and skin as delicate as a butterfly's wing in Santina's arms next to his son.

Santina looked up at Angelo, diamonds of tears dusting her cheek. 'They'll be *fratelli di latte,* milk siblings.' Making the sign of the cross with her rough, worn hands, she added with a sob, 'Poor Bella, poor Jacobo.'

Angelo watched the baby search for Santina's nipple, tiny feet kicking, clenched fists punching.

'She has the eyes of an angel.'

'And the lungs of a devil.' Santina guided the baby's mouth towards her breast. 'She's going to be a handful, this one.'

Angelo nodded.

It was the death of one Bella; the birth of another.

CHAPTER 2

Jacobo sat on the veranda. Swirls of cigarette smoke wafted above his head. He inhaled deeply. In his lap lay a copy of the newspaper *La Stampa*. He was reading about *il Duce*'s latest exploit, an activity that had become his morning obsession. He glanced up and watched Bella playing a game of jacks with Rico. Hair of orange flames nestled in waves against her cheeks, and when she grasped the ball and jacks in one hand her lips spread into a smile. Every now and then she would look up at her father, eyes meeting fleetingly across the veranda, then quickly return her gaze to the game.

Jacobo sipped the coffee Signora Franca had made him. She was a widow from Capo Bagno and walked two streets to the Fratta, three mornings a week, to help with the household chores, cook *aquacotta,* chicken livers and creamed *baccalà* the way they liked it, in the traditional Jewish fashion. Lea Servini, the teacher in the elementary school and the sister of Jacobo's friend Davide, had suggested they shared her. With an absence of women, Cosimo and Jacobo had found themselves hurtling around in an unknown sea with a house to maintain and a child to care for. Jacobo had to admit that Signora Franca made life easier for him and his father, with her cheery manner and boundless energy, ordering the men around, spring cleaning the house and providing rules and order.

Jacobo looked up. Bella was there in front of him. Beside

her stood Rico, their fingers entwined. They stared at him; grass green eyes full of mischief that Jacobo still found disconcerting, and Rico's charcoal eyes, soft like those of the calves on Angelo's smallholding.

'We want to eat breakfast together on the veranda before we go to school,' Bella said in the Monterini dialect. 'Rico's eating polenta!'

'No, Bella.'

'*Per favore, babbo.*'

Cosimo peered around the black door of number 110 Via Meravigliosa. 'In this house it's pasta and Italian. And *cornetto* for breakfast eaten at the kitchen table.' He beckoned Bella into the kitchen. 'After breakfast, you must learn your Hebrew letters, Bella. You're up to *tet*, remember.'

'I want to eat polenta with Rico outside on the veranda.' Bella pointed towards Rico, gazing shyly at the square tiles of the veranda.

'But Signora Franca has prepared fresh *cornetto* and hot chocolate for your breakfast,' Jacobo replied.

Bella grabbed Rico's hand. Eyes narrowed, jaw clenched, she inched towards the Ghione side of the veranda.

'I said no!'

'But why not?' She stamped her foot.

There it came, the insistent manner Bella had of digging and pushing to get her own way. And she's only seven, Jacobo thought. He stared at her for a few moments, then stabbed the cigarette out with the heel of his shoe.

'Do what you want.' He tried to call out her name. As always it lodged in his throat, a sharp strip of glass. When she was born, he'd fought against calling her Bella. Not appropriate, he'd told Angelo a few days after the birth. Too painful.

But like most things in Jewish Monterini, the matter was discussed in the synagogue, in the bakery and in the bookshop.

'It's important to respect our customs, Jacobo,' Rabbi Coen had insisted during the seven-day mourning period of *shiva*. 'A baby is named after a dead relative.'

'Don't we have enough dead relatives to choose from, Rabbi?' Jacobo made a sweeping movement with his arm across the mantelpiece where the photographs of his mother, and brothers killed in the Great War, smiled back at him.

'*Dai* Jacobo.' Cosimo had encouraged him, leaning heavily on Jacobo's shoulder as if this would help him make the correct decision. 'What the rabbi says is right. It shows respect, a continuation of the generations. The baby will understand more clearly where she's come from.'

But Bella didn't seem to know where home really was. Was it the shiny black door with the silver *mezuzah* that Jacobo and Cosimo always kissed before entering the house; where they ate *challas* on Friday evenings and went to the synagogue on *Shabbat*? Or was it the door where grey paint flaked to the floor in twirls, behind which the laughter of Rico's twin brothers filled the air? In that house the furniture was chipped, wine was poured at breakfast and the Monterini dialect drifted out to the veranda. In the Levi home there were silver candlesticks, photographs and sadness. Only Italian was spoken. But Bella was a child of the alleyways; the dialect came naturally to her, threading her into the fabric of *contadino* life.

Jacobo readjusted his tie and walked into the kitchen. Very little had changed in the house. Cosimo had installed a washroom at the back so the washing could be done at home rather than down at the *lavatoio*. The kitchen with red tiles covering the floor, the large oak table and dresser lined with jars of ingredients had not changed since Bella had died. Jacobo always found that comforting.

He accepted another *caffelatte* from Signora Franca. She gave him a disapproving look. Was it because he was caught dreaming of the past and had probably ignored her offer of a second coffee, or because he had allowed Bella to do what she wanted?

He sat down at the table next to his father and picked at a *cornetto*. The flaky pastry brushed his lips.

'You need to be firmer with Bella, Jacobo.' Cosimo peered at his son with a look mixed with love and concern.

The sound of Rico and Bella's laughter echoed across the veranda. Signora Franca raised her eyebrows, her lips pursed.

'I'm not saying anything but...' She turned towards the stove and placed the warm pastries on Cosimo's plate. 'You're the father after all. And look at what she wears all the time. Boys' clothes!' Signora Franca pointed towards the children, the flesh of her upper arms hanging flabby and loose, reminding Jacobo of a flesh-coloured, upside down umbrella. 'That's not how *il Duce* likes young ladies to dress, you know, in dungarees and boots bought from the cobbler at the corner of the street.'

'Well, I do make sure she learns her Italian grammar,' Jacobo said indignantly as if it were the most important acquisition for a young girl growing up in an Italian village in central Italy, where dialect floated from the tongues of the locals. He ignored Signora Franca's comment regarding Mussolini's dress code and was secretly proud of Bella's insistence on dressing like a boy.

'There are other things to focus on besides Italian grammar,' Cosimo said, removing his spectacles and wiping them with the corner of the tablecloth. 'You need to be firmer with her, more involved in her life. You can't just let her roam around the village doing whatever she likes.'

'I find it hard to look at her, let alone discipline her.' Jacobo hesitated. 'Sometimes it's easier to ignore her.'

He sat back on his chair and glanced through the door on to the veranda where the children were spooning polenta and *panzanella* into their mouths. When Bella was born, so violently

18

on that June night, Jacobo's life was tossed in the air, shaken around and forced to settle like molten lava on the remains of a once solid soil. Nothing relieved his loss in those early years. He had simply wanted to lie down on the fresh earth of his dead Bella's grave and remain there. Seven years on and Jacobo was still lost. All that was familiar was his Monterini; its cerise sunsets and Etruscan tombs, the family bookshop and the friendship of Angelo next door.

After breakfast, Jacobo walked along the cobbled streets of the Fratta with the honey-coloured houses piled one on top of the other like building blocks from the games he used to play with Angelo as lads. He tipped his hat to the Zerulli bakers, made his way across the piazza and climbed the stairs to the bridge that led him to his bookshop in Via Cavour.

It was here in Monterini, amidst the shelter of the olive groves and the purple vineyards, that Jacobo's great, great grandfather Avraham Levi had arrived in the 18th century, in search of a refuge after the massacres of Monte San Savino. He had found acceptance amongst the *contadini* of Monterini who continued their subsistence farming, unperturbed by the strangers with their long beards and dark coats, strange customs and mournful prayers.

Avraham Levi established a printing press and a Jewish bookshop, selling religious texts, versions of Jewish poetry and stories written in Ladino. When Jacobo took over from Cosimo, he sold the printing press to the De Benedettis and expanded the direction of the bookshop. He changed the name to La Libreria Speciale and introduced works on comparative religions, philosophy, literature and his great interest, the writings of the Kabbalists. He moved his bookshop from its established position in the Jewish Ghetto, over the bridge to Via Cavour in the newest quarter of the village. This was where it stood now, next to Café del Giorno, surrounded by modern, box-like houses with red bricks and square windows.

Jacobo stopped in front of the wide facade of the bookshop. His assistants Nanni Manduro and Marlene Elmi were waiting for him on the pavement. They nodded shyly at each other, their eyes darting around to see if anyone was watching them. Jacobo raised his hat to Marlene. He delved into his jacket pocket and removed a bunch of keys, his right hand twisting the fabric of his trousers to stop his arm from reaching out. How difficult it was to remember not to shake hands in this new regime of rules. The traditional handshake had been forbidden earlier that year by Renato Ricci. Now only the Roman salute was allowed. Jacobo didn't feel comfortable greeting his fellow villagers in this way, stamping his foot and stretching his arm out in front like the war-loving emperors of the past. It felt sinister, undignified.

Unlocking the door of the bookshop, Jacobo stared at the volumes bound in red and black leather and sighed. So many of his favourite texts were now banished from view. Gone were the recently banned political writings of Antonio Gramsci and Carlo Rosselli, now stacked neatly in boxes at the back of Jacobo's office and in the house in the Fratta.

'Communists,' Rabbi Coen had uttered when Jacobo removed the works from the bookshelves.

'Mussolini's right to ban them,' Signor Mazzi the kosher butcher had said. 'He knows what's good for our country!'

Amongst Jacobo's clients were wealthy Jewish families from Rome who drove past Monterini on their way to Sienna or Florence and stopped at the bookshop to buy a *Haggadah* for Passover, a biblical text or the latest Pirandello play. Usually Jacobo enjoyed learning about their lives, the new courses at the universities. Even the latest scandal never failed to entertain him. But no longer. Gone were the intellectual discussions of the Kabbalists, the Torah, the debates, the gossip. Now only one name moistened his clients' lips; a single breath, pronounced in honeyed tones of respect:

Il Duce.

Jacobo's clients spoke only of *il Duce*'s benevolence towards the Jewish communities of Italy; sentences laced with his goodness, his understanding of national socialism, his imperialism, his desire to keep Italy afloat, hauling it out of the depths of poverty inherited from the Great War.

But Jacobo wasn't so sure. They didn't hear the words whispered in the breeze whenever Mussolini's name was mentioned: '*Pericolo, stai attento*. It's harmful, beware.'

Jacobo didn't know where it came from, only that it echoed through the Etruscan tombs, over the rooftops, playing with his imagination until he could no longer breathe.

CHAPTER 3

Augusto: the sunflowers nodded at the sun like obedient schoolchildren and the air was filled with the smell of jasmine. Jacobo sat under a peach tree, sipping wine Angelo had poured from an aged green bottle. He had never been particularly fond of Angelo's vintage, but he was grateful for the peace of the surroundings, the rows of vines, the clicking of crickets. He had brought his work on the Kabbalist Isaac Luria and a handful of political journals that he couldn't read in public. The sun streamed down on the fields, yellow and wasted; the branches of the olive trees wilted and desperate in the scorching heat.

Jacobo glanced up from his reading. Angelo was teaching Bella and Rico how to take cuttings from the mature vines, how to increase the crop by layering the plant. He noticed the way Angelo bent over the children speaking in the Monterini dialect; how his hand brushed against Bella's head or smoothed Rico's arm. It struck Jacobo how his own hand always lingered somewhere near Bella, and then dropped awkwardly to his side.

'Volcanic soil is the best,' Angelo was explaining to the children. Black, grainy soil streamed through his fingers, just like the Fiorina waterfall on a stormy night. 'Rich in sulphur and calcium.'

Bella nodded at Angelo, her short curls bobbing like violent waves in an orange sea. Rico stood close beside her, black fringe covering shy eyes, arms the colour of burnt almonds. Jacobo knew how much Bella loved the afternoons when she and Rico were allowed to run through fields of nodding sunflowers to help Angelo at his smallholding. She called it a farm, but it was a grandiose name for a field, half a dozen vines, two olive trees, a cow and a pig. When Angelo had insisted Jacobo join them on Wednesday afternoons Bella seemed excited. She showed Jacobo how she'd learned to pick an olive, so it didn't harm the fruit, how to plant saplings and how to press the udders of a cow so the milk landed in the bucket and not on her face. But after several weeks, her interest in Jacobo had waned.

Jacobo put down his copy of the mystical journey of Isaac Luria, placing it on top of the banned writings of the Rosselli brothers. Removing his spectacles, he walked over to the row of grapes that Angelo had been tending all afternoon. He broke off a small bunch and popped several in his mouth. He chewed silently. The sweetness of the grapes hit his lips, a taste of summer, intense yet delicate. Jacobo allowed the juice to linger on his tongue, relishing the delicacy of the flavours.

Clasping his grey hat to his head, he moved over to a vine on the other side of the pasture. He reached out for some plump, ripened grapes and tasted them, his tongue prodding and pocking at this new bunch. The same sun, identical soil but these grapes were tart just like Angelo's wine.

'*Venite. Venite subito*,' he beckoned Bella and Rico who were kneeling on the earth cutting back weeds. Obediently they came, barefoot, the skin of their arms rubbing against each other.

'Try these,' Jacobo passed them the bunch he'd just tasted. The children sucked the grapes between their teeth, their eyes squeezed into narrow slits as if Jacobo had just insisted they suck a barrowful of lemons.

'*Brutto*,' replied Rico shuddering.

'Sour,' added Bella.

Jacobo took each child by the wrist and marched them back to the row where Angelo tugged at an angry weed, his broad back sheltering the fruit like a parasol.

'Now try these.'

They placed the grapes on their tongues.

'*Che buono*,' said Rico.

Jacobo turned to Bella. 'Which are better?'

Bella pointed to the bunch where the delicate skin clung to the swollen fruit. 'These, *babbo*, definitely these. They're much sweeter.'

Rico nodded in agreement, eyes widening.

'That's exactly what I thought.' Jacobo placed his arms across his chest with satisfaction. 'You see this bunch here, the sweet ones?' He lowered his head towards the children. 'Well, these are the grapes from the row *zio* Angelo has been working on for the past few weeks.

'And these,' he wiggled a bunch in front of their eyes as if dangling purple flies. 'These nasty ones are from the vines at the other end of the *campo*. He hasn't worked on these for a while now.'

The children stared at him.

Jacobo rubbed his chin with his finger and thumb. He walked back to his seat underneath the peach tree and picked up his book. He couldn't concentrate. His thoughts were unravelling. Why were the grapes where Angelo had been working sweeter than the others? Was it the soil, the angle of the sun?

Somehow Jacobo knew it was neither the Monterini sunshine nor the volcanic earth. It was something to do with Angelo himself; his language was nature, he understood the seasons, could almost smell the rain or the snow. He knew when the earth felt too thick, too grainy. Jacobo often heard him humming Monterini folksongs as he stood by the vines stroking the fruit, fascinated by the varying shades, from silver grey to the greens of the mountain trees, from smoky pinks to the reds of the velvet curtains in Jacobo's sitting room. To Jacobo they all looked the same but for Angelo they were like people with a soul of their own.

Jacobo placed his book back on the ground and walked to the edge of the pasture. There was a thin hedge dividing Angelo's field from the adjacent one. Leaning his weight against the hedge, Jacobo reached over and snapped off a bunch of grapes. He tasted them, then spat them out, wondering if anyone had noticed. The neighbour's grapes were insipid, even a touch sour, by far inferior to the ones Angelo had been working on for several days.

Jacobo returned to his chair and pondered over the question of the grapes. Was it possible? Could it really make so much difference? He decided to spend more time trailing Angelo around the vineyard, probing and tasting to see if it really was true: the grapes loved the sound of Angelo's voice.

Several Wednesdays later, Jacobo planted himself in front of Angelo, a bunch of grapes resting on each smooth palm. 'I've discovered something.'

Angelo looked up, hand twisted around a weed.

'The grapes can hear you. They respond to the sound of your voice when you sing the Monterini tunes, the melodies. The juice is sweeter. Even the children agree.' Jacobo took a deep breath. He felt awkward in his suit and grey hat next to Angelo with his face smudged with streaks of magenta, his overalls trailing on the ground and his wide, muscular arms engrained with mud. Angelo always seemed so free, chanting his way through his labour with the melodies of their youth, stopping only to down a tumbler of red wine.

'I've been watching them for a while now,' Jacobo continued.

'You'll think I'm mad, but the grapes love it when you sing.'

Angelo's lips parted into a toothless grin. He hesitated, as if embarrassed, then leaned forward. Bending over Jacobo, he kissed him on both cheeks. 'I thought it was me who was mad. I knew they liked the music, deep down in here.' Angelo banged his chest with his fist. 'But it seemed impossible.'

Angelo twisted his hands. Dark brown on the upper side, they were lined with purple furrows on the palms. Jacobo was hit by the smell of grapes and earth, *la terra*, always lingering over them, even after Angelo scrubbed them. It was the smell of the *contadino*. He wondered if Angelo felt self-conscious standing there in front of him dressed in dungarees, his face dusted with earth. Was Angelo aware of the dusty smell of books hanging over Jacobo, the cologne he rubbed behind his ears before work?

Those differences between them had always existed. In a village like Monterini it was difficult to escape the boundaries class and religion imposed upon them. But a thread united them too; Jacobo wasn't sure if it were merely memories of their childhood games, skimming pebbles in the Piccolina river, discovering the cold water of the Fiorina waterfall just as Rico and Bella did now. Or was it the bonds formed through hardship and pain? During the Great War, Jacobo knew the Ghiones would have starved if his father had not slipped *lira* notes under the slit in the doorway. Angelo's feet would have turned blue in the icy Monterini winters when the paving stones of Via Meravigliosa were coated with snow, if Cosimo had not left a pair of boots wrapped in newspaper outside the door of the house with grey shutters.

In gratitude, Angelo continued to provide the Levis with courgettes and peaches, wine and cheese. On that terrible June night that caused Jacobo's muscles to ache and his skin to tingle with fear whenever the memory swept over him, Angelo had scooped up baby Bella, caring for her, loving her as if she were his own. Jacobo knew he could never repay Angelo for the attention, the love, but maybe he could find a way to help Angelo improve the flavour of his crop.

'If it's music that makes the grapes grow stronger, tastier, that's what you'll give them. And you never know, you may produce a crop that outshines all the others. It could become the best loved wine of the province!'

They chuckled, swept up in dreams and hopes, strengthened by the warmth of the sun, the smell of wild roses.

～～～

'My grapes can hear!' Angelo exclaimed to Santina a few weeks after Jacobo's announcement. He had been afraid to tell her, afraid she would laugh, or worse, hit him with the back of her hand as if he were Rico or the twins and had just been caught stealing *panini* from the table when her back was turned. 'They love my voice, my music. I always knew it.'

'*Che stupidaggini*!' Santina shrugged her shoulders. Her hair streaked with premature silver lay buried under a patterned scarf. She'd been pretty in her youth, with the sombre eyes and dusky complexion that Enrico had inherited, but hard work and financial worries had aged her. At thirty, her breasts sagged; the skin beneath her eyes shaded with inky half-moons.

'I haven't got time to listen to you jabbering on about grapes and music. What nonsense.'

'Jacobo thinks they can hear. He says if I sing to them, get workers to help me, the wine will be better than any in the area. It could make us rich.'

'Us rich? On grapes and a pig?'

'And two fields of vines,' Angelo insisted. 'And don't forget the olive trees and the cow.'

Santina snorted. 'Dream on, Angelo. We're *contadini*,

remember. Peasants don't get rich in Monterini.' She turned her back to him, the black shawl over her shoulders rising with each inhale of breath. 'The sun must have fuddled Jacobo's mind, probably all that *vino* you two drink every Wednesday afternoon.'

Angelo took a gulp of red wine from the tumbler he was holding. 'Jacobo doesn't like my wine. He screws up his face whenever he drinks it, thinks I don't notice. But just imagine if he's right, Santina. Maybe singing to them will make a difference. Folks may love the taste. And if it works…'

'You'd think, with his brains, he'd know better.'

Angelo blocked his ears with his hands. He wasn't just a peasant, he reminded himself, he owned the smallholding his father bought just before he died with money he borrowed from the Levis. A *contadino* with land! That made him a level up from the *contadini,* didn't it?

'Jacobo's discovery could mean more money, fewer worries.'

'You're a fool. The whole village will make mincemeat of you. "*Pazzo,*" they'll whisper. "*Pazzo,* crazy man!"' Santina handed Angelo his morning *caffè con la ricotta*. Her lips slid into a smile, her eyes softened.

Encouraged, Angelo added, 'Maybe I'll even be able to buy a donkey! Jacobo's right. I've known it for years.'

He paused.

'But I was too scared to say. Jacobo has given me courage.'

Santina was no longer listening. She grabbed a pile of sheets and towels and trotted down the steps and along the alleyway to the *lavatoio* for the weekly washing trip.

❧

Despite Santina's protestations, Jacobo and Angelo noticed how the grapes appeared sweeter, more fragrant, when they spun the folksongs of Salone through the air like sweet incense. It was as if fertiliser had been added to the soil. When Angelo spoke his voice was gruff, like the sound of a shovel scraping against the earth. When he sang, the sound was gentle, melodic, like the chirping of birds. Even on the Sabbath, Jacobo and Bella would trundle down to the fields, after the service at the synagogue, and weave Jewish tunes in and out of the Monterini melodies. Soon the hymns from the Sunday service resonated across Angelo's fields, and verses of Christmas carols could be heard floating through the vineyard in summer. Like a basket woven with different threads, the grapes were interlaced with two cultures.

And the vines flourished.

With every note of the litany, with each Hebrew song, their juice sweetened, promising a perfect harvest.

At first Jacobo was reluctant to sing. He was embarrassed in his *Shabbat* suit and hat, walking up and down the rows of vines singing Hebrew prayers. But something urged him to encourage Angelo to sing; a churning sensation deep inside, a drawing down of his muscles, as if something was rinsing through him. No words, no feelings, just sensations as deep as the ones he felt whenever Mussolini's name was mentioned. It impelled him to show Angelo the way, to sing with him, believing that somehow, it would improve the quality of his wine, even provide him with a supplementary income. He remembered the taste on his tongue: nectar. If Angelo could produce wine as full and rich as those grapes, it could change his life.

Early autumn, Jacobo suggested finding a name for Angelo's wine.

'Something catchy, I think,' he announced one evening, stepping on to the veranda where Angelo was sitting, watching Bella and Rico play jacks on the steps. Rays of evening sunlight streamed through gaps in the houses streaking their hair with gold.

The street was awash with the pre-prandial sounds of plates clattering, *brodo* bubbling and men swapping stories of the day's events, cigarette smoke swirling above their heads.

'You'll need it for this year's production,' Jacobo continued.

'You really think I need a name?' Angelo's eyes were glued to the ball Bella was bouncing on the tiled floor. He appeared to be paying more attention to the children than to Jacobo's idea.

'*Certo.*' Jacobo's voice ached with irritation. Why didn't Angelo see the importance of this? It could help his family through the winter months of hardship, an added income to the staple diet of olives, vegetables and grapes. Could he not see that an excellent wine with the hint of honey, sunshine and warmth could double, even treble his income?

Jacobo stopped mid-thought. Of course, he couldn't. Angelo had left school at the age of ten. Jacobo wasn't even sure he could still read. Business and making money were as foreign to Angelo as digging potatoes out of the ground was for Jacobo. His face flushed with shame. He knelt on the floor of the veranda in his suit and touched Bella's arm. She looked up. Her eyes, greeny-grey in the twilight, remained fixed on Jacobo's face; eyes that were so much like her mother's, it sent a stab of pain coursing through him.

'*Sì, babbo.*'

'Can you help *zio* Angelo think of a name?' Jacobo crouched next to her, unable to rest his gaze on her face. Her presence continued to unnerve him, even now after all these years. 'Or perhaps you can think of something, Rico?'

'*Vino,*' Rico said, thick black hair curtaining his eyes.

'What do you think?' Jacobo asked Angelo.

'*Vino Ghione,*' Angelo chuckled.

'*Vino degli Angeli!*' Bella announced, scooping up the remaining ten jacks. '*Ho vinto*, I've won.'

'*Brava* Bella. *Brava*,' Jacobo shouted with equal excitement and clapped his hands. He wondered how his daughter had devised such a pertinent name so quickly. Wine of the Angels. It was perfect.

'It's only a game, *babbo*.'

'I think he means your name for my wine, not the game.' Angelo laughed bending forward, his broad shoulders blocking out the remaining rays of speckled sunlight. 'It's good, don't you think, Rico? And my name is in it too.'

Rico shrugged and threw the ball into the air. 'Who cares!'

'It's the only real name for your wine,' Jacobo said. 'What a clever choice, Bella, pure brilliance.'

All the tiny muscles of Bella's face relaxed. Her lips parted into a radiant smile, her freckles strengthened by the heat of the sun, merged into one another. Her hair now reached her shoulders. Jacobo hadn't notice it grow.

Rico pulled Bella down the steps of the veranda urging her to listen to Gino Bonito play his mouth organ at the corner of Via Bel Fiora. She turned her head and glanced back at her father; her lips stretched into a grin.

Jacobo couldn't remember ever seeing her look so happy.

CHAPTER 4

It was a clement day in February. Jacobo was walking along the San Gianni path surrounding Monterini. He loved to stare at the crevices towering above him, feel the texture of the rock against his fingers like shavings of an aged *parmigiano*. Sometimes he placed his cheek against the surface of the *tufo*, feeling it pulsate against his skin, smelling the dampness and sensing the breath of the stone.

Crocuses carpeted the borders of the San Gianni path. A blanket of forget-me-nots stained the earth blue. Jacobo raised his head and watched the reflections of the sun dance on the round window of the Beit Israel synagogue. He shielded his eyes with a rolled-up newspaper. He had taken to reading the paper during his morning walks, instead of with his *cornetto* at home in Via Meravigliosa. The newspaper articles were beginning to agitate him, and he didn't want to alarm Cosimo and Bella or embarrass himself in front of his customers and staff at the bookshop. He had to watch what he said. Mussolini was loved by young and old, regardless of wealth or religion. With *il Duce* came a fresh vision of youth, prosperity.

Hope.

He sat down on a bench and opened the early morning edition of *La Stampa*, smoothing the edges. Lighting a cigarette, he leaned back and inhaled the fumes of tobacco mixed with mildew and early spring. On the front page *il Duce*'s face beamed at him, lips swollen into a smile. He was leaning over the Pope, embracing him, eclipsing him with his solid frame. Mussolini had consented to the teaching of Catholicism in every Italian school and had agreed to the establishment of the Vatican City. The Pope had finally accepted the Fascist Party, and the Lateran Treaty was signed.

A victory for them both.

Above the branches, over the rooftops and between the sheets of washing flapping in the wind came the words: '*Pericolo, stai attento*. It's harmful, beware.'

A single, soft breath like a sigh. There'd been occasions in Jacobo's life where he'd been afraid. His childhood fear of the priests still nagged at him whenever he saw them, those '*fratti*' who scuttled across the Fratta, from the cathedral to the San Benedetto Monastery, coats trailing behind them, black hats perched on their heads like helmets; eyebrows arched into worried frowns.

But this was different.

Pericolo, stai attento.

The words sifted through him, filling him with dread. Where did they come from? He wondered whether he imagined them. He sat back, the wooden slats of the bench digging into his spine. Clouds streaked with a rosy hue floated above the spires of Monterini, the musty smell of wood burning reached his nostrils. Nothing in the village had changed, but somehow Jacobo knew things would be different. He returned his gaze to Pope Pius XI and shook his head. The Pope had accepted a party that believed only one way was right.

'Why did you give him the power, dear *Papa* Pius?' he whispered to the morning air. 'It's a mistake.'

Swallows swooped above him, marking the arrival of an early spring. And yet those words continued to float on the breeze.

Pericolo, stai attento. It's harmful, beware.

33

Before making his way over to La Libreria Speciale, Jacobo walked up from the San Gianni path, past the cathedral and the monastery and down the crooked, uneven steps that led to the Beit Israel Synagogue.

Rabbi Coen was locking the iron gates. His eyes twinkled but his eyebrows formed a V shape, a look that suggested to Jacobo both surprise and amusement.

'Jacobo, you've just missed the morning service!'

Jacobo shoved *La Stampa* against the rabbi's beard, a nest of soft clouds trailing beyond his chin to his chest.

'Have you read this, Rabbi? This agreement with the Pope, it feels sinister. I'm worried.'

'You're overreacting, Jacobo. I often speak with Mayor Baldini and our village lawyer Signor Bruscalupi. They reassure me *il Duce* is good for our country. I believe them.'

'But Rabbi, Mussolini's changing tack. He knows no limits. We need to be aware.'

A lopsided grin appeared on the rabbi's face. Jacobo wasn't sure if he was mocking him or trying to pacify his concerns. Rabbi Coen reached forward and patted Jacobo's arm.

'Jacobo, you and I, we're intellectuals not politicians. Several Jews in Monterini and many from the big cities are members of the Fascist Party. They support him. They say Mussolini is our friend. We've nothing to worry about.'

Jacobo questioned the rabbi's certainty. Maybe he thinks I'm *pazzo*, a little bit mad, he wondered, just as the *contadini* had thought Angelo when he announced the birth of *Vino degli Angeli* the previous year.

'I wish I could believe you, Rabbi.' Jacobo thought back to that fateful June night when his Bella had died. Then, there were no words seeping from the cracks in the wall, just a feeling, as black as the starless nights in Monterini after a violent storm. He had known then she was dying. Nobody had believed him, but he had known, and from that feeling he had lost her. Something was dying now, Jacobo was certain.

He glanced around. Feeling secure in the safety of the synagogue, he placed one hand under the rabbi's elbow and with the other shook his hand. It felt bony and cold.

'You're a good man, Jacobo,' the rabbi said. 'And you mean well. But don't let fear steal your soul.'

As he retraced his way back up the steps, Jacobo couldn't help thinking that the rabbi was wrong.

Jacobo's solemn mood continued throughout the day. When he arrived home after work he sat on the veranda. Signora Franca had opened the black shutters, allowing the spring breeze to blow away the mustiness of winter.

Jacobo drew on his cigarette; blue ribbons of smoke coiled above him.

In the street, children rolled coloured marbles on the paving stones; men in suits holding *Il Corriere della Sera* and Mussolini's paper *Il Popolo*, mingled with *contadini* in shirtsleeves and cloth caps. Women huddled together in packs. Boasting of the tastiest recipe or who perfected the most economical dish linked all the women of Monterini like beads in a chain, regardless of class and wealth. Each swore her *pane*, *fettucini* or *fegato* was superior to that of her neighbour.

Bella and Rico ran up the steps. Overalls rolled up to their knees, they stepped over pots of hyacinths scattered across the tiles of the veranda.

'We're going to have a celebration.'

'We need one.' Jacobo stubbed out his cigarette, removed his hat and wiped his feet on the doormat. In the kitchen Signora Franca had left a plate of *crostini* and a bottle of Angelo's *Vino degli Angeli* next to an envelope with Jacobo's name written in neat, bold letters.

'Signora Franca said it's from Maestra Lea.' Bella nodded her head towards the letter. 'But I haven't done anything wrong in school, *babbo*, I promise.'

Jacobo opened the envelope, read the contents, then folded it and placed it in his jacket pocket.

'What is it, *babbo*?' Bella asked.

'So, when's this celebration?' Jacobo ignored her question.

'Any minute,' Rico answered. '*Eccolo*, here it is.'

The clip-clopping of hooves echoed in the street. Bella and Rico scrambled back on to the veranda and down the steps as Angelo appeared round the corner of Via Meravigliosa. He was pulling a raspberry-coloured donkey with a triangular white patch on its nose.

'This is Rodeo.' He grinned, scratching his head as if he couldn't quite believe his luck. 'I'm the proud new owner of a donkey!'

A few coarse hairs peeped through the neck of Angelo's vest. The neighbours from the Fratta bustled around him, clapping him on the back and shouting *auguri*. Angelo shook himself free, his eyes seeking Jacobo's.

'We've done it, Jacobo. I've bought a donkey!'

'You've done it, Angelo, it's your voice they love.'

Angelo's wine had become a success. The taste of sunshine wet the lips, scoured the back of the teeth and flushed the throat. Although Santina still refused to believe it had anything to do with the Salone melodies, the harvest had been promising and the popularity of the wine had spread throughout the town.

Angelo led Rodeo down the crumbling steps below the house into the *cantina*, which served as a storehouse for his wine and now as a stable for his new workmate. The children carried the bottles and the *crostini* on to the veranda and Jacobo poured the wine into glasses. Angelo joined them, raised his glass towards his friend and with a large smile said, 'Thank you, Jacobo.'

Jacobo had stood by Angelo's side, loaned him money to employ more workers, encouraged him to fill his fields with song. He knew Angelo could never have bought a donkey without his help. He smiled back and lifted his glass. 'To friendship.'

Santina appeared on the veranda, arms crossed over her chest. She scowled but her eyes sparkled. 'Us with a donkey! Whoever would have thought it.'

They clinked glasses as the words *chin chin* echoed up to the rooftops.

CHAPTER 5

The fields were dusty brown in the stifling heat. Angelo put his hand on his back and eased himself up. It was hard work in the height of summer, but the harvest promised to be a good one, the fruit was ripening on the vines, firm, healthy looking grapes. Angelo sang every day with the help of Gino Bonito and his mouth organ, and some local boys who performed in the cathedral mass. They walked up and down the aisles pruning, singing and weeding. On Wednesday and Saturday afternoons, Jacobo joined them along with Bella and Rico.

Angelo knew he had been the laughing stock of the village; he'd heard the whispers along the alleyways and outside Roberto's bar in the piazza where he drank his grappa most evenings. Many of the farm workers thought it was luck or prayer that created a good Sangiovese wine. But like Jacobo, Angelo sensed the grapes could hear. He knew they welcomed the sound of voices drifting in the breeze. He was certain they responded to the Salone melodies.

Angelo packed up his belongings and joined Gino Bonito at the corner of the field to catch the cart back into town. Bella and Rico were waiting for him as usual in the piazza.

'*Babbo* said he wants to make an announcement this afternoon.' Bella ran up to him, orange flames streaming behind her, cheeks hazelnut brown from the afternoons in the smallholding.

'Perhaps he is going to buy a donkey like my *babbo*,' Rico suggested.

'What would my *babbo* need a donkey for? He spends all day with his books. No, it's something else.'

Angelo's eyes settled on the child he had cherished as if she were his own daughter. He had fallen in love with her green eyes and piercing lungs that very first moment when he lifted her onto his shoulder and stroked her back. Even when Santina gave birth to the twins Mateo and Carlo four years later, Angelo had to remind himself he was the father of three children not four.

He loved watching her play hopscotch with his sons, help Santina knead dough or sit at the table in either of her two homes, forming the letters of the Italian or Hebrew alphabet with a dedication he could only marvel at. He who could barely read and had no idea where to start to form a letter with a pen. When Bella sat with Rico, guiding his pencil into shapes and patterns, Angelo's heart would swell.

He looked at her now. Eyes shining with anticipation, she bubbled with excitement like an overboiled pot. His own eyes felt heavy. How will she manage, he wondered, when she finds out?

'Have you seen the news?' Jacobo asked, brandishing a copy of Mussolini's *Il Popolo* in Angelo's face as he climbed the steps up to the veranda.

'You know I can't read the paper! And I've no time for nonsense.' Angelo responded with the Roman salute. He had little interest in politics, didn't care about government reforms. He saluted everyone as he didn't know what else to do to replace the handshake. He frowned at the word *squadristi*, Blackshirts, looked on naively at the mention of *I Patti Lateranensi*, the Lateran Treaty, and shook his head in ignorance when Jacobo spoke of the Rosselli brothers and their organisation Giustizia e

39

Libertà. He was one of the *contadini* and none of this made any sense to him.

Fascist? Anti-fascist?

What did it matter as long as there was food on the table and his grapes continued to ripen with the warmth of the sun and the sound of beautiful voices?

'But it's not nonsense,' Jacobo continued. 'Every day, there's something else. First, *I Patti Lateranensi*, and now almost every single Italian has voted for Mussolini's latest legislation.'

'What's legis— something, *babbo*?' Bella asked, eyes wide with interest. Her hand reached towards her father. Jacobo didn't notice. He answered eyes blazing, gaze fixed on Angelo. 'Only fascist members of Parliament can be elected from now on. No other parties are allowed. That's it, he's done it. Mussolini now has total control.'

'No politics please.' Santina stood on the veranda sandwiched between two pots of lavender. '*Vai, vai*, let's go.' She ushered everyone across the tiled floor.

Angelo watched her waddle through the door of the Levis' house, her black dress tight around her bottom. Why does she always have to dress like a widow, he wondered. Jacobo's the one who's widowed.

But not for long.

Angelo had noticed the smart envelopes with black ink delivered by Signora Franca from Maestra Lea. He'd watched the sorrow from the past years, as prominent as bushy eyebrows or a sharp nose, dissolve from Jacobo's face. It seemed to be sudden, almost overnight. The grief the whole village associated with Jacobo had thawed like a heavy snow in springtime leaving a thin coating of joy.

Angelo crossed the kitchen into Jacobo's sitting room. A wooden table stood by the large window overlooking the valley. On it were several glasses, a bowl of olives, a basket of *crostini*

40

and slices of *sfratto*. Bella stood by her father's side, her arm almost but not quite touching the leg of his trousers. Next to her stood Rico and his brothers, Carlo and Mateo. Santina sat next to Cosimo on a chair overlooking the valley. The sun glinted through the wide window and the olive trees swayed in the light breeze. In the distance a dog barked.

There was a knock on the door.

'*Chi è?*' Bella's eyes were as round as the apples in the orchards. Nobody knocked in Monterini.

'*Vieni* Bella.' Cosimo stood up, reached out his hand and led Bella across the kitchen to the half-open door.

A head of hair the colour of soft wheat peeped through the gap in the door and Maestra Lea stepped into the room, clasping the small, plump hands of her two daughters. She wiped her feet neatly on the doormat, and with a sharp nod, indicated to Luciana and Elena to do the same. Behind them was Signora Franca. She was smiling broadly.

Bella's mouth gaped open as she stared at her teacher.

'Have you come for *babbo*'s announcement?'

'Of course.' Lea's dusky eyes sought Jacobo's across the room. She bent down and kissed Bella on both cheeks. 'Weren't you expecting me?'

'No.'

'*Entrate. Entrate.*' Jacobo hurried the guests back into the sitting room with an unfamiliar eagerness. The creases at the corner of his eyes when Jacobo talked about Mussolini were now ironed into the smoothness of his skin. His suit hung loosely on his shoulders and his black hair framed his face. He looked handsome with his prominent cheekbones, strong mouth and inky eyes that melted the hearts of the women in Monterini in the way that Angelo with his pockmarked skin, unwieldy frame and self-conscious manner could never do. He had returned to the Jacobo Angelo remembered as a child: the handsome lad with the intelligent smile.

Jacobo nodded to Angelo to uncork the bottle of white *Vino degli Angeli*. Coughing to attract the attention of the company in the room, he beckoned Lea to his side. Luciana, the eldest, clung to her mother's skirt and twirled a piece of hair around her finger. The little one, Elena, sucked furiously on her thumb. Angelo thought their manner displayed both timidity and fear.

Jacobo's words floated across the room. 'So, we wanted you all here... delighted to announce... wedding in September...'

Barely registering Jacobo's words, Angelo looked across at Bella. Her skin whitened and her face crumpled, but her eyes shone deep jade. His muscles ached for her. He placed his hand on the heart side of his shirt, hoping its pressure would stop the pounding.

'Bella and I will be moving to the Ghetto.'

Angelo's sharp intake of breath echoed around the room. This was news to him too.

'*Felicitazioni.*' Cosimo walked over to his son and soon to be daughter-in-law and kissed them both. He ruffled the hair of Luciana and Elena and smiled across at Bella who was crossing her arms against her chest. She looked like a warrior defending herself against an enemy.

'*Non vengo.*'

'What do you mean? You have no choice.' Jacobo was used to confrontation.

But so was Bella.

'I'm not coming! I'm going to stay here with my *nonno.*' Bella walked over to Cosimo and threaded her fingers through his. The muscles of her jaw clenched and tightened as she spoke. 'I want to live next door to Rico. You can marry Maestra Lea and move to the Ghetto, but I'm not coming with you.'

'Does this mean you didn't already tell her?' Lea's glass lay untouched in her delicate, pearl-coloured hands. Flecks of worry filled her eyes as they wandered from Bella to Jacobo and back to Bella. 'You should've warned her, children need to know these things before they happen.'

Jacobo stared at Lea, his mouth gaping open, as if the idea had only just occurred to him. Softening, he leaned towards his daughter and breathed gentle words into the air. 'Be reasonable. It's a five-minute walk to the Ghetto.'

'I don't care.' Bella stood hands on hips, nose flaring like Angelo's donkey, Rodeo.

Signora Franca looked across at Jacobo, her lips pinched together. She raised her eyebrows and nodded in the direction of Bella as if to say: 'You're the father, do something with your wayward child.'

Angelo had heard her whispering to the neighbours, that Jacobo left Bella to live her life without rules, without discipline. And it was mainly true. For seven years Jacobo's life had been dictated by grief and loss. It was a mercy there was enough of them around to help raise his daughter.

Bella's voice became stronger with the attention she was receiving. 'I'm not coming. This is where I live.' She pointed to the white walls of the room, the vista stretching across the west side of Monterini, the fields speckled with sheep and goats; the silver branches of the olive trees. 'And this is my family.' She nodded towards the Ghiones.

Angelo's heart lurched. He understood. How could Bella and Jacobo move away, even if it were only to the Ghetto, a few streets away from Via Meravigliosa? It could have been a different continent.

'You live with me,' Jacobo said.

'Why?'

'Because you're my daughter.'

'But you don't really love me, so it won't make any difference if I come with you or not.'

43

Silence chilled the room, like an unwelcome frost in summer. Even the twins were quiet. Only the sound of Signora Franca's tut-tutting echoed through the air.

Jacobo stood tall. He was breathing fast. He walked over to his daughter, eyes narrowed into leaden slits, veins pulsing on his forehead. He raised his hand, paused as if trying to reason with himself. Then his hand came down and slapped his daughter's cheeks.

Uno. Due.

Angelo could almost imagine the sound reverberating across the room. Santina scolded and hit their sons whenever they were cheeky or disobeyed. It was a regular occurrence. He'd even heard his wife gossiping with Signora Franca about how soft Jacobo was, how he should try to control Bella more. A good slapping would do the trick, one of them had said. Yet this reaction seemed out of place from the distant, detached Jacobo who casually ignored Bella's remarks and behaviour, preferring to read his books about religion or discuss the latest political scandal.

Angelo turned his gaze to Bella. Her cheeks flashed red, from anger or the imprints of Jacobo's hands, Angelo wasn't sure.

'*A camera. Subito!* Your room. Now!'

Bella inhaled deeply, her eyes spitting grass-green sparks of hatred. Her shoulders shook as she moved across the room towards the stairs.

'I hate you.' She shot her father a look of defiance. 'I'm not going to my room. I'm leaving!' Turning abruptly, she traced her way through the kitchen, her footsteps echoing across the veranda. Nobody stopped her.

And they didn't even have the chance to raise their glasses and shout *auguri*!

CHAPTER 6

Bella flew down the stone steps to the cobbled streets of the Fratta. The clatter of crockery echoed along the alleyways as late diners cleared away the remnants of their meal. Notes from a mouth organ soothed the air. That's Gino, Bella thought as she wiped tears away. She wondered about stopping and telling him her problem. But her legs kept running.

She passed the cathedral where pigeons balancing on the stone pillars picked fleas from each other's feathers. Bella had always been terrified of the cathedral, shrouded in dark shadows and so much larger than the Beit Israel Synagogue, so much less familiar. She always refused to look at the statues on either side of the wooden doors; two giant stone scholars dressed in long robes, each holding a key and a cross. They were not frightening like the gargoyles and lions dotted around the palazzo, yet there was something real, something terrifying about the huge crosses they were holding. She shut her eyes as she passed by just in case they came to life. Maybe they would capture her and punish her just as her father had done.

Tears of rage still scarred her cheeks as she ran down to Capo Bagno at the far end of the village. The area had been named after the public washrooms, fashioned out of the golden *tufo* stone, with troughs carved into the floor and walls. For centuries the women of Monterini had washed their clothes in this secluded spot. Bella whispered through the slats, 'I'm not moving.'

She jumped down the uneven steps, winding from the summit of the village to the San Gianni path.

'I don't want a mother, not even Maestra Lea.'

She shook her head at the village towering above her, then paused, breathless. She was heading towards the old Etruscan roads, the *cavi*, as they were called by the Monterinesi, beyond the boundaries of the town, forbidden as a playground by anxious parents.

She had never been so far from Via Meravigliosa on her own. But she didn't care. She touched her cheek. It was the first time her father had hit her. She wasn't sure if that was making her shoulders shake with anger, her breaths short and puffy. Or was it because she might have to leave her home? She was nine. Surely, she could stay in the Fratta with her *nonno* and live next door to Rico.

Bella stopped running.

She was very close to the Piccolina river but not the part she was used to where she skimmed pebbles with Rico. This was territory she had never seen before. A blanket of bulrushes surrounded her and along the river's edge were yellow foxgloves, ferns and palms with leaves as a large as a person. She stepped slowly over bracken, watching to check the ground was safe. Angelo always warned her there were vipers by the river, she should tread carefully.

She raised her eyes.

In the distance, a figure was moving towards her; a tall woman, swaying gracefully from side to side. Long, white robes twisted around her body. Her eyes were shaped like half-moons and her hair was coiled on top of her head like a stack of black bowls. It reminded Bella of paintings she had looked at in history books with her *nonno*.

The figure stopped by some reeds at the edge of a rock, a few steps in front of Bella.

'*Seisma! Calya* Tanaquilla.'

Bella stared for a moment. 'What does that mean?'

'It means hello, my name is Tanaquilla.'

'Strange name.'

'Tanaquilla? It's Etruscan, like my language.'

'My *nonno* taught me the Etruscans were a fierce people...' Bella hesitated. 'But they vanished, just like the Romans and the ancient Greeks.'

'Is that so?' Tanaquilla closed her eyes, long pencilled lashes fanning her cheekbones.

'*Sì, sì.* Monterini is built on a rock, full of Etruscan caves. *Babbo* told me there are hidden tombs. I'm not supposed to come down here. Not even with Rico.' She paused; her heart was racing. She wasn't sure if it was because she had run faster than ever before in her life or because she was standing opposite this strange-looking person.

As if reading her thoughts, Tanaquilla said, 'You're breathing too fast.' She smiled gently, her eyes silver and watery blue.

'You have different coloured eyes.'

'And you have fierce green ones.'

The tension melted away.

'Have I met you before?' Bella knew everyone in Monterini. If someone came to visit or buy a book from her father's shop, she always knew if they were a stranger to the town.

'Maybe.' Tanaquilla leaned her head towards one side. Her skin was pale, luminous. Her pupils seemed to glow. 'Once before, but there was no need to remember me then. Today you're upset. So perhaps you needed to see me.'

'How do you know?' Bella's cheeks flushed with excitement.

'Because I'm a haruspex! I'm learning to tell the future. At least, I'm in training. I knew you would be coming to see me today. And I knew you would be sad.'

'But how?'

47

'I'm learning to observe the shape, colour and markings of the organs of animals. That's how I interpret the messages of the gods for the future.'

'The insides of animals?' Bella screwed up her nose. 'That's disgusting.'

A smile crossed Tanaquilla's lips. 'It isn't easy to be a haruspex. But there's another way you can divine the future. It's what I was doing before you arrived. Do you want to see?'

There was something about this figure that entranced Bella, something familiar yet unusual at the same time. She wondered if she could trust her.

Again, as if sensing her feelings, Tanaquilla stretched out her hand. 'You need to trust, deep down inside.' She placed both hands on Bella's shoulders, long fingernails softly touching Bella's skin, and turned her to face the river. Bella felt the air against her cheeks, the clouds above her. Everything was still, as if the waters of the Piccolina had stopped flowing; as if everything around her had merged into her.

'You must listen, Bella, to the whispers, to the magic. It's all around you.'

Bella turned her face towards Tanaquilla. 'I never told you I was called Bella. How did you know?'

Tanaquilla laughed. A deep, soulful laugh. It seemed to come from the earth below and echoed to the mountains beyond the village. 'The same way I knew you were sad. Look, I'll show you.'

They walked through veils of leaves to a clearing in the undergrowth, stepping over branches and nettles. Tanaquilla pulled a curtain of ivy to one side. Behind the foliage was a cavern carved into the rocks. Specks of sunlight glinted through the forest curtains. Inside, the light was dim, the air fetid with the scent of rotten leaves, like the musty smell of *zio* Angelo's *cantina* after a heavy rainfall.

In the centre of the cavern was a stone column. A pile of large lava stones, reddish brown, golden *tufo* and dark green *peperino* had been stacked beside the column to form an enclosure of several small squares. In one of the enclosures, three eggs, cut in half, lay upright.

Tanaquilla led Bella over to the stones, indicating a spot next to the eggs. Obediently, Bella sat down. Tanaquilla pulled her robes behind her and placed herself cross-legged next to Bella. She pointed to the eggs.

'You see, a haruspex can substitute the sacrificial animal with an egg to divine the future. I have cracked these eggs today and, from their internal makeup, I knew you would visit me.'

'How?'

'This side here tells me I would be visited by a young person, probably a girl. Look, can you see the light colouring? It means the person could be angry. Sad too.'

'I'm both.'

Tanaquilla poured the contents of the egg onto one of the *peperino* stones. Placing her index finger over a muddy-coloured patch, Tanaquilla explained. 'You see, it shows me your life, right here. This bit means everything will change.'

'Oh, that's already happening.' Bella frowned. 'My *babbo* is going to marry a widow from the Ghetto. She's quite nice, I suppose. She always gives us a *caramello* after our spoonful of cod liver oil. It's to prevent rickets, you know.' She paused and clenched her fists. 'But I don't want to leave our house in the Fratta. Or *nonno*, or Rico. I want to stay there forever. And I don't want a mother either. I don't need one.'

'Everyone needs a mother.'

'Not if it's *zia* Santina.'

Thoughts of Bella's own mother had floated around her over the years, tickling her chin, flicking her hair, playing with dreams. But she only needed to look next door. Occasionally

Santina was motherly, warm and loving. Mostly she was noisy like a steam train, running after Rico and the twins, stick in hand, cussing in a fit of temper if they touched the freshly baked bread or ate too many overripe peaches. When they disobeyed her, nothing was more bitter than her wrath. Even the *marah*, the horseradish, that scalded her tongue during Passover was preferable to Santina's rage.

'I don't need one. Not even Maestra Lea. Even though she's kind and never shouts.'

Tanaquilla leaned forward and peered closely at the mixture covering the stones. 'Well, this is what it tells me.' She guided Bella's finger through the contents of the eggs. 'Look, right here. This shows change. But it's only the beginning. And it's not so bad. You see there?' She whisked Bella's finger through the air to a dark brown coloration on the other side of the stones. It looked cloudy, heavy.

'Like tears.'

'No, not tears. It's movement. You will go backwards and forwards for many years and then it will stop.'

'Stop? Why?'

Tanaquilla's eyes narrowed as she stared at the murky colouring. 'You come home.' She looked up. One silver and one blue eye searched Bella's. In the distance, the metallic notes of church bells spun through the afternoon air.

It was four o'clock.

Bella jumped up. 'I have to go.' She brushed down pieces of twigs that clung to her overalls. 'I'm in so much trouble.'

'One more thing. There's blood in the vitellus. That means there's an omen in the egg. You must watch out for it.'

'An omen? What's that?'

'Don't worry, it can be good or bad. Remember to keep listening, feeling. That's the main thing. Sense what's going on around you, just as if you're in a dream. And I'll be there somewhere.'

Bella nodded. She felt calm and safe with this person with odd colour eyes, who spoke about omens and read the future from eggs.

They walked along the river to the old Etruscan road. The rocks of the *cavi* towered above them, menacing, magical. Tanaquilla waved at her, then sauntered back towards the clearing, her robes swishing around her feet. Bella watched her for a moment, then leapt up to the road coiling around Monterini. She climbed the stone steps through layers of *tufo* rock to the village above. Panting, she reached Capo Bagno. Bending forward to catch her breath, she scanned the valley; the reeds guarding the riverbank, the bulrushes swaying in the soft wind, the dark green ferns. Above them the hills rippled with olive trees, vineyards and lavender. Bella wondered if Tanaquilla was still standing there, white robes billowing in the breeze, surrounded by her canopy of green.

Who was she?

A real person? A dream?

She blinked twice, hoping Tanaquilla would still be there. She was gone.

Above Bella's head crows circled, smudges of black in the aqueous sky. Like distant thunder moving closer, the village awoke; shutters creaked open inviting the afternoon light back into the houses; voices flung words into empty streets. There was nothing out of the ordinary from any other day in Monterini.

On the morning of his wedding, Jacobo woke at six. In the lemon dawn he saw his Bella float before him, hair blazing, eyes smiling, blowing him kisses just as she'd done the evening he'd lost her. Then Lea's face appeared, with its intelligent eyes, wheaten hair and neat button nose.

'You'll come with me now. Say goodbye,' he almost heard her say.

A wild laugh filled the room.

He blinked. The faces had vanished.

He had to pull himself together, this was an important day after all. Jacobo looked out towards the west side of the valley. In the distance, Monte Amiata stood formidable and strong. He would miss the valley, the way it folded into itself, deep ridges, verdant and lush, stretching out before him; the Fiorina waterfall; the Etruscan tombs.

He kicked the sheets onto the floor in a tangled mess and padded across the tiles to the other side of the room. He opened the black shutters, light filtered through from the street. The clattering of carts and donkeys' hooves clip-clopping on the stones greeted him. Paolo Zerulli, the baker, stopped his wagon in front of the steps leading to the veranda and the Ghione and Levi households.

'*Il pane eccolo*.' He waved two loaves of Monterini *pane di compagna* fresh from the oven at Jacobo. 'Good luck for the wedding, Jacobo. *Auguri*. Time to move on.'

A clatter from downstairs in the kitchen made him jump. Signora Franca was already preparing breakfast. She was partly responsible for the union between Jacobo and Lea Servino, bearing missives between them, encouraging, cajoling. Jacobo knew the entire village had plotted and schemed, clucked and gossiped, inching him towards this day as if he were a crumb of food, brought by an army of ants towards their nest. Before he knew it, he was leaving the Fratta and marrying the Ghetto's widow, with her laughing eyes and two small children. For a moment, he wondered if Lea was only marrying him as she needed a husband to support her and her daughters.

'She's too proud for that,' he mouthed aloud. Lea was an independent woman, a gifted teacher. She loved poetry and read widely. She was certainly no Mussolini housewife. In fact, Jacobo had found an unexpected ally in Lea when it came to Mussolini.

He remembered her as a little girl, she was the younger sister of his friend Davide. She would often hide behind her mother's skirt, just as her eldest daughter Luciana did now, too shy to peep her head into the warm night air, too reserved to greet him. At school, their paths barely crossed; at the synagogue Lea was hidden behind the carved wooden awning of the women's gallery. When Lea's husband Luigi died as suddenly as Bella, with no warning, no goodbye, Jacobo came to pay his respects. Like Jacobo, Lea was left widowed, her daughters Elena and Luciana to raise alone.

Jacobo moved over to the oak chest standing next to the window. He opened the top drawer and took out a photograph in a gilt frame. It was the one of his Bella on her wedding day, smiling at him, eyes full of hope and love. Her hair hung around her heart-shaped face, not like the tangled curls his daughter had, but smooth and rich, like velvet curtains. He stroked her face, searching to see if he could make out the freckles that splattered like brown stains across her nose and onto her cheeks.

The door of the bedroom creaked opened. Cosimo stooped across the room, his smile fading when he noticed the photograph in Jacobo's hand. He was already dressed in a dark suit, white hair combed to one side, beard clipped.

'You're starting a new life, Jacobo. Give it to me.' Cosimo plied the photograph from Jacob's grasp. 'I'll keep it for Bella.'

Jacobo shrugged himself out of his dreams. It was absurd to still feel this connection to his dead wife, but there was something pulling him, tempting him. The wild laughter rang again in his ears, yet he knew his father couldn't hear it. A shiver of fear raced down his spine. He watched as Cosimo tucked the photograph of dead Bella inside his jacket, patting it as if it would be safer hidden away. The wrinkles around his father's mouth relaxed. His voice, gentler when he spoke, rinsed away pain like healing waters.

'The memories must stay hidden in here.' Cosimo touched his heart. 'You have the chance of a fresh start, so does little Bella. She needs calm, rules. Lea will be good for you both.'

He laid a cool palm on Jacobo's cheek. 'Now get dressed, it's a big day.'

※

When Jacobo walked on to the veranda with Cosimo and Bella later that afternoon, he looked up at the opaque sky and thanked God the sun had spared him. September could bring sheets of freezing rain when the villagers would bolt their doors and warm their toes against the stove. Or it could deliver days of blazing heat when old and young would fan themselves with newspapers, splashing water from the fountains onto flushed faces.

Jacobo smoothed the sleeve of his suit hoping it would hang on his body more comfortably, his hat would not stick to his hair and his palms would be less moist when he planted the wedding ring on the finger of his new bride.

Angelo was leaning against the door of his house, the jacket he had worn for his own wedding straining at the waist, buttons aching. Gone were his cloth cap, overalls and braces. He reached out towards the sky, then checked himself, his arm thumping down on his thigh. Jacobo smiled. He was touched Angelo had remembered how much he hated the Roman salute. Angelo glanced up and down the street, pulled Jacobo close and kissed him on both cheeks.

'*Auguri*. No salute today! Especially for your wedding.'

Jacobo gave him a friendly punch and smiled.

'We ought to leave,' Santina urged the wedding party. She picked a stray thread from the lapel of Jacobo's jacket, then added, 'You look the perfect bridegroom.'

The faded blue dress with puffed sleeves that she saved for Easter and Saint days was stretched across her chest. By her side stood her three sons, shifting uncomfortably in trousers and shirts Santina had no doubt borrowed from neighbours. Jacobo was touched by their effort to look well-groomed for his wedding day.

'We better be going.' Angelo placed his arm under Jacobo's elbow. 'We don't want to keep her waiting.'

The wedding party crisscrossed the alleys from the Fratta to the Ghetto, ducking under white shirts and blue overalls drying in the sun. They passed the *frantoio*, where the olive oil was processed, the *matzah* ovens, the *mikvah* and the rabbi's house.

As they approached the synagogue, music wafted out from the open door into the courtyard. The iron gates were open to allow guests to arrive and take their places on the wooden benches. Stepping down towards the courtyard, Jacobo hesitated. The muscles in his neck tightened, he could hardly breathe.

'She'll make you happy. Both widowed, both young. Shame she doesn't live in the Fratta.' Angelo dug his suited elbow into Jacobo's waist.

'Not you too, I've had this all morning from Bella.'

Jacobo had heard Bella moaning to Rico on the veranda and knew she hadn't even bothered to pack her clothes and toys. She was furious to be moving, furious to be wearing a dress instead of her customary dungarees. Now she was slouching next to Rico, her small face creased into a grimace.

Jacobo beckoned her to him. His hand wavered in front of her, playing with the air, almost touching her. Then it crashed to his side. He took a deep inhale, pointed through the entrance and down the aisle towards the *bimah*, the raised platform in the centre of the synagogue. Luciana and Elena were already seated, hands folded in their laps, hair brushed back from their faces and held in place with slides. They were wearing identical pale lemon dresses patterned with pink flowers. They looked neat and tidy sitting quietly listening to the Hebrew tunes.

Jacobo glanced down at his daughter. She was wearing the new powder blue dress the tailor in the Ghetto had made especially for her. Three times Jacobo had led her along Via del Ghetto to undress behind the curtain and stand barefoot on the stone floor, whilst Signor Sadun, pins fanning his lips, tucked and pinched, shortened and lengthened the various pieces of material around her calves, waist and shoulders. Standing there now, hands on hips, scowling furiously, she looked as if she had just returned from helping Angelo at the smallholding. There was a stain by her chest and another near the hem. White socks curled halfway down her legs; her black shoes were scuffed. A russet nest of hair partly covered her forehead and eyes.

Jacobo sighed. 'Look, Elena and Luciana are sitting nicely in the front row. Go and sit with them.'

'No,' she hissed. 'I'm staying with Rico.'

'Bella. Can't you do as I say, just for once?'

'*Va bene*,' she smiled sweetly. 'But don't make me move to the Ghetto. *Per favore*.'

The humming of the Hebrew melody *Osei Shalom Bimromav* drifted from inside the synagogue above the heads of the guests and out to the courtyard.

A swishing sound made them turn. Lea stood behind them. She had come out of the antechamber where brides were supposed to wait quietly, unseen by future bridegrooms. In one hand she held the hem of her dress as if worried she may slip.

'Why don't you and Rico sit over there, right in the front row with my girls. They are much younger than you and need to be looked after. You would both do the job so well.' Lea's gloved fingers stretched out towards Bella and Rico; her eyes smiled at Jacobo.

'Can I stay at home then? In the Fratta with *nonno*, Rico and *zio* Angelo?' Bella asked again, tugging at Jacobo's jacket.

'Go and sit down and I'll think about it.'

Lea bent down and took Bella's hand in her own. 'I'll discuss it with your father, as long as you promise you'll come and live with us as soon as you're ready.'

Bella nodded and grabbed Rico's arm. As they ran over to the front row to join Lea's daughters, she whispered, loud enough for Jacobo to hear, 'Told you I'd get round them.'

Jacobo turned his gaze towards his nearly new wife. Her white dress hugged her body, accentuating her breasts and slight waist. The sleeves stretched down her arms to meet her gloves. She glanced at him shyly. Her eyes were dark, much like his own, and her hair was pinned up into a bun. A veil stretched from the pins down her back to her hips. It was a different material from the dress; older, greyer. Lea had brushed her lips with red and her cheeks glowed with a silver shimmer. Jacobo wondered if it were make-up. Or traces of sunlight catching her pale skin across the courtyard.

'I shouldn't be here. It's bad luck, you know, to see the bride before the ceremony,' she laughed. 'But I don't believe in those things. It sounded like you might need a hand with Bella.'

'I always need a hand with Bella.'

Silent moments burdened the space between them.

'You look beautiful, by the way,' Jacobo spoke finally.

'It's my old wedding dress. I hope you don't mind. I didn't want to be extravagant and buy a new one. The veil belonged to my mother. I'm sorry, I should've asked you.'

Lea was widowed when Elena, now almost four, was just a baby. Her parents had left Monterini to find work in Poland years ago. Even with her teacher's salary, it must have been a struggle to bring up two young girls alone. Jacobo felt a wave of affection rush over him. She was attractive, in a different way to his first wife, and he appreciated how she had just spoken to Bella and Rico, firmly but with warmth.

Lea raised her lashes and a look of love fluttered through the air towards him. In that moment he knew she cared for him.

'Don't make her come,' Lea said gently. 'Let's wait a while. Take it slowly, give her time.'

'Maybe you're right. For a short while.' Jacobo needed to get both Bellas out of his mind. Concentrate, he instructed himself. He watched Lea glide away, his eyes resting on a line of white buttons that stretched from the back of her neck to her waist. In a moment he would be following her into the small antechamber. He would be lifting the veil over her face, checking in the traditional way that she was the right bride.

Under the white sheets of the *chuppah*, the wedding canopy, Jacobo was calmed by the sweetness of the roses Signora De Benedetti had woven around the posts.

Moments away from marriage, he watched Lea step towards him, her dress sweeping the tiled floor. From the corner of his eye he noticed the headstones of the cemetery glistening in the sunlight. It seemed that the graves were shrouded in a film of auburn mist. He shut his eyes. A soft breeze rose, slipping away memories, banishing old ghosts.

Jacobo stretched out his hand to welcome his new bride and whispered a silent goodbye to the old one.

CHAPTER 8

In the weeks following the wedding, Angelo was haunted by memories. Each morning he woke with a nagging pain in his chest. He wondered why he breathed with difficulty, why the gentle cadence of music brought little comfort. Even singing to his grapes failed to revive him.

'I must be ill,' he said aloud one evening as he led Rodeo along the San Gianni path to his stable. Bubbles of sweat sprouted on his forehead. He refused an *aperitivo* at Roberto's bar, ate barely a spoonful at lunchtime and his glass of wine remained untouched on the table.

He nodded at Pino Petri, reading *Il Popolo* outside the barber's shop, offered a laboured smile to Gino from Naples. Feeling old and weary, he shuffled down Via Meravigliosa, watching the dust coat his boots. Santina was standing on the veranda, pinafore covering her dress, hands folded tightly across her chest.

'What is wrong with you?' she hissed through clenched teeth. Angelo looked up at her from the bottom of the steps, clasping the iron railings with his earth-coated hands. 'You look sixty years old, shrivelled and hunched, just like your father, may he rest in peace! What kind of a husband are you?'

'Good evening to you too.' He pushed past her, muttering under his breath. He sidled through the kitchen to the washroom at the back of the house. With the extra money Angelo had earned from *Vino degli Angeli*, he'd bought some wood and had built a small washroom. Each day his sons would haul buckets of water from the fountain in the street to the kitchen and Santina would heat the water over the fire. Now everyone could wash in the house instead of down at the river with the other *contadini*.

He was hoping to get some peace, alone in his washroom. But no, Santina was knocking on the door with the soup ladle.

'Angelo, for pity's sake?' Santina's voice echoed through the planks of wood, rising each time she bashed the soup ladle against the frame. 'I've been greeted with a gloomy face for the past few weeks. You've hardly spoken to our sons. You've jumped at me whenever I've opened my mouth.'

Angelo soaked the purple patches on his arms, watching the bubbles of soapy water disappear into his skin. Why couldn't the woman leave him alone? His mind drifted to the soft, rolling fields at his smallholding, the sun kindling his crops with a warm glow. His beautiful, calm grapes never tormented him with questions. His donkey waited for him graciously in the *cantina*, rubbing its soft fur against his arm, nuzzling its head into the palm of his hand. The pounding on the washroom door brought him back to the present with a jolt.

Angelo wiped his hands, opened the door and faced his wife. Her long nose was heightened by puffy, russet patches under her eyes. Hair scooped up on top of her head covered by a chequered scarf, pinafore hugging her portly belly, she resembled the corpulent, old women of Monterini who dressed in black and waddled down the streets stumbling over the cobblestones. At night they sat outside their homes, eyes squinting in the light of the oil lamps as their fingers, like dancing spiders, threaded patches of embroidery nestling on their laps. It wouldn't be long before she would be joining them, old and fat, he thought as he looked at her.

'Well?' she scowled, her cheeks plump and rosy.

Angelo shuffled over to the kitchen, sat down at the oak table and stared out of the window. Apart from the small washroom, the house had remained much the same over the years. It was smaller than Jacobo's, more functional. There were no ornaments, no photographs and the windows were tiny, without the view of the valley that Jacobo enjoyed. But the walls of both houses were made of *tufo* rock, breathing air into the house in warm weather and blocking it like a sentry during the freezing months of winter, when snow coated the streets and the fountains trickled icicles.

'Maybe I'm ill. Thought of that? You offer me no sympathy.'

Santina placed the ladle in a pot that was bubbling on the stove. She stirred it. An aroma of beef stew filled Angelo's nostrils. She turned towards her husband, arms folded across her bosom. 'It's Jacobo. You haven't been the same since he left.'

'*Sei pazza.*' Spitting words as if spitting out a heavily salted dish, Angelo reached across the table and poured himself a drink from the carafe of red wine.

'Do not call me a mad woman,' Santina yelled, her face so close to Angelo he could see the egg whites of her eyes, the little flecks of yellow and red. Wisps of silvery hair sprouted from her scarf.

'Jacobo is a few streets away. I can see him, any time.'

'*Esatto.* But it's not the same, is it?' Santina turned to remove the bread from the oven. Placing it on the table, she took a cloth to hold the loaf in her left hand as she cut it slowly with her right. Angelo tore chunks from the slabs she was cutting and rolled them into small balls. He dipped the balls in the wine and placed the soaked pieces in his mouth. As he looked up, he noticed the flesh on Santina's face soften, an expression of kindness flit across her eyes. His wife was often brash with him and the children. It was her way, he accepted it, sometimes even enjoyed the bickering. He found it easier to deal with than her sympathy, probably because it was so rarely offered.

'He's moved away. You miss him, that's all.'

Angelo yearned to scream at Santina, tell her not to be so stupid, sympathy didn't suit her. But he knew better than to call her *pazza* again, not so soon anyway. He took a gulp of wine. 'It was good enough for Bella. She didn't leave.'

'Only because she ends up getting her own way.' Santina bent over Angelo. He could feel her breath on his cheek. 'It makes sense for them to live in the Ghetto. Lea grew up there, her girls are used to their home.' She straightened up and moved back to the stove to check on the stew.

'It's empty without him.'

'It's a change that's all and, in this village, we're not used to change, no matter how small.' Her voice was quieter now, gentler. But it didn't last long. As he slipped more wine-stained crumbs into his mouth, Santina spun round and whacked his hand with her ladle.

'Enough bread before the meal! Get your sons and let's eat. He got married, that's all. Be pleased for him. And for the sake of *La Madonna*, please try and cheer up!' She made the sign of the cross.

Angelo wiped the crumbs from his lips with the back of his hand, walked across the stone floor and out on to the veranda. Santina was right, he should be happy for Jacobo. But somehow, he knew the heaviness in his chest would only vanish if Jacobo were living next door, watching the same sunsets and sipping the same wine. His comfort was their Wednesday afternoons. The memories floating above the shared bottles of *Vino degli Angeli* would not vanish with a marriage or a move. Each week Jacobo was there, his arms full of books and newspapers, his head full of rage at Mussolini's latest exploit. Angelo would have to comfort himself with that.

'*A tavola*,' he called to his sons, sprawled across the middle of the street playing marbles with Bella.

She looked up at him and waved, green eyes dancing, lips breaking into a smile. Angelo waved back. Whilst she was still there, in the house next door with her chatter and vitality, a part of Jacobo still remained.

~~~

When Jacobo stepped over from the Fratta to the Ghetto, he was hit by an unexpected wave of sentimentality. It was down these cobbled streets that Avraham Levi had wandered searching for the perfect place to settle.

In this, the most ancient quarter of Monterini, the sun fought its way through tiny alleyways. Without verandas to divide them, houses clung together. There was no space for idle chatter, whiling time away with neighbours. Children didn't play hopscotch or sing the nursery rhyme, *doman domani*. But the synagogue was close by and so were most of the other Jewish families; the De Benedettis, the Servis, the Spizzochinis, as well as Rabbi Coen.

In many ways, Jacobo felt nourished by his new life in the Ghetto. Although it only took him a handful of minutes to cross Via Roma and return to the Fratta, there was something about the sombre Ghetto streets that suited him. He wondered whether it was the lack of bustle and chaos he had been so accustomed to or whether it was simply the fact he was now living in the traditionally Jewish part of Monterini, close to his roots, close to his fellow *ebrei*.

The Kabbalist Isaac Luria said there exists a divine spark of energy in every created thing. Jacobo sensed that spark in the glittering stained-glass window of the Beit Israel Synagogue, in the dense, sweet smell of *challas* baking in the ovens on

Friday mornings in preparation for *Shabbat*. He detected it in the *sfratti*, laid out on trays in the Servi's bakery; little batons of pastry filled with almonds and dates. He recognised it in Signora Servi's smile, in the press of her fingers as she handed him a packet of pastries.

Jacobo had always been more interested in the intellectual and philosophical side of his religion, with tradition playing a smaller part in his life. Now he felt nurtured by the communal events when Lea would invite the De Benedettis or the Spizzochinis for the Friday evening meal, remembering it was in fact Luria himself who introduced the concept of *Kabbalat Shabbat*. The lace tablecloth, the kosher Monterinese wine, blessings over the candles, the meal of artichokes and sautéed veal gave him a new sense of belonging. It helped to eclipse the fear that had haunted him for some time. Or perhaps it merely helped to contain it.

Several months after the wedding, Lea encouraged Jacobo to invite Bella to join them in the house in Via Zuccarelli.

'It's time for Bella to move in with us,' she announced one morning at breakfast.

At the table, in front of him lay a copy of *La Stampa*, with a photograph of Mussolini driving a racing car blazoned across the front page. Jacobo shook his head and dipped a piece of *cornetto* into his *caffelatte*.

'Look at this, Lea,' Jacobo said. He pointed to the paper, ignoring Lea's comment. 'Yesterday he was playing a violin, last week winning a chess game. I even saw him in the paper jogging the other day. What's he trying to do?'

'To portray himself as a super man, I guess,' Lea said. She tilted her head to obtain a clearer view of the page. 'I saw a photograph in *Il Popolo* and he was flying a plane. Next we'll see him making a meal and washing the clothes.'

They laughed.

'So, what do you think about Bella? What should we do?'

'Wasn't it your idea she should stay in the Fratta?'

'I thought it was best at the time, what with us getting married, so many changes. But she needs to be with her father.'

'Why? She's happy in the Fratta. It's what she wanted, isn't it? She's with *babbo*. She has the Ghiones next door. She's fine.'

'I'm sure she's fine. And yes, it's what she wants. But I'm not sure it's best for her.' Lea emphasised her words with authority as if she were talking to one of her pupils. Jacobo wondered if she found his distracted air annoying and felt the need to scold him. He always felt distracted when Bella was near him or her name was mentioned.

'Her place should be with her father and with me and the girls. She needs a real family, love, support. Not that she doesn't get that from your father, of course. But she's getting older. The Ghiones, well, you know... they are wonderful people but...'

'But what, Lea? The Ghiones love Bella, they treat her like their own.'

'I know they do.' There was a pause. 'Last week I saw Rico wearing the costume of the *Balilla*.'

'Are you sure?'

'Well, yes. Lots of young children in Monterini have joined up but it's not good.'

Jacobo couldn't imagine Angelo sending his sons to the *Opera Nazionale Balilla,* Mussolini's fascist youth group. Over the past few years, the *Balilla* had grown in popularity. From the mountains of the north to the beaches of the south, children were demonstrating their allegiance to *il Duce*. But Angelo?

'I saw all three boys running to a meeting last week,' Lea continued. 'I was surprised Mateo and Carlo were allowed to join. They're so young. I thought you had to be at least eight.'

'How do you know that's where they were going?'

'It was pretty obvious. Black shirts, fez-like hat with a tassle and picture of an eagle, greeny-grey trousers. They resembled *squadristi,* little Blackshirts.'

'Hmm.' Jacobo tapped Mussolini's crumpled smile with the back of his hand. He couldn't imagine Angelo's three boys marching off to meetings dressed in the uniform of tiny Blackshirts. It didn't fit with Angelo's view of life.

'We're being told at school to encourage the children to join. Orders of the ONB. Part of furthering their education, or something like that.' Lea licked the froth from the rim of her coffee cup. 'But, of course, we ignore it.'

'This is the new imperialist fascist state, remember,' Jacobo said. 'We're surrounded by fascists, even in Monterini. But Angelo? He's never been interested in politics of any description. As long as he's got his wine, his grapes, he's happy.'

'Don't worry.' Lea placed a hand on Jacobo's arm and turned her face towards him. 'Angelo's not a fascist, I shouldn't have mentioned it.'

She paused, took a breath. 'The thing is, I would like Bella to live with us. You're her father.'

She touched Jacobo's cheek, then pulled her hand away. Jacobo reached out and caught it. He stroked her arm. Her skin was smooth and taut. Shyly, he pulled her towards him. He held her for a moment feeling the weight of her body against his, breathing in the sweet smell of her. His arm dropped to his side. He so much wanted to be part of Lea's life, to be included, yet something hindered him. There was a space between them and Jacobo didn't know how to fill it, how to step between the gaps. His eyes wandered over to the windows of Lea's kitchen with the view of the cemetery surrounded by vineyards. There was a flicker at the corner of his eye, something was pulling him.

He shut his eyes.

He could feel Lea's breath on his cheeks. She entwined her fingers through his with the determination of a *contadino* steering his donkey through fields of stones.

'We're a family now, Jacobo.' The words blew softly through the air and melted on his skin.

'I don't know why but I often forget about Bella. When I realise, it always seems too late.'

'Well, it's not too late now.' Lea's lips parted into a smile. 'She belongs here with us, not with the Ghiones.'

Maybe Lea was right. Maybe it was time to bring Bella over to Via Zuccarelli, to the spindly, crooked house that had belonged to Lea's father Samuel. But with Bella living in Lea's house he would have less excuse to trudge through the autumn rain to the Fratta; to sip *Vino degli Angeli* with Angelo; to delight in the smells of pine trees, the sounds of donkeys braying.

A few days later, Bella and Rico appeared at the house in the Ghetto. It was a dismal day, the golden walls of the village stood murky grey against the thundering sky. Lea ushered the children into the kitchen where Jacobo was hunched over the evening paper. Hands on Rico's shoulders, Lea nodded over his hat towards Jacobo, her lips mouthing the words. 'You see, I told you.'

'Look who have come to see us,' she said aloud.

'Well Rico, what's this?' Jacobo pointed to the uniform.

'I'm a *balilla*.'

Rico had recently grown, his legs long and tapering beneath his green shorts.

'I can see.' Jacobo rose from his chair and walked over to the boy. Taking Rico's chin in the palm of his hand he asked, 'Why, Rico?'

'We all have to be now. It's the new *Italia*. And it's fun.'

'I want to join the *Piccole Italiane* so I can go with him. It's for girls.' Bella nodded. Her grass eyes sparkled.

Jacobo's gaze met Lea's across the kitchen. 'It's impossible, Bella, you're a Jew.'

'So what? Please *babbo*. *Per favore*.' She ran over to Jacobo and flung her arms around his waist.

Jacobo stiffened. 'No.'

'But why, *babbo*? It's fun and I want to go with Rico. Even the twins are allowed. They go to the *Figli della Lupa* for younger children. Ask *zio* Angelo if you don't believe me.'

'It's out of the question,' Jacobo repeated. A necklace of sweat beaded his throat. 'Mussolini is dangerous for this country, you'll have nothing to do with these groups, do you hear me?'

Bella sighed and rolled her eyes to the ceiling. '*Andiamo*,' she mouthed to Rico, grasping his hand and pulling him towards the door. As they marched down the steps, she whispered in the Monterini dialect, 'I'll get round him, I always do.'

But her father heard.

Voice like crushed pebbles, he shouted into the dusky Ghetto streets, 'Not this time, *signorina*. *Il Duce* is stronger than us all.'

CHAPTER 9

Bella arrived in the Ghetto on a cold day at the beginning of November. Rico accompanied her. The streets were gloomy, the sky heavy with clouds. She carried a bag of books, and a spare pair of dungarees. Rico carried her small Pinocchio and her favourite faded yellow blanket, the one Angelo had used to cover her hours after her birth. They crossed the piazza, the bare branches of the cedar trees stark against the blue-black sky. At the entrance to the Ghetto, they faced each other. Bella placed her belongings on the ground and hugged Rico.

The clouds parted allowing a slither of sunlight to blush their faces. Bella waved, then stumbled past the *matzah* ovens and the kosher butcher.

'My goodness, your new sister is an educated girl,' Lea declared to Luciana and Elena as they greeted Bella on the steps of the house in Via Zuccarelli.

'I take after my father,' Bella said softly. She followed Lea down the narrow hall into the sitting room and placed her belongings on the floor. The house was smaller but more elegant than the Via Meravigliosa house. The floor tiles were polished and shiny, and a smell of disinfectant wafted through the air. There were candlesticks on the table and photographs on the windowsill of Lea and her girls, the Jewish community celebrating a communal event in the synagogue. The photograph of Lea and her first husband Luigi had disappeared. Replacing it in a silver frame was one of Jacobo staring shyly at the camera in his wedding suit and Lea, face partly covered by her veil, was looking at Jacobo. Glass ornaments dotted the shelves and flower-filled vases splashed the walls with purples and pinks.

'But you look just like your mother.' Lea knelt down next to Bella and lightly touched her head. 'She had hair just like you, orange curls that lit up our dull streets and those unusual green eyes. And lovely freckles that splashed her face, just like yours. She was very beautiful, you know.'

'I never met her.' A flush of warmth rushed to Bella's cheeks. 'And I don't think about her, hardly ever.' She paused for a moment then spoke slowly as if weighing up her words. 'Is it bad that I don't miss having a mother?'

'You can share ours.' Elena rested a head of dark ringlets on Bella's shoulder. A podgy hand grabbed Bella's slight one.

'No thanks.' Registering the look of pain on Elena's face and the quizzical look on Lea's, Bella reshaped her answer. 'I don't need a mother. I have my *nonno* Cosimo and *zio* Angelo and *zia* Santina and all the people in the street and, of course, Rico. And Carlo and Mateo.'

'Your *babbo* too,' offered Lea quietly.

'Oh.' She nodded. 'I forgot about him.'

'How can you forget your own *babbo*?' Luciana's lashes glistened. 'I won't forget mine. Ever.'

Bella gazed at Luciana's milky white cheeks, her skinny arms. She'd noticed how the older sister often hid behind her mother, whilst Elena, the younger, more playful one, brazenly chatted to everyone. Luciana was fragile, sad and seemed to really miss her *babbo*. Bella needed to answer thoughtfully.

'I think it's because he forgets me,' she said.

'Well, not anymore. I'm here to remind him.' Lea pointed to a shelf at the back of the room. 'Come on, *signorine*, find a

71

place for Bella's books. And then you two can show your new sister her bedroom. It's the one I slept in when I was a child. I used to love it. It's pink and green and in the morning the sun shines right through the windows and the whole room has a rosy, warm colour.'

'I hate pink,' said Bella coolly as she followed Elena and Luciana out of the room. 'It's my worst colour.'

Every day after school, Bella returned to her old neighbourhood with Rico. They played hopscotch on the paving stones and ran down to the river. He showed her the special handkerchief he wore to the *Balilla* meetings. It looked just like the Italian flag. They laughed as she tied it around her head like a scarf. Sometimes Angelo would take them on his donkey, Rodeo, down to the fields. They helped him trim the weeds around the vines or jump on the vats of grapes with their bare feet. Sometimes Jacobo joined them. He would sing to the grapes with Angelo, and then sit under the peach tree, reading his religious texts, ploughing through newspapers, his eyebrows arched into a frown at the discovery of the latest Mussolini exploit.

In the evening, Bella returned to the Ghetto. She did her homework, played with Luciana and Elena, ate dinner with her new family; *acquacotta* or mushroom *risotto* followed by chicken with artichokes, and read avidly after they had washed the dishes.

She soon became accustomed to the narrow, dimly lit alleyways of the Ghetto, the intricate fountains and the spindly houses. Her father and Lea pointed out homes where generations of Jewish Monterini families had lived. They showed her where Avraham Levi had settled in the Vicolo del Ghetto. She tried to imagine her ancestors walking through Via Zuccarelli, Vicolo Canaletto and Vicolo del Ghetto; tiny alleyways that curled and twisted through the Ghetto to the piazza. She ambled to school with Lea and her new sisters, past the Jewish library, the *matzah* ovens, the *cantina* where the kosher wine was made and through the Ghetto arch.

On Friday afternoons she waited patiently to collect *challas* from the Jewish bakery and munch on a discarded piece of *sfratto*, too poor a quality to sell to the Monterini clientele. She became friends with Signora Servi, the baker's wife, and quickly learned, if she hung around before closing time, the signora would greet her with a bag full of leftover *tozzetti*. She winked back at the kosher butcher Signor Mazzi and waved to Signora De Benedetti.

Sometimes she helped Salamone Spizzichino light the candles in the synagogue in his role as *shamas*. This was her favourite pastime in her new life in the Ghetto. Salamone's eyes lit up when Bella appeared every Friday evening at the entrance of the Beit Israel Synagogue. His back was hunched, and he walked up the aisle in a crooked way, bending his whole body from side to side. Bella had to crouch down to talk to him. His hair was whiter than the snow coating the summit of Monte Amiata in winter. Salamone led her down the aisle, his hand holding the long stick that, with Bella's help, would light all the candles for *Shabbat*. Bella felt important when she stood next to Salamone on the *bimah,* the raised platform, and looked up at the tall column guarding the Ark behind which the Torah lay wrapped and hidden.

She became accustomed to helping Lea and her stepsisters prepare for *Shabbat*, rushing with Elena to buy *challas* from Signora Servi or collect fresh almonds from the *contadini*. She loved to stroke the green husks and pop one or two in her mouth on the way home. She enjoyed helping Lea and Signora Franca prepare stuffed artichokes for the *Shabbat* lunch and arrange the fresh fruit in layers on Lea's best crockery.

Lea always insisted that the three girls wore clean, pressed clothes for *Shabbat*. At first Bella resisted, preferring her dungarees and boots. As the weeks passed, she began to enjoy the ritual of ironing her skirts, polishing her shoes and together with her stepsisters threading a piece of lavender through her hair.

In time, Bella became used to dividing her days between the Ghetto and the Fratta, learning to live with the choices others make. The quiet calm of her new quarter embroidered with the fabric of Jewish life seemed a natural repose from the bustling chaos where her *nonno* and Rico still lived. She jumped across the few streets from the Ghetto to the Fratta, studious and diligent in one; playful, high-spirited and chatting loudly in the Monterini dialect in the other.

For months Bella searched for the figure with eyes like half-moons and white robes billowing around her ankles. At first, she tiptoed alone to the spot by the river where she first met Tanaquilla. Then she took Rico, without telling him why, and made him promise he wouldn't tell anyone where they were going. Venturing out into the wilds of the *cavi* had been fruitless. The bulrushes swayed silently in the wind, the path remained untrodden and empty. Only the smell of rosemary and fennel reached her nostrils.

When she had almost given up hope, Bella saw Tanaquilla again.

She was playing hopscotch with Rico on the steps leading down from Capo Bagno to the San Gianni path. It was early evening and, at first, they didn't hear a rumbling noise growing closer and closer. Stamping boots on the cobbled streets, a hum that grew more intense, revealed a throng of men in black uniforms.

Amongst the faces, Bella recognised Signor Petri the blacksmith with Gino Bonito and other villagers of Monterini.

They were marching, arms outstretched. Some carried the black fascist flag, adorned with the emblem of the fasces, the bundle of wooden sticks and a blade resembling an axe. The children watched quietly as the men stormed past them shouting, their feet crunching on the cobblestones. The sky was alive with crimson streaks.

Bella looked up. Above the stream of black uniforms, between spires and red tiled roofs loomed Tanaquilla, a statue, draped in white robes. She screamed.

'It's only a fascist march, silly. Come on, let's go back and play.'

'No, Rico, there's something over there. Look.'

'Is it a dog? Or a bat? They make me jump too sometimes.'

'It's daytime, *stupido,* there are no bats.'

Bella squeezed her eyes shut, then opened them. Tanaquilla was still there gazing at her, hands crossed over her chest. Her fingernails were long and painted black. Her silver and navy-blue eyes had such an intense depth they made Bella think of the starless night over Monterini in winter. Tanaquilla's lips parted into a thin smile. Despite the excited banging of her heart against her chest, Bella was flooded with a feeling of calm. She sensed this figure with strange clothes and funny customs meant her no harm.

Bella threaded one arm through Rico's and, with her free hand, pointed upwards, towards the spire of the cathedral.

'It's something over there.'

'I can't see anything.' Rico squinted. 'Must have run away.'

The uniforms continued to thunder past. Above them Tanaquilla swayed, a twig in the breeze.

Palms on Rico's shoulders, Bella placed him in front of a gap in the houses. 'There, look ahead Rico, straight ahead. What can you see?'

'Houses, washing on lines. Lots of trees, some swallows,

a magpie and loads of *signori* in black shirts rushing past shouting.' Rico's voice was clipped, he was breathing heavily through his nose. Bella could tell he was irritated with her. Perhaps he thought she was playing one of her games when she would pretend to hide and then jump out from a secret place and scare him. But this time it was no game.

'Look, there's a *signora*. Can't you see her?' She ached for Rico to see Tanaquilla.

'You're being silly. I'm going home.' Rico spat out the words. The dimple that appeared when he smiled had vanished.

Bella's hand dropped to her side. Rico couldn't see Tanaquilla.

The sea of fascists disappeared towards the piazza. The stamping sound of their boots echoed through the alleyways. Bella and Rico walked back towards the Fratta. As they reached Via Bel Fiora, Bella turned. Tanaquilla was still there, hovering behind her. She looked out of place in her robes and hair like stacked bowls. She lifted her hand and placed it behind her ear, tilting her head forward as if listening to something. Then she disappeared behind the mountains.

It's only me who can see her, Bella thought. She wasn't sure if the knowledge made her feel special or more alone. She tried to remember what Tanaquilla had told her the first time they met, something to do with listening, sensing, knowing Tanaquilla would be around, somewhere.

CHAPTER 10

That same afternoon, Lea returned from school and slung her books on the kitchen table, eyes black sparks of fire. Two tiny red blotches appeared on her cheeks. She was breathing heavily. The three girls were sitting at the kitchen table. Bella was doing her homework and Luciana and Elena were cutting out paper shapes and sticking them on to pieces of white cardboard, chatting to Bella about what they had done at the *asilo*.

'Where's your father?' Lea asked Bella, her voice urgent, shriller than usual.

'At the bookshop, I suppose.'

Lea walked into the hall and picked up the telephone. 'Jacobo Levi. It's urgent.' Silence seemed to last forever. The words blew out of Lea's mouth like gusts of wind. 'Jacobo, *sei tu*? I'm fine. Yes, the girls are fine too but something awful's happened.'

A long pause. Bella remembered what Tanaquilla had said to her, how she placed her hand behind her ear that very afternoon as if urging her to listen. She put down her pen and followed Lea into the hall. She sidled up to her, hoping to hear her father's voice.

'I had to swear an oath today, promising to defend the fascist regime,' Lea continued. 'We all had to do it, all the teachers, all over Italy, apparently.'

Bella leaned closer to the receiver, but her father's voice was too faint. Lea raised her eyebrows in surprise and gently pushed

Bella away, her head nodding in agreement with what she heard at the other end of the line.

'And what's more, from now on, all schools and all newspapers have to write the date like this...' Lea glanced down at Bella. 'Remind me of the date, Bella, my head's a blur.'

'The thirteenth of November.'

'Well, instead of writing the thirteenth of November 1929, we now have to write the thirteenth of November of the seventh year of Mussolini's reign.' Lea's voice was croaky, her chest heaving. A tear streaked her cheek. As if remembering Bella was close by, she brushed it away and smiled, a watery half smile. Bella reached for her hand as Lea said, 'Jacobo, I'm frightened. Whatever will he do next?'

⌾⌾⌾

Jacobo's reply was lost somewhere in the telephone cables between Via Zuccarelli and the bookshop on Via Cavour. Or perhaps heard only by the operator in the post office in the new part of the village. The lines on Jacobo's forehead deepened as he held the receiver in his hand and stared at the ceiling, thinking of his clients and the other villagers who had dismissed his worries about the new fascist ruler with a brisk wave of their fine-suited arms.

'He's good for Italy, good for us. He's our friend,' some of the prosperous Jews from the big cities had declared, encouraged by Mussolini's determination, direct manner, daring approach.

'Today Italy, tomorrow the world,' they'd insisted, quoting their leader. There was nothing wrong with fascism, they reminded Jacobo. Many Jews belonged to the party. After all, Mussolini wasn't anti-Jewish, *non è vero?*

But Jacobo had always sensed he was a force to reckon with. Even the rabbi and Jacobo's own father had come to Mussolini's defence in the past: 'That Benito, such a nice boy.' Only Lea had understood. She alone shared the same fear, the same worries, knowing that as his popularity grew so did *il Duce*'s power. His beliefs were becoming increasingly alarming:

Single vision.

No other political parties.

Control of industry, schools, the press, the police, the Catholic Church.

An empire to beat all empires.

Jacobo replaced the receiver and sat back in his chair. He looked out from his office at the back of the bookshop, to the red brick houses of the new part of town. Heavy clouds hung in the sky, stark and menacing.

Despite their agreement on the views of Mussolini, Jacobo had never discussed with Lea the familiar feeling that echoed around him when a new ruling was made. That tingling sensation across his back, along his jaw; the smell of sulphur that itched his nostrils. Sometimes he tried to push it to the back of his mind, even pretend it wasn't happening. But danger lurked in every corner, every crevice.

Dinner was a grim affair. Jacobo forked ribbons of pasta into his mouth, eyes vacant, face pale. Lea motioned to the girls to clear away the dishes and make room for the *polpettone al limone*. Bella leaned across the table, gazing at her father.

'Well?' Jacobo stared back from behind his round-rimmed spectacles.

'The *signora* said there was blood. It means there's an omen in the egg.' She measured her words with care. 'At first, I thought it was the wedding, but that's been fine. Then I thought it was moving here and that's really been fine too. So maybe *il Duce* is the omen?'

'What do you mean?' Jacobo cocked his head to one side. His eyes settled on her, waiting for an explanation.

'I mean an omen can be good or bad, can't it? And there was a fascist march today and this new rule about the date. And because I saw her again, it made me think about it.'

'Saw who?' Jacobo's quivering lips were in contrast to his voice, which remained calm. 'Think about what?'

'The omen,' Bella said, emphasising the words and raising her eyes to the ceiling with irritation.

'What omen? Who told you this, *cara*?' Lea placed a hand on Bella's arm.

'It's nothing,' Bella sighed. 'Just someone I met, well I think I met her, but I'm not sure. She didn't seem very real. And Rico can't see her, only me.'

'What are you talking about?' Jacobo's words were jagged, as if he had forgotten how to breathe. Placing his hands on the floral tablecloth, he leaned forward. The stares of father and daughter merged across the dinner table, the inky eyes of fear transfixed by the wild eyes of youth. 'Who did you meet? Or think you met. Which *signora*?'

Bella had never told them she had ventured as far away as the forbidden *cavi*. She may have been punished, banned from seeing Rico for several days, or perhaps a week without *caramelli*. Now, as she started to relate the events of that afternoon, when her feet carried her beyond the boundaries of the village, the words tumbled out, bumping against each other in their excitement to be heard. In breathless bursts she described Tanaquilla, their conversation, the eggs in the clearing. She even ended with an account of the last sighting that very afternoon.

The muscles along Jacobo's jaw clenched. A snorting sound could be heard as the breath escaped from his nose, reminding Bella of Angelo's pig at the smallholding. *Zio* Angelo always used to explain that when the pig was anxious or frightened it would snort and puff. Bella giggled as she looked at her father and thought of Angelo's pig.

Jacobo shoved away his chair, strode around to Bella's side of the table. He cemented his hands on her shoulders. The giggles froze on Bella's lips.

'*Vietato*. Forbidden, it's forbidden.'

'What is? What have I done?'

Silence grew around them.

Luciana's lips began to quiver. Her round, hazelnut eyes opened wide and misted over. 'Why is he angry?' she whispered to her mother, not daring to glance at her stepfather.

Lea shook her head, glancing from Jacobo to Bella. She beckoned Elena to her, stretching her arms around her two daughters, pulling them towards her, protectively, motherly.

Jacobo took a deep breath as if trying to control himself. 'It's forbidden to converse with spirits or witches. Whatever they are.'

Bella had expected her father to be cross with her for venturing down to the *cavi*, all alone. But he hadn't mentioned that. She couldn't understand why he was mentioning spirits and witches. She crossed her arms over her chest and glared at her father. 'Tanaquilla's not a witch. She's Etruscan!'

The colour vanished from Jacobo's cheeks, his face cavernous, almost ghostly in the twilight. He stooped over to the bookshelf in the corner of the dining room. He reached up for a tattered, leather-bound volume and thumbed through the pages of his *chumash*, the Hebrew prayer book.

'*Eccolo*,' he said at last, thrusting the book under Bella's nose. 'Leviticus, chapter twenty, verse six. It states clearly: "It is prohibited to have any connection with spirits after death."' Jacobo pushed his spectacles further up his nose as he squinted at the small letters written in Hebrew on the right and Italian on the left.

'Aren't you being rather dramatic, Jacobo?' Lea's arms tightened around her daughters. Elena buried her head in the folds of Lea's skirt. 'The person Bella is talking about is just an

81

imaginary figure, you know the sort of thing children do, it's very common.'

'I'm not a baby,' Bella said. 'I'm nine! I know what's imaginary and what's real. She's a person, a strange one but a person all the same, even though there's a funny smell around her, a bit like eggs, or the sulphur springs outside Monterini.'

The skin of Jacobo's face blanched. The tension in the room took on a life of its own, as if a real being was breathing the air. He clasped the *chumash* and with trembling fingers fumbled back towards the beginning of the book.

'Book of Exodus, chapter twenty-two, verse seventeen: "You shall not suffer a witch to survive." Are you a witch, Bella? Are you?'

Bella shook her head. 'I'm not a witch *babbo*,' she cried. 'I'm not a witch.'

Her words mingled with Luciana's sobs. Elena's face was still buried in Lea's lap, arms tight around her mother's waist.

Lea snatched the book from Jacobo's hands. 'Enough! What on earth has got into you? You're frightening them. Look, my daughters are quaking.' Lea pulled Bella to her and stretched her arms around all three girls.

Jacobo's skin was ashen. He stepped back, breathing as if each breath was catching in his throat. He stumbled towards the table and sat down. 'I'm upset by today's news, I'm sorry.'

Placing his chin on his hands, he looked at Bella. She wondered whether her skin was as pallid as his, if her eyes flashed with the same anger. An unforgiving calm settled over her father. When he spoke, his voice was soft and feathery.

'Bella, please shut this out of your mind. And don't mention it ever again.'

And she didn't.

Not until it was too late.

PART TWO

Forbidden Love: 1937–1943

CHAPTER 1

Bella opened the door of the secondary school and raised her eyes to the sky. The air was sultry. She stepped out, casting a glance at Monte Amiata swathed with clouds. Droplets of rain splashed her arm. Her eyes filled with tears. It seemed to happen a lot lately.

Bella saw Rico less these days. It was more than the physical separation of the Ghetto and the Fratta. Three years ago, Rico had left school, older than most of the other farm workers, but young to end his education. Jacobo had begged Angelo to let him stay on, telling him Rico was intelligent, would continue to do well in his studies. Angelo would hear nothing of it. He needed Rico with him, the grapes were flourishing. Why did he need to pay more workers to sing to them when he had an able farmhand in his young son?

'What good are words and sums if you can't eat?' she remembered hearing Angelo say, one summer evening after school.

But she missed Rico. They'd been bound together since birth, tripping in and out of each other's kitchens, sharing sweets and marbles and sometimes even clothes. This familiar love, nourishing her through childhood, what use was it now when she hardly saw him?

She tried to remember the last time. It was five or six weeks ago when a carpet of lavender stretched across the fields and the sun turned their arms chestnut brown. They had spent the afternoon with Angelo at the smallholding. Since then the weather had turned; murky skies marked the beginning of autumn.

A hand brushed Bella's shoulder. She flipped round, almost dropping her schoolbooks. 'Rico! You frightened me. What are you doing here?'

'I was passing. Why are you standing here, staring at the rain? You'll get soaked.' He unfolded a raincoat. 'I brought this for you. I could tell it was going to rain. I smelt it.' He winked at her. 'Sometimes it's useful being a *contadino*.'

A warm feeling flooded through Bella. She wondered if Rico had passed by specially to see her, whether he missed her too.

He placed the raincoat over their heads and shoulders, his bare arms bronzed from working in the fields. He was a good head taller than her. If she stood on tiptoes, she just about reached his shoulders. He had Angelo's height but was slim and wiry, aching with muscles. Rico had not inherited the pockmarked face or tough, sandy hair of his father. His face was compelling rather than handsome, with knowing charcoal eyes. Black strands of hair fell across his cheek and down to his neck.

'I'll walk some of the way with you.' He smiled an open, gentle smile, touching her elbow with his free hand. It sent a ripple through her and made Bella feel quite giddy. He guided her through the school gates with their ornate cast iron railings. The rain was coming fast, the sky bruised with clouds. To keep dry they had to walk close together, the flesh of their arms rubbing against each other.

'I don't see you much anymore.' She turned her head towards him and wondered what it would be like to stand with him under the *chuppah*, the wedding canopy at the Beit Israel Synagogue. The thought quickly vanished, there could be no wedding, the rabbi would never bless them.

Rico lowered his eyes. She detected a flicker around his mouth as if he were about to say something, then he looked at her again.

'It's true, it's been a few weeks.'

'When I come to see *nonno* in the Fratta, you're rarely around. Signora Franca says she never sees you when she's cleaning the veranda or helping *nonno*.'

'So, you miss me, do you?' He poked her in the ribs. A whooshing sensation raced through her. The other girls in Monterini often spoke of the boys they fell in love with. They remembered the exact second. Vera Todi from the Fratta told Bella how an arrow full of love pierced her heart when she saw Guiseppe Petri washing himself in the fountain. But when it came to Rico, Bella couldn't recall a day, a month or a particular second when her arrow struck. As they stood there under the raincoat, she simply knew she loved him.

She always had.

They walked over the bridge and down the stairs to the old town, retracing steps they had taken every day as children. They passed the lions, wet and shiny in the downpour as if they were freshly polished. When they came to where the road forked, the Ghetto in one direction, the Fratta in the other, they stopped.

'Walk back with me to the Ghetto?' She placed her fingers lightly on his arm. His muscles tensed beneath her touch. He nodded agreement, his dark eyes watching her intently.

'It's very wearing at home. Things aren't good for us. Us Jews, I mean.' It was easier to talk about the current situation, than focus on the churning inside her each time their skin touched. '*Babbo*'s constantly preoccupied. He brings home all the newspaper clippings from the morning. He thinks we are about to be swallowed up by the fascists.'

'*Zio* Jacobo's been saying that for as long as I remember. Nothing's going to happen. You Jews, you're just like everyone else. There's no difference.'

'*Babbo* certainly doesn't think so. You know Rico, he even makes a note of what he's heard on the wireless and reads it out to us over lunch. We have a day by day account of who said and did what.'

'At least you learn what's going on.'

'Sometimes, I'd rather not know. And Lea thinks *babbo*'s right. She doesn't trust Mussolini. Never has. Her mother and brother still live in Kraków and they send us letters about what's happening over there. And we have cousins in Berlin, on my mother's side. Some rulings were passed in Germany last year, you see, the Nurenberg Laws. *Babbo* told me they're making life difficult for Jews living there. He says they have become almost like non-people.'

'But it's different here.' Rico stepped across a puddle of water and guided her around it. Monterini was a dangerous place when it rained. Their shoes slid on the wet cobblestones, water curled around their feet and splashed their calves. Balancing the raincoat and Bella's books as competently as tightrope walkers, they jumped over the torrents gushing down the narrow streets, splashing the golden *tufo* walls of the houses.

'What if *babbo*'s right? Mussolini sent the *capo* of the fascist police to Berlin last year. He met Himmler. He's the new head of the German police. *Babbo* says he's a very dangerous man.'

'Just block your ears when he tells you these things. I do it all the time to *mamma* as soon as she starts her nagging. You should try it.'

Bella gave a half smile. All she wanted was for him to understand the fear that crept up on her as swiftly as mist in summertime; the worried whispers she heard along the alleyways of the Ghetto, her father's deep scowl when he read the papers, his insistence that things were going to get worse.

But Rico didn't understand. How could he? And now he was telling her about the *Avanguardista* movement he had joined, Mussolini's Blackshirt youth group, who pledged their allegiance to *il Duce*. According to Jacobo, many of them were thugs, accosting those who didn't join the party. There were rumours of violence and attacks, late at night or in people's homes. She'd never witnessed anything like that in Monterini, maybe in the big cities to the north and south, but for Rico to be associated with it seemed wrong to Bella.

'You're not a fascist, Rico.' She touched his hand; it was as rough as a spade. 'Why on earth are you a member of the Blackshirts?'

'Just felt like being part of something, I guess. I don't know enough about it, only what I hear at the blacksmith's or in the fields, or in Roberto's bar. I know Mussolini is building an empire for us in Africa; the war in Abyssinia is going well, they say. Everyone's waiting to hear if he's conquered it yet.'

The differences between them choked her like ivy around a grapevine. Suddenly she felt like a stranger to him. She couldn't explain the tight feeling in her lungs, the way her stomach churned as if she were permanently sick, so different from the fluttering and tingling when he touched her. And she wasn't even sure if it were her absurd feelings for Rico or her fear of the future that was causing her sadness.

She swallowed, then said slowly, 'My father believes what Mussolini is doing in Abyssinia is terrible. It's imperialistic, against the beliefs of the Roman Catholic Church, he says.'

Although Bella questioned Jacobo's outrage at what was going on, part of her wondered whether he could be right. And now she questioned Rico's blind faith in where the leader of their country was taking them.

Rico was looking at her strangely. 'Bella, *me ne frego*, who gives a damn.'

'That's the motto of the Blackshirts,' Bella said. Was he mocking her? 'You shouldn't be quoting them.'

A cloud crossed Rico's face. He resembled the shy, insecure boy she remembered from their childhood, always hiding behind her, waiting for her to take the lead. She wondered if she had offended him.

'I don't always understand what's going on. You do, you're educated,' he said.

'Just because you've left school doesn't mean you can't learn or discover new things.' Bella's eyes searched his, but all she could see were his long lashes, his gaze fixed on the wet cobblestones. 'We could look at the newspapers together. Maybe even read some of the anti-fascist literature and really discover what's happening. But we'll have to keep it a secret. What do you think?'

'Maybe.'

They had reached Lea's house in Via Zuccarelli. She invited Rico to join them for lunch. He refused politely, bending to kiss her cheek. He smelt of sweat, earth and sweet rain. She breathed it in, hoping she could keep the scent of him alive.

Later that afternoon, Bella finished reading Dante Alighieri and was learning by heart a poem of Gabriele D'Annunzio, both set texts for her Italian literature class at school. She looked up from her books and out of the window across the view to the east side of Monterini. It had stopped raining. The olive trees glistened and streaks of lilac sketched the sky.

She made a decision; she would move back to the Fratta.

She wanted to spend more time with Rico, feel his presence near her. She wanted him to recognise how she felt about the political situation, even if he didn't fully understand it. She barely did herself. She tried to listen and sense a picture of things but became more confused. Her *nonno* Cosimo was older and frailer, she was sure he would be happy to have some company. Then she could rifle through the contents of her father's texts hidden in chests in her grandfather's house. She would teach Rico what she discovered. They would learn about the different sides to the political debate, and that way they could spend more time together. She would tell her father she was showing Rico there was another side to Mussolini's imperialistic views. It would be like the old days, spinning pebbles in the Piccolina, playing hopscotch on the streets of the Fratta, never out of each other's sight.

Bella decided to mention her new plans to her father that evening after dinner. Jacobo was sitting on the settee in the sitting room. On each side of him were her stepsisters, an arm draped over their shoulders. Their heads were bent close together. He was explaining something to them, and although Bella couldn't catch the words, she was fascinated by the way they were sitting; relaxed, at ease, free from the tension that lay between her and her father. They resembled a real family. She felt like an uninvited guest.

Luciana now eleven had just started secondary school and was pointing to a line in a book she was reading. Her hair had grown longer and lighter, but her hazelnut eyes still darted this way and that whenever anyone spoke to her. Sometimes Bella heard the teachers calling Luciana a frightened rabbit, saying she was too scared to talk in class or raise her hand. Yet here she was chatting to Jacobo about the Pirandello play she had been asked to read, excited by Jacobo's questions, interested by his comments.

On the other side of Bella's father, Elena was leaning across his lap. Her outstretched hand played with the buttons of Jacobo's shirt. He didn't seem to mind and bent his face towards her, his black eyes, usually so gloomy when he spoke to Bella, seemed to dance. He stroked Elena's head and nodded keenly when Luciana made a comment he deemed important.

Bella coughed. They all looked up. Elena jumped off the settee, grabbed Bella's hand and pulled her across the room. She was a plump nine-year-old, who loved Bella's company and would spend time in Bella's room chatting endlessly about what she had done at school, who her friends were.

But today Bella shrugged her off. 'Not now, Elie, I need to talk to my *babbo*.' She noticed how she'd emphasised the word.

Elena opened her mouth to say something then snapped it shut and ran back to the settee, jumping onto Jacobo's lap.

'What is it, Bella? I'm helping Luciana with her homework. What's that book you've got in your hand? Is it D'Annunzio, another fascist you're reading?'

'Yes, *babbo*, a set text for my Italian literature class.'

'Of course, only fascist authors allowed in fascist schools. Have you heard what our *Duce* has done today, Bella?'

A knot of anger pulled at Bella's insides. She didn't want to hear what had happened. 'I've decided to move out,' she said quickly. 'I'm going back to live in the Fratta.'

She walked out of the room, knowing her outburst would soon fade through her father like a ghost, one of the many. Some he chose to conquer, but most he chose to ignore.

She heard the protestations of her stepsisters as she walked through the hall, past the kitchen where Lea's back was bent over schoolbooks, her elbow sliding away from her waist, as pen crossed page.

Jacobo appeared silently by Bella's side, his fingers twirled round her wrist.

'What's this all about so suddenly?'

'It's not sudden,' she lied. 'I want to move back to the Fratta, that's all. *Nonno*'s on his own, he's always happy when I'm with him. Signora Franca told me he gets lonely. And anyway, I didn't think you'd mind.'

'Well, I do mind.' His eyes weighed her up, examining her face, as if looking to see whether there was something he was missing. Was he sad she was planning on moving out or just confused at her sudden decision?

'But why? It's not as if I'll be far away.'

'We need to stay together. We don't know what Mussolini will do next. This conversation is an old one. I'm tired of it.' His tone suggested indifference.

'I'm tired of it too. It's hard listening all the time to whatever Mussolini is or isn't doing and how we'll all be treated in the same way as the German Jews. I want to learn on my own, make up my own mind.'

And why don't you put all the effort you put into the political situation into me, she yearned to say. Why don't you talk to me like you do to Luciana and Elena? Why can't you do that, *babbo*?

She grabbed her coat from the stand in the hall where all the winter coats were kept and below which the outdoor footwear was stacked. She didn't bother to change her shoes. She stepped out in her slippers to the clouds darkening the doorway, wrapped up by the cold, night air. She didn't turn to see the expression on her father's face. But she heard deep sighs. She wondered whether he uttered the words, 'Don't leave.'

Or whether she imagined them.

CHAPTER 2

Only stray cats walked along the streets of the Fratta searching for refuge from the rain. The inviting smell of wood fires, the pungent aroma of donkeys filled the air. Bella climbed up the steps to the veranda. The pots of autumn flowers had been cleared away and were now standing in a corner piled one on top of each other.

Instead of going straight into her grandfather's house, Bella pushed open the door with the grey shutters and stood on the threshold.

'What a nice surprise on such a cold night.' Angelo faced the door as if he'd been waiting for her to appear. '*Mia piccola Bella*. Come in.'

She had always been his little Bella, as precious as a single grape, he'd told her, as beautiful as the strips of gold over Monte Amiata at dusk.

'Are you looking for Rico?' Santina looked up from her embroidery. She was sitting in front of the fireplace, her fingers dancing with the needle. 'He's in the *cantina* cutting more wood for the fire.'

Bella shrugged her shoulders and lifted her eyes towards Angelo. 'Actually, I want to see you, *zio*. I need to ask you something.'

Angelo's lips parted, showing his few remaining teeth, uneven and yellow. He pulled up a chair and motioned for her to sit down. He walked over to the dresser and brought a bottle and two glasses to the table.

'Nobody usually asks me anything,' he said, his voice deep with pride that she had come to seek his advice.

'Unless it's about grapes!' Santina snorted from her corner by the fire.

'This isn't about grapes. You know me, I know little about that kind of thing. Except how to sing to them.'

'But you can drink and enjoy it. *Chin chin.*' Angelo clinked her glass and winked at her.

Bella took a sip. 'Mmmm. *Zio*, it tastes like honey and warmth, almost as if you can hear the music when it touches your throat. I don't remember your wine ever tasting this good.'

'Good harvest,' Angelo smiled. 'And good voices this year. That's the difference.'

'*Stupidaggini,*' Santina held her tablecloth close to her eyes to examine the cross-stitching.

'Can you believe this woman! Eight years we sing to our grapes. Each year the wine gets better and better and still she doesn't believe it.'

'*È vero.*' Bella laughed.

Santina shook her head. 'What did you want to ask my genius of a husband then?'

'Nothing to do with wine. I wondered whether you thought *babbo*, I don't know, he seems so different these days. I remember him being distant when I was younger, not quite here most of the time, not interested in anything apart from his books. But now I see him with my stepsisters, caring and attentive. I don't remember him like that, certainly not with me. Then there's this Mussolini issue. He seems obsessed with him.

'He changed years ago.' Angelo took a gulp of wine. 'Gradually, bit by bit. The Mussolini thing is not new.'

'And me? Has he changed towards me, do you think?'

'Changed towards you? He loves you. Made you leave the Fratta to live with him. You're his world.'

'But I don't think I am.' She gazed down at her glass. 'I've decided to move back here. We'll be neighbours again. Won't that be nice?' She jumped up and ran around the oak table to kiss Angelo on both cheeks. She didn't tell him the real reason for her move: the desperate need to be near his son, to feel Rico's breath on her face.

It was not long before Bella was sleeping in Jacobo's old room in Via Meravigliosa. At one end of her new bedroom, the windows breathed over the street to the braying of donkeys, the clattering of carts. At the other were the hills, bluey grey at dusk, pale yellow in the dawn light. Branches of trees, bare and spindly, stretched towards the sky like fingers of a skeleton.

Bella lay in the same bed where she'd been born, where her mother had fought for her life. None of this bothered her. All that mattered was knowing, on the other side of the wall, in the room he shared with Mateo and Carlo, was Rico. At night she lay under the sheets, her thin body pressed against the wall. She tried to imagine his heart beating, hear his breath moving through the layers of rock. Occasionally she called out to him, but the *tufo* was too solid to allow lovesick whispers to permeate its walls.

She read newspapers each morning, cutting out articles and facts that could be of use in their programme of learning. She taught Rico about imperialism and racism, showed him how Mussolini's intervention in the Spanish Civil War was viewed by most intellectuals as unacceptable. She made sure Rico knew when the Rome Berlin Axis agreement was signed. She scoured the shelves of books considered unacceptable to the fascist regime.

One day, balancing on the tips of her toes, Bella pulled out from beneath a pile of religious texts, Ignazio Silone's

Fontamara. Ignazio Silone reminded her of Rico. He was the son of a small landowner, embarrassed by his peasant background. He yearned for more. He dreamt of change. He wrote what became known as the bible of the *contadini*. She sat on the floor of the sitting room, her back pressed against the bookshelf. She turned the pages avidly, seized by the stories of hardship and discontent.

'It's Rico's story,' she whispered to herself, swallowing up the writing, wishing she could transfer the ideas to Rico's mind. Every now and then she raised her head and looked towards the wall separating Cosimo's house from Angelo's, knowing Rico was there.

The following morning, Bella woke in the early hours and continued reading. She read about the rebellion and struggle of the *cafoni* of *Fontamara* amidst the onslaught of fascism. The world was changing for the people of *Fontamara* just as it was for herself and Rico.

The front door of Rico's house slammed shut around five. Angelo and Rico were setting off for the fields. At seven, Bella dressed and went down to the kitchen for her breakfast. She declined her *caffelatte* and instead drank *caffè con la ricotta* and a glass of red wine. She licked her lips. It was the start to the day for all the *contadini* of Monterini.

'What's got into her?' Signora Franca looked at the empty wine glass standing next to Bella's book on the table, her thick eyebrows arched into a V.

'That's what I was wondering,' Cosimo answered. 'She's behaving oddly this morning.'

'Don't talk about me as if I'm not here,' Bella snapped. Her eyelids felt heavy, she wasn't sure if it was from waking before dawn or the effects of the wine.

'None of that lip!' Signora Franca tapped her arm. 'This is

not the breakfast of a properly brought up young lady.' Signora Franca's lips twitched as she spoke. Born in the Fratta, she had married Signor Franca, the Jewish owner of the haberdashery in Via Roma. It had been a scandal at the time, and Bella had been too young to remember the details. All she recalled from the gossip woven between the Ghetto and the Fratta was that by marrying the Jewish haberdasher, Signora Franca had clawed her way out of the confines of her class. Now she was glaring at Bella, her mouth tight, the mole on her left cheek brown and shiny.

Bella closed the pages of *Fontamara*, hoping Signora Franca had not caught sight of the title. She grinned at her grandfather, an inclusive smile, knowing whatever she did was fine with him.

'Lay off the *vino* in the morning, even if it is Angelo's,' he whispered. 'We don't want to upset her, do we? She might stop coming here to keep this place clean and tidy.'

Bella threw her arms around Cosimo's neck and kissed his cheek. It was flat and smooth despite his white hair and beard.

Bella was seized by a sudden urge to see her father. He would know about the *Fontamara*, it had been hidden amongst his forbidden books. He would be the only one she could talk to. She decided to pass by his bookshop on her way to school.

The damp air hugged her shins as she sauntered through the streets, across the piazza and up the stone steps leading to the bridge, which linked the old village to the new one. Jacobo usually opened the bookshop by eight and would take himself to the bar next door, sipping his espresso in silence as he browsed through the pages of the morning paper.

She stopped in front of Café del Giorno. Jacobo was sitting in the corner near the window, cradling a porcelain cup in the palm of one hand. He swayed backwards and forwards, head lowered, eyes shut behind his spectacles; tranquil, at peace.

'*Babbo*?' Bella wavered, afraid to disturb Jacobo's reverie. A soft feeling fluttered through her as she watched him sitting there, looking vulnerable, gentle. Seeing him like that it was hard for her to believe there was always a chasm between them. She so wanted this awkwardness to vanish, for him to stroke her head and guide her with soft words, just as she had seen him do with Luciana and Elena.

His eyes flickered open, his pupils, almost navy blue. 'Is everything all right? *Nonno*?'

'*Nonno*'s fine. Relax. I wanted to come and speak to you. Don't look so shocked.' She wondered why there had to be a reason for her presence. Couldn't he simply be happy to see her?

And then he said, 'Not shocked, pleased.' Jacobo nodded towards an empty chair and made a sweeping gesture towards the bar. His eyes lit up. He seemed genuinely happy she was there. A sensation of warmth washed through her, filling her chest.

'What were you doing, *babbo*, just before I arrived?' Bella removed her coat and placed it on the chair next to Jacobo's. She settled herself down opposite him.

'Praying, dreaming, my usual.' A faraway look crossed his face. 'Coffee always helps me to concentrate.'

'I thought religion had been eclipsed by politics.'

'There's always time for prayer and meditation, Bella. It helps deal with the politics.'

'Not for me.' She paused for a moment and then produced the book from under her coat. 'I need your help.'

Jacobo glanced at *Fontamara* and blanched. 'Put it away, quickly. It's highly inflammatory. We could get into trouble for just looking at it. Where did you get it?'

'From your bookshelf. At home.'

'You must never show it in public.' Jacobo walked to the counter and paid for his coffee. He placed a hand under Bella's elbow and guided her into the street. They walked in silence until they reached La Libreria Speciale.

Marlene and Nanni were waiting for Jacobo at the corner. Their lips parted into a smile when they saw Bella. They nodded *buongiorno*, glanced warily up and down the street. Nobody offered the Roman salute. Marlene kissed Bella on both cheeks. Jacobo unlocked the front door. They followed him inside.

Bella looked around the bookshop. It had changed since her last visit. It appeared smaller, more huddled together, almost as if it had shrunk. There were piles of leather-bound tomes on the counter, in the middle of the room and dotted around the floor. The walls were lined with the same familiar shelves, heaving with books, but in Bella's eyes it all appeared disorderly, run down.

As if reading her mind, Marlene said, 'It's a bit of a mess, it needs a good tidy up.' She removed her hat and fluffed her hair. She took a lipstick from her bag and painted her lips bright red without using a mirror. Nanni hung his coat on a wooden stand by the door. There was a button missing from his jacket.

Jacobo turned down the narrow corridor to the left of the room. With a sweep of his head, he beckoned Bella to follow him. At the end of the corridor he opened the door to his office and ushered her inside.

'You should've known better than to bring that book out in public. We could've been arrested.' Jacobo walked round his desk and slid into his chair, cheeks pale, muscles of his jaw twitching.

'Don't exaggerate, *babbo*.'

'It's directed against the fascist regime; its lies, the violence, the indoctrination.'

'I thought it would be helpful for Rico.' Bella pulled a chair from the corner of the room and sat down opposite him. 'It's very much his story.'

'It's the story of the *contadini*.'

'I thought Rico should read it. It's about change and...'

'Nobody here wants to learn about change,' Jacobo interrupted. 'Neither the *contadini* nor the educated.'

'But I want Rico to see he has a right to education, to knowledge. Life's not just about grapes!' She took a breath. 'Maybe he should join the *partigiani*? Is he still too young?'

'He's sixteen, Bella.' Jacobo's eyes narrowed. 'Is that what he wants? Or what you want for him? Remember, it's an offence to belong. It's an offence to do anything these days. Soon it will be an offence to pray in the synagogue or eat *pane azzimo* at Passover.'

'*Babbo*, you're exaggerating again. Mussolini would never do that.'

'I wish I could be that sure. But something...' he shuddered. He was gazing ahead, his skin like glass as the colour drained from his cheeks.

Bella turned around to see what Jacobo was looking at. Her nostrils twitched. A faint smell of sulphur filled the room. 'What is it, *babbo*?' She placed her hand on her father's arm. Does he see Tanaquilla, just like me she wondered. She dismissed the thought. No, how could he? He had forbidden her ever to mention it.

'It's nothing.' Jacobo shook his head. He was breathing heavily, eyebrows knitted together in a frown. He had retreated from her. An invisible presence had lodged its way between them, slipping away their moment of closeness.

'I'd better leave. I'll be late for school.' Bella rose from her chair, hesitating, wanting to say so much. She longed to ask why he often appeared so unnatural with her; longed to tell him about the strange presence that showed up every now and then in her life. But the words melted on her tongue.

'Thank you for coming to see me.' The frown had vanished

and Jacobo's skin had returned to its usual hazelnut hue. 'It's rare to be on our own, without the others. We should do it more often.'

'Do you mean that?' It felt as if Bella's entire body was smiling.

Jacobo nodded. 'Leave me the *Fontamara*. I'll drop it off later. Better not have it anywhere near school. If you give it to Rico, make sure he reads it in secret. It may upset *zio* Angelo.'

Bella walked around the desk and handed Jacobo the book. His hand lifted in the air, near her cheek, hovered then dropped to his side. Bella paused, then bent forward and planted a kiss on his forehead. It felt smooth and soft. She could smell the scent of his cologne, strong yet sweet.

She couldn't remember ever having kissed him.

At the entrance of his office, she turned. Her father had placed his palm on the spot where her lips had touched his skin.

CHAPTER 3

On the twenty-first of June 1938, Bella and Rico celebrated their seventeenth birthday. It was almost dawn and Bella was sleeping when a pattering sound hit the windowpane behind her bed. A summer storm, no doubt. She pulled the pillow over her head. When the noise persisted, she sat up and reached for the clock by the side of her bed. She blinked as she noticed the arms pointing to ten to four.

'It can't be hailstones, it's the middle of June.' She slipped out of bed, undid the clasp and opened the window. Rico's face stared up at her in the inky night. She leaned out of the window and noticed his arm, paused, ready to shower her with pebbles.

'What are you doing? You'll wake up the whole of the Fratta.'

'What day is it today, Bella Levi?'

'The anniversary of my mother's death.'

'You've never given a second thought to this day being anything other than our birthday.' The last two words left his lips in a heightened whisper. 'Quick, climb down, I've brought a ladder.'

'I'm just wearing my nightgown.'

'No one's awake. Come on, we've only got one hour.'

Bella hiked her nightgown over her thighs and climbed onto the window ledge. The air was thick with heat of summer night. Balancing there, for several seconds she took a deep breath and smiled. She turned and climbed down the ladder. Rico was waiting for her, arms extended.

'*Auguri.*' His lips brushed her cheek. '*Vieni*, I want to show you something.'

Bella's nightdress flapped around her legs as they ran, fingers entwined like the vines in Angelo's vineyard. They slipped through the Fratta to Capo Bagno, down the steps towards the San Gianni path and along to the river.

'I have a present for you,' Rico said between jagged breaths. He stopped and handed her a small box hidden in the pocket of his trousers. They had sometimes celebrated their birthdays together with a tower of profiteroles or a glass of *frizzante* for the adults. They had never bought each other presents.

'This isn't what we usually do.'

'True, but I wanted to thank you, you know… for helping me… the reading, the learning. You've opened my mind.' Rico hesitated. 'Open it.'

Bella sank down on the rocks where they used to skim stones in the waters of the Piccolina. She untied the ribbon and opened the box. An onyx necklace slid between her fingers like one of the vipers hiding along the riverbank.

'But this belonged to your *nonna*. You can't give it to me.' Bella shook her head as she held the gift close to her chest.

'Why not? My *nonna* always said I should save it, you know, for… well… for the person I care about.' Rico's eyes had a softness she had not seen before. Maybe once or twice when he helped Angelo's cow give birth last spring, or when a lamb or rabbit caught his attention. But she'd never noticed such tenderness cross his face when looking at her.

'Isn't this one of the original Etruscan jewels your grandfather found in the *cavi*?'

Rico nodded, looking at the ground. He crossed his arms around his body as if to protect himself. 'Do you understand why I'm giving this to you today?'

Bella moved towards him. She needed to touch him, stroke

his hair, maybe even kiss it. She started tapping him playfully with the back of her hand.

'No.' She wasn't going to make this easy for him.

'It's for you because it's our seventeenth birthday and I want you to have it.'

'Why?' Bella grabbed the collar of his shirt. Her heart beat so fiercely her ribs hurt, as if someone had stuck her in a bodice and was pulling too tightly.

'You know why. You've always known.'

'No, I don't. You hide your feelings from me.'

'I'm hopeless.' Rico's face fell in upon itself, as if his bones had shifted.

'You're not. You're intelligent and sensitive.' She dared to place a hand on his arm. How bronzed it was; how clearly defined were the muscles. She ached to run her fingers over his taut skin, touch his cheeks, feel his lips against hers.

'I don't have clever words like you and *zio* Jacobo. All I know is, I simply want to be with you from the second I wake until I close my eyes. And even then, I see your face in my dreams.'

Bella placed her hands on Rico's shoulders and lifted her face towards him. He bent his head forward, brushing her mouth with his lips, soft kisses flowing like water down a mountainside. She hoped they would never stop.

'I've always loved you, Rico,' she whispered when she pulled away from him. 'Even as a baby.'

'Well, that's silly.' He twirled his finger through a strand of her hair. 'You certainly couldn't love me as a baby.'

'Oh, but I did. I was born loving you.'

He kissed her again and she told him how she only felt whole when he was by her side. Without him, she felt as if a part of her had vanished. Stroking his cheek, she told him how much she loved his face, touching his arm she told him how she admired his strength.

Rico unclasped the onyx necklace, tied it around her neck. Bella tucked it inside her nightdress. She nuzzled her face against him. She wanted to remain there forever, enveloped in his strong arms, feeling the breadth of his solid chest, smelling him, tasting him.

'We better go back, before someone notices we've gone,' he whispered the words into her ear. She placed her hand on his mouth to stop them. Fingers clasped, they climbed back up to the stirring village, avoiding the San Gianni path. It meant a hard climb over rocks and boulders laced with bracken and stinging nettles. Neither of them felt the plants rubbing their ankles.

The sun had risen over the horizon, a gold stain in the dawn sky. The shutters of Angelo's house were wide open. Shouting echoed through the windows; the smell of coffee wafted in the air. Their lips touched briefly, tenderly. Rico helped Bella scale the ladder. She blew him a kiss from her room and watched him stumble over the bracken, wondering what on earth he would tell Santina.

'Thank God *nonno* sleeps late and is rather deaf.' She smiled to herself. She'd dreamt of this moment, waited for it, always knowing that it could only ever be a dream. She loved him and now knew he loved her. But this was not going to be easy. When she thought of a future together, imagined them standing under the wedding canopy in the Beit Israel Synagogue, her dream splintered. She tried to push the thought to the back of her mind. Today was their birthday. All that mattered was that he loved her.

Rico turned to look at her, cheeks flushed with happiness, face full of hope. She smiled and blew him a kiss.

The pattern had begun.

CHAPTER 4

One ruling followed the next; a tumbling stack of cards. In July 1938, a law was passed banning all literature which failed to promote the fascist viewpoint. The back room in Jacobo's bookshop was stacked with non-fascist material. With the help of his assistants Nanni and Marlene, Jacobo smuggled books across the bridge and into the house in the Fratta to sit alongside *Fontamara*.

The writings of Antonio Gramsci, reviews by political refugees Treves, Nitti, Modigliani and Turati and their anti-fascist newspaper *La Liberta* were locked away in trunks and covered with lace tablecloths. Jacobo was grateful the women of Monterini spent so much time embroidering.

Walking along Via Meravigliosa with the last carton of reviews, Jacobo watched Signora Petri sweeping her porch, squabbling with her husband the blacksmith and chatting with her neighbours all at the same time. He envied her sense of freedom, her lack of fear. He stooped down and placed the forbidden material on the cobblestones. Above him, women leaned out of their windows to chat to their neighbours, relating snippets of gossip, competing over recipes, grandchildren and the size of *zucchini*. Further along the street, children splashed water from the fountains onto their bare arms.

A clip-clopping revealed Angelo and Rodeo, a basket of olives balancing precariously on the donkey's back. Angelo welcomed Jacobo with a beaming smile.

'Come by for a glass of *vino* before lunch,' he said.

Jacobo bent down to pick up the illegal material.

Nothing had changed for Angelo and the other inhabitants of the Fratta. They shrugged their shoulders at the annexation of Austria or naming Mussolini the First Marshal of the Empire. None of it bothered them. They tended their crops, provided food for their families, enjoyed lavender sunsets, and took pleasure in the pinks and purples of the oleander stretching across the valley.

Yet again, those familiar words rinsed through Jacobo.

Pericolo, stai attento. It's harmful. Beware.

A perfect place. Amidst a backdrop of perfect fear.

And it was just the beginning.

Early September, Jacobo was alone in his office sorting through orders for a client in Grosseto, when he heard a commotion at the entrance of the bookshop. He looked up. A knock on the door and Lea's face peered into the room. The hat with a blue feather that she always wore at the Scuola Bertolucci had slipped to one side. It made her look unkempt.

'What's happened? Why aren't you teaching?'

Lea's lips quivered. She stretched out her palm and led Jacobo back along the corridor, past piles of books. Jacobo had never seen so many people in his bookshop at the same time. Some were weeping, others were staring vacuously, deep frowns settled on their foreheads. A small crowd was huddled over a newspaper. Rabbi Coen shook his head, Dottore Gianni Vetrulli, the old doctor's son, gesticulated wildly. Jacobo's father was watching them, his shoulders bent under an invisible weight, his arms folded around his body.

Everyone was talking at once.

'How could he...? So bad... What next... Come to this...'

'Lea, for the love of God, what's going on?'

She took a deep breath. 'You always thought something like this would happen. You were right and we're finished.'

It was as if molten lead was sliding over Jacobo, shifting his limbs, realigning his body, shrinking him. Gianni Vetrulli placed *La Stampa* in Jacobo's outstretched arms. Jacobo focused on the headlines.

PROVISIONS FOR RACIAL DEFENCE IN FASCIST SCHOOLS.

He bit the inside of his cheek. Reaching out for Lea's hand, he read through the new law. Jewish teachers, members of staff, heads and directors of every educational establishment were to be suspended from service. Jewish children would be forbidden to attend schools and universities. And it wasn't only schools. Composers, writers, politicians and medics were now without work. He read to the end of the paper where the ornate signatures of four men bore witness to these laws:

Vittorio Emanuele, Mussolini, Bottai and Di Revel.

Hammering in his chest, a rash exploding on his skin, Jacobo wanted to scratch himself, scratch away every inch of pain.

A voice from deep within:

'I warned you. I warned you. *Pericolo, pericolo.*'

Jacobo's eyes sought out the rabbi's. His head was lowered. A tear trickled from the corner of his eyelid, down his arched nose. It dropped onto his beard, enveloped in the thick, white nest. 'Jacobo, I'm sorry. You never trusted Mussolini. We didn't listen.'

'They won't win.' Jacobo breathed the words into the air, unsure where this sudden strength, this determination came from.

'They've won already. No Jews employed by the fascist state can work. I'm no longer a doctor. It's all I've ever wanted to be, just like my father.' Gianni raised his arms in defeat, cheeks sucked in, eyebrows arched in an angry gesture. His thick, brown hair was ruffled and unkempt, his voice raw. He had been Jacobo's friend since they first went to *cheder*, the Jewish Sunday school. Under the prying eyes of Rabbi Coen, they had studied, giggled and left as soon as they could, legs running down the alleyways to find Angelo and head to the river. 'At least you have the bookshop, Jacobo. It's privately owned, they can't take that away from you.'

Jacobo placed his palm on his friend's shoulder. Within minutes the initial overwhelming sensation had shifted. He had always feared the worst and now it had happened he felt strangely in control, almost vindicated. A warm churning sensation spiralled through his body, filling his chest and throat. The years of wondering what Mussolini would do next, waiting for each ruling to unravel, seemed to fold into one. He'd lived with fear and uncertainty, when others thought he exaggerated. They always assumed he was searching for problems where none existed.

'We'll form our own school,' Jacobo said after a long pause A sense of purpose he hadn't experienced for a long time flushed through him. 'Nothing will stop our children from learning. I'm self-employed, I can still work, so can Signor Servi, Signor Mazzi, Signor De Benedetti. We'll help those who can't.'

'So, we're back where we were centuries ago,' the rabbi said. 'Pushed behind those Ghetto walls, like in the days of Count Medici.'

'Nothing ever changes,' Cosimo added. He'd been quiet, hunched in the corner of the bookshop. Jacobo walked over to his father and placed his arm around him. Cosimo's sharp shoulder blades dug into Jacobo's wrist, the bones on his face seemed to have shrivelled.

'It will be all right, *babbo*,' Jacobo said.

They had to survive. There was no other choice.

CHAPTER 5

Octobre sixteenth: a day of darkness.

All over the country, professionals like Lea packed away years of dedication into bags. Stripped of the right to earn a living, they were spat out like rotting vegetables.

Lea stood in her classroom and wiped away a stray tear with the back of her hand. Through the window she watched the children assembled in the playground. Pencils poked over the tops of satchels strapped to their backs. Luciana stood alone in the corner, biting her thumb. Although nearly thirteen, Lea noticed how vulnerable she looked, her eyes skittering around the playground, white socks crumpled by her ankles. Elena was huddled amongst a group of pupils. They were stroking her hair, packing books into her bag. And there was Bella, fiery reddish hair forced into an unruly ponytail, gazing ahead in that vacuous way of one who has received a shock.

Or is in love.

A gentle tapping. Lea turned her head. The head of the school, Signor Roselli, was standing by the classroom door. When the laws were first announced, Signor Roselli told Lea he had spoken to Signor Bruscalupi, the village lawyer. There was nothing they could do. Personal intervention could not improve the fate of the teachers and pupils at the mercy of Mussolini, Victor Emmanuel et al.

Lea's knees buckled. Signor Roselli's hands cupped her

111

elbows. It was common knowledge in the village that she was his favourite, another rumour born through a whisper and breathed into the world.

'We're like orphans,' she said, her voice unfamiliar, cavernous, as if she had to dig deep inside to find it. 'But worse; we're orphans in an orphanage that no longer wants us.'

'No one condones this, Maestra Lea. No one.' Pain flittered across Signor Roselli's angular face, with its deep furrowed forehead and wide set eyes. He was a tall man, with square shoulders, a slim waist. He always wore a dark, loose-fitting suit and a stiff oval-shaped hat. Never once had Lea seen him without his hat.

'After years of your commitment and professionalism, we are being forced to let you go.' Signor Roselli's shoulders shook as the words tumbled from his lips. 'It's unjust and cruel.'

'You have no choice.' Lea nodded in the direction of Mussolini's portrait on the wall of her classroom. 'He's taken away the freedom to choose and my heart breaks for our village.'

'Monterini won't let you down,' Signor Roselli said. 'We'll visit you every day and we'll bring worksheets and books and all the new changes to the curriculum.'

Lea sniffed back tears. They melted through her; words, water, anger.

'Thank you for everything, Signor Augustino. Now I have to face the children with strength.' She reached out her palm, wondering whether he would accept it, or whether his arm would float up in front of her. Under the watchful eyes of Mussolini, the headmaster grasped her hand between his and shook it. He leant forward and placed two kisses on her damp cheeks.

Lea peered round the classroom, scouring for the last time, sheets of writing on the wall, paintings and designs. She picked up her briefcase and walked through the corridor, down the stone steps to the playground. Reaching out for the hands of the two smallest children, she nodded to Bella to do the same. Bella grasped the hand of Aldo Vetrulli, the doctor's son.

'*Andiamo.*' Lea's voice trembled. 'Walk out of the gates. Heads high. Don't talk, don't look back.'

And they left, the Jewish teacher with her Jewish pupils; all Monterinesi who just happened to go to the synagogue on Saturdays rather than the cathedral on Sundays.

A menacing sky hung above the procession of teachers and pupils. Bella wondered how the streets, which moments before seemed familiar and welcoming, could now appear so unfriendly. She could have sworn she saw the face of *il Duce* leering at her in the swirling clouds. Not a profile vision as allowed in official events, but Benito, with his large face and ample nose twirling and whirling into unrecognisable shapes. As she watched the clouds, she seemed to hear Tanaquilla's warning buried deep inside her:

"An omen. Tread carefully."

She wondered if Tanaquilla was nearby, watching them trudge through the streets. Since that afternoon many years ago, Bella had never spoken about Tanaquilla. She often felt her arms tingle, her body alive, a force through the soles of her feet. It was a visceral sensation; a compelling magic she couldn't put a name to, couldn't make sense of. Deeper than words. Deeper than hearing a sound. She wondered whether it was what Tanaquilla had meant by listening. And sometimes she wondered whether Lea had been right and Tanaquilla was merely a childish fantasy.

Bella didn't know what was real anymore. Being banished from school, walking like an outcast through the streets of

Monterini, felt like fragments of an unbearable dream. She tried to concentrate on the sole thing that felt real to her; her love for Rico.

The procession crossed the bridge and crept down the steps towards the piazza. Above the rooftops, smoke rose like grey shadows. The golden *tufo* rock, which usually glistened in the sunlight seemed colourless against the leaden sky.

A door opened and an elderly man with a bald head and unshaven face stared at them. The braces of his dungarees hung loosely around his hips. He was stroking his chin with weathered hands. Bella wasn't sure whether his dark expression was one of contempt or pity.

The upstairs shutters flew open. Two women with wrinkled skin craned their necks to watch them. They didn't smile, not even with their eyes. More villagers appeared in the doorways of bars, shops. Others peered down from the windows of their homes. Young children got up from their games of jacks and hopscotch and gathered together.

They all watched in silence.

As the group of pupils crossed the piazza, Bella saw Signora Franca. She was standing under one of the cypress trees talking to Clara the midwife. The women smiled at Bella. When Bella was younger, Signora Franca often recounted the story of how Clara had delivered her, and Dottore Mazzola had tried to save her mother. A look of concern spread across Signora Franca's plump face. She clasped Clara's hand and pulled her towards the procession. The two women squeezed in behind Bella. They gripped her shoulder with plump fingers.

Pino Petri the blacksmith was watching from the bar. He stamped out his cigarette, pulled his cap down and followed Signora Franca and Clara into the procession. Then the barber, Fernando, walked out of his shop, scissors still in his hands, and stepped in behind Pino. The coal merchant followed, then the tailors of Via Roma and the manager of the Monte dei Paschi bank. One by one they joined the group of pupils and teachers; the butchers from the Ghetto and the Fratta; the bakers Carlo and Paolo Zerulli; Carlo Roberto the organist.

And the footsteps grew louder on the cobbled streets.

Gianni Vettruli stepped out of his surgery, his surgical bag overflowing with medicines, bandages and thermometers. His face was dark with shadows. Next to him stood Dottore Mazzola, his arm fastened around Vetrulli's shoulders as if he couldn't let go. Dottore Vetrulli nodded to Bella and took his place in the procession next to her and his son Aldo. Mazzola stepped in beside him.

They were all there: Catholics and Jews, professionals and *contadini*. Everyone had joined in, walking alongside those that were banished, in a silence heavy with unspoken words. Bella could almost feel empathy pouring from their skin.

⚬⚭⚬

Jacobo sat by the window of Roberto's bar. He was holding a copy of Benedetto Croce's literary magazine. *La Critica* was aimed at anti-fascist, Italian intellectuals and Jacobo was taking a risk, one he refused to take when Bella showed him a copy of *Fontamara*. But it was Jacobo's way of saying thank you. Like Jacobo, Croce had questioned Mussolini for years. He'd been one of the few Italian intellectuals who refused to sign Mussolini's questionnaire on racial background and was now under house arrest.

There was a thumping sound, like the stamping of footsteps. Jacobo looked up. He took a deep breath wondering whether it was another fascist march. Thump thump, clunk clunk. The noise grew louder. Jacobo folded *La Critica* and placed it inside his jacket. Then he noticed the wave of human bodies turn the corner and come into view; small children, *contadini* in dungarees and cloth caps, the bank manager, the lawyer, villagers from every corner of Monterini. At the front of the crowd was Bella, eyes shining, face like a waxed candle.

'The whole village has come out. Maybe they're protesting?' Roberto gestured to Jacobo from the counter where he was pouring espressos laced with grappa into small white cups.

Jacobo rose. He'd felt confused at first, unsure what was happening. Now he understood. 'This is no protest. This is solidarity,' he said. This was the town he'd lived in his entire life, home to generations of Levis. He felt strangely bereft yet grateful at the same time. 'I love you, Monterini,' he whispered as he stepped on to the street.

The sun sliced through the clouds, an orange stain in a dark sky. A hand brushed Jacobo's shoulder. It was Angelo, wearing blue overalls, face smeared with purple marks and fine earth. His smile was guarded as he placed his arms around Jacobo and hugged him. Jacobo was struck by the scent of wine that seeped from Angelo's clothes, from his hair, his skin; his *Vino degli Angeli*, wine of the Angels.

Angelo pointed towards a group of men wearing the grey suits and flat caps of the fascist police. 'Look, there's Ugo Grazzi. We used to play with him, Jacobo, remember, when we were lads.'

Jacobo looked across at his old friend, now living in Grossetto and head of the Salone police force. Their eyes met. Grazzi nodded, then lowered his gaze. He was larger than Jacobo remembered with a portly belly and wide, strong shoulders. Jacobo could just make out a thick moustache over his upper lip. He wondered how Grazzi felt seeing the villagers come out in sympathy for the Jews who'd lost their jobs, their right to an education. Then he wondered why Grazzi was back here, in Monterini on this of all days. Was it to check the new rulings were carried out? He dismissed the thought and turned his head towards Angelo.

'The police can't join in, no matter how liberal their views may be. But at least they're here.'

This was more than solidarity, Jacobo realised. This was a village in mourning. It reminded him of a funeral cortege with its silence, its unproclaimed grief. Monterini was saddened by the absence of liberty, morality. Oh yes, even morality was missing from Italy now. And when that goes?

Jacobo threaded his way through the crowd to Bella. Cheeks milky pale, eyelids heavy, she turned her face towards him. Her irises gleamed with an intensity Jacobo had not seen before, green sparks like jewels glinting in sunlight. He wondered how on such a dark day in the history of the village she could look so beautiful, so deeply happy.

It was only much later that he understood why.

Like separate stitches in a cloth, the community was sewn together, making a fabric more closely interwoven than ever before. Lea and Gianni Vetrulli set up a school in the synagogue compound. Desks were made by some of the village carpenters, chairs and benches donated and books and stationery appeared as if by magic. A room on the lower floor functioned as a surgery, with needles, medicines and bandages supplied by Dottore Mazzola. The top floor became the classroom. A section at the front was allocated to the younger children, taught by Lea with the help of Bella. At the back, three rows of desks were set aside for the older pupils.

Signor Roselli and Maestra Virginia dropped by the school daily, bags brimming with finely sharpened pencils and bundles of white paper. Determined all students of the village would have an equal right to education, they checked their work and supplied snippets of knowledge.

Jacobo marvelled at how easy it was for everyone to come together to form a new type of community; one born of necessity. Vetrulli taught science and mathematics, Rabbi Coen religious education. Jacobo was asked to teach literature, philosophy and ethics, not by law a subject required for *maturità*, but one considered suitable in the circumstances. Geography was taught by Signor Servi and history by Claudio Pazzi who owned a haberdashery on the Via Roma. With a passion for the humanities and a love of imparting knowledge, these shopkeepers led the students through the Vie Cavi to explain Etruscan burial rites and the Roman use of aqueducts.

Despite all the years of fear, Jacobo now breathed more freely. It had happened and, after all, was it so bad? The fields were abundant with crops and animals. Food appeared on tables; money passed from one enterprise to another. Those not employed by the state helped the newly jobless. With the help of the *contadini* there was enough to survive.

Jacobo also knew he was lucky. Private enterprises were permitted and Jacobo was able to keep his bookshop, although further changes had to be made. Copies of Alberto Moravia's *Gli Indifferenti,* religious texts and anything deemed remotely 'anti-fascist' were tucked away in boxes, hidden under the seats of the synagogue and in the deep caverns sprawling beneath Monterini; a secret underground of rock-lined passages and niches constructed by the Etruscans and used by one civilisation after another.

Anti-fascist leagues and communist groups, which sprouted like seeds, secreted away more books and magazines. Copies of the fascist reviews *Opere Pubbliche* and *Sul Mare* took pride of place in the bookshop window, with Pirandello's plays dotted in between. Religious texts with a Catholic theme were still permitted, but Jacobo felt it safer to relegate them to shelves at the back of the bookshop. Just in case.

When members of the Fascist Party entered the bookshop, stamping their feet and raising their arms, the hairs on Jacobo's neck still bristled, a wave of fear rinsed through him. But the words he was so used to hearing, the familiar sensations, the faint smell of sulphur, had all but vanished.

CHAPTER 6

When the sun blushed the mountains and the cockerels greeted the day, Rico leaned over the layers of hair spread on the pillow and delivered a fresh kiss to Bella's cheek. Before leaving, he knelt by the side of the bed. Clasping her hand in his, he traced his lips along the veins in her arm.

Bella did not worry they would be caught. No point in fretting about the future, it was too unknown. Her life was peppered with a sense of excitement despite the racial laws. Each night she knew her lover would be there, tapping on her window. His hands tarnished with the juice of grapes would grasp her body with a tenderness she had until now only dreamt of. She would feel his breath in her ears and on her face. Her skin would tingle as his lips met hers.

At night they whispered their dreams of what life would be like in another era. Would they live in the house with the grey or black shutters? Would their children be farmers or intellectuals? Jews or Catholics? Bella immersed herself in these games, whirled into their private fantasy. Deep within, she knew how impossible these fantasies were. They could never be married under a *chuppah*, the wedding canopy, in the Beit Israel Synagogue, *never* share a home, nor raise children. But, if he knew this, Rico kept silent.

Each day he became more learned. He had read *Fontamara*

and *Vino e Pane*. Together they devoured the works of Gramsci, Nitti and Rosselli at night, hiding the books under the covers of Bella's bed. Around them, Monterini was changing, but their love was fuelled by a sense of purity and adventure, in a world they no longer understood.

⁌⁍⁌

At the end of November, Angelo was sitting in his kitchen wondering for some time when his son would join him. He enjoyed his time with Rico and the twins. Santina would bustle around them making coffee, sliding a spoonful of fig jam onto chunks of bread. She would feed them with commands and snippets of gossip, seemingly discovered during the night. They would hear but not listen, nod but not register. Angelo enjoyed this unacknowledged conspiracy with his sons.

That morning he was agitated without Rico. 'For the love of God, where is he? We'll be late.'

'You've got plenty of time, don't fret.' Santina was not used to being interrupted. She banged Angelo's cup of coffee on the table, wiped her hands on her apron and waddled upstairs to the room Rico shared with his two brothers. A few moments later, she reappeared, scratching her head.

'He's not here.'

'What's he up to now?' Angelo slurped his coffee and with his finger wiped lumps of ricotta from the rim of the cup. He stood up and opened the door. The sky was pregnant with leaden clouds, the air damp, darker than usual. The clip-clopping of donkeys indicated the start of the day for the *contadini* of Monterini. In the distance a church bell chimed. Stepping out to the veranda, Angelo peered up and down Via Meravigliosa, lights from the houses blinked at him through the near dawn light. He wandered around the side of the ochre-coloured

120

buildings to see if Rico had climbed down to the *cantina* to get his donkey ready for the daily trip to the fields.

Rodeo stared at him over the wooden door. Angelo frowned and looked up, just as Rico's legs emerged from the upstairs window of the house next door.

'What's going on?' he shouted, causing Rico to totter on the ladder. Through the open window, Bella's arms grabbed Rico's shirtsleeve.

'*Non è vero!*' Angelo exclaimed. 'You get down here at once, young man!'

Bella's ashen face withdrew from the window as Rico climbed down the ladder. Despite the early morning air, Angelo's cheeks were burning, his heart heavy.

'What do you think you're doing? You're children!'

Rico jumped down from the last few rungs of the ladder. 'We're not children, and we love each other. That's all there is to it.'

'Love each other? That means you can climb into her bedroom, does it? And what if your mother had seen? Oh my Lord, we can't tell your mother.' Angelo grabbed Rico's ear and pulled him around the house towards the veranda. 'You're in big trouble, *mio figlio*. This has to stop, you understand?'

He let go of Rico's ear but grasped his wrist. Rico shook it free and glared at his father, eyes darker than starless nights in Monterini.

'You can't stop us.'

'Oh yes I can. This is Bella, our Bella, what are you playing at? You could ruin her reputation.'

'Her world is falling apart, and you care about reputation!'

Rico had never spoken to him in this way. A wave of fury tumbled through Angelo. How dare Rico take such risks and talk about love as if they were doing nothing wrong. How dare he feel no shame? Without thinking, Angelo bent forward

121

and slapped Rico across the cheek. Hearing his son's gasp of surprise, he turned his back and climbed up to the veranda.

Santina stood on the doorstep, nostrils flaring like a donkey. 'Where've you been? I've been waiting here with your breakfast.'

'*Niente*. It's nothing. Get the boy some coffee.' Angelo's gruff reply had the desired effect. Santina cursed, then turned with a huff towards the kitchen.

'Not a word,' Angelo hissed. 'Drink. Collect your things. We're going to work.'

'You can't just hit me because you don't like it.'

'Not now, Rico.'

Angelo lowered his head to enter the house. He picked up his coffee cup and licked the remnants of ricotta trailing along the rim. Maybe he should talk to Bella? But how could he possibly discuss such a delicate matter with her? Rico said they loved each other. He believed him but what should he do? Forbid them from seeing each other? Order them to marry?

Angelo sat back on his chair and wondered whether he should tell Jacobo. He was worldly and knowledgeable. He'd been married twice, met important people every day in the bookshop. He would know how to handle the situation. He'd be angry, of course, worried about Bella's reputation, no doubt. They were young, it was true, but many couples in the village married at such an age. It wasn't that unusual. The families were close, they cared about each other. In fact, this could be a blessing at such a terrible time in the history of the Italian people. He made up his mind. He would go and speak to Jacobo.

⌘

She knew he'd seen her. She slid against the wall, hiding herself from view, feeling the blood drain from her cheeks. Perhaps Rico would say he had found a ladder and was rousing her as she'd been sleeping in of late. One thing she knew for certain, she didn't want her father to find out. He would be cross, horrified even. And she couldn't bear the thought of the distance she had felt most of her life widening and engulfing her, just when she needed her family, her community. Standing there in her bedroom, by the open window, Bella realised just how much she needed her father.

She pulled a white jumper over her head and slipped into a brown skirt. These days she refused to wear black, the colour of the fascists. She tied her hair back and picked up a woollen shawl from a shelf in her wardrobe. She hoped she would look older, more austere, purer. She sat on her bed waiting for the minutes to pass into hours. She heard her grandfather's footsteps on the landing, the clattering of plates in the kitchen, the raucous sounds of Signora Franca's voice. The smell of freshly baked bread wafted through the house.

She opened her bedroom window, inhaled the musty autumn air then walked down to the kitchen, calm and controlled. At the bottom of the stairs, she heard chattering coming from the kitchen. It was her father's voice. Angelo had wasted no time. She stood outside the door, her hand resting on the handle, unsure whether to enter or to retrace her steps up to her bedroom.

'Bella? Is that you?' Jacobo opened the kitchen door.

'*Buongiorno, babbo.*'

His face was thinner, lined with ladders of wrinkles, skin stretched even more tightly across his cheekbones.

'You're here early.' The words caught in Bella's throat.

'Mussolini has just broken diplomatic ties with France. An end to the *accordo amichevole* he signed with Laval a few years ago.' With a flick of his wrist, Jacobo motioned for her to join them at the table.

For once, Bella was grateful Mussolini was still the main thing on Jacobo's mind. So, Angelo hadn't reached him yet. Or perhaps he was hoping to catch her out. She brushed her lips against Jacobo's cheek and reached for the *caffelatte* Signora Franca had prepared. Her hand was shaking.

'What's wrong, Bella? Are you ill?'

'I'm fine, *babbo*. Just tired.'

She sat down and took a slice of bread spread with Signora Franca's apricot jam, whilst Jacobo read *La Stampa* in silence. His usually intense eyes looked dull behind the spectacles. Was he there for a reason or was the morning's unexpected visit one of life's curious coincidences? Her breathing calmed, the ache in her abdomen settled. It's fine, she repeated to herself, it's fine.

The door to the veranda flew open. Bella jumped. Angelo stooped into the kitchen, lowering his head under the doorframe. He bent down to kiss Jacobo and Cosimo on both cheeks, nodded *buongiorno* to Signora Franca and stared at Bella with a look of disbelief. His refusal to kiss her, pained her. Her throat was parched but gulping down coffee didn't seem to help. She coughed nervously and piled the cups into a small porcelain tower. She took them over to the sink.

'I need to speak to you later, Jacobo. Alone.' Angelo's screwdriver eyes bored into Bella, twisting and turning.

'It's not like you to sound so serious. Of course, come to the bookshop this afternoon, around five is good for me.'

'*Andiamo, babbo.*' Bella's voice, barely a squeak, was unfamiliar even to her.

'What's wrong with you this morning?' Signora Franca barked.

Bella remained silent. Her gaze flittered between the men in the room. There were deep furrows at Cosimo's temples. Jacobo was frowning and Angelo's expression was deep and dark as if the sun had disappeared from his face and would never return.

Angelo worked in silence. He bent down towards the earth, digging and tilling, his hunched back facing his son. His hands pulled roughly at leaves. At ten o'clock, when a ray of sunlight burst through the clouds, they stopped. Angelo poured his *Vino degli Angeli* into Rico's glass. They dipped chunks of Santina's *pane di campagna* into the tumblers of red wine. Eyes of father and son met fleetingly; each time Rico's fiery blackness darted in the opposite direction.

Words formed on Angelo's lips, but he bit them back. He didn't doubt for a moment that Rico loved her. He loved her too. She was as good as his own daughter. *La mia piccola* Bella, that's what he'd always called her. What could be better than to have Bella as his daughter-in-law? He pondered this thought as he picked up his fork and dug manure into the ground, muttering to himself like a priest at prayer.

At lunchtime, they downed their tools and returned in icy silence to the village. At the corner of the piazza, Rico raised his head. 'Might snow.' His voice was as hollow as the *cavi* surrounding Monterini.

'Not yet.' Angelo sniffed the air. 'No smell of snow. Air's not ready.'

'You can't stop us.' The words sprung from Rico's lips, little darts digging into Angelo's skin.

'Can't I?'

'I'm going to marry her. What are you going to do? We're almost adults.'

Angelo gazed up at the turrets of the palazzo, wishing he were imprisoned inside and didn't have to deal with his rebellious son. He was unaccustomed to the role of disciplinarian; family thrashings were usually Santina's domain. But Santina was oblivious to the morning's events. Angelo would have to deal with this himself.

As he turned to face Rico, he noticed the clenched jaw, the

angry pout. And the love deep in those black eyes.

'Just stay away from her for a while,' Angelo replied, softness threading through words.

A tired sadness settled over Angelo as he made his way that afternoon across the bridge to La Libreria Speciale in Via del Corso. Although he had difficulty in making out the letters, he gazed at the copies of Pirandello's *L'Amica delle Moglie* watching him from behind the glass window. His lips moved slowly, attempting to sound out the shapes.

When Angelo left school at ten, Cosimo had begged his father to allow him to continue his education. Without the knowledge to read and write, Angelo would never rise above the class of the *contadini*, despite the family's smallholding. But Angelo's father had insisted he was needed on the land. Angelo thought back to those long evenings, after a day shovelling the earth and pruning the vines, when Cosimo helped him form letters with black ink and make sounds out of strange shapes. All to no avail. He was still illiterate.

The bookshop was dustier than Angelo remembered, books piled one on top of the other, without the order and glamour that had made it famous in the region of Salone and beyond. Nanni Manduro, Jacobo's assistant, was wrapping up a leather-bound volume of *L'Italia di Mussolini* for the mayor, Luigi Baldini. The mayor lifted up his arm in the greeting of the Roman salute. Angelo returned the movement.

'Jacobo's in his office. He's expecting you.' Manduro indicated towards the back of the bookshop.

Angelo shuffled down the corridor. At the closed door of Jacobo's office, he hesitated. How would Jacobo react to the news he was about to tell him? With the back of his hand, Angelo wiped droplets of sweat from his forehead.

'Angelo! *Benvenuti.*' Jacobo's voice echoed through the

door as if sensing Angelo's arrival. Angelo cleared his throat and entered the room. He needed to get this matter off his chest, share the worry. He settled himself onto the chair on the other side of Jacobo's desk, twisting his hands in his lap. Jacobo cupped his chin with his palm and leaned forward, staring at Angelo through his round-rimmed spectacles.

'Is there a problem?'

Words formed shapes in Angelo's mind. He didn't know which ones would sweeten the impact on Jacobo. He cleared his throat. 'I caught Rico escaping from Bella's bedroom this morning.' The sentence flew out in one breath. The relief Angelo felt vanished as soon as he noticed the shadows darken Jacobo's face. Even his nose seemed thinner, bonier than usual. 'I've told him to stay away from her but apparently they're in love.'

Jacobo's knuckles turned milky white as his fingers clasped the edge of his desk. 'Bella wouldn't allow Rico to come to her room at night.'

'She has, she does. I saw it.'

'It must stop.'

Jacobo thumped the table, then jumped up from the chair, spectacles falling from his nose. He fumbled to replace them. The harshness of his tone, the way the table shook as he slammed his fist emphasised his displeasure. Angelo couldn't remember ever feeling so uncomfortable in Jacobo's presence. He didn't know what to say. Silence blanketed the room as thick as winter fog.

'But they love each other.' Angelo finally spoke. 'They want to get married.'

'Marriage isn't an option. We have to stop this now. There are too many differences because…' Jacobo stopped short as if measuring his words.

'Because what?' An overwhelming feeling of pain surged through Angelo. He suddenly felt like a stranger to the man he'd known all his life. 'We're not good enough for you, are we?'

'That's not what I'm saying. Bella's a Jewess. Mixed marriages are forbidden.'

'Rico doesn't think of Bella as a Jewess, but as a friend.'

'According to Mussolini's ruling last year, we're not part of the Italian race!' Jacobo's eyes flickered; Angelo wondered if it were through anger or fear. 'No, Angelo, you must never think of marriage.'

'But why not?' Angelo persisted, like a child refused a *caramello*. This was not what he'd expected. He knew Jacobo would be upset, angry even, but he'd thought the idea of matrimony would calm him, help him to see a way through the tangles, even bring a sense of joy to the families. As the day had unravelled and Angelo had become accustomed to the shock of seeing Rico leave Bella's bedroom, the idea of a marriage had lifted his spirits until it had almost eclipsed the original reason for his visit with Jacobo.

'I understand this is upsetting, Jacobo, but I thought you'd see marriage as the best solution. Rico loves her, you can see it in his eyes.'

'It's the wrong time for them. We mustn't encourage them to think of a future together.'

'Others have married, before the laws. Look at Signora Franca. To have Bella as my real daughter... well, you know, Santina and I, that's how we see her already.'

Jacobo sank back in his chair. He removed his spectacles and rubbed them with a corner of his jacket. When he replaced them, Angelo could see his hand was trembling.

'Marriage is out of the question for many reasons. They are much too young. Bella's taking her *maturità* this summer, she wants to study, become a teacher, maybe a journalist, when these ridiculous racial laws are lifted.'

Angelo looked around the office with its mahogany desk and shelves full of files and important-looking documents. For the first time he felt ill at ease in Jacobo's company. When he spoke, his voice sounded unworthy, 'So, later then?'

'Not later. Not ever. They can't see each other anymore.' Jacobo stared down at his desk, his fingers pressing against the wood.

The room was filled with shadows.

That evening, Angelo prowled around the kitchen like a hungry fox, grunted at his three boys, ignored Santina and ate dinner in silence. He slammed a bottle of *Vino degli Angeli* on the table, causing them all to jump.

In truth, he was more wounded by the conversation with Jacobo than Rico's behaviour the previous night. The more he reflected on it, the more drained he felt, as if someone had put him through one of the mangles in the washroom at Capo Bagno and squeezed too tightly. Yes, the children should be supervised more closely. Yes, times were hard. But life had always been hard in some form or other. He remembered winters of famine, when frozen rivers and hardened earth produced not a crumb. He'd gone to bed at night, his stomach gnarled with hunger.

There was always something. Suffering, hardship, poverty were part of everyone's destiny, always had been. There was the Great War when Monterini was stripped of one villager after the next. Angelo's father had been killed at Caporetto, Jacobo's two brothers in Dalmatia. Then Bella's death and the birth of baby Bella had shaken them all. And now there was this nonsense with Mussolini and Hitler, this silly ruling against the Jews, which surely would not last long. As for mixed marriages, Angelo was certain they were only forbidden between Italians and Africans to promote Mussolini's war efforts in Abyssinia. Hadn't the Jews always managed in Monterini? There was no difference in the quality of their lives nowadays. The whole village joined together to provide what they needed for their school. Olives, wine, potatoes and oil were supplied by the *contadini*. Nobody went short. They almost seemed proud of their own resilience.

Angelo couldn't understand why Jacobo was so upset about Bella and Rico marrying. The religion wouldn't be a problem. Padre Giacomo would sort it out. Maybe they wouldn't have a full mass. But how could they tell them they couldn't see each other anymore?

They were best friends, after all.

CHAPTER 7

On one side of the valley, the Piccolina river snaked between black and green smudges of trees. On the other, just beyond the village walls, lay the white gravestones of the Jewish cemetery, encircled by stiff poplars, those guardians of the dead.

Bella chose a spot where she could peer at the river. She liked to hide beneath the long strands of bulrushes. She was like the women in the synagogue, screened behind the intricately carved, wooden awning; hidden yet present.

These days she yearned for space and silence, away from the clattering of Monterini, away from her stepsisters, the makeshift Jewish school. She felt trapped in the room above the synagogue where students of all ages huddled together. The musty smell unhinged her. It was not much better in the house in the Fratta. Since Angelo had discovered her nighttime escapades with Rico, she felt uncomfortable being there. So, she escaped with her schoolbooks to a place of silence and calm. Not even Rico knew where she hid.

A tingling sensation washed through her, a gentle ache. Bella sniffed the air. A faint whiff of sulphur touched her nostrils. She looked up. Tanaquilla was there, swaying gently above the cemetery. It had been many years since Bella had seen her. Sometimes in her dreams, she felt Tanaquilla's breath slip across her brow. She sensed the sulphuric smell. And all the while her father's words from many years ago echoed through her: *Vietato. Vietato. Vietato.*

Bella reached out her arms. The vision flickered, like a passing spirit through the branches of the olive trees, hovering. Then she was gone.

Bella scanned the horizon. The winter sun slid through smoky clouds. It glistened on a vehicle looping across the mountain road towards Monterini. A beam of sunlight caught its side, speckles of light dancing like coloured insects in the air. The engine roared as it climbed towards the entrance to the village. Two further vehicles followed behind. As they turned the sharp bend in the road and sped past the spot where Bella lay hidden, she became aware of colours and shapes on the side of the car.

'*Dio mio.*' The hairs on Bella's arms stood erect. 'What are they doing here?'

She sprang to her feet. How dare they intrude upon the peace of Monterini? She brushed the dirt away from her skirt, collected her books and pencils and started to run along the San Gianni path, past the old Etruscan caves. Two more vehicles turned the last corner. As they passed the cemetery, she flung out her arms with an instinctive desire to protect her mother from the enemy; the mother she so rarely thought about. She sprinted along the track, past the Ghetto washrooms up to the piazza. She had to warn the village before the motorcars arrived.

Dottore Mazzola was sitting at a table outside Roberto's bar. Bella stopped in front of him panting and puffing.

'*Cara*, what's the matter?' He placed his cup on the table.

'Didn't you see the cars, climbing up to Monterini? What does it mean?' The words flew from her lips.

'Which cars?' One of the Zerulli brothers was unloading loaves of bread strapped to his donkey's back.

'There were three of them with swastikas on the side and

they're coming here.' Bella tried to remember which brother it was, they both looked so similar, with their angular faces and thick black beards.

The baker's full lips parted into a smile. 'I heard some cars, but it's nothing.' The noise from the engines had disappeared. The town was quiet, save for the banter of the bar, the trickling of water from the fountains.

Dottore Mazzola drained his coffee cup, took hold of Bella's arm and steered her across the piazza towards the Arco, the ancient entrance to the village. Three cars were parked in front of the commune, which housed the office of the mayor, Luigi Baldini. Bella found herself in the midst of a crowd of villagers. They were walking around the vehicles, inspecting the design, expressions of intrigue stretched across their faces. They had probably never seen such beautiful cars before; donkeys, of course, and carts for the animals. Even the occasional truck was visible in and around Monterini. But these were different. The grey metal gleamed, suggesting wealth, glamour, possibilities. Bella watched the awed fingers of the Monterinesi glide forward to stroke the sleek finish.

'What a sight in a village full of donkeys!' Angelo appeared by Bella's side and just behind him, almost out of view, stood Rico. They watched the swastikas shimmering in the afternoon sunlight, as if mesmerised. A strange feeling came over Bella. Was this a warning from Tanaquilla? After all, she had just flashed in front of her. Bella closed her eyes and tried to remember what she had seen. Had Tanaquilla placed her hand around her ears, encouraging Bella to listen, to be careful? Or had she dreamt it? She was unsure what was real or imaginary.

A young priest approached the group, his face crisscrossed with lines of worry. It was Don Philippe, the new assistant to Padre Giacomo. There had been rumours about him circulating in the village. Some called him an upstart from the north with newfangled views; others questioned his links with the partisans. She'd heard certain villagers whispering the word *partigiano* as he walked by, his long black cloak swishing against the cobblestones.

Don Philippe gestured to Dottore Mazzola. 'Mussolini is driving to Florence with members of Hitler's SS. I heard it on the wireless this morning. They have to pass through Monterini.'

'Maybe they've come to have grappa with the mayor?' volunteered the organist Carlo Roberto who was standing close to Bella. Some of the villagers collapsed in giggles, lips parted displaying rows of yellowed teeth.

'Do you mean they are actually inside the building?' Bella asked. 'I have to tell *babbo*.'

'Calm down, it's a harmless visit.' Rico inched towards her, a look of longing spreading across his face. They had been told not to go near each other unchaperoned, and for the last couple of weeks they had avoided each other in public.

'How do you know it's a harmless visit? We live like strangers in our own village because of them.' She didn't care who heard her. The stress of the past months wound around her like thread around a cotton reel. Rico didn't recognise the dangers, didn't feel the tension that crept through her, all her waking hours. He had lost nothing. He could still work freely, go to church without a worry, and even play at being a partisan.

'It's only when freedom has been taken away that you realise how sweet it tastes.' Bella's whispered words dangled in the afternoon air. Rico would never understand how the lack of liberty gnawed away at a human being until all that was left was an empty core. She loved Rico, but at that moment, she felt distanced from him, as if the years of friendship, their tender moments had evaporated.

The old, iron doors of the commune opened with a clatter and out walked Monterini's mayor, pursued by an entourage of clucking officials. Luigi Baldini's moustache was parted like a fringe into two long threads that curled at the ends. He surveyed the crowd and with a huge smile turned to usher out his guests.

Up went the hands. Click went the heels.

Benito Mussolini sauntered down the steps with two men wearing the uniform of Hitler's SS officers. In his dusty green jacket tinged with orange stripes and gold emblems, *il Duce* was taller and more handsome than Bella had imagined. He smiled flirtatiously at the crowd like a dashing film star. Behind them were Mussolini's henchmen, his *squadristi*, with their turtlenecks, black ties and strange hats. They stood close to their leader, the tassels from their fezzes dangling over their eyes, strutting in front of the crowd of Monterinesi peasants. They were nothing more than thugs. Vermin, hand-picked by Mussolini to work as his militia. Mussolini pinched the cheek of Carlo Zerulli's nephew and ruffled the hair of Clara Todi's granddaughter.

He dazzled them all.

It made Bella want to vomit. She yearned to thump him right across his gleaming medals, tell him how he had ruined her life. But she stood in silence, nails digging deeper and deeper into the palms of her hands.

Just before sliding into his car, Benito turned and knelt next to a group of children sitting at the side of the road. He placed his hand in his pocket and pulled out a fistful of toffees and handed one to each child. He stood up and beamed at his people.

A vision of strength, of beauty.

A new Jesus.

With his long nose and sculptured features, he reminded Bella of a taller, more robust version of her father. Mussolini blew a kiss to the crowd and disappeared into his limousine. The two SS officers stamped their feet and gave the Roman salute, the one Hitler borrowed from *il Duce*.

'*Heil* Hitler,' they shouted.

'*Heil* Hitler,' echoed the crowd.

'That's Kessler and Priebke,' Don Philippe muttered under his breath. The officers bowed their heads and climbed into the second vehicle. 'They're Hitler's Gestapo here in Italy.'

The cars reversed out of the square accompanied by a trail of dust, stray cats and waves from the crowd. Some villagers even cheered. Several children ran behind the cars, hurling whoops of excitement into the air.

They walked back through Via Caldorello and Via Bel Fiora to the Fratta. Late afternoon dampness wrapped itself around Bella. She glared at the houses, winter pansies adorning the doors, tattered paint on the walls. For the first time in her life, she was uncomfortable in the narrow alleyways with crumbling walls and stone fountains. It was as if this village, the Fratta, which had always felt part of her, was no longer her beloved home. It had become tainted with the presence of evil, hidden behind a mask of acceptability, accessible to everyone. Well, almost everyone. She felt so alone.

'I'm going to the Ghetto to see my father. He's there in the school. I need to see him, tell him what's just happened. This can't be good news for us.'

Angelo nodded at a poster of Mussolini plastered on a wall between two houses. 'These laws will stop soon, you'll see. Mussolini's not against your religion. Never has been.'

His voice was laced with a simplicity that infuriated Bella. She looked at Rico. His fingers fidgeted beside him as if he were on the point of taking her hand. But no show of affection was permitted. They had promised.

'You're an Italian like all of us,' Rico said.

'I'm not!'

She needed to get away from them. An overwhelming urge to be in the Ghetto with those who understood, took hold of her. She kissed Angelo on both cheeks, and nodded at Rico, who was drumming his fingers above his right eyebrow. It was their secret code. Twirling the hair meant down by the Piccolina river; a hand on the stomach meant in one of the disused *cantine* on the San Gianni path. Rico was asking her to meet him at an old Etruscan tomb behind the *cavi*.

'*Arrivederci*,' Bella said without copying the movement of Rico's arms to confirm she understood the location. Her arm hung like a wooden log by her side. She gazed past Rico to the hills beyond. She would meet him later, but right now she needed the arms of someone else to hold her, stroke her forehead and whisper: 'It will be all right, my darling daughter, it will all be all right.'

CHAPTER 8

Bella ran along Via del Ghetto until she reached the Beit Israel Synagogue. She flew down the steps leading to a terrace with a stone wall and an iron balustrade. She stopped, took a deep inhale of breath and narrowed her eyes. In the distance, the Jewish cemetery spread out in front of her, the white gravestones shimmering in the sunlight. And around them swirling shapes flitted past the poplars, over the cedars, across the village walls. Bella creased her eyes shut. When she opened them they had disappeared.

Inside the synagogue complex, Bella bounded, two steps at a time, up to the first floor. Jacobo was sitting in the corner of the room, which now housed the school for Monterini's Jewish children. Next to him were Gianni Vetrulli, Dottore Mazzola, Lea, Rabbi Coen and the Jewish baker Signor Servi. Bella was surprised to see Don Philippe amidst them.

'*Babbo*. I need to talk to you. Something terrible has happened this afternoon.'

'We know,' Lea uttered looking up. 'Dottore Mazzola came to tell us straight away. It's all right, *amore*.'

'But *il Duce* was here, in Monterini, with some German officers. What does it mean for us?'

'Don't worry, *cara*, we're discussing the situation with Don Philippe.' Vetrulli looked up.

'*Babbo*, I'm scared.' Bella placed her palm on her father's shirtsleeve.

'We're working things through, Bella.' Jacobo tugged his arm away. His tone was gruff. Since the discussion with Angelo, Jacobo had become even more remote with Bella. He had forbidden her to see Rico, and barely spoke to her. When he did, his voice was laced with remnants of rage. He hadn't forced her to move back to the Ghetto and she knew he found it hard to look at her, so she kept away. But now she needed her father, her community.

Bella's face came close to Jacobo's and she could feel the breath from his nostrils against her skin. 'Well, tell me what you're working through! I need to know. You're not the only one Mussolini has it in for.' She clenched her fists, squared her back, her chest protruding forward. She wondered whether she resembled one of Mussolini's *squadristi* gearing up for a fight.

Jacobo glared at her, his eyes inky dark, glinting with anger. He turned towards the others. 'I apologise for my daughter's behaviour. She should know better.'

'But I'm frightened. It's as if they've sprinkled Monterini with poison, yet it all felt so normal, so acceptable.' She sniffed, fighting back tears. '*Il Duce* even gave *caramelli* to the children and ruffled their hair.'

Lea rose and pulled Bella towards her. As her stepmother's arms encircled her, Bella watched her father's back. It was motionless. Only his head bent a fraction lower. Bella rested her gaze on Jacobo's black hair, noticing for the first time that it was thinning, and a small circle of pale flesh had appeared in the centre. The hairs around were peppered with grey. Her eyes followed the line of view from Jacobo's pupils, out through the window to the tall poplars lining the alleys of the cemetery. For a moment she wondered if he saw the swirling shapes too. Was one of them her mother, laughing at her from her bed in the earth, as if she were saying: 'You'll never get him, little Bella, Bella the imposter. He's mine. He always will be.'

Standing there in the makeshift school in the old synagogue, Bella felt the warmth of her stepmother's arms and knew Lea had tried to love her. But it wasn't enough. In the confusion of that afternoon, she realised all she needed was a gesture from her father, a word, a hug. One kiss would have been enough to leave Rico behind and to embrace her destiny with a full heart.

She was met by the silence of her father's back.

Cosimo was reading in the back room of the house in Via Meravigliosa when Bella entered. He smiled and held out his hand. She sat on the floor beside him and buried her head in his lap. Her grandfather stroked her hair as she recounted the events of the afternoon. She told him about her visit to the synagogue complex, how Jacobo was not able to comfort her. She did not reveal how she had left the Piazza del Commune feeling disappointed with Rico and Angelo and closer to her father and his views than ever before. And she did not tell him how moments later she was flung back again, like a crumb of unwanted bread, catapulted from one camp to the other.

'It's because of her,' Bella announced, lifting her head and nodding towards the top drawer of the dresser where old sepia photographs of her mother gathered dust.

'Because of whom? Your mother?'

'It's as if we're competing for his affection. And she always wins.'

Cosimo pulled Bella up so she was kneeling in front of him. He looked into her eyes. 'Where did you get this nonsense from, *signorina*?'

'I suppose in here.' She tapped her heart. 'I just know it. I wouldn't mind, if it were Lea. At least I'd have an equal chance. But how can I compete with a memory?'

'It's not a memory for him. He sees her when he looks at you. You're very similar. But only to look at. That's where it

140

ends. She was very different from you. She didn't have your questioning intellect, your intuitiveness, or your stubbornness. All that is from your father, and that's what's so hard for him. He doesn't know how to deal with you, as he doesn't know how to deal with himself.'

Bella unfolded her legs and stood up. She gazed out of the window into the night embroidered with stars.

'I think the truth is, he can't forgive me.'

'What, for looking like her?'

'No, for living, instead of her.'

Cosimo ran his wrinkled fingers along his jaw. He tried to speak, hesitated, then closed his lips. A small, pearl-shaped tear slid across his cheek. When it reached the contour of the jaw line, it wavered. Bella knelt down again and smudged it against his skin with her finger.

'*Nonno*, don't cry.' She squeezed Cosimo's hand.

'Your father loves you.'

Bella shuffled; the stone floor was beginning to freeze her knees.

When Cosimo left that evening to meet Alfredo Mazzi for grappa and a game of cards, Bella wrapped herself in a coat and scarf and walked down to the Etruscan tomb. She climbed under the wooden door; a deterrent for intruders, an inadequate impasse for determined lovers. Rico was crouching in the corner by the steps leading to the tomb. He was lighting candles. The golden walls of the *tufo* rock appeared eerie, the air smelt damp. Bella shivered.

Rico looked up. His eyes smiled but his lips remained in a solid line. His hand reached for her, lingered in the air, unable to touch her.

'Am I losing you?' Rico's olive skin appeared pallid by candlelight.

'Rico. You'll never lose me.' She stepped towards him. He clasped her hands, tugging them around his waist, pulling her closer. Guiding the way, he led her down the steps into the darkness of the tomb. Bella was comforted by the moistened walls, the crumbling stone, even the dust and dirt felt safe compared to the toxic sensations that had seeped through her that afternoon. Rico kissed her nose, her eyelids, her lips, holding her hair tightly in his clenched fist. Each kiss burnt out the memory of Mussolini's visit, each touch washed away the fear. The warmth of Rico's embrace stopped the pain she felt when near her father. At the same time, a ripple of guilt wrapped itself around her, squeezing until she was breathless.

Later, as they were scrambling up the hill towards Monterini, Rico grasped Bella's hand. 'Let's just tell them we're getting married.' His breath was hot against her cheek.

'It's impossible! You know that.'

'Don't you want to?' Rico's voice was edged with an impatience that was rare. He stopped moving and let Bella's hand drop to her side. 'We're almost eighteen! What do you think is going to happen next? It's time. We'll tell them what we want.'

'You don't see the obstacles.'

'And you only see obstacles.'

The moon emerged from behind the rooftops; the *tufo* was silvery grey in the darkness. Black shadows danced across the stone. All around her the valley was still.

'It's not the right time to dream.'

How could she explain the sensation pulsing through her, the fear she experienced, the knowledge that he didn't understand, couldn't share her anguish. For him nothing had changed, his life continued in the same rhythm, whilst she felt like a stranger in her own village.

Rico caught her wrist. He held it tightly. 'Sometimes I

wonder if all this is an excuse.' His voice remained gentle but there was prickliness to his words. 'I know you love me. But maybe you don't want to marry me.'

Bella shook her arm free. He was wrong to think these matters were simple; she was a Jew living under the racial laws. She needed her community, the safety of the synagogue more than ever. She reached out for his face. Her fingers touched his wet cheek. She sighed. For the second time that evening she felt tears on the face of a man she loved. She pulled him to her and stroked his hair. It was tangled and matted. Her lips reached for his. She kissed him again and again, hoping it would reassure him.

When they reached the village and climbed the hill towards their homes, Bella was sure she saw a figure watching them from a window.

'Look,' she pointed. 'I think Angelo has seen us. We'll be in trouble.'

'It's not my father we have to worry about,' Rico stated calmly. 'It's yours.'

CHAPTER 9

The river was covered with an icy film, animals shrunk into pens. A chill surrounded the village, fighting its way inside coat collars, up stockinged calves and through gaps under doorways. It numbed the senses, froze the heart.

Like the air surrounding Monterini, the friendship between Jacobo and Angelo suffered a severe drop in temperature. Gone were the days sipping *Vino degli Angeli* on the veranda. The bridge to their hearts had been blown apart.

Jacobo's complexion faded to wintry white, his face became as furrowed as Angelo's fields. Each morning when he shaved, Jacobo counted the grey hairs sprouting on his head and examined every wrinkle. He wondered where the Jacobo with his elegant nose and refined bone structure had gone. All he saw was a pasty, middle-aged man with hollow cheeks and shadows as huge as pillows under his eyes.

The daily news plunged him into fresh depths of despair. They had not received letters from Lea's family in Kraków for several months. After the government broke the agreement with France, Mussolini announced his new pact with Japan and Germany. Even Chamberlain's visit to Rome had no effect. Mussolini was on a journey, one that Jacobo had predicted many years before. With each announcement of gloom, Jacobo sank deeper inside himself, shoulders hunched, bones fragile.

The situation with Bella and Rico added to his load. A

few days after Angelo appeared in his office, Jacobo discussed the option of moving to the Fratta with Lea. She'd refused. She needed to be near the Jewish school, near her community, particularly now, she'd said. Who knew what would happen next? Jacobo didn't want to separate Bella from his father, he was too frail to manage alone, even with Signora Franca's help, and the Ghetto house was too small to house them all.

He wondered whether they should arrange a marriage for Bella with one of the boys from the community. She was too free, always had been. When he mentioned it to Lea, she looked at him astounded.

'Jacobo. She's seventeen, eighteen this year. You've given her a free rein for so long and now you're trying to control her.' She was cutting up vegetables into paper-thin slices for a lamb stew. Despite the cold air between them, Angelo had left bunches of carrots, polished cabbages and potatoes piled into towers on their doorstep. Signor Mazzi the kosher butcher at the end of Via Zuccarelli had plenty of meat and thanks to Jacobo's bookshop they were still able to earn a living.

'They've been friends all their lives. The entire village has waited for them to fall in love,' Lea continued.

'Only the Catholic half of the village!' Jacobo leaned across the table to pinch a slice of carrot. He nibbled as he listened to his wife.

'You brought her up believing we were all the same.' Lea wiped her hands on her apron, picked up a pencil and opened an exercise book to start her marking. After a moment she looked up, her face flushed. 'Why don't we speak to our rabbi? He'll know what to do. It's such a tricky question and your families were always so tight. Maybe it's not such a bad idea to introduce her to someone. There are lots of eligible Jewish boys in Monterini. And if not, there's Favore and Montore. She's stubborn, thank God. She'll never do anything she's not happy with.'

After lunch, Jacobo walked back to La Libreria Speciale. He crossed the piazza, waved to Gino Bonito, then stopped in his tracks. Bella was standing by the fountain, deep in conversation with Angelo and Rico. Her woollen hat was pulled tightly around her ears. She was twisting her gloved hands. Slouched next to her, Angelo was shaking his head. Rico's face was flushed, his hands gesticulating wildly, reminding Jacobo of the swallows swooping across Monterini in springtime.

'*Buona sera*,' Jacobo said, smiling at the vision of Angelo and Rico towering above Bella, protecting her. Then he wondered why they were there, huddled together, staring at him in startled embarrassment.

'We were just talking about you, as it happens,' Rico said. 'In fact, it's quite a good moment for you to appear.'

'Rico, no,' pleaded Bella. 'Not now.'

'What's going on?' Jacobo said.

'Not now, Rico,' Angelo repeated Bella's words.

'*Sì, sì*, now's fine, *babbo*,' Rico insisted.

The intensity in his eyes reminded Jacobo of something he was familiar with but couldn't quite put his finger on. And then he understood. It was the same force he had encountered many times in the irises of his daughter; hollowness to the pupils, flickering red veins. Was it hope, courage or sheer determination? Jacobo hadn't seen that look of fervour in Bella's eyes for some time. It had waned, whilst Rico's had deepened. A quiet, simple child. An embarrassed, uncomfortable youth. But the man he was becoming stood triumphant.

'*Zio* Jacobo, we have something we want to tell you,' Rico ignored the others and reached out for Bella's hand. Her face turned the pale yellow of marzolino cheese.

Jacobo glanced from one to the other; Rico, with his solid face and dark eyes bearing into him like needles; Bella, nose and mouth screwed up as if she were trying not to cry; and Angelo,

146

kind, harmless Angelo, shaking his head of straw as he gazed at the ground.

'We're getting married,' Rico announced.

'Marriage is something you usually ask permission for, Rico,' Jacobo said. His voice was raspy. He tried to remain calm despite the pounding in his head. He was stunned at Rico's courage. Were we like that at his age, he wondered.

'We knew you'd never give us permission,' Rico continued, squaring his shoulders.

'I knew nothing about this, Rico's just told me now,' Angelo said. 'But it's no surprise.'

'And you, Bella?' Jacobo turned to his daughter. 'You know it's impossible.'

'I don't want to hurt you.' Bella looked at Jacobo as words tumbled from blue lips. 'And I don't want to disappoint you.' She turned to Rico, brushing tears from cheekbones.

'You're both so young.' Jacobo's calm was fading. 'There are many problems, as you both know. Legal problems, religious problems.'

'You know how I feel.' Angelo's voice sounded like grinding metal. 'There's always a way.'

'*Zio* Jacobo. We want your blessing. It's important to us,' Rico said, adding with a hint of malice, 'but we can get married without it.'

Another blanket of gloom fell from the sky.

'You'd do that?' This boy seemed so much more of a man than Jacobo had ever felt. What were they rearing them on these days? A diet of resilience, desire and determination? This was what Mussolini advocated. But Rico was clearly not a fascist. If he were, he certainly wouldn't be contemplating marrying a Jewess.

'We love each other,' Rico replied. 'We just want your blessing.'

Jacobo glanced at Bella. She rocked backwards and forwards, hugging herself, her lips set in a long thin line. She reminded Jacobo of *la pazza* Rosellina, the crazy woman from Capo Bagno whose fiancé deserted her just after the Great War. Ever since, the poor thing had whiled away the hours outside her house, rocking herself into madness.

'Bella!' Jacobo shouted.

Bella raised her head, her cheeks the colour of sand. She was biting her lips, her eyes moving from Rico to her father. Jacobo's hand skimmed past her hair, played with the air in front of her face, then landed on her cheek. He stroked her skin. She smiled at him. He placed a hand around her shoulder but addressed his words to Rico. 'You'll never get my blessing. I need to talk to Bella. Alone.' Jacobo spoke gently, measuring his words, as if Bella had already joined Rosellina in the world of the insane. He took her hand, placed his lips on her knuckles.

This singular act, like a gust of wind, changed the course of events in the lives of these Monterini citizens.

Momentarily.

As Jacobo led Bella away from the piazza towards the Ghetto, words floated around them. Jacobo thought he heard:

'Don't change your mind.'

Or was it: 'Don't let him change your mind?'

Bella fell into Jacobo's arms like a child into a pool of toffees. That evening after Elena and Luciana had gone to bed, they sat around the table with a pot of coffee and a plate of *biscottini* Signora Franca had left in the kitchen. Bella had insisted that Cosimo be present. Jacobo asked two questions:

'Do you love him?'

'Yes.'

'Do you want to marry him, despite the prohibition?'

Bella sucked in her breath. She began to cry. Jacobo stretched his arm across the table and wound his fingers around Bella's wrist. He stroked her skin. 'You are about to make the most important decision of your life. You have to be sure, not only for yourself but for Rico and for us too. It will cause pain if you marry him and pain if you don't. You have to work out which is the easiest pain to bear.'

Bella watched her father's lips move. His elbows were on the table and his chin was cupped in his free hand. Behind his spectacles, inky eyes watched her, smiled at her. Her father was breathing her in. She was, at that precise moment, the centre of his world. Bella loved Rico but she needed her father more.

It was decided.

Bella would once again move in with Jacobo and Lea. She would be nearer to the makeshift Jewish school. Her *maturità* would occur in May, so she needed all the help she could get from Lea, Signor Roselli and the other substitute teachers who had emerged since the racial laws were announced, rushing to the synagogue as soon as their work in the government school had finished, bringing supplies, fostering morale, helping to keep the students educated.

Bella's hardest challenge was Rico. For several days she lay low. When they met on the veranda and he touched his collarbone, head or elbow, she promptly looked the other way, pretending not to notice the meeting place of his choice. After a week, she muscled up the courage to visit him. It was the day she had pencilled in her notebook as her moving day to the Ghetto.

Winter sunlight bled through the narrow gap between the alleyways. Bella stood outside Angelo's house. A shape was visible behind the half-opened grey shutters of Rico's bedroom.

'Rico?'

She called him again. A few moments later, grinding could be heard in the street as Rico flung open the shutters and looked down at her from the window. He knows why I'm here, Bella thought. Had she come with good news she would not be standing shivering on the veranda. She would have searched for him in the vineyard days ago. She would have rushed up to him with her happy news. '*Sposiamoci*,' she would have screamed to the rooftops, pummelling him with her fists, smothering him with kisses. 'Let's get married.'

'Please come down, I need to talk to you.'

'No.' His voice was distant, unforgiving.

'Rico, I can't talk to you from here. We're not alone.'

Behind each door were ears, yearning for a snippet of gossip to mull over during the empty hours of siesta. Bella wondered whether Signora Franca was standing by the kitchen door of their house, ears pricked in anticipation of the news. She had never approved of Bella's friendship with Rico and never wasted an opportunity to tell her.

In the street, a group of children were playing marbles, another chased stray cats. Just like we used to do, Bella thought, in a different era, in another lifetime.

'If you've got something to tell me, say it from there.'

He looked like a stranger; eyes narrowed into thin slits, skin papery and shiny. He was no longer the man who had held her in his arms in the Etruscan tomb, the man who had awoken each cell in her body with his kisses. Why did he refuse to come down and talk to her? She hated him. But above all, she hated herself and the harm she was about to cause.

'Rico, I can't marry you,' she whispered the hurt, trying to send it up to him gently. She was sure beyond each wall, behind every closed door, others were listening to the words intended for him alone. She could sense the fluttering of lace curtains in the windows behind her.

'I can't,' she repeated. 'Don't ask me why. Don't try and understand. I don't either.'

Rico's body stiffened, his face unwieldy as if made of steel not skin. He was like the statues of the knights outside the cathedral. Not a hint of sadness oozed from his pores. He leaned forward and reached for the shutter.

It closed with a jolt.

Bella was left alone in the street, eyes glued to Rico's bedroom, the sight of his stone face etched in her mind. As she turned towards the house with the black shutters, she imagined her neighbours facing her, pebbles in hands, ready to slay her for breaking Rico's heart. All at once, the same sulphuric smell she associated with Tanaquilla surrounded her. She raised her head and glimpsed the white Etruscan figure shimmering above the rooftops of Monterini.

It was a flash; surreal, fragmentary. Perhaps merely a shape in the clouds? Bella shivered. She wanted to escape from Rico, from her visions of Tanaquilla. She wanted comfort, normality. So, she ran towards her grandfather, the one who had always been solid, dependable and loving.

Cosimo helped her pack her belongings into her suitcase. He didn't question her, he merely hummed '*Finiculi Finicula*', the song Gino Bonito had imported from Naples, folding her skirts and blouses with his arthritic hands. When the last pair of socks and the final book had been packed, Cosimo made Bella some fennel tea.

It was early evening when Jacobo came to collect her. The sun shone through the window, warming three generations of Levis. Bella glanced around the sitting room with its family photographs and view of the Piccolina. She could just picture the entrance to the Etruscan tomb where Rico had entwined her in arms longing to be loved. She would not feel those solid, safe limbs around her ever again. She looked out at the yard where Rico used to bring his father's ladder and climb up to her bedroom window.

So many memories. It would kill her if she stayed in this house any longer. Was this how her father had felt when her mother died; surrounded by constant reminders that burrowed into his skin, forcing the wound to expand not heal? Pain that had to be carried day in day out.

Bella picked up the bags containing her clothes and books and stepped out to the veranda with Cosimo and Jacobo. She glanced across to number 109. Jacobo nodded as if reading her mind. For the first time, she knocked on the grey door. For decades doors and windows had swung open, delivering sunshine and laughter into the Levi and Ghione households. For years the families had shared birthdays, barmitzvahs, weddings and christenings. No longer would the customs of religion embroider the lives of the families of 109 and 110 Via Meravigliosa.

There was a sound, then Angelo appeared in the doorway, his vest and overalls clinging to his body. Giant shadows crossed his eyes.

'I've come to say goodbye.' Bella's voice cracked. Angelo beckoned to Santina and together they walked on to the veranda. The emptiness between the two families vibrated like a live being, with a heart and soul so apparent it was almost visible.

'You're leaving again?' Santina barked the words through clenched teeth. She wiped her hands on her apron. The smell of simmering apples wafted around them as they stood awkwardly in the gap between the two houses.

Bella nodded. She placed her arms around Angelo's waist. Resting her hair of flames against his chest, she whispered, '*Mi dispiace*. I'm sorry.'

'We'll miss you.' Angelo's voice was muffled. She lifted her

152

eyes to the window above where Rico slept with Carlo and Mateo. Was he listening behind the shutters?

She knew she was breaking his heart.

All of their hearts.

But not her father's. His heart was at peace.

CHAPTER 10

Bella lived in a fog. Haunted by the past and fears for the future, she escaped by immersing herself in her studies and banishing thoughts of the Ghiones from her mind. Everywhere she went in those early days of her breakup with Rico was tinged with the presence of Tanaquilla. She sensed the white robes swirling around her as she trekked from Via Zuccarelli over the bridge to Via Cavour to drop off a letter for Jacobo or to collect some worksheets from Scuola Bertolucci. She heard the swish-swish as she stepped on the cobbled streets, her nostrils filled with the smell of burnt eggs.

Imagination or reality?

Was this now the omen?

At every turning point of her life she had asked the same questions. Always shaking her head, always reprimanding herself, wondering whether she was going mad.

As the weeks wore on, the risk of encountering Rico lessened. He seemed to have disappeared. She imagined he too was in hiding. Then a rumour arose that he had left the village. No one knew where he had gone; at least that's what they told her. He had vanished, as swiftly as wolves on Monte Amiata. There was speculation amongst some of the Monterinesi that he had joined the *partigiani* near Modena. Others insisted he'd joined a monastery in the Abruzzo. Bella assumed the Monterini gossipmongers had concocted this rumour; priesthood was definitely not Rico's style. Not even a grieving, love-stricken Rico.

Then another whisper floated through the village. Even though Bella didn't trust it, her heart lurched whenever she heard it. According to their old friends from the Fratta, Rico had become one of Mussolini's *squadristi*, his uncouth, vile henchmen; his Blackshirts. This piece of tittle-tattle didn't fit in with what she knew of Rico, his convictions and feelings since they had started to read together, to discover the truth of the reality they were living in. But then again Rico hated her. Maybe he would join the fascists to punish her. He had dabbled with the idea before.

After weeks of avoiding the Fratta, Bella began to spy on the old house in Via Meravigilosa. She visited Cosimo again, lingering on the veranda, playing hopscotch with the children in the street in the hope of discovering where he was. But the veranda was always empty, the shutters closed, and the twins tidied away as if Angelo and Santina had known in advance of her visit.

'Where is he?' she wondered, staring at the grey shutters as the colourless weeks trembled into months.

It was an unseasonably hot day towards the end of May. Cloudless sky spread over Monterini. Swallows swooped across the spires; pigeons nestled in the cracks of the village walls. Geraniums sprouted from plant pots and windowsills with splashes of reds and pinks.

Bella was crossing the piazza on her way to spend two postprandial hours with Signor Roselli as last minute preparation for the *maturità* examination. Siesta emptiness, save for Gino Bonito and Carlo Zerulli, fanning themselves with their hats under the shade of the cypress trees. She stopped at the fountain to watch swallows cool themselves from the spray squirting out of the carved mouths of the lions. She bent forward to trickle water on her forehead. Someone grasped her arm. She whirled around.

How different he looked.

His face the colour of faded oak, the stubble around his chin like rust. He was breathing deeply, his hand still clasping her arm.

'*Mi fai male*, you're hurting me.' She looked around, frightened that someone would see them and blow the rumour along the alleyways of Monterini.

Rico relaxed his grip, but his fingers were glued to her skin. 'Do you have any idea what you've put me through these past months?'

She replied by frantically shaking her hair in all directions, a mirage of reddish lights. 'No, I mean yes, I do. Of course, I do.'

'No, you don't.' He let go of her arm, his eyes watching her with disdain.

'Rico, it's been difficult for me too. I've no idea where you've been. Nobody in your family will talk to me. I've tried to visit *zio* Angelo and *zia* Santina, it's as if they've disappeared.'

'It's easier to disappear.' He stared through the fountain spray to a place beyond the valley where the Etruscan tombs glinted in the sunshine.

'Have you joined the *partigiani*?' Bella whispered the words. His eyes continued to gaze ahead, without a flicker. 'There are many rumours. Some say you've gone to Turin to join the Giustizia e Libertà. Others say you've been hiding in the Modena area. Some even think you've become a monk.' She hesitated then said, 'Or a fascist.'

'Is that what you think? I've become a fascist?' His face like stone resembled the carvings dotting the water fountains around Monterini. 'Maybe I have. Maybe you're right. I've left because of you, that's all you need to know. I'm here today to collect some things, but I won't come back.'

'You won't come back? You love Monterini.' She didn't know what had shocked her more; the thought that he was now an ardent supporter of Mussolini or that he would never return to Monterini.

'I love it less than I thought.' Rico kicked a pebble. 'Anyway, there's nothing to stay for. There's so much out there, whole new worlds I never even dreamt of. Ways of life I would never have thought possible, especially for me. Some of it's awful, scary, but it's life. I'm learning so much.'

His skin flooded with warmth. Within seconds, he resembled the old Rico, her Rico, yet tougher, more resilient. With dismay, Bella realised this change had nothing to do with her.

'You've changed.'

He bent towards her, his lips touching her ear lobes. Trembling, she felt the warmth of his breath against her face. 'I know. I've seen what's really happening outside the walls of this village. It changes a person.'

He stepped back to scrutinise her. She dressed differently these days. Gone were her daring scarves and brightly coloured shirts. Grey skirts and short-sleeved, white blouses were her new fashion. Even her hair was less unruly, as if tamed by a new mistress. Would he notice the sparkle had gone?

'You look different too,' he said, as if reading her mind. 'More old-fashioned. You've become one of the Monterini *signorine* through and through. Mussolini would be proud of you.'

'Thank you! Is he proud of you?' There was defiance in her voice, goading him to tell her. She needed to know which rumours were true. Had he become a fascist after all just to spite her?

Rico lowered his eyes. 'Maybe he is proud of me. Whatever

I've become, it's because of you. It's your fault.' He stepped back, eyes narrowed as if to survey her more clearly. 'I've just realised what's different about you. You don't smile any more.'

Bella's hand flew to her lips and touched the thin, paralysed line.

'It doesn't suit you. Your face is lost without its smile.' He turned away from her. She watched him cross the piazza and disappear in the throng of donkeys and *contadini*. When she could no longer distinguish his straight back and matted hair, she sank down onto the edge of the fountain.

She was no longer part of his life.

On the morning of the *maturità*, Bella walked to her old school alone. She was the only girl taking the final exam from the segregated Jewish school. In the playground, she recognised Nicoletta and Paola, two of her old classmates. They were not forbidden to study at the Scuola Bertolucci. They nodded shyly, then turned away from her.

Bella stood alone, clutching her satchel. She stared at the azure sky. Was Tanaquilla perched somewhere on a rooftop gazing at her? Did she sense her isolation? She had not appeared since the evening Bella had left the Fratta, but Bella knew Tanaquilla was somewhere above the spires, floating around the silvery branches of the olive trees.

When all the other students were seated in the classroom, Signor Roselli emerged to escort Bella to a desk assembled in the corridor. She sat down alone. Her eyes fell on another empty desk close by. The Bella of the pre-racial laws would have asked who the unexpected guest was. This new Bella sat down silently, opened her satchel and stacked her pens and pencils neatly in front of her. Next to them, she placed the flask of black tea Jacobo had prepared for her earlier that morning.

The door of the classroom was still open, and Bella could

see her peers standing to salute the Italian flag. Most of the boys wore the black shirts, black knickerbockers and black caps of the *Avanguardista*. She wondered which ones would graduate to join the *Fasci di Combattimento*, Musolini's black-shirted bodyguards. These were the lads she and Rico had played marbles with in the streets of the Fratta. They had licked each other's ice creams at Roberto's bar. She couldn't have imagined any of them advocating the Blackshirts' motto of *me ne frega*, I couldn't give a damn. But then again neither would she have imagined taking her national exams relegated to the corridor of the Scuola Bertolucci.

There was a new flavour to the wall display. The old map of the world had been replaced with a large map of the Mediterranean coastline, highlighting the achievements of Italian colonisation. With amusement, Bella observed a selection of creams, cleaners and waxes at the bottom of the poster. No doubt to remind the girls of their position in social colonisation. Next to the poster was a slogan. Bella leaned forward, almost knocking over Jacobo's flask of tea, in an attempt to decipher the words.

'War is to the male what childbearing is to the female.'

What a relief Lea wasn't present to witness Mussolini's propaganda in her old school. Above Bella's head, Benito smiled bewitchingly behind the gilt frame.

'You're killing us with your lies,' she whispered to him.

She was interrupted by Signor Roselli ushering a tall, slender boy to the empty desk next to hers. As he folded his limbs onto the chair, he offered Bella a sympathetic smile. It was Michele Coen, one of the few remaining Jews in the nearby village of Favore.

That day Bella loved Michele Coen. Her heart sang with gratitude towards him, for not leaving her alone in the corridor with her flask of tea, her pencils and the glaring profile of *il*

Duce. She had someone else to look at, another being to inhale the same poison.

'*Ciao.*' She smiled at him with warmth.

'It's only you and me. We'll show them,' he whispered, nodding towards the classroom full of poised pencils. Corn-coloured hair with flecks of gold hung across his face, revealing pale blue eyes.

Signor Roselli looked at them sharply. 'There is strictly no talking. Any misdemeanour and you will be sent home immediately. These are the rules of the establishment and the government.'

Speech over, he winked at them. 'Good luck. And yes,' he whispered, nodding at Michele, 'make sure you show them.'

Bella and Michele's arms moved symmetrically, carving patterns through the air as they endeavoured to inscribe all they had learned. There was courage in their knowledge, a determination to prove they were as able as their peers, despite the lack of formal schooling. When the whistle blew at one o'clock, Bella felt renewed strength. She sensed it was partly due to the boy with lemon hair and a smile as wide as the Fiorina waterfall.

During the break, Bella and Michele sat in a corner of the playground and shared the flask of tea and some bread with *taleggio*. They talked about the paper they had written, discussed their answers.

'What's happened to Rico Ghione?' Michele asked her suddenly. 'We heard in Favore that he left the village. There're all kinds of rumours about him. Apparently, he's now one of Mussolini's key supporters. Knows him personally, it seems.'

'How should I know?' Bella asked, heat spreading across her cheeks and down to her neck. She tried not to show how much this disturbed her. Just another piece of gossip, she told herself, don't listen to it.

Michele looked taken aback. 'Well, you and he were almost joined at the hip. When you and Rico broke up, it was more of a talking point than Mussolini's latest conquest.'

'But we kept it completely hidden.'

'Not very well.' Michele laughed. He continued to tease her. 'Either that, or you totally underestimate the love of gossip in our mountain villages. We even knew about it in Favore. And I dare say the citizens of Rome and Florence speak of nothing else.'

Bella gave him a playful punch. 'Well, it's over now. He's gone. Out of my life.' Her legs swung backwards and forwards as they sat together on the school wall. She was surprised how calm she felt sitting next to Michele. The usual fluttering around her heart, the way her tongue got caught up in her mouth whenever Rico was mentioned, seemed to have disappeared.

After the break they had to wait until the future *squadristi* had filed through the school and taken their place in the classroom. Paola and Nicoletta inched past them, the only girls in a sea of black shirts. Bella smiled. They lowered their heads, their eyes glued to the ground like a spider's legs to its web. Were they embarrassed for themselves or for her? She felt the fury of the betrayed.

Michele reached over and squeezed her hand. It lasted a second but was enough to comfort her. When the class was finally seated, Bella and Michele were motioned towards their desks, their footsteps echoing across the silent classroom. In the corridor two solitary desks awaited them, alone and together.

The afternoon session had begun.

And Bella's heart had been stirred.

CHAPTER 11

On a grey February evening the following year, Michele Coen walked through the Ghetto streets to Via Zuccarelli. He stood in the sitting room, surrounded by books and newspapers, and asked Jacobo if he could marry his daughter.

From the moment Rico had disappeared and a spark had ignited between Bella and Michele, Jacobo had been dreaming. He had prayed for a day such as this. He had thought about it as he walked along the San Gianni path, imagining what it would be like to have Michele Coen as his son-in-law.

'You may, Michele. You may marry my daughter, if she'll have you, that is. I assume you've asked her?'

'I thought I'd get your blessing first, Signor Jacobo. Then if you agree, I'll ask her.' Jacobo's heart was pumping fast. Michele had asked for Jacobo's blessing! He had respected him, cared about what he thought. He grasped the boy's hand. 'Ask her now.'

Jacobo stepped into the narrow hall and shouted up the stairs. He had to cough several times just to get the words out of his mouth.

Bella walked into the sitting room, her hair like a cape floating behind her. When she saw Michele, her mouth opened into a half smile. Her pale lashes blinked furiously. The rust-coloured freckles blended together as she screwed up her nose.

'Michele, I didn't know you were here.'

'Tell her why, ask her,' Jacobo ordered.

Michele twisted the hem of his jacket with his hand. He wasn't classically handsome; his flaxen hair and pale complexion gave him a limp look as if he were recovering from flu, and his limbs hung on his body almost as if they were borrowed from somebody else. But when he smiled, his face resembled Monterini on Saint days, bright with flags and candles. He was smiling now, eyes fixed on Bella.

Jacobo could tell he loved her. From the moment Michele appeared regularly in the Ghetto, Jacobo noticed how his eyes followed her. At the makeshift school as she showed a pupil how to translate from Latin to Italian, Michele's eyes were glued to Bella. Only the other day Signora Franca had pulled Jacobo aside and with a forceful wink which made her mole tremble said, 'This is a much more suitable match for our Bella. About time she came to her senses. Wonder what's taking them so long.'

Jacobo had merely smiled, but his heart had not stopped hoping.

'I came to ask your father if I could marry you.' Michele bit his lower lip. His fingers scrunched the faded border of his jacket. 'I'm sorry it's not the most romantic location. I wanted to take you to the thermal baths at Favore and ask you to share my life, this strange life, whatever we can make of it. But your father said to ask you now. So, do you want to marry me?'

To Jacobo, the silence in the room was unnerving. Why won't she answer him, she must love him, she spends so much time with him? His daughter was looking at him with a wistful expression on her face, her eyebrows arched, her lips slightly open, revealing delicate white teeth, which reminded Jacobo of the pearl necklace he gave his Bella, her mother, the day they wed. Maybe he would offer it to his daughter as an engagement present. His thoughts were running away with him and still she hadn't answered. Come on, he urged her silently. He's kind. He's handsome in a way. He's educated; he's one of us. We'll be safer here all together.

'*Sì*,' Bella replied, biting her lip. 'I do want to marry you, Michele.'

Jacobo was sure his whoosh of relief could be heard through the streets of the Ghetto. He clapped his hands and shouted *mazel tov* so loudly that Lea and the girls ran into the room, their faces a mixture of worry and excitement. He pulled Bella and Michele into his arms. Bella's slender body seemed to crumple into him. Tears wetting his lashes, Jacobo blessed them with the traditional Hebrew prayer: 'May the Lord bless you and keep you; may the Lord turn his face to shine upon you and be gracious unto you.'

It rose above them, floating over the spires and streets of Monterini, through the cemetery and towards the Etruscan tombs.

Jacobo was preparing to lock up the bookshop and return home for dinner. It was later than usual, and Nanni and Marlene had already left. He twisted the key in the lock, slid it into his trouser pocket and placed his felt hat on his head. As he turned to leave, he stopped abruptly. Angelo was staring at the shelves of books in the shop window as if considering which one he might buy. Jacobo hadn't spoken to him for several months. He occasionally saw him leading Rodeo to the vineyards or drinking grappa at Roberto's bar. They averted their eyes. It was better that way. Whenever Jacobo made a visit to the Fratta, the door to Angelo's house was shut.

Their lives had drifted apart. But memories are etched into skin like carvings on a tree. All Jacobo wanted was to slap Angelo on the back, invite him to drink an *aperitivo*, just as they used to before the racial laws; in the days before love had ruined friendship. Then, it had all been simpler. Jacobo looked around to check nobody was watching and reached out his hand. 'It's good to see you.'

Angelo's fist remained glued to his side; Jacobo's hand dropped like a leaden weight.

'Jacobo, I'm not a man of words, not like you. I'm good with my hands but these won't work for what I need right now.'

Jacobo stared at those large, familiar hands he'd seen a thousand times. Hands that picked grapes, made cheese, brought calves into the world; that touched the earth as if it were lace.

'What do you need, Angelo? Come inside, so we can talk.'

Jacobo peered at him closely. Angelo's cheeks were hollow, his expression vacant, as if something had disappeared from his soul.

'I heard about the wedding, Jacobo, I found out yesterday. We don't understand it. We were family in every possible way.' He hesitated before breathing the words into the air. 'It was as if they were betrothed at birth. Everyone thought so.'

'Except me.'

'So, this has nothing to do with those laws, after all.' Angelo's face turned the colour of the gravestones in the cemetery. Jacobo could almost touch the pain. 'You never wanted our families to become one, not for a moment.'

'Of course, you felt like family. You meant a lot to me and still do. But we need to be with our own kind, especially now. Surely you can see that?'

'You sound like *il Duce* himself.' Angelo's voice was crisp, like the sound of scrunching leaves.

'Well, maybe I do. He's the cause of it, after all. Everything's upside down, our lives are upside down. We're not who we were.'

'But before, before all this, if it had been then? Would you have let them marry?' Angelo's eyes sought Jacobo's. Deep, full of hope, they begged him as if his life depended on it. Jacobo was moved by their power. He lowered his gaze. Was it better to be kind or honest? He struggled with the dilemma and his heart sobbed.

'Would you?' Angelo repeated, raising his voice.

'No,' Jacobo whispered, truthfulness winning over kindness. 'Probably not.' He could barely comprehend his own words, but he knew Angelo had heard.

'Seven generations, this bond. Seven generations. And you bite through it without a moment's thought?'

'This doesn't break the bond.' As he spoke, Jacobo knew it was a lie, but he couldn't bear the pain he was causing his friend.

'They love each other, Jacobo. And you won't let them marry.' Angelo straightened up. He towered above Jacobo. He pointed his index finger at Jacobo, prodding him with courage born from anger. 'I spit on you, Jacobo Levi. I spit on you.'

Jacobo grabbed Angelo's arm. 'I didn't tell her not to marry Rico. She made up her own mind.'

'They were in love.'

'They were too young.'

'They were seventeen, she's barely eighteen now.'

'This is what she wants. Nobody's forced her.'

'You've broken our hearts.' Angelo spat hot words into the frosty evening air, his voice jagged. A crowd was gathering on the street around them.

'I loved you like a brother, you know that.'

'You pretended we were the same, as good as you.'

'Jacobo and Angelo, that's how it was. That's not changed.'

'And Rico and Bella! That's how it always was. And always should be. But it was a lie.' Angelo moved closer to Jacobo, his fist attacking the air between them with little punches. Swirling patterns radiated into swipes, jolts, thrashes.

They grabbed each other.

A hand, a wrist, a knee. Anything their fists could sink into.

They punched, thrust after thrust, rolling on the floor, hair matted to their faces, dust from the street stuck to their coats, unstoppable, unforgiving. Angelo's cap flew from his head. Jacobo grabbed a handful of yellow hair. As crimson strands of winter sunset streaked the sky, they remained glued together. The crowd around them ballooned.

'Shame on you both. At your age too!' Signora Franca barked at them.

'As if we don't have enough going on around us, we have to fight one another!' Rosa Vetrulli, the doctor's wife, wrung her hands in despair.

Jacobo and Angelo ignored the cries. Hats discarded on the roadside, shirtsleeves flapping in the breeze, they fought as if the world existed for them alone. They were held in the fight by the arms of the other, attached by an invisible thread, by a moment of madness.

Neither man saw Bella standing behind the crowd, tears slashing her cheeks. She watched as the memories flooded back: wine under the peach tree, singing along the rows of vines, stamping her feet in vats of grapes.

'Help us please, somebody help us,' Bella cried.

Next to her stood the woman with half-moon eyes and white robes. And the stars were their backdrop.

CHAPTER 12

The wedding was set for the tenth of June, before the sweltering heat of summer wrapped itself around the village and the energy of spring was more than a distant memory. In the weeks leading up to her marriage, Bella lived in a daze, not daring to question her choices, knowing only the closeness she experienced with her father was as precious as the engagement band on her finger.

Every *Shabbat* morning, she accompanied him to the synagogue. She watched him from the ladies' section at the top of the building, smiling up at her, his grandfather's *tallit* spread over his head and shoulders. He in turn accompanied her to the *mikvah*, holding her bag when she went inside for the ritual bath, waiting patiently until she emerged, washed and cleaned, ready for her new life with Michele.

It was the day before her wedding. Bella walked from the Ghetto to the Fratta, under a sapphire sky knotted with wisps of clouds. She wanted to try on the pearl-coloured dress her mother had worn when she married Jacobo. Weeks earlier, when helping Cosimo with the Passover cleaning, Bella had stumbled across a bundle of silk wrapped in sheets and tucked neatly away at the back of a cupboard.

'How strange we've never seen her wedding dress before. Maybe it means I should wear it.' She paused. It had always been unsafe for Bella to mention the feelings and sensations she experienced. But this was her grandfather not her father. 'Do you think it's an omen, *nonno*?'

Cosimo screwed up his eyes, his skin papery, fragile. Veins stretched across his temples like blue webs. 'Who knows? Maybe your mother is watching out for you. If you believe that kind of thing.'

'Do you?'

'Possibly. And you?'

Bella hesitated; should she mention the figure that haunted her, that appeared when she least expected? She feared she would appear foolish. Underneath the hesitation was the warning Jacobo had screamed at her years ago. *Vietato*. Forbidden.

'There's a magic here, no doubt,' her grandfather continued. 'Layers of civilisations built one on top of the other. Etruscans, Romans, Counts, *contadini*, Jews. And now fascists. Something has to remain in the soul of Monterini. That's what I believe.'

Bella stroked the soft silk and placed it close to her nose. The smell of sulphur overwhelmed her. She looked around. She listened. There was no swish-swish of robes, only softness to the air, a serene silence. And still she couldn't tell him.

'And *babbo*, does he think so too?'

'No good talking to your father about this. He backs away. We aren't supposed to meddle, you know. Let the dead lie, let past centuries be in peace. That's what it says in our Torah.'

Bella lowered her head, her body stiffened. 'I think I'll wear the dress.'

Bella thought about this conversation as she stepped across the veranda. She glanced up at the Ghiones' door. It was shut tight despite the warm June air floating through the village. She hadn't seen or heard of the Ghiones since the fight between her father and Angelo. A shudder coiled down her spine. Had they closed the door on purpose, suspecting she might be there? She tried to dismiss the thought, but it festered like a scratched wound.

She walked through the open door and crossed the kitchen, calling out to her grandfather. The house was calm, quiet. She padded upstairs to her bedroom. Her mother's dress fanned the bed; little beads around the neck and waist sparkled like freshly polished jewels. Although slim, Bella was thicker around the waist than her mother had been and Signor Sadun, Monterini's tailor, had let out the seams. Bella stepped out of her skirt and undid her blouse.

A scraping noise came from the kitchen, footsteps on the stone floor.

'I'm up here, *nonno*,' she called out. 'Just trying on my dress.'

She pulled on the wedding dress and placed her hands around her neck to reach for the buttons. Fingers clasped hers, strong and warm. She jolted round feeling his breath stain her body.

He was leaner than she remembered, with silver shadows highlighting the delicate skin under his eyes. Gone were the long strands across his forehead. His hair was now short, almost shaved, making him appear boyish and haggard at the same time.

'What do you think you're doing? You can't just barge into my room. You scared the life out of me.' The words came out like puffs of smoke, barely audible.

There was no smile, no flicker of tenderness. Rico looked her up and down, a smirk stretching from cheekbone to cheekbone.

'So, you're getting married?'

'You should leave.'

'To him, Michele Coen. You'll regret it.'

'It seemed a good idea.' Words faded.

'A good idea! You don't love him.'

'How do you know? Of course I do. I'm marrying him. Anyway, it means nothing, love.'

'You're wrong.' Rico's fingers encircled her wrist. 'Without love there's nothing. You'll see.'

'It's you who's wrong.' Bella untangled herself from his grasp. 'Love changes. It can grow or disappear. People change.'

'No, they don't. I see that now, every day. Their views may change but the core never changes. It stays the same.'

'You've changed.'

'I still love you.'

'Please leave.'

'I know you feel the same.'

'I'm a shadow of the girl you grew up with.' I must stay strong, I must stay strong, Bella repeated silently, amidst the clamouring of her heart.

Rico's voice softened. 'And you don't realise how good you have it in Monterini. I hear about it every day, from France, from Germany. Even here, up in the north. People hiding, dying. Orphans, hundreds of them. It's another world out there.'

He cupped his hand under her chin and forced her to look at him. He was still forceful despite a tender soulfulness. 'You'll regret it, Bella Levi.'

'Please leave. It's my wedding day tomorrow. I'm doing the right thing. It will be good for me.'

'Why?'

She couldn't answer. She felt the rising and falling of her chest as she tried to concentrate on breathing; anything to forget the touch of his skin.

'No one is equal these days. No one.' He walked towards her bedroom door. 'You'll never truly escape me, Bella Levi. You'll look at him and think of me. You'll lie next to him and wish it were me. You'll have his children and wonder what ours would have looked like. This is your last chance. From tomorrow I'm your history.'

Then he was gone, footsteps disappearing into endless night.

171

Bella stood at the entrance of the Beit Israel Synagogue. The fragrance of wild roses and lavender her stepsisters had picked on the San Gianni path earlier that morning and wound around the pillars of the *bimah* wafted along the narrow aisles and pricked at her nostrils. Humming of Hebrew melodies; smiling faces; sunlight filtering through the windows drifted through and around her. The soulful notes of the marriage ceremony floated up to the sky, stained fuchsia in the early evening light.

She had been swallowed up in a fog of arrangements and decisions: the wedding, her mother's dress, where she and Michele would live. She was a witness, a silent ghost, like her dead mother or Tanaquilla, watching as she was carried along on this cloud that was her life. She wondered how it had ever happened, how she had agreed to marry Michele and move to Favore, that God forsaken town in the mountains. When she was younger, she had fantasised about leaving Monterini, but she had never envisaged living in that village with its ageing population and bleak winters. Stone houses clung desperately to the mountainside. There was no school, no library, no grinding of crickets in the summer, no lizards leaping out of cracks in the walls. It felt remote, unfamiliar, barren.

Did she love Michele?

She knew only that the war in Europe wafted around them like a bad smell. How long before the odour would gag them all? She knew life was fragile. She knew money, education and position meant nothing. One intake of breath and it was all gone.

She heard voices in her head telling her to run in different directions: her father's, Angelo's, Rico's. Since his appearance the day before, Bella felt Rico's presence everywhere; in the cool alleyways, in the warm air around her, even here at the synagogue. When they were young, he used to wait for her on *Shabbat*, by one of the stained-glass windows. He would lift himself up, resting his feet on a large stone, so he could stare at her during the service. She had always been unable to tear her eyes away from the shadow behind the blue, green and red fragments of glass. Now she couldn't tear herself away from the memory of him the night before; his teeth glinting, his soot-like eyes hounding her, pulling her further and further into his snare.

Jacobo appeared beside her and offered his arm. 'Are you sure you're all right?' A worried frown etched his forehead. 'Is it the dress? Maybe you shouldn't have worn it?'

'It's not the dress.'

'Your hair, it looks like you haven't even combed it. And you look pale.' Jacobo's fingers played with her hair, tucking unruly clumps under the thin veil.

'I'm fine, *babbo*, let's go, they're waiting for us.'

She placed her hand on her father's arm. His suit was fraying at the cuffs and there was a kidney-shaped stain just where her fingertips touched the fabric. He, who always used to be so well dressed, so polished. He was breathing fast, there was an excited air about him, as if he didn't quite believe he was walking his daughter to meet her betrothed under the *chuppah,* the wedding canopy.

The crowd rose as they entered the building. Dotted amongst family and friends were a few select members of the Jewish and Christian communities. Padre Giacomo had retired, and his assistant Don Philippe had taken over all official duties. He sat in the front row in between the mayor, Luigi Baldini, and the *vescovo*. The mayor had thought it fitting to invite the bishop, particularly in the current climate. Angelo and Santina had been invited. They were nowhere to be seen. Bella's gaze drifted towards the *bimah*, the platform in the centre of the synagogue, where Michele stood waiting, arms outstretched, eyes silky blue and full of hope.

She stopped at the bottom of the steps, motionless, transfixed. Her father's elbow nudged her, digging into her ribs. As she struggled up the steps, her eyes focused on the tiled patterns of the floor. Michele reached out for her hand, pulling her next to him. He had cut his hair and his skin was scrubbed and shiny. His lips opened into a shy smile. He breathed her in, she felt his love. It touched her as she stood next to him under her *nonno*'s prayer shawl, draped over their heads in the traditional Monterini fashion. A silent prayer fluttered around her heart. 'Please let me love him. Please let me forget him.'

Both men entwined in her thoughts, both men inseparable yet worlds apart.

The music stopped. The rabbi spoke. She heard the chink of breaking glass, the whoops of *mazel tov*, the cries of *auguri*. Michele's arms encircled her waist, sweeping her towards him. His mouth touched hers. They were man and wife.

⌾⌘⌘⌾

The crowd spread on to the terrace. Jacobo and Lea had organised a modest celebration; it was hard times after all. Everyone helped to prepare food. Signora De Benedetti had made artichoke salad, Signora Palli aubergines and Signora Franca had prepared *crostini* topped with *pecorino*, tomatoes and courgettes. *Sfratti* and *cantucci* biscuits were provided by the Servis and placed fetchingly on a dish belonging to Jacobo's grandmother. The rabbi had made sure there was a plentiful supply of kosher wine to toast the lucky couple with a *l'chaim*.

Jacobo passed around the beakers of wine, kissing guests on both cheeks and accepting their good wishes for the marriage of his daughter. For the first time in a long while, he let joy filter through him, unclenching muscles, blowing away the dust of fear that settled in every cell.

Up until that last moment when he stepped down the aisle, his daughter clinging to his suit sleeve, he was filled with dread. It was similar to the old feelings, when every move Mussolini

174

made would cause his nostrils to quiver, those familiar words to smother him. He thought back to the numerous times he had quarrelled with Bella, fighting over where she should live, whether she should belong to Mussolini's youth group, how she should study. He remembered all those moves, Fratta to Ghetto, Ghetto to Fratta. She had worn him down, this fireball of a daughter, with whims and ideas she clung to with a determined cunning.

Even when Bella let go of his arm and sidled up to Michele, pale, eyelids lowered, Jacobo feared she would back out. When Michele placed the gold band that had belonged to her mother on Bella's finger, Jacobo heard the breath rush out of his lungs. He wondered if his relief was obvious to everyone. But all eyes were fixed on the bride and groom.

She was married, safe. Now here she was standing next to Michele, her wild hair as orange as the burning sun, chatting to the rabbi, holding Elena's hand. Was she happy? He couldn't tell. Her face was flushed and there was a glint in those grass eyes.

His reverie was blighted by a clamour in the street. Yelling, loud cries. Suddenly the alleyways were brimming with people, arms gesticulating wildly. Jacobo opened the iron gate of the synagogue and climbed up the steps with Rabbi Coen.

'What's going on?' Jacobo caught a child by the arm. It was Maurizio, Clara Todi's grandson. Maurizio shrugged his shoulders and mumbled, '*La gue...rra, la gue...rra.*'

A group of men were leaving the *frantoio*, the oil press, shirt sleeves ruffled up to their elbows, waistcoats flapping over their bellies, faces wrinkled with worry.

'Terrible news.'

'It's the end.'

'What's happening?' Jacobo wished they'd say something. Nobody seemed to be making any sense. They ran past him, ignoring his questions. Jacobo was relieved to see Dottore Mazzola pass the synagogue. The doctor stopped when he noticed Jacobo and placed a hand on his shoulder.

'I know it's your daughter's wedding today, Jacobo. I'm sorry to change the mood but the news is bad.'

'What is it, *dottore*?'

'We've just heard Mussolini on the wireless, speaking from the Palazzo Venezia. He's declared war on France and England. Italy has now entered this blasted war.'

Jacobo felt heat from somewhere near his intestines rise up to his face like a violent wave. The passageways of his throat tightened, restricting free circulation of breath. Everyone was talking at the same time.

'Do you think it will be over soon, *dottore*?' Rabbi Coen's eyes were dark with fear.

'*Non lo so*. I don't know. In Rome they're saying it'll be over in a matter of months but I'm not sure.' Mazzola adjusted his hat, gazed at Jacobo and the rabbi. 'I think it's going to be hard for all of us. But for your people, it will be a catastrophe.'

Jacobo turned to look at the crowd still celebrating on the terrace. They were unaware of the news, although some faces were turned towards him, wondering, enquiring, eager to hear what the commotion was about. Others were sipping wine, wiping flakes of pastry from their lips. An eagle spiralled above the rooftops; water trickled from the fountains. The fields beyond were splattered with red poppies; cerise and white oleander swayed in the breeze. Crickets clamoured in the distance. Nothing else seemed to have changed in this perfect place.

'Whatever will happen to us next?' Jacobo said aloud.

Only the village heard the whisper. Only the village knew the truth. Monterini and the white-robed woman who watched from the clouds.

CHAPTER 13

Italy entered the war and the hammering began. Almost immediately battles were lost, territories relinquished. Jealous spasms seized *il Duce*'s heart. Hitler, his one-time protégé, was busy annexing countries, winning battles and igniting Mussolini's desire to be as great a conqueror as the German leader.

All over the country people continued their lives as best they could, suffering the injustice of a war most did not want. Rumours of starvation trickled through town to village. Losses mounted up one by one. News that the British had destroyed Rodolfo Graziani's troops in the Cyrenaica area of Libya silenced the jubilant fascists, as did the Greek army's victory on the Albanian border, squashing Italian soldiers as if they were ants on a hot day.

In Monterini they survived, reminding each other it was worse in the south where whole villages were invaded by their German 'friends', or in the north where the communists reigned. News of hunger in Rome sent shivers coursing through veins. At least, in Monterini, fields heaving with crops surrounded them. It was business as usual at the blacksmiths, the bakeries and the bookshops. The Monterinesi continued to pray in the churches. To the joy of Don Philippe, weekday mass became almost as fashionable as the Sunday variety.

All men between the ages of eighteen and fifty-five were

called up to fight alongside Hitler's troops. Like feathers from hens on Saint days, husbands and sons were plucked from fields and shipped off to join Mussolini's soldiers. One by one they disappeared, Pino Petri, Paolo Zerulli, even old Gino from Naples.

Monterini was empty. *Vuoto.* A *sfratto* without dates. Those that were left clung to each other as if with every passing breath they would be swept off the *tufo* cliff and buried in the Etruscan remains below. Women joined new ranks within the furrows of the fields, tilling, pruning, harvesting; doing what up till now had always been considered the work of men. They climbed ladders, collected olives, carried buckets of grapes to be harvested, sinking their bare feet into barrels of purple juice. Even the sweet melody of female voices could be heard rising above the rows of vines in Angelo's vineyard.

And the grapes prospered.

Due to a minor wound inflicted on his tibia during the Great War, Angelo, with the help of Dottore Mazzola, was kept out of the enrolment. He continued to work on his land, producing cheese and olive oil, selling the meat of his animals and some stock when he needed extra money. There was a plentiful supply of vegetables to keep the family and neighbours alive. The harvest of 1940 was a good one and Angelo's wine, considered not a luxury by the Monterinesi but a necessity, continued to be drunk for breakfast, lunch and dinner. *Vino degli Angeli* was the best loved wine in the area of Salone and profits increased.

Jacobo's bookshop suffered but survived. There was little money, but books were still sold and when necessary so was the odd candlestick or silver kiddush cup. Jacobo scuttled backwards and forwards from the bookshop to the Jewish school dividing his day between selling copies of texts acceptable to the fascist regime and teaching students who were not.

For Bella, life was miserable. Favore was embedded higher in the mountains than Monterini and was surrounded by tar-coloured, unmanageable rock. Winter weighed down on her.

January breath.

With the onset of war, shops closed, houses emptied, and the alleyways appeared ghostly in the winter light. Bella hated the Coen house in the Ghetto area of Favore, just past the ancient stone arch. It had been a beautiful house once. When the racial laws were announced, Michele's mother sold half to her neighbour Signor Boscani. Now the Coens lived in three small rooms, cowering together by the stove to keep warm.

Bella knew her marriage was doomed.

Weren't they all doomed? It was Italy in the racial era. The country was at war. Breath was bated on the lips of all who lived in the area of Salone. What did it matter if her heart was hardened, her future written in stone and passed over to a man she didn't love? It pained her to think she'd used Michele. He hadn't asked to be used, only loved.

On that first night as she lay with him in the marital bed, his mother's snores breathing through the walls of the next-door bedroom, she knew she couldn't let him touch her. No fingertips, lips or gentle strokes could ever replace those of her first love.

'My only love,' she sobbed into the pillow as Michele's fingers jumped across her chest and down the contours of her stomach. He tried to woo her, surprising her with soft kisses on her eyelids when she was asleep. He would search for poems of Guido Gozzano, Amalia Guglielminetti, the poets of the *Crepuscolarismo* movement, which he knew she loved. Nothing could tempt Bella back into his world. Like a butterfly, her wings flitted around him, longing to escape.

Every day she and Michele caught the bus into Monterini. Bella taught with Lea at the Jewish school and Michele helped

Jacobo in the bookshop. Bella missed the olive trees and vineyards, the golden *tufo* rock, the monastery and the palazzo.

'Why don't we move to Monterini?' she begged Michele time after time.

'You know I can't move, *cara*, I've told you. I can't leave *mamma* alone. She's crippled with arthritis.'

'And I need more than this,' Bella whispered under her breath. But he heard. He always heard. He turned his white shirt and black braces away from her. All she saw was the tousled, lemon hair. And she felt his heart shrinking.

Every day Bella wondered how she had let things run out of control. She had galloped along beside her fate, as if there were no choice. As a teenager she dreamt of discovering cities with beautiful people, libraries full of books, museums and theatres. She'd imagined herself in cafés, on wide boulevards in Florence or Rome, sipping espresso from pretty, porcelain cups. Now each night, as she lay next to her husband and felt the frozen air of Favore suffocating her, all she dreamt of was returning to Monterini. As the months slipped by, she became thinner and paler. Whispers wafted from village to village, carried by raindrops and scattered like seeds. But only she knew the truth. The day she moved to Favore with her new husband, Bella stopped living.

Her saving grace was a tiny balcony where she would stand for hours staring at Monte Amiata, bluey black in the distance. The crooks and curves of the mountain reminded her of layers of satin. Rico used to watch the same view from the back window of his bedroom in the Fratta. She wondered if he ever witnessed the changing colours of the landscape, the russet orange as autumn approached, the dazzling stars at night? Perhaps they were breathing the same air, sharing the same thoughts.

But Rico had disappeared.

'Why did you do it, Bella?' Michele asked one bitter cold

evening. He was lugging some wooden logs through the front door into the kitchen, a gift from Signor Boscani to help the Coens fight the freezing nights.

'Do what?' Bella was reading by the fire, her hand clasping a shawl around her shoulders. Michele's head was dusted with snow. As he removed his coat, a layer of snowflakes made circles on the stone floor.

'Marry me, Bella. Why did you marry me?'

Her breath caught in her throat like a sheet of glass. She stared at Michele's trembling mouth and she hated herself.

'You don't even have an answer.' Michele threw the logs on to the fire. He was panting heavily through his nostrils.

'That's not true.' Bella jumped out of her chair, her book falling on the floor. She pulled her shawl tightly around her shoulders and ran over to her husband. She grasped his shirt collar.

'You saved me, remember? If it wasn't for you, I would never have got through the *maturità*.'

'Is that a good enough reason to marry someone? You made me think you cared for me. But you don't love me, do you? Be honest.' Michele grasped her wrist with his thumb and forefinger, just as Rico used to do. Bella felt the pain again in her heart.

'I will learn to.' I must try, she scolded herself. He's a good man.

But deep within she knew the truth. She had cheated him, just as she had cheated herself.

There was nothing she could have done. Her fate was sealed long ago on a cloudless day in 1921. And so was his.

It was late February. The wind had blown the snow away from the front door of Michele's house onto a pile of logs stored at the side of the road. Sugary patches dotted the rooftops and pathways of Favore. It was Saturday, *Shabbat*. Michele had risen early to walk to Monterini with Signor Gabriele, the only other Jew left in Favore. They went almost every week to meet Jacobo and pray in the synagogue together. Bella usually stayed in bed, wrapping the blankets around her and reading in the early morning light. That day she got up with Michele and made coffee for him and his mother. She took the steaming cup and some *pane di campagna* Lea had baked into the room at the back of the house where Michele's mother Carla slept.

'Stay here, *mamma* Carla, it's too cold to get up. I'll be reading by the fire if you need me.'

As he prepared to leave Bella turned her head, and Michele's lips brushed her cheek, not her mouth. He glared at her, eyes smouldering, then placed his fingers under her chin. He nudged her towards him, digging into her skin, forcing her to look up.

Lips touched lips.

Michele left the house, banging the door behind him. He stumbled down the path towards Signor Gabriele's house, head bent, back swaying gently. She wished she could run after him, grab his coat collar and kiss him with the passion he desired, the passion he deserved. But she remained by the window watching him.

She washed in icy water, dressed then sat by the fire, book in hand. But she couldn't read. Her bones ached with emptiness.

'I must get out of here. I cannot bear this depressing, hateful place a moment longer.' She reached for her coat and scarf. 'I'll be back soon, *mamma* Carla,' she called as she ran out of the house, treading carefully along the snow-clad paths. She waved at a cart trundling along the road. It was a farmer she recognised from Monterini.

'*Vad' a San Colombo.*' He spat out the words in dialect with a toothless grin.

'*Benissimo,*' she replied, hugging herself. It was heart-warming to hear Monterinese again.

San Colombo was a tiny compound of fields and smallholdings where Angelo's grapevines and olive trees rustled in the wind. It was a brisk walk from Monterini. Descending the mountain, the air warmed, snow faded. Rays of sunlight tickled her skin and as they reached the pastures of San Colombo Bella's spirit improved.

'Why does the sun never shine in Favore?' she asked the *contadino*.

'Because it's closer to God's anger,' he replied with a wink.

Bella thanked him for the ride and jumped to the ground. 'Spring always comes early to Monterini,' she reminded herself as she looked around, shielding her eyes from the dust of the farmer's cart. Yellow broom and purple and pink crocuses splattered the path with colour. Bluebells stretched towards her. She tilted her head to one side. Soft notes trembled through the air. It was the familiar sound of Angelo singing to his grapes.

Bella's chest tightened. She had not seen him since the evening Jacobo and Angelo had fought in the dusk-tinged streets of Monterini.

Before her marriage, before Favore.

Before her heart had died.

Angelo looked up. A rosy haze flooded his cheeks. Was he happy or embarrassed that she was there? She searched for something gentle to say but the words came out barbed, a deep wound. 'Why can't life be simple? Like it used to be.'

He didn't answer. She moved towards him. 'I used to love it here.'

Angelo's eyes softened, yet the silence between them remained palpable, unwavering. His cheeks were still rough and pockmarked and deep grooves had settled on his temples and above his mouth.

'It wasn't my fault, *zio*,' she blurted out, unsure, hesitating.

Pools of water filled her eyes. 'I just didn't know who to please first.'

'*Lo so.*' Angelo's voice was impassive. 'I know.'

Bella took a step towards him. She placed her arms around his waist, smelling the earth on his shirt, breathing in the vapours of wine on his breath. For a moment he pulled back, then he touched her head with his hand.

For Bella, it seemed as if they stood there for ever, enveloped in the soft fog of memories. She saw herself and Rico running through rows of purple and white grapes, screaming songs to the mountains in the distance, her father sitting under the peach tree, tumbler of red wine planted by his feet, grey hat shielding his eyes from the sun as he read from the books of the Kabbalists.

'That was when I was happy.' Her tears splattered onto Angelo's shirt.

'I know,' Angelo repeated, but softer this time.

Rough fur rubbed Bella's arm. She looked up and saw Rodeo, Angelo's donkey. Laughing through her tears she rubbed Rodeo's nose. 'I remember when you bought him, *zio*. How can I remember when I was so young?'

'It was a big day,' Angelo chuckled. He tickled Rodeo's ears. '*Vino degli Angeli* was a success. You thought of the name.'

'It was when we all felt free.'

'Not me,' Angelo sighed. '*Contadini* are never free.'

She gazed up at this tall man whom she had always thought of as a father. Suddenly she realised the meaning of the word trapped. Angelo had done well; his wine was a success. He probably had more money than he could have ever hoped for. But the shackles of his class still restrained him. It was clear they were all trapped in one way or another.

'So maybe now we really have something in common,' she whispered with a sad smile.

The following day, Bella left Michele and his mother and caught the Sunday bus full of villagers from Favore travelling to Monterini for mass. A gentle sun warmed the crocuses on the outskirts of the village. When Bella arrived at the house in the Fratta she noticed Jacobo's bicycle resting against the wall. She glanced up at the house next door then pushed open the front door and stepped into the kitchen where Jacobo and Cosimo were sitting at the table, sipping coffee from chipped cups. Replacing crockery was a luxury from a previous life.

'*Ciao*.' Bella stepped round to kiss them on both cheeks.

'How nice to see you.' Cosimo pushed himself up and walked to the stove to pour her a cup. 'Sit, *cara mia*. Look, I have some parsnips and carrots here and a few potatoes. Angelo left them at the door only last night.'

'Phew! We're running out.' Bella sighed as she took the vegetables from him. She decided not to mention her trip to Angelo's smallholding the day before. 'Michele and I would starve if we didn't have all of you down here in Monterini. There are hardly any farmers in Favore.'

She picked up a potato and held it against her cheek. 'Thank God for Angelo.' She inhaled the earthy smell.

'He told me Rico was back. Did you know that?' Cosimo asked.

Jacobo glanced at him and Bella noticed the lines on her father's forehead sink deeper into the skin. His eyes swam with anger as if he were willing his father to stay silent. She wasn't fooled.

'You knew?' she asked Jacobo, hands resting on her hips. 'And you didn't tell me? Did you want me to bump into him in the street?' She wondered why Angelo hadn't mentioned it the day before. That was the one thing Angelo and Jacobo had in common, they still treated her like a child.

'I didn't think it was important.' Jacobo twiddled with the buttons of his jacket and gazed out of the window.

'Not important! He was my best friend, *babbo*. Surely I'd want to see him if he came back.'

'You're a married woman, Bella. It isn't appropriate to be seen dallying with another man.'

'Dallying! What do you mean, dallying? Where is he? Where's Rico?'

'Does it matter?' Jacobo sighed. 'Rico is the past. It's your husband you should be devoting your time to.'

'How can you take food from Angelo and Santina and say Rico's the past? It's a touch hypocritical!'

'Angelo is a good man.' Jacobo lowered his eyes. 'Whatever has happened between us, he's a good man and he cares about our family.'

'Where's Rico, *nonno*?' Bella turned her attention to Cosimo who had got up to stoke the fire. It was cold in the room despite the stove and the spring air. She pulled her scarf tighter around her shoulders.

Her grandfather seemed oblivious to the tension rising in the room. 'He's down by Villa Sofia, not sure what he's doing there, you hear a lot of gossip from people in the street, *le pettegole*, you know what they're like these village gossipers. He's back, that much I know.'

'Thank you, *nonno*.' Bella kissed him. His skin had become powdery with age. Death skin. But she didn't care, she loved him. 'I miss you, *nonno*, I wish we could come back here.'

'So, come.' Cosimo stroked her head. 'I don't know why you ever went to live in that miserable village.'

'I'd love to move back here. Favore is destroying my spirit.'

'It's out of the question.' Jacobo thumped his fist on the table, making them jump. 'You can't leave your new home, you've responsibilities now, you're a wife.'

'But I hate it there. The wind rattles through our room at night. The village is like a ghost town. I'm so miserable. At least

186

let me come back with Michele and be here with the people I know and love.' Bella sank to her knees by Jacobo's chair. She stretched up her arms, grasped the lapels of his worn coat. 'Please, *babbo*.'

He shook her free with an air of exasperation. 'Bella, you must go back to your husband and continue the life you've chosen.' Jacobo enunciated the words slowly as if talking to the child flitting through memories.

'Chosen!' Bella spat the word at him. She dropped her hands and sighed. 'Really, *babbo*, what choice did I have?'

'Nobody forced you,' Jacobo's voice was calm. 'It was your decision.'

'But only because I wanted to make you happy.'

'When did you ever do anything to make me happy?'

'I've only ever wanted to make you happy, but the problem is we've never, ever understood each other.'

'The problem is, we understand each other too well.'

'I can't see how.' Bella sniffed hard. She walked through the kitchen and opened the door. Then she was gone, snapped up by the spring air.

She stood by the steps at the bottom of the veranda, comforted by the smells of burning wood coming from the neighbouring houses. She didn't know what had made her more cross. The fact that Rico was back, and nobody had told her, or the fact that she had married a man to please her father? Because that is what I've done, she realised. She leaned against the wall of the Ghione house and closed her eyes.

'I just have to get away from that ugly place. We'll be fine if we can live here together. I know I can make my marriage work in Monterini,' she said aloud.

A hand brushed her shoulder. She opened her eyes and saw Angelo dressed in his Sunday best.

'I saw you leave. This is for you.' He handed her a crumpled envelope. His voice was cold, distant, and so different from the day before when he held her in the fields by the smallholding stroking her hair. 'Be careful,' he added as he climbed up to the veranda and disappeared inside the house.

Bella cradled the envelope, touched it to her cheek. It's from him, from him, she hummed silently. She placed it to her lips then slid it into her pocket. Instead of walking over to the Ghetto to visit Lea and her stepsisters, she ran down Via Meravigliosa towards Capo Bagno. She skipped down the steps to the San Gianni path and ran towards the spot by the Piccolina, where she'd first met Tanaquilla. Only then did she open the envelope, unfold the paper and read the words that brought the sunlight back into her life.

CHAPTER 14

I t began with a note:

> *Meet me tomorrow, 17.00. Villa Sofia.*
> *Come alone. I need to trust you.*
> *Rico.*

All day Bella sat in the Jewish school with Lea. Her hand stroked the note hidden in the pocket of her jacket as she leaned over the heads of the children and pointed out mistakes in grammar and spelling. She corrected their tenses, explaining the use of the *congiuntivo*, how important it was to write Italian precisely, correctly. At midday she walked back to the house in the Ghetto with Lea and her stepsisters and helped to prepare *aquacotta* for the family lunch. Things were tougher since the outbreak of war and Lea had to let Signora Franca go, despite protestations she would work for nothing.

Jacobo, Michele and Cosimo arrived as usual just after one o'clock. Bella, stomach tight with excitement, coaxed spoonfuls of vegetables and egg into her mouth. She wished away the minutes until she could see him. And all the while she stared at her husband and her father chatting happily together, knowing she was betraying them both.

Just after four o'clock, Bella excused herself from her school duties explaining she had an errand to run. She sprinted through the Ghetto and over to Via Meravigliosa. Cosimo played cards with his friends in Roberto's bar every afternoon, but the front door was open as usual. Bella waved at Signora Petri and crossed the veranda. Pansies lay shrivelled in broken pots, a stool lay on its side against the wall where paint peeled onto chipped terracotta tiles; so different from the veranda she remembered from her childhood.

She crossed the kitchen, noticing pans piled high in the sink. Potatoes and carrots crisscrossed the kitchen table, more gifts from Angelo, no doubt. She ran upstairs to her old bedroom. Everything was in the same place, the bed against the wall next to the window with the vista over the mountains. The patchwork eiderdown relatives had given to Jacobo and her mother as a wedding present lay strewn across the bed. Even the sheets were rumpled as if she still slept on them. Nothing had changed from that last afternoon nearly a year ago, when she had tried on her wedding dress and Rico had appeared.

Except for her.

She had changed.

Bella rummaged through the top drawer of the oak dressing table, next to the window overlooking the Fratta. The lipstick she had used on her wedding day was buried under a pile of linen. It was an old one of Lea's; nobody could afford lipstick anymore. With her finger she smoothed some of the red gloss on her lips, then on her sallow cheeks, pinching them until they glowed. What would he think of the shabby skirt hanging from her hips, her cheekbones sharp as any table edge? Or her dull, sad eyes? The usual verdant brightness had faded to murky grey. Like dishwater, she thought. But he had asked to meet her, she reminded herself. She placed the lipstick back in the drawer. Her fingers touched the pearl necklace Jacobo had given her to mark her engagement to Michele. Bella had never worn it, but she placed it around her neck and did up the clasp, hoping it would add some allure to her wasted appearance.

She ran down to the *cantina* and brushed the cobwebs and mice droppings off her old bicycle. She lifted it on to the street and shut the door gently. She looked up. Angelo was watching her from his kitchen window. Their eyes briefly met.

Bella rode through the village bumping over the cobbles of Capo Bagno, down to the San Gianni path, noticing as if for the first time, the fennel and broom by the roadside, the spires of the cathedral and the sinuous meandering of the Piccolina. Violets, ruby red cyclamens and yellow crocuses spread along the path in patchworks of colour. Above her, Monterini towered, its crumbling walls and jaded houses pale against the soft sun. As her scrawny legs pushed the pedals of her bicycle, Bella wondered why Rico had chosen this meeting place and not the Piccolina or the *cavi*? Why Villa Sofia and not those ancient caves where they had made love the evening Mussolini came to Monterini?

What does he want, she wondered for the hundredth time, her stomach twisting with nerves. As she flew along the roadside, butterflies danced above her head. She sniffed the air. There it was, that memorable smell, that familiar presence. She tilted her head and sensed the swishing of white robes. It was as if Tanaquilla was urging her on, encouraging her to meet her only love.

'My Tanaquilla,' Bella whispered to the air. 'My Tanaquilla.'

Villa Sofia was high up on a hill, like a fortress guarding and protecting Monterini from invaders. Bella wheeled her bicycle through the gates. An army of olive trees greeted her. Silvery grey leaves shimmered in the afternoon sunlight.

Rico was sitting on a stone bench under the shade of a willow tree. At the rattling sound of the bicycle, he looked up.

191

He took it from Bella's hand without touching her and propped it against a tree. He stared at her with frozen eyes. This was not the reception she'd hoped for.

'Are you alone?'

'Of course. But I don't understand. Why here?'

'You'll see.'

'Didn't the house used to belong to Signor Romano? I heard he left after the racial laws were announced.'

'Yes, that's right and he told us to use it.'

Us? What could he mean by us? Here they were together in the forgotten garden of an empty house, alone yet strangers as if centuries had passed between them. Rico kept his gaze lowered, his mouth pinched into an angry O shape.

'What do you mean?'

'I can't explain.' His voice was so faint Bella could barely catch his words. His hair had grown long again and lay recklessly across his left eye. There was an elegance to the way he held himself, a confidence she had never seen amongst the *contadini*. It was as if he felt at home in his body, as if he knew himself.

Placing one solitary finger under her elbow, Rico led her through the tangled remnants of a once cherished garden. Ragged rose bushes lay twisted and gnarled on mounds of untamed beds, weeds curled around hyacinths and bluebells. Steering her around patches of crocuses they approached the front of the house. The pale-yellow paint looked tarnished and was peeling in places. The shutters on one of the upstairs windows flapped against the wall, making a clapping sound like thunder across the valley. Villa Sofia appeared unloved and unlovable in the late afternoon light.

'Thank you for coming,' he mumbled. 'I didn't know if I could still trust you.'

She longed to say, you know you can trust me *amore mio*,

nothing has changed. But she remained silent, knowing it was Rico who had changed, who had drifted away from her.

Rico shrugged his shoulders. 'You're here, that's all that matters. Does anyone know? Michele? Your father?'

'Of course not.'

'Good. I'm going to show you something very important. And very secret. Can you cope with it?'

'What are you talking about?'

'You'll see. Come with me.' He motioned her to follow him.

Bella had envisaged this meeting in a myriad of ways, running over in her mind how Rico would wrap her in his arms, whispering how he had dreamt of holding her. He would smother her face with hot kisses and tell her his plans to whisk her to safety, maybe to Switzerland. He would breathlessly convince her he'd never stopped loving her and beg her to leave Michele.

When she saw him sitting under the willow tree with his icy smile, something warned her that her dream would disappear like mist. She recalled the words he'd said on the night before her wedding. She should have known there were no second chances.

Rico guided Bella up the stone steps fanning the entrance to Signor Romano's villa. What could be so important, so secret she wondered. Rico pushed open the front door and beckoned her to follow.

Bella stepped over the threshold and took a deep breath. Nothing could have prepared her for the sea of pale, dark-haired children staring at her with a sorrow that pierced her skin.

A group was huddled together in the middle of the hall. Above them an elegant chandelier hung from the ceiling, its crystals swaying in the breeze of the open door. Another group of very young children were sitting on worn, brown suitcases placed next to the staircase that spiralled to the floor above. All the girls wore their hair in long braids stretching down from their ears to the middle of their backs. The boys had cropped hair and wore short trousers. Their clothes, hanging from skeletal limbs were more like rags; torn and soiled in places. Bella gasped. These children had clearly not washed for days. She placed her hand in front of her mouth in an embarrassed gesture.

What struck her most was the silence hanging like a shroud over the room with its peeling wallpaper and filthy floor. It was as if the children had come from the dead; ghosts filling the grand entrance of Villa Sofia with sadness and fear.

Bella's eyes sought out Rico's.

'They don't speak Italian.' His voice echoed in the silence of the room. 'No French either. Mainly Serbo-Croat. There are a few Poles, a few Hungarians. Some Germans.'

'Who are they?' Bella managed a whisper. 'They're so skinny, so sad!'

'Refugees, mainly Jewish. Here illegally.' Rico nodded towards a tall, slim figure with thickset arms and wide shoulders. Flames of hair similar to Bella's framed his face, red stubble lined his jaw and upper lip. A few straggly, rust-coloured hairs above his eyes were the remains of his eyebrows. A young boy with shorn hair clung to his jacket sleeve, a tiny girl wrapped skinny, dirty fingers around his trouser leg. Their eyes were dull, listless, set in faces ravaged by hunger.

'That's their leader, Georges Barantova. He's from Russia but he's been living in Berlin, teaching music at the university. He was forced to leave. He's a communist, but one of the lucky ones.'

'But why here? What can we do for them? It's hard enough for us as it is!'

Rico turned to face Bella with eyes of steel. 'You've no idea what's going on in the rest of the world. Can't you see how much easier it is for you in Monterini compared to what others have to deal with? And you were the one who taught me, remember? You were the clever one.'

Bella bit her lip. Heat rose from throat to face.

'*Sono ebrei,*' Rico added, bending towards her, almost touching the skin of her ears with the soft, full lips that used to caress every crease of her body. She tried to concentrate on what he was saying. 'Most of them are Jewish, just like you, but less lucky.'

'I'm sure this must come as a huge shock to you.' Georges Barantova, the man Rico had pointed out, moved towards Bella and took her hand. He spoke in perfect Italian with a subtle accent, his voice gentle, calm. 'All of us in this beautiful house, all skinny and dirty and frightened, all relying on you.'

Bella saw months of pain in the sucked-in cheeks and yellowy-grey skin. What could she do for these people? She could barely manage her own life tucked away in the middle of a mountain.

'Me? How can I possibly help you all?'

A small round figure shuffled towards them from the other side of the hall. It was Don Philippe, the young priest with the long cassock and the modern ideas. Bella remembered seeing him for the first time at her wedding. She was surprised he had dealings with Rico.

Don Philippe squeezed Bella's arm and, as he smiled, his eyes shone like endless stars. 'Rico said you'd help us. Maybe in time your stepmother too. And perhaps your father, with his contacts, his knowledge. We need people we can trust. It could be dangerous, you see.'

'Their parents have been deported by the Nazis, mainly Jewish but some are from communist and Roma homes too.' Barantova nodded towards the crowd of children. 'The parents

195

have disappeared. Possibly dead. These children are more or less orphans.' He whispered the word orphans.

'They will die if we don't help them,' Don Philippe added. 'You are our only hope.'

Bella surveyed the room. Apart from the chandelier the entrance hall was bare. She wondered if Signor Romano had sold all the furniture. Or had it been stolen? She peered through the grand archway leading into other rooms; all stark, empty. The sight of these miserable souls staring at her, blank expressions, no smiles, seemed incongruous in this grand mansion with its winding staircase, high ceilings and impressive bay windows. The strength of the silence surged through her. She glanced at Rico, but his eyes refused to meet hers. At least he still believed in her. He had brought her here to meet these orphans, to be part of something important. And, although she hadn't truly believed the rumours, a sense of relief flooded through her. Rico had definitely not joined Mussolini's Blackshirts.

Don Philippe placed a palm on Bella's arm. 'They've been brought here at great risk by the organisation Delasem. It helps Jewish immigrants escape persecution. The owner of Villa Sofia has offered the house to hide them here.'

'We have to teach them Italian,' Rico interjected. 'They need to be passed off as Catholic orphans. They must learn the Monterini dialect to get by in emergencies. If anyone hears German or Serbo-Croat in these parts, it could be the end for all of us.'

'But why me?' Bella said.

'Because Rico said you're a good teacher,' Barantova explained. 'Patient and kind. He said you taught him. And he said we could trust you.'

She wanted to fling her arms around this man with hair as wild and orange as her own. Despite everything, Rico still trusted her.

'And you're Jewish, aren't you? You understand the situation these orphans are in.'

She was tempted to tell them how hard life was in Monterini, no schooling, no work unless you had a private business like her father, lack of money, privileges, esteem. She wanted to relate all of this, but the words caught in her throat. She remembered what Rico had said about the situation in other parts of Italy and abroad. She only needed to look at these faces the colour of slate, bodies deprived of food and stinking, to realise their eyes had seen more horrors, their souls witnessed greater suffering.

These children, so different from her; no language nor culture in common, tied only by a single bond of faith. In their simple faces Bella recognised herself, in their frightened expressions she saw Luciana, Elena and the children she taught at the makeshift Jewish school. And we only had to move from one school to another, she reminisced silently, not country to country.

She turned towards the three men: the bald priest with sparkling eyes and pregnant belly under the black cassock; the Russian communist with his thick moustache, unruly hair and maudlin gaze; and Rico the partisan peasant who wanted only to be more than he already was. It dawned on her that one of the rumours swirling around the rooftops of Monterini was true; these men were all *partigiani*, partisans involved in an illicit operation, doing what they could at great risk to save these children.

'We're all trying in our own way to survive the madness of this world,' she said at last with a sigh.

'Will you help us?' Don Philippe asked, arching his eyebrows.

'I will.' Bella smiled. For the first time in months a grain of joy fluttered around her own orphaned heart.

CHAPTER 15

The news of orphans at Villa Sofia spread through the village faster than an epidemic of typhoid. Catholic orphans from the Salone area was the story whirling through doorways. Whether anyone doubted this Bella never knew. The villagers seemed to welcome the news with an unquestioning acceptance, unusual in a village of gossipers. But it was wartime; gossip was restricted to who was in love with whom and who had baked the most unpalatable bread.

A few days later, Rico arrived at the house in the Fratta clasping his left shoulder. He climbed the steps leading to the veranda, dragging a rifle in his free hand and leaving a trail of crimson drops along the stones of Via Meravigliosa.

'A hunting accident,' he declared loudly for the benefit of the street. By some coincidence Dottori Mazzola and Vetrulli happened to be sipping *Vino degli Angeli* with Angelo in his kitchen, surgical bags brimming with bandages, disinfectant and needles. The two doctors stitched up his wound and Dottore Mazzola signed the papers declaring him unfit for call-up. When Mazzola delivered it to the commune, Signor Baldini stamped the form with a smile.

The orphans began to settle into their new home. Furniture was borrowed and built with the help of local carpenters. Food was scavenged, begged or bought with money Don Philippe, by some miracle, had access to. Slowly the children's cheeks filled out, their waists thickened, colour returned to their complexions. A working day was quickly set up. Mornings were split between conquering the Italian language and task-based assignments. Milking cows, learning how to become cooks, carpenters and tailors were the main skills required.

The aim of the organisation Delasem, Barantova and Don Philippe informed Bella, was to keep the children safe and equip them with skills needed to set up communities far away from Italy. When the war was over and the time right, they would be ready and skilled to be farmers in Palestine.

Bella's day was now divided between teaching at the Jewish school in Monterini and at Villa Sofia. She left Favore at the crack of dawn, hitching a lift with a local farmer and arrived at the villa at six to have breakfast with the girls and start her first lessons. At eleven she cycled to the Monterini Synagogue school to teach till one. With no time for lunch with her family in the Ghetto, she would cycle back to Villa Sofia munching on a slice of bread or some left over *panzanella* and begin the afternoon lessons at two.

As news of the orphanage spread, new helpers were recruited. Soon members of the Jewish community or those close to Don Philippe who could be trusted helped with the enormous task of passing off these orphans as Roman Catholic Italians. Low profile was the key to keeping them safe, the priest insisted, and speaking the Monterini dialect as much as possible.

'We're safe in Monterini, even if there are members of the Fascist Party around,' he whispered to Bella one day. 'That's why we chose here. It would never have worked in the north, and the south is German territory. But we still have to keep our eyes and ears alert. You never know who might betray us.'

Life was breathed back into Villa Sofia. The sound of voices bubbled through the rooms and out of the windows into the sunflower fields beyond. As she leaned over the girls with their shy eyes and intelligent smiles, pointing out the rules of Italian grammar, Bella felt herself waking up from the dead. Suddenly she had a real purpose to her life. She was barely in Favore, rarely saw Michele and her days were spent watching Rico as he taught the orphans how to milk cows and how to make a table from a piece of wood.

They hardly spoke. But their eyes knew. Occasionally she would look up from the Italian verbs she was teaching a group of children and catch his stare. Loathing, she thought. It pained her so much she could barely breathe. She looked down, not brave enough to witness that look of hatred, and contented herself by being near him. Feeling his presence, imagining the touch of his skin was enough. Sometimes she heard his voice speaking gently to one of the orphans: '*Sei brava. Hai fatto bene*. You're good. You've done well.' She closed her eyes and pretended his words were intended for her.

Bella became close to three of the girls. Marianne and Camilla were German, Tamara was from Yugoslavia. Marianne was slim and carried herself in a refined elegant manner, whether she was writing lists of Italian words to learn or was baking bread. Her short, dark hair framed her face and curled at the ends towards her mouth, giving her a heart-like appearance Bella found very fetching. She was the oldest of the girls and mothered the other two. She checked they understood everything they were taught, and ensured they uttered the words in dialect with the correct intonation.

Camilla reminded Bella of Luciana. Her eyes constantly skittered around as if danger lurked in every corner. She was fairer than most of the other children with thick lips that quivered when Bella taught her the Monterinese words for family members. It was only later Bella discovered her parents were shot before her eyes for not wearing the yellow star.

As they prepared a saucepan of fig jam or a pasta dough Marianne and Camilla confided in Bella. They spoke of their past, where they lived, the schools they attended. They had been stowed away by neighbours, ex-colleagues of their parents in disused cellars, old barns living on scraps, mice their only companions. Until Barantova found them. Bella marvelled at how the girls told these stories in their new dialect, eyes dry, faces like slate, as if the horrors had happened to someone else.

At eleven, Tamara was the youngest of the three. She told Bella both her parents were communists like Georges and had been captured for their political beliefs. In a composed manner she recalled the day Nazi soldiers burst into their apartment in Belgrade and forced them on to the landing and down the stairs. Tamara had been learning the piano with a neighbour who lived on the same floor of the building. At the sound of shouts in German they opened the front door to witness Tamara's parents thrust down the communal staircase, the soldiers' pistols digging into their ribs. The soldiers assumed Tamara was the piano teacher's daughter. Her parents didn't look round to say goodbye, not even with their eyes, Tamara told Bella. For a while she was hidden in the cupboard where instruments and sheets of music were kept. Then Barantova saved her.

Bella was astounded at how quickly Tamara adapted to the language and the lifestyle of her new life. She soaked up the sentences in both Italian and dialect and was soon helping Bella teach the complications of the grammar, the precise form of the Italian language as opposed to the wayward freedom of dialect where words were swallowed or dropped at random. It was a challenging job to teach Italian and Monterinese side by side. In the end, Bella succumbed to the dialect of her youth, easier for most of the orphans to grapple with, without the restraints caused by exacting clauses and tenses.

There was a boy who captured Bella's attention. Salamone Papo from Sarajevo was the youngest child in the Villa. When he first arrived, his skinny legs could barely carry him, and Bella estimated his age to be no more than two. He was almost bald, and his cheeks were sucked in, giving his face the eerie appearance of old age. At first, she found it hard to look at him, his deathly appearance disturbed her. Within weeks Salamone transformed from a sickly toddler into a healthy four-year-old. His face filled out and brown sprouts of hair appeared on his scalp.

Salamone became known as Rico's little shadow, following him from the carpentry workshop to the fields, crouching down on his small legs, watching as Rico demonstrated milking to the older boys, guiding their hands over the udders of a cow and giggling when they were all splashed with milk. The contours of Rico's face softened when Salamone ran up to him screaming in his new Monterinese dialect. If Rico looked up and saw Bella smiling at him, the muscles around his mouth tensed and he would grab the young boy's hand and walked away.

It was better this way.

Rico and Bella lived like strangers, side by side and Bella knew Jacobo witnessed this. Despite the pain of knowing Rico no longer loved her, Bella had to be convincing. She watched the creases around her father's eyes soften, his jaw relax when he stopped by to teach at the orphanage. The distance between her and Rico fooled others into thinking her feelings had evaporated.

Only she knew the secret of her heart.

From the beginning of April, it began to rain and continued for several weeks making the journey from Favore to Villa Sofia hazardous. The chestnut trees glistened with raindrops; the sky was stained with purple clouds. The wheels of the carts churned in layers of mud. Bella would often have to jump out and run through sheets of rain to Monterini arriving soaked and shivering, her long hair sliding down her back like wet snakes.

Pale blue patches circled Bella's eyes; her skin appeared sallow. She folded her skirt over a belt to stop it falling past her slender hips. One afternoon, when Jacobo was visiting the villa to teach Bible stories to a group of young boys, he pulled Bella aside, eyes scanning her face behind his spectacles, creases appearing on the bridge of his nose. How often had he looked at her in this searching manner?

'You look thin and pale. What's the matter?'

'You know exactly what's wrong, *babbo*. I'm unhappy. I mean, I love it here, working with my orphans, but the stress of keeping their identity a secret weighs me down. And I hate where I live. I despise the long journey, I'm forever tired and hungry.'

'Maybe the journey is too much for you. Your work here is far too important to give up. Perhaps now is the right time to come back.'

'Really, *babbo*?' She could come back home?

'Speak to Michele. As long as he agrees to come with you, that is. Tell him I think it's a good idea. The house in the Fratta is too big for *nonno*. Lea and I were thinking of moving back. Things are tough, it's impossible to keep two houses going, let alone three.'

'I will, *babbo*, I'll ask Michele tonight.'

'Besides, I can see the good Rico is doing for these children. And I watch you both, Michele has nothing to fear.'

Bella skipped along Via della Riforma, whispering to the stones that she would be back for good. A flutter of white skipped by her side. Bella had noticed the white robes and slanting eyes amidst the faded faces of the orphans, whirling around her as she worked. At the end of each day, Tanaquilla was there, hovering above the drenched, shiny leaves of the olive trees, as if guarding Signor Romano's old house. This ghost from the past who had predicted she would move:

Backwards and forwards.

From the Fratta. To the Fratta.

But only the phantom in white robes knew it would be her last.

Bella decided to wait until the end of the Jewish festival of Passover to broach the subject with Michele. Preparations were already in full swing. The communal ovens were scrubbed and polished, the flour ground, koshered and prepared for the ritual baking. Since she was a child, Bella had watched the women with scarved heads and aproned bellies manoeuvring the long steel forks into the ovens to cook the *pane azzimo* for Passover. For years she'd enjoyed watching Signora Coen and Signora De Benedetti mix the flour and water with their mature, well-practised hands, their fingers moulding and manipulating the dough into honeycombed circles. She loved the fresh smells of this ritual baking, the preparation of almond cakes, cleaning the utensils in Lea's house until they sparkled.

That year Bella arranged with Signora Coen to bring a group of children from the villa to observe how they make *pane azzimo*. Part of their education as good Catholic orphans, she suggested with a wink. The boys giggled but the girls displayed genuine interest in the process. It then followed that a demonstration was made down at the villa and before long Don Philippe and Rico had their sleeves rolled up and their hands dipped into the unleavened flour. Bella could not help laughing as she watched the *contadino* and the priest engaged in this ancient Jewish tradition.

Some of the orphans had not celebrated Passover before, and those that had were unused to the sefardi customs of rice balls and unleavened pasta. Bella made *sfogliette* with unleavened flour and showed Marianne and Camilla how to roll out thin pieces of pasta and bake it immediately to stop it rising. Her heart swelled as she watched them explaining to Tamara and a boy from a Roma village in Hungary why these customs were important, how relevant they were to all of them in the villa, regardless of their background and religion.

'It's the first time it really makes sense to me,' Marianne said, munching on a piece of freshly baked *pane assimo,* her lashes washed with tears.

On the last day of the festival, Bella helped Michele's mother wrap the Passover dishes with newspaper to be stored under the bed until the following year. She decided to broach the subject of the move with Michele as they undressed for bed.

'I want us to move back, Michele. To the Fratta. What do you think?'

Michele buttoned up his pyjama top and raised his head to look at her. 'What difference where we live? I lost you a while ago. In fact, I don't think you were ever mine.'

'That's not true.' Bella reached for his hand and placed it close to her lips. 'I promised you I would try to love you and I am trying. It will be better for us in Monterini, you'll see. I'll be happier there.'

'Why? Because he'll be next door?'

'Of course not.' The veins on Bella's neck throbbed. 'I'm worn out with the journey and my work. I need to be at home near my family.'

'And what does your father think about this?'

'*Babbo* has agreed. They're going to move too. It makes sense to live in one house for the time being.'

'So, you've worn him down, bit by bit. Poor Jacobo. He finally agreed and now it's my turn.'

Bella dropped hold of Michele's hand. 'Is that how you see it? I wear people down till I get what I want?'

'In a way. But I can't fight you anymore. Look at you, deep circles under your eyes, skin and bone. You're slipping away from me.'

'If we leave here, I believe we'll have a better chance. It'll be easier for us in Monterini.'

Michele shrugged his shoulders. She moved closer towards him, placed her arms around his waist. She felt the points of his ribs dig into her flesh. She lay her head against his chest. Slowly, she undid the buttons of his pyjamas and raised her head to his lips.

A few days later, Bella and Michele moved back into Bella's old bedroom with the view of Monte Amiata to the east and the Fratta to the west. Bella opened the window to breathe in the familiar sounds; the clamour of carts, the clopping of the donkeys' hooves against the stones. Her nostrils tingled with the aroma of sweet pastries, intermingled with the pungent smell of cat's spray and smouldering metal from Pino Petri's forge.

She had come home.

There was a sense of familiarity and warmth that she had never truly experienced in the Ghetto house, despite Lea and her stepsisters' attempts to welcome her. She wondered whether it was because she'd been born in this room, her mother fighting to bring her into the world. It wasn't just Rico that her heart was attached to, it was the feeling of being where she belonged. If she leaned out of the window and closed her eyes she could imagine the sound of dialect spinning through the air; Santina's shrill voice shouting at Mateo and Carlo and Angelo's deep chords telling her to calm down. She felt the years floating away.

But it was different now. It was no longer the Monterini of a former era. War raged around them; on the Albanian border, in the Ethiopian desert and at home in the hearts of those who used to love.

Not only her and Rico.

But her father and Angelo.

A few days later, Jacobo arrived with Lea, Luciana and Elena and bags and boxes full of precious things Lea couldn't bear to leave behind. Elena threw her arms around Bella. She was taller now and her hair had grown down to the middle of her back. Despite her whoops of delight at living with Bella again, she seemed quieter, more subdued. No wonder, Bella reminded herself, they were living under racial laws, they couldn't go to the Italian school or play with Italian friends.

Luciana took Bella's hand and kissed it. 'I'm pleased you and Michele are living with us. I feel less afraid.'

Bella was touched by the gesture; she put her arms around her stepsister. How thin she was, how pale. Tiny blue veins stretched across the translucent skin below her eyes. There had always been a sadness to Luciana, which now seemed to sink into her bones.

'I'm happy too, it's how it should be, all of us together.'

Suddenly the house in Via Meravigliosa was fuller than it had been for years. Cosimo told Bella it reminded him of the years before the Great War, when Jacobo's brothers and mother were still alive. He assured her he enjoyed seeing all the rooms filled with the noise and bustle of the new guests. In contrast to the soulless silence of the house in Favore, Bella felt uplifted by the presence of so many family members.

Signora Franca had been recruited back to help, interfering in her old familiar manner, bossing them around and cooking the combination of Jewish Catholic dishes that had been part of Bella's youth. The kitchen was filled with the smell of baked artichokes, ricotta filled *tortelli*. Despite war and lack of delicacies, Signora Franca still seemed to find cod and chickpeas or salted anchovies, bossing everyone around as she cooked and cleaned.

Bella smiled inwardly when Signora Franca elbowed her in the ribs if Michele entered the room and she hadn't greeted him. She would scowl if Bella didn't stand on tiptoes and stretch up to plant a kiss on his lips. Bella didn't grumble. She was home, that was all that mattered. Even Michele seemed to be more relaxed. It was as if he trusted her more, or perhaps he felt he could keep a better eye on her. He mentioned Rico much less and even nodded at him once when they met on the steps of the veranda.

Bella wanted Michele to feel the move was the best thing for them. She tried harder. She reached out for his hand, brought him *sfratti* the girls baked at the villa, cutting up little pieces and placing them between his lips. She told him what she was teaching the children, how they were improving. She recounted snippets Marianne and Camilla related of their previous lives, the food they used to eat, how their parents were important at the universities, the hospitals. How suddenly everything changed. She spoke about Tamara and her life in Belgrade. She told him how the flesh on the little girl's arms and legs had thickened; her skin now the colour of burnt almonds. When she arrived home after a long day, muscles aching with fatigue, she would sink on to their bed and reach for Michele's hand. All in the hope of making him believe she loved him.

When she watched him across the table helping himself to Signora Franca's *aquacotta*, crumbs of bread caught between his teeth, she wondered whether she'd ever really loved him. Then she hated herself; it wasn't his fault. He was a pawn in the game; a game he didn't know he was playing. And she pitied him.

The frost between Angelo and Jacobo began to thaw. Angelo had always left a basket of potatoes, green beans and tomatoes, depending on the season, outside the door of 110. But now a slab of *pecorino* cheese and bottles of *Vino degli Angeli* were lined along the wall of the veranda in a display of alternating colours.

One day, Bella saw Jacobo placing newspapers and cigarettes by the door of the house with grey shutters. She wondered whether he waited behind the black door hoping Angelo had noticed the gifts; whether Angelo listened for the sound of uncorking bottles, clinking glasses.

On her way to the villa one morning, she saw Angelo leading another donkey down to the *cantina*. She'd heard *Vino degli Angeli* was now bottled, labelled and transported all over the region and beyond. Jealous whispers floated on Monterinese lips that wealthy fascists were clinking their glasses of Angelo's wine as far away as Torino and Napoli. Some even wondered whether *il Duce* himself had sampled the drops of wine warmed by the Monterini sun and embraced by the voice of its people. The irony was not lost on Bella. She imagined Benito toasting Erich Priebke, the German captain of the SS police force *Sipo*, with a beverage devised and improved by the observations of a Jew.

'Another donkey, *zio*.'

'Rodeo *due*. That's what I'm calling him.'

'Well, you must be doing well.'

'Beyond my dreams, Bella.' He smiled, an open, almost forgiving smile. 'I owe it to him.' He tilted his head towards her house. 'Your father. The singing was his idea.'

Bella felt a rush of warmth flood through her. Maybe, just maybe the rift could be healed.

'I'll never forget what he did for us. You know the Germans love *Vino degli Angeli*?'

'The village talks of nothing else.'

'I can almost call myself prosperous.'

They laughed. Bella popped her hand in Angelo's. 'Maybe you can forgive him?'

A shadow crossed Angelo's face, but he held on to her hand. 'I owe your father a lot, but some things are hard to forgive.'

Hope vanished as quickly as it arrived.

CHAPTER 16

By the summer of the following year, the orphans resembled the children of Monterini, skimming stones in the Piccolina, diving into the waterfalls of the Fiorina and running across the fields collecting leeches for Dottore Mazzola. Bella had worked hard on their grammar and vocabulary. Some of the younger children had almost forgotten their mother tongue and chattered away in both the national language and the local dialect as if they had been born in one of Monterini's spindly houses.

Bella was proud of her bunch of orphans, so dissimilar to the hollow, wearied faces she witnessed that strange day in February. When she thought back to the sight of those sad ghosts standing bedraggled in the empty rooms of Villa Sofia, she realised how much the children had changed.

One clement day, Bella took a group of children to visit the cemeteries of Monterini with Mario Celeste, a Jewish lawyer who cycled over twenty kilometers each day to teach history at the villa. First, they visited the Catholic cemetery with its tall poplar trees and the adjacent memorial garden to the Monterini soldiers of the Great War. Mario described the battles of Isonzo and Caporetto whilst Bella pointed out the names of Rico's uncles and her own, scratched on grey tombstones and shaded by the branches of an oak tree.

'Shall we take them to the other cemetery now?' Bella suggested.

Mario shifted nervously. He sucked in his breath. Bella arched her eyebrows, wondering why he was concerned. Then she knew. Mario had only recently moved from Torino to the nearby town of Gradole. Perhaps it wasn't safe to visit a Jewish cemetery in Torino? She placed her hand on his arm.

'It's fine here. Come, I'll show you my mother's grave. But listen carefully, everyone. You are Italian Catholics, remember. When you enter the cemetery make the sign of the cross.' She nodded at Daniele and Simone who were playfully attempting to stamp the sign of the cross on the other children. 'But don't overdo it! And don't forget, we always have to be on our guard.'

She led her group of orphans down the main road snaking Monterini. The cemetery was a short walk outside the village walls and when they reached the large iron gate Bella ushered them through. Tall poplars lined the aisle leading to the graves. Bella clutched her straw hat to her head and with the freedom of the little girl who used to skip along the rows of grapes with Rico, she skipped around plump-leafed cacti and blue and white oleander. Marianne, Camilla and Tamara followed her, curious to inspect the graves of Bella's ancestors. Bella stopped by a wild rose bush. The red flowers were wilted and withered in the heat. Clumps of rosemary and thyme filled the gaps by the grave.

'But it says Bella Levi!' Marianne exclaimed, pointing to the name carved on the gravestone. Her velvet eyes searched out Bella's.

'It's my mother's grave. I was given her name.' Bella's voice was acid calm. She sniffed the air.

'Isn't it strange to see your name already there on a grave?' Camilla said gently, in a perfect Monterini accent.

Bella shivered.

Chilled skin.

Her nose quivered with that familiar smell, pungent and biting. And then she looked up. White robes flapped above her;

eyes sometimes watery blue, sometimes deep navy, but always slate-like. At that moment, Bella wished she hadn't been cursed with this spectre, appearing before her at odd moments of her life, never knowing when and where she might pop up. Bella hated her.

She sealed her eyes shut. Scared of what she might sense, fearful of what Tanaquilla might tell her, she didn't dare look at her name on the grave. It was as if her ribs were punched, her tummy churned by an overwhelming sensation. Like burning. The sulphur smell faded away. When she opened her eyes, the white robes slipped into the clouds.

'I never knew my mother. She died when I was born, you see,' Bella said.

Tamara slipped her hand into Bella's. 'Then you're an orphan like us, aren't you, Maestra Bella?'

'Yes, I suppose so. Perhaps half an orphan.'

She suddenly realised how pertinent the word orphan felt to her. Most of her life she had felt alone. She had her *nonno* and Angelo and Santina next door. But how well did she know her father? How much a part of his life had she been? As she looked at the grave of this other Bella Levi, she wondered how different it would have been if her mother had survived.

At lunchtime, Bella cycled back to the Fratta and parked her bike at the bottom of the steps. She was late and the street was already empty. Around her was the clattering of dishes, the smell of *brodo* stewing. The air was heavy with heat, the sun burnt her face and shoulders.

She stormed into the house. 'Why did you call me Bella? Why did you give me a dead woman's name?'

Jacobo was standing by the window. He turned away from the view of the valley and Bella noticed how withered he'd become. His summer suit drooped from his shoulders and

213

his trousers hung from his hips like limp curtains over a tiny window frame. Speckled, grey hair, listless eyes.

'I have no idea,' Jacobo answered, his glasses perched at the end of his nose. He scrunched his eyes as if trying to recall. 'I think I was encouraged to, I'm not sure. So much of those early days passed me by. I lived in a fog, back then, you see.'

'Why is it bothering you now after all these years?' Michele asked. He was sitting at the table drinking a glass of water. His braces had slipped down to his waist and his hair was dishevelled. 'It's not important. We're at war, in case you've forgotten. The British are bombing Rome and you're worrying about your name. It's pathetic!'

They lived in the same house, slept in the same bed, yet an icy river, too treacherous to cross, still flowed between them, despite all Bella's attempts at kindness. When Michele threw stones into the river by caustic remarks, Bella usually chose to ignore the torrents. That day her temper had been tickled; her mood dampened by a gravestone. She placed her hands on her hips and spat words from her mouth.

'How dare you call me pathetic, in front of my family. I took the orphans to the cemetery today as part of a history lesson with Mario. A way of forgetting the bombings in Rome and Grosseto, if you must know. I showed them the Jewish cemetery too and we saw my mother's grave. Why do you always dismiss my feelings so flippantly, Michele?'

'Because you dismiss mine. It's my way of survival.' His eyes were stormy blue, piercing her with a hatred so palpable she grasped the arm of a chair for support.

Lea entered the room with her daughters. They were carrying a bowl of rice and a plate of courgettes. Lea placed the bowl on the table and wiped away a wisp of hair with the back of her arm.

'Please don't fight, you two.'

Grey moods between Michele and Bella lay over the house like a shroud. Everyone could sense the strain. Lea had tried to placate them at the beginning, humour them, help them. But as the weeks spun into months she had yielded to the tension, knowing whatever she did or said she couldn't change Bella's heart, couldn't stop the pain from rising above Michele like a thick, black cloud. It imbued them all; another personal tragedy, amidst all the others.

'You've seen your mother's grave before, Bella,' Lea said in an attempt to change the mood.

'I know. But this time it made me shiver to see my own name written there.' Like an omen, Bella thought.

Jacobo's eyes were glued to the spot where Monte Amiata rose into the powder blue sky, his mouth locked into a single, silent line. Bella followed his gaze. Above the mountain a single solitary white cloud shimmered. Within that cloud a shape formed. She was sure it was Tanaquilla. She blinked. The wisps dissolved, the shape vanished, and the sky was once again a clear, resplendent sapphire.

The feeling of doom lingered over Bella. She tried to shake it off by throwing herself into Pirandello's *Sei personaggi in cerca d'autore* with the older children. Don Philippe decided it was far better for the children to be seen studying an author popular with the fascist regime. Keep the local *fascisti* happy, he insisted. Good Catholic orphans studying 'approved' texts.

'Low profile, no complications, no partisan theory or forbidden writings,' he whispered constantly into the ears of his fellow helpers.

With an astonishing competence, the children threw themselves into the complications of the play. Most of them had been well educated in their native country. The older ones were accustomed to the literature of their land, knowledgeable in the geography and history of their countries. Most of them Jews, all in Villa Sofia, with their various cultures, different languages, no common thread to Bella or to each other; but for that link of faith. What did it mean to them and to her? She was cocooned in a town where everything had always been permitted, where she had been *una ebrea libera*, a free Jew. From secret whisperings with Marianne or Tamara under the blankets at night, or alone in the fields full of sunflowers, Bella knew that Rico had been right. They had been fortunate in Monterini despite *le legge razziale*. Did she not still live with her family, her *nonno*? Nobody here had been snatched away from sobbing parents, nobody had been hidden in darkened rooms with rats nibbling their ankles and rancid water to drink. *Grazie a Dio*, Bella thought, for the organisation Delasem, which had saved the lives of these seventy-two little souls. And thank God that Monterini was their home.

Yet the sense of foreboding she experienced at the cemetery was spreading. She felt it in her toes and along her spine, even in the air around her.

Destiny.

Omen.

The sensation had always been there, ever since that first encounter down at the river with the figure in white robes. It lurked somewhere, curled inside her, squeezing until she could no longer breathe.

It was *Shabbat*. Cosimo, Jacobo and Michele returned from the Beit Israel Synagogue and after a quiet lunch everyone escaped to their rooms for a rest. Michele lay on the bed watching Bella reading, his gaze so intense she looked up.

'What is it?'

'Just watching you, hoping one day, you'll want to come and join me here in our bed.'

He'd left her alone for a while, hadn't harassed her or forced her to make love to him. She'd tried to be friendlier, sliding her hand down his back, or sweeping his hair away from his eyes. She related things the girls told her at the villa, trying out the German words they had taught her in secret whispers, when nobody else was around.

'I'm lost and lonely.'

Bella closed her book. She crossed the room and climbed on to the bed next to him, tucking her legs under her, leaning back on her calves. She pressed her thumb against a tear sliding down Michele's cheek.

'Oh Michele, we're doing so well here, back in Monterini. We're happy, aren't we?'

'Are we?'

'I know it's hard for you leaving *mamma* Carla in Favore, but you visit her and we're together with my family. And I'm trying so hard, surely you can see that?'

'I can see you try hard when your father's around.'

'What do you mean?'

'You hold my hand, touch my cheek, rub my back, but only when he's there. The rest of the time you're vacant, distant. Like I don't exist. It's cruel.'

Bella's cheeks burnt; waves of heat sifted through her. Was she really cruel? She was trying so hard to convince them all.

Michele was sobbing now, loud, passionate cries. She was sure it would wake her father and Lea. 'You've destroyed me. I know you didn't mean to, but that's what you've done. You took my love and then you returned it, half-digested and covered in spit.'

She grimaced. The image sickened her, but she understood his suffering. She knew only too well how it felt to love someone who didn't care, who greeted you with icy smiles and a hardened heart. She pulled a lock of hair away from Michele's forehead.

His eyes flashed with love or anger or hatred. She couldn't tell which.

'There's nothing left of me, Bella, I'm just a shell waiting for you to trample on me. I wake up in the morning, I don't know if you'll smile at me or scowl. If I get half a smile, I feel joyous. I come home from the bookshop where I work with your father and I wonder, will she say hello, or will she just ignore me.'

'Is that really how you see me? I'm so sorry. I've tried, God knows I really have, but...'

'But not enough,' he interrupted her. 'Because your head is always here.' He nodded towards the bedroom wall.

'Michele, I married you, I chose you, nobody forced me. I may like to pretend sometimes that I was forced, but I wasn't. I chose you.'

'Then I'm sorry you regret your choice.' He wiped away tears with the back of his hand. He reached out for Bella's hair, clutching it as if it were a rein and she were his mule. His pale blue eyes gleamed with a new emotion. He pulled her back down on the bed, pulling at the buttons of her shirt, fumbling for her breasts. She let out a sharp cry. He parted her legs, roughly, with a force she had never witnessed before and unzipped his trousers.

'Michele, no I can't, not now.'

'You're my wife, Bella. Remember that, my wife.'

As he entered her, Bella saw Rico in front of her, mouth snarling, pupils burning. Her Rico, the *contadino-partigiano*, the saviour of the Jewish orphans, mouthing the words he had spat at her the night before her wedding.

Later that evening, Bella sat alone on the veranda, legs tucked up in front of her, arms cradling her knees. Clouds brushed across the sky, mint green in the cool light. The faded notes of a mouth organ folded through the air, then Bella heard squeaking from the side of the house. Pulling her shawl around her shoulders, she jumped off the chair and walked across the veranda. A mouse with a long, spindly tail was caught in a trap. She bent down. It kicked its tiny legs, trying to break free. Soft, frightened eyes pleaded with her.

'You're trapped like me,' she whispered. 'Trapped and desperate to break free.' She leaned forward, unclipped the spring. Shaking itself free, the mouse tumbled out.

'What have you done, Bella? We get rid of them, not save them!'

Bella spun around. Angelo loomed above her, eyes half playful, half scornful. Stooping down, he reached forward and touched the top of Bella's head. His hand was warm, familiar, loving. So different from Michele's touch, only a few hours before.

'I had to let it go, *zio*.'

You see, I'm that pitiful creature, I'm trapped like the mouse, even my orphans are freer than me. The words screamed silently, prisoners in her head, but she knew somehow Angelo understood. He placed his hands under her elbows and drew her up to standing. With his thumbs he traced a tear line on her cheeks, then parted his lips, a smile full of sorrow.

The stars pricked the sky and the moon slid behind the spire of the cathedral.

CHAPTER 17

At the villa, Bella had grown accustomed to the strained atmosphere between herself and Rico. She was simply happy to be near him. Whenever Rico passed close by, Salamone Papo clinging to his leg or riding on his shoulders, she would breathe in the air, hoping to catch the earthy scent of grapes, wet soil, wild flowers; all those familiar smells that reminded her of how close they used to be.

Their relationship was now one of efficiency, a word here, a nod there, warnings on how to behave in Monterini, what to say if confronted about the presence of orphans at the villa. It reminded her of the relationship between Jacobo and Angelo, an abyss crossed only by vague mutterings, but without *Vino degli Angeli* to soften mood and assuage resentment.

She loved to watch Rico play with Salamone, swinging him high in the sky, listening to the little boy's giggles, knowing Salamone's happiness and health were partly due to Rico's affection. He has done this, she thought, he has helped Salamone recover. Sometimes, when she watched Rico stroke Salamone's cheek, or joke in dialect with the older boys, she felt a pang of unwanted jealousy settle in her chest. If only he would say something nice to her, acknowledge her presence, just once. She had learned to live with fear and uncertainty. Surely, she could bear this aching love that choked her, engulfed her to the extent she could barely utter a *buongiorno* when their paths crossed.

Then things changed.

One morning, in the middle of an Italian class, Bella looked up and noticed Rico watching her from the open door. His face was smooth, uncreased. Bella felt a frisson deep in her belly. As their gaze met, she noticed something resembling tenderness in his eyes, a flicker of a smile around his lips.

She didn't hear Tamara respond to her question when to use the *congiuntivo*, didn't feel the little girl tug at her sleeve and call her name. She was lost in a moment of intimacy, a quiver of hope. Then he turned and walked out of the room, the sound of his boots crunching across the tiled floor.

They met in the post-prandial hours, just before siesta. Bella was leaving the Fratta to return to the villa and Rico was helping Angelo carry bottles of wine into the *cantina*. It was rare for him to be at the house in the Fratta, most of his time was spent with the orphans. It felt strange seeing him with Angelo, unloading *Vino degli Angeli* from Rodeo's back in the sweltering heat. Memories of her childhood flooded her, momentarily eclipsing sadness.

Angelo wiped his brow and bent down to kiss Bella. His eyebrows and hair were almost white now, like soft wisps of clouds. She inhaled the deep scent of fields, the smell of the *contadino*; the safe smell of her youth.

'*Mia piccola* Bella, how are you?' Angelo handed her a bottle of red wine and enquired about her father. A silent rapprochement had occurred between Angelo and Jacobo; a subtle attempt to claw back the remaining threads of friendship. Instead of leaving bottles of wine outside the Levis' front door, Angelo would appear on the veranda with two beakers of *Vino degli Angeli*, just as Jacobo turned the pages of his newspaper. At first, they drank from either end of the veranda. Then one day Cosimo beckoned Bella over to the kitchen window and pointed to the two men. They were sitting side by side, chairs drawn close together, backs against the wall.

'We survive, *zio*, always thanks to you and the other villagers who deliver goods to our doorstep. You look well.'

There was something different about Angelo. He had aged, it was true, and still looked ungainly as if he didn't know how to support his limbs. But there was something else. Bella cocked her head to one side, wondering what had changed. As he started to talk about the year's harvest, she observed a new confidence, a self-assurance that she'd never noticed before. He still dressed and talked like a *contadino*, always addressing her in dialect with an odd smattering of Italian, but there was an air of wellbeing about him. A result of the success of *Vino degli Angeli*, she decided. Angelo had gone up in the world. And her father with his frayed clothes, loss of income, had gone down.

Many people in the surrounding villages and towns had felt uncomfortable buying books from a Jew. La Libreria Speciale now opened only two days a week. The strain of not working was evident on her father's pinched face. The change in eating habits from pasta, meat and pastries to rice, vegetables and the occasional meat broth had made his body gaunt.

As Angelo climbed the steps to the veranda, Rico loitered behind. He had remained quiet, busying himself with unloading bottles of wine. Bella nodded and turned towards her bicycle, parked on the other side of the street. Rico grabbed her arm. A shiver of excitement shot through her. She shook her arm free, but he took her hand. He held it. Suddenly she didn't care who saw her, Michele, her father, any of the neighbours.

'*Ti ringrazio*,' Rico whispered.

'Why are you thanking me?'

'For what you've done. At the villa, with the children. You just came. You trusted me despite the dangers. I've wanted to thank you for a while now, I just couldn't. I'm sorry.' His face

222

was crisscrossed with worry, as if he wasn't sure how to speak to her, what to say, how she would respond. It had been so long since they had been alone together, so long since they had spoken.

He let go of her hand.

'You can always count on me.' This sudden act of kindness from someone usually so remote gave Bella courage. She tapped at her heart. 'Nothing's changed in here. You need to know that.'

She fixed her gaze on the deep chestnut of Rico's eyes, then she took a breath. 'I came to the villa because I wanted to be near you. Be part of something important to you.'

'Stop, don't say anything you'll regret.'

'I expected you to know how I was feeling. I expected you to understand me. I couldn't admit, even to myself, that my reasons were selfish. And they were, at first. But now I love Villa Sofia and those other wonderful souls, determined to save our orphans, Don Philippe, Georges, Mario. And those children mean more to me than I could ever have imagined.'

'It doesn't matter why you came to the villa. It only matters that you did. You've taught the children how to be Monterinesi, you've given them hope. We're all grateful.'

'But it's me who's grateful, Rico. They've given me hope. You all have.' She bit her lip, her eyes fixed on the contours of his face, noticing the flicker of his eyelids, the thickness of the lashes. She noticed the muscles of his throat jump and dance and how he ran his tongue against his bottom lip.

She held her breath wondering whether to continue. Was she brave enough to say what her heart was truly feeling? The smell of sulphur was everywhere, on her skin, on him, in the space between them. She closed her eyes. She didn't want to see Tanaquilla floating near her. She didn't want to listen. The words poured out of her, a scattered stream of sound.

'And it means I can be near you. Breathe in the smell of you, watch how you've grown and changed. And it doesn't matter that you hate me because I'll always love you despite the fact I'm married, despite the racial laws and despite this huge chasm between us.'

His face was thick with sadness; she ached for him, a longing so great she could barely stand. She reached for her bicycle for support. The sun slithered through the gaps between the houses, staining rooftops with scarlet patches.

When she turned around, he'd gone, vanished into the heat of the afternoon.

PART THREE

Jacobo and His Angel: 1943–1946

CHAPTER 1

Raindrops, like pale grapes, fell from the sky. Then the sun smiled through the cracks in the clouds and touched the pores in the rock, tempting the village back to life.

Angelo sat on the veranda, head buried in his hands. The rain soaked his shoes, dirt from the trucks sprinkled his overalls. He lifted his head and turned his gaze towards Jacobo's house. The door swung open. Paint peeled at the edges, there was a crack across the centre Angelo hadn't noticed before. If he closed it, he would shut away the years and they would be gone. This way he could still hear the memories flying like birds through the open doors of his youth. The laughter, shouts, the cries that had echoed all around them as they grew from boys to young men and old fools.

They had left.

The Levis, the Servis, the De Benedettis, Rabbi Coen; vanished like mist on Monte Amiata. Angelo scratched his head trying to make sense of the news he had received from Don Philippe, the young priest he didn't much like or trust. He had run up to Angelo in the piazza just as he was returning to the Fratta with Rodeos one and two. The priest looked shrunken, wounded, his shoulders heavy.

The Jews had left the village.

Santina tugged at his arm, awakening him from his reverie. 'Have you heard what's happened?' Santina's voice was urgent; her skin ashen, eyes rimmed red. Next to her was Signora Franca, her face like soft candle wax, as if eyes, nose and mouth had melted into one with no distinguishing feature. Strange what shock can do, Angelo thought.

'It's terrible, Angelino. Our village has all but died. My dear husband will be turning in his grave. Thank the Lord he didn't live to see this.' Signora Franca's face rearranged itself, her brown mole wobbled as she spoke.

'We have to do something.' Santina was still tugging at his arm.

'I need to think.' He shook his arm free. He wanted them to go away, leave him in peace, work out what to do next.

'You stupid fool.' Santina swiped the side of his head. He barely felt it. His body was numb, as if his bones had crumbled.

'You who never thinks. How come you choose this moment to be a great thinker? This is the time for action, not thinking.' Santina grabbed Angelo's shirtsleeve, her hands gnarled and knobbly, the blue veins bulging. Signora Franca pulled at his braces.

Angelo staggered up and followed his wife and Signora Franca across the veranda. Wisps of grey hair escaped from the back of their scarves and curled like tiny snakes around their necks. He stopped at the open door. It felt wrong to enter Jacobo's house, sacrilegious, like breaking open the Etruscan tombs scattered all around Monterini, by the river, along the *cavi* and within the mound of *tufo* directly beneath his feet. Thousands of years ago families had lived there, slept on floors, cooked for their children; working, praying, surviving. And then they were gone, eradicated in a Roman whim. Was it to be the same now, he wondered. Repetition like birdsong or a prayer, through centuries of civilisation. He made the sign of the cross. He remembered that Cosimo and Jacobo used to kiss the *mezuzah* on the side of the door, whenever they entered the house. Angelo placed his hand to his lips, touched the metal cylinder and stepped across the threshold into the kitchen.

Nothing had changed, yet there was something in the air.

Was it grief?

Or abandonment?

Rooms don't have feelings, Angelo reassured himself. Atmospheres are made up of people not sensations. Yet if grapes can feel, why can't rooms? He surveyed the kitchen. Crumbs glistened on the white tablecloth. Plates and cutlery lay abandoned. A large saucepan filled with squares of carrots and potatoes was perched on the stove. A broom leaned against the wall and on the floor vegetable peelings mingled with specks of dirt.

'I'll clear up.' Santina squeezed Angelo's hand. He could tell she was crying, he could sense the shaking of her shoulders, the muffled voice. Angelo's hand swung out in front of Santina.

'Leave the room as they left it. It will wait for them.'

'The Germans will see it's an empty house. They'll guess Jews lived here.'

'She's right, it's a large house for Monterini, they might use it to house their soldiers or even their colonels.' Signora Franca came out of the sitting room holding a thin, oblong box in one hand and a letter in another.

'We'll say it's our house. We'll move some things in here and live in both places.' Angelo swallowed hard. 'Leave the broom where they left it, and the pan on the stove.'

'And the crumbs?' Santina did not smile.

'You can get rid of the crumbs. We don't want them to think we didn't care.'

Signora Franca shifted herself onto a chair, tore open the envelope and read in silence. When she raised her head, her lip was trembling.

'It's from Lea. She's left me her mother's jewellery, both her wedding rings and the rings that had belonged to Bella, Jacobo's first wife,' she added as if she needed to remind them. 'She asked me to wear them, to keep them safe, and if I need to, to sell them.'

'Was there any message?' Angelo asked. 'For me?'

'No. She just said to burn the letter.'

Patterns of sunlight tinged the tiles of the veranda. Angelo had moved some of the Ghione possessions into Jacobo's house to make it look occupied whilst Santina and Signora Franca cleaned, tidied and packed away candlesticks, photographs and silver cups into boxes. The white porcelain plates remained where the Levis had left them. Santina had transferred the stew from the pan into a dish. The crumbs had gone, the kitchen gleamed.

'We're going over to the Ghetto,' Signora Franca said. 'See if anyone's left.'

'If hunger didn't kill us, and the last war didn't destroy us, then neither will this,' Santina said.

Angelo followed the women through the Fratta across Via Roma to the Ghetto. The streets were eerily silent. Doors creaked open, as if the inhabitants had just walked to the bakery or the synagogue, or were washing clothes in Capo Bagno, pounding the fabric with a ferocity that was dear to all the women of the village. The usual clattering of crockery, chattering of villagers seemed nothing more than memory churning its junk of old bones.

'What should we do?' Angelo shrugged his shoulders in despair. Monterini had been torn in half and he didn't know who to turn to. In the past before the freeze between them, he would have gone straight to Jacobo or Cosimo, who in turn might have talked to the rabbi, who for good measure might have informed the priest.

'Padre Giacomo!' Santina shouted as if reading his mind. 'Let's ask him. Or the new one, Don Philippe.'

'They're on their way.' Angelo recognised the voice of Dottore Mazzola. He turned. The doctor was carrying some sacks in his hand. His face seemed pinched and deep grooves cut across his forehead and around his mouth. Angelo felt the pressure of the doctor's hand on his arm. 'We must go into every empty house, tidy and clean and remove all valuables.' He passed a sack to Angelo and the two women. 'Mark everything; who it belongs to and what it is. Then hide it.'

They entered house after house, the air sliced with sorrow. 'Can it be their grief?' Angelo whispered. 'Or is it mine?'

'It's collected grief,' Signora Franca said. She entwined the fingers of both hands and shook them in front of Angelo. 'In this village we are bound together.'

In Via del Ghetto they met Clara Todi.

'The De Benedettis have gone,' she sobbed. 'I've been their neighbour for fifty-six years. Signor De Benedetti always helped us, even though he was a fancy businessman. He never forgot my family.'

Angelo knew the De Benedettis well. Simone had been a friend of Jacobo's. They had all played together as children, down at the river, under the waterfalls, running along the *vie* and *viccoli*.

'Look.' Clara pressed a smooth, rectangular, wooden box against Angelo's belly. 'They came to see me moments before they left. They gave me this box.'

When Angelo reached for the box, Clara protectively pulled it close to her bosom. It was made of burnt oak with tiny, reddish jewels embedded into the corners and centre; too large to be a jewellery box, too small to be a chest.

'Signora De Benedetti asked me to guard it for them. I didn't ask what it contained. And I won't look. She said there were things inside that belonged to the family. Things from the past, heirlooms I suppose. She said they were sentimental objects and she didn't want anyone else to have them. "Keep this box safe for me, Clara," she'd said. "If I don't return, you can keep it."'

Angelo, Santina and Signora Franca walked to Lea's old house in Via Zuccarelli. Signora Franca untangled a key from a large bunch tied to a belt around her waist. When Jacobo and Lea left the Ghetto, Jacobo had told her to keep the key. Just in case, he'd said, almost as if he knew. The shutters were closed. Even though the house had been empty for months, photographs still hung on the wall and a white, lace cloth adorned the dining room table.

Angelo bent his head to one side as if listening for something. But voices and souls no longer lingered in this house.

They had been gone too long.

The synagogue complex was bustling. Angelo was relieved to see Dottore Mazzola and Padre Giacomo packing up school books into boxes. The baker Paolo and the blacksmith Pino were stacking the chairs and moving the desks into the corner of the schoolroom. Signora Petri was sweeping the floor. She handed Santina a bucket and pointed to a mop leaning against the wall.

Like the houses in Monterini, the synagogue had been carved into the rock as if naturally erupting from the *tufo*, an explosion of shapes, colours and stained glass. Someone was crouching in the corner, next to the Ark containing the Torah. Angelo recognised the bald head haloing a black cassock. It was Don Philippe. He was shovelling prayer books, silver cups, prayer shawls and skullcaps into a sack. He stood up and opened the wooden doors of the Ark. He reached up for the Torah.

Angelo remembered Jacobo telling him it was the most

important item in the synagogue. '*Padre,* this is a sacred book. Leave it where it belongs.'

Don Philippe swivelled round to face Angelo, an expression of puzzlement and amusement flashed across his face. Angelo was wary of this young upstart from the north, with his newfangled ways. His eyes were too sparkly, his voice too soft. He didn't like the way the young gathered around him as if he were the latest version of Jesus. Whispers circulated across trees and fields, sidling through open doorways, slipping under cracks in the shutters.

Partigiano. Partigiano.

'We have to hide everything,' Don Philippe whispered, his lips brushing Angelo's ears. His voice reminded Angelo of toasted hazelnuts on a winter's day, gentle, soothing. 'If we don't, the synagogue will be ransacked. Rabbi Coen told me to gather everything, the prayer books, the shawls, the silver trinkets. We have to hide it all. But their Torah, we must bury.'

'Bury? In the earth? Are you sure?'

'It's their custom. If the community is banished these precious scrolls must never be destroyed. They're to be buried. Then, if they return, we'll find them.' Don Philippe looked straight into Angelo's eyes. 'We must hurry. Very soon Nazis will surround this town. They'll crawl through our streets, take over our homes, our churches and our lives.'

'But the Germans are on our side,' Angelo said. He couldn't make sense of this war, fascism, Mussolini. They were only words. The Germans loved his wine, that much he was grateful for.

'Trust me. I know what the Nazis are capable of. Very soon their tanks will be winding round the hill towards the village; grey uniforms will march through our alleyways. Our women will be forced to serve pasta and *brodo* to our German guests.'

'But why did our Jews disappear so suddenly, without a word, without saying goodbye?'

'Because the Nazis will kill them if they stay. Anyone hiding Jews will be shot. I told Rabbi Coen the whole community must leave. It's our duty to rid Monterini of its Jewish presence, you understand?'

He picked up the Torah and handed it to Angelo. 'Unscrew the silver handles. Take off the coverings. The rabbi told me to wrap them all separately. They're to be buried separately too.'

Don Philippe began to fill the sacks, alternating books and prayer shawls. 'We must make sure nobody takes anything that doesn't belong to them. We're here to hide and protect whilst they're gone.'

'Until they come back?'

'If they come back.'

It was dusk. Angelo was tired. He had been working in the synagogue for most of the afternoon. His head hurt and his soul ached. It struck him they needed to decide what to do with the bookshop. Should they bolt the door and throw away the key? Should they burn the anti-fascist literature Jacobo had hidden in the *cantina*? Angelo hurried over the bridge and along Via Cavour. The bookshop was empty, the doors locked. Angelo walked back to the Fratta, choked by the heaviness of the air. Out of the shadows a black arm touched his shoulder. He jumped.

'*Padre*, you terrified me.'

The light from the streetlamps shone on the inky circles beneath Don Philippe's eyes. Was it fatigue or stress, or the starkness of the lighting that had aged the priest a thousand years? 'You look tired, *Padre*.'

Don Philippe's eyes flitted nervously, scanning the empty street. He placed his hand on Angelo's arm, drew him into a recess where a stone fountain and a dancing bear hung together like lovers in the night. Don Philippe gestured to him to drink.

234

Angelo bent over the fountain, and with his palm ladled drops of water into his mouth. The priest leaned next to him mouthing, 'You can be proud of your son, Signor Ghione.'

Angelo lifted his head out from under the tap. 'What do you know about my son? It can't be through church?'

'Sadly not. But we're close friends. Enrico is a good man.'

Close friends with Don Philippe? Santina had berated him many times for knowing so little, for spending his days singing to his grapes whilst gossip spread around him like a batch of measles. Santina always knew who had argued with whom, who was betrothed to whom, almost before it happened.

'My son keeps himself to himself. He doesn't tell me what he's up to. We don't speak a lot. I hear the rumours, I say nothing.'

'He's helping the orphans to adapt.'

Angelo lifted his head and banged it hard on the metallic ridge of the tap. He rubbed it with the back of his hand.

'Rico helping orphans to adapt. Adapt to what?'

'A new culture, new language. He's keeping them safe. He's an asset to us at the...' His voice trailed into the distance; eyes fearful as if he'd said too much. Angelo had heard mutterings about the priest, his political affiliation. At times Angelo had wondered about his own son. He placed his hand on the young priest's arm.

'Don't worry, *Padre*. You don't have to say any more. Sometimes things have to be kept secret, even from a father.'

'Fascists are swarming through Monterini like ants towards a pot of fig jam. They're everywhere. Some you know, others you don't. Anyone could be an enemy. Rico has to be careful, you understand?'

Angelo nodded. A sudden worry for his son tugged at his heart. He noticed a dark shadow flit across Don Philippe's face. The priest grabbed Angelo's hand.

'You may find there's a lot to cope with, Signor Ghione. It's a challenging time and the Lord works in strange ways. We have to deal with what's put in front of us, even if it crosses our boundaries, our beliefs in what's right.'

Then he left, a misshapen silhouette ebbing into the blackness of night. Angelo scratched his head, wondering what he could have meant.

CHAPTER 2

The eighth of September 1943: the day they discovered that Maresciallo Badoglio had surrendered to the Allies. All over Italy and allied Europe people rejoiced but for the Levis it was a calamity. The Germans were heading north, and Jews were no longer safe. Not even in Monterini.

Jacobo stood in the kitchen, wringing his hands. Through the slit in the door, the sunlight streaked his hair copper grey. 'Pack up your things everyone. We've got to get out! We're no longer safe here.'

They stared at him, silenced by his wild eyes. Lea spoke first. 'What is it, *caro*? What's happened?'

'Mussolini's gone. We've joined the Allies.'

'But that's good, *babbo*, it means the war's over,' Bella said.

'Not for us Jews. The German army will be here by dawn. The whole community is leaving Monterini.'

Nobody moved.

'Pack the essentials but take something warm, a coat, a blanket.'

'And the lunch I've just cooked?' Lea pointed to the stove with a flick of her wrist.

Jacobo let out a frightened laugh. 'Are you mad, Lea? Our lives are at stake and you're thinking of eating!'

'What about my mother?' Michele said.

'The rabbi has sent someone to the communities of Favore

and Montore. She'll be hidden. There's no time to waste, just leave everything as it is.'

'I'm too old, Jacobo, I've lived here my entire life. I can't leave now.' Cosimo's voice was strained, helpless, as if he had already given up.

'You have no choice, *babbo*. We're leaving.'

Bella's nostrils flared but no smell of sulphur greeted her, no swish of white robes. So, this is it, she thought, this is finally the omen. Monterini coughs up its cargo of Jews.

Upstairs in the bedroom, Bella and Michele placed a change of clothes and two books into a knapsack. Bella reached into the top drawer of her dressing table and took out a photograph of her mother in her wedding dress. She kissed the faded face of that other Bella and tucked it inside Moravia's *Gli Indifferenti*.

She followed Michele downstairs forcing back tears. As she watched the back of her husband's neck, they spilled onto her cheeks. Would she see Rico's neck, olive toned and thick set, ever again? What about all the orphans? Would they be safe? She swallowed hard and placed her hand on Michele's shoulder to steady herself. He turned around and smiled at her and, in his expression, she thought she saw love. Or was it merely satisfaction that she would now be his alone?

Everyone stood in the kitchen. Lea was forcing woolly hats on Luciana and Elena.

'It's still summer, *mamma*! We can't possibly wear our winter clothes.' Elena pushed her mother's hand away.

'We may need them!' Lea insisted. 'We don't know how long we'll be away.'

Bella placed her knapsack on the table. '*Babbo*, there must be another way. This is too drastic. Surely, we don't have to run away like criminals?'

He stepped towards her and placed his palm on her cheek.

'You know what the children at the orphanage have been through at the hands of the Nazis, don't you? We'll be killed if we stay.'

Bella's eyes searched the house. She stared at the large window in the sitting room overlooking the valley, the olive trees burnt gold in the sunlight; the silver candlesticks on the sideboard; the trinkets and photographs of a family, a lifetime. There were pieces of her everywhere; in the house, in the streets of the village, at Villa Sofia.

Jacobo slipped on his coat despite the blistering heat and was helping her *nonno* dress into warmer clothes. It struck her how comically nightmarish the situation was. She wanted to pinch herself back into reality, into the safety of what she'd had only moments before.

They stepped on to the veranda. Jacobo moved towards the door of Angelo's house. He stood there for a moment, looking small and out of place in his winter coat. He raised his hand to open the door, then changed his mind, ushering them down the stone steps to the street.

Cosimo and Bella looked up at number 110.

'Goodbye home,' she said and blew a kiss. 'Goodbye Rico,' she whispered. She reached for her grandfather's arm. He felt sunken and shrivelled next to her. He didn't look back at the house, home for generations of his family.

Luciana slid her palm into Bella's. 'I'm frightened.'

She had no words of comfort; the air had been smashed out of her lungs. She searched for Tanaquilla above the spires and rooftops. The sky was a calm blue, with patches of silky, grey clouds. Only pigeons swooped above her head.

At the entrance to the village, Bella stopped. She couldn't move her feet. It was as if she were chained to the stone slabs of the piazza, her ribs punched by some unknown force. A chugging, pulling sensation within mirrored the juddering, pulling thoughts of her mind. She grabbed the sleeve of Michele's coat.

'I can't leave.' The words were muffled, barely audible even to her.

'Don't think about it, just keep moving.' He placed his hand under her elbow, his fingers squeezing. Encouragement or a warning? Bella wasn't sure. She shook her arm free and reached out to stroke his cheek, but her arm fell clumsily to her side. Countless times she remembered her father's arm reaching out and landing with a thud by his thigh. She knew exactly how it felt.

'This has nothing to do with you.'

'It has everything to do with me.' Michele paled, skin almost translucent, irises ice blue. 'If you loved me, you'd come with us. If you stay, I'll hate you, and hatred is dangerous.'

'What's happening?' Jacobo turned towards them.

'She's not coming with us.' Michele spat the words out before Bella had a chance to speak.

Jacobo's eyebrows arched into two points. 'Of course she's coming, Michele, she's part of our family. She has to leave, like us. There's no choice.'

'I'm staying, *babbo*.'

Luciana and Elena grabbed her arms. 'Don't leave us.'

'*Per favore Bella, per favore*,' Cosimo begged like a small child.

'You can't stay here all alone, Bella.' Lea wiped away tears with the sleeve of her coat.

Only Jacobo was quiet.

His arms reached out to her, his eyes pleading. No words could have had the same effect. Bella felt herself swaying, pulled in by those deep dark eyes of hope. If she went with them, they would all be together, they would be happy. And what about her? The churning increased, it was as if her insides were pinching, pulling and burning all at the same time.

Then Bella listened. She listened like Tanaquilla had told her to.

'I can't, *babbo*. *Mi dispiace*. I'm sorry.'

Jacobo's face was washed with pain. He was melting before her. Suddenly it all made sense, his looks, his moods, his way with her throughout the years. Everything came together in that one moment, that one expression. Grief.

Bella's gaze moved from her broken-hearted father to her grandfather. He was standing between her stepsisters, a withered arm hung limply around each girl. She wasn't sure if her *nonno* was comforting Luciana and Elena or they were propping him up, holding his anguish on their tiny shoulders.

And still she couldn't leave Monterini.

Jacobo came close to Bella, his long straight nose digging into her cheeks, his breath hot against her skin.

'I lost her, now I'm losing you.'

'No, *babbo,* you'll never lose me. I'm choosing to stay in Monterini, that's all.'

'Then you're no longer my daughter.'

'Was I ever truly your daughter, *babbo*? Was I?'

A gasp, deep and prolonged, echoed around the square, above the cedar trees, beyond the Etruscan tombs.

He turned and walked away from her.

Bella sank to the ground, the stone of the piazza cold against her knees. She watched as they walked into the unknown: her father, Lea's hand against his spine; her sisters balancing her precious *nonno* between them. And her husband with a look of steely hatred as he mouthed the word, '*Traditore*. Betrayer.'

Then she saw her, a shimmer floating above Michele as he passed the stone lions and stepped through the Arco. Tanaquilla's long robes swirled above Michele's head. She could almost hear the swishing sound.

She was alone in the square.

She wondered how many Jews remained in Monterini. There were the orphans, of course, but they were being passed off as Catholics. It dawned on her that she too had the same choice. She would renounce it all; her religion, her marriage, her family. She would stay for her Catholic-Jewish orphans.

But also, for him.

And for herself.

CHAPTER 3

Santina was not in the kitchen when Angelo returned to the Fratta. The stove was empty, the table bare, Rico nowhere to be seen. He wondered if his eldest son knew what was happening in the village. He needed to find out what Rico really did at the orphanage and what his connection with the priest was. Most importantly, he wanted to talk to him about Jacobo. Angelo had a feeling Rico might know what to do. He was involved in something, that was clear from the priest's comments, and if it were something clandestine, something against the regime, then maybe Rico would know how to help Jacobo.

He walked back to the veranda. The door to the Levi house was still open. Santina was standing in the kitchen, an apron tied around her waist, her back to the open entrance. When Angelo tapped her shoulder, she turned.

'We've been through all the houses; cleaning, hiding, sorting.' Santina slumped into a chair, exhaustion etched across her face. 'I keep wondering where they are, what they're doing.'

'Jacobo knows the area well. He'll know where to hide.'

'*Signor* Cosimo's old. It's warm now but the weather can turn at any moment. He'll never manage out there in the cold and dark. His arthritis will be terrible. He'll need his medicines.'

'Medicines will be the last thing on their mind! They'll need to find somewhere to hide. Don Philippe told me they'll be killed if the Nazis find them.'

'But only if they find them!' A voice drifted towards them; a gentle whisper broken by tears flickering at the edges of the words.

She was there, enveloped in the black night. A shimmer from a streetlamp cast shadows across her face. A grubby white dress hung from her slender shoulders down to her ankles. Her unruly hair scraped back accentuated her nose and sharp cheekbones. Her eyes shone silvery green.

Next to Bella stood Rico, their hands entwined. He was wearing a brown faded jacket Angelo didn't recognise. His hair lay neatly combed across his scalp. The breath moved heavily in and out of his chest.

Angelo and Santina gazed at the couple. Their intake of breath, frozen into a moment of time, echoed through the dimly lit kitchen. Santina was the first to move. The sudden scratching noise of her chair on the stone floor broke the silence, drawing them back into the reality of their world.

'What is she doing here? She should have left the village hours ago?' Santina screamed.

'*Zitto, mamma*! Shush.' Rico closed the front door, then slid his arm protectively around Bella's shoulder. A bunch of heather tied together with white ribbon hung from her hand.

Angelo staggered towards them, dragging his legs. His heart was banging furiously in his chest. What have these foolish children done?

'Bella, you must leave Monterini. You must join your husband, your family. You're a Jewess. You're not safe here.'

'There's no Bella,' she answered softly. 'From now on I'm Maria Cristina Ghione.' There was defiance in her voice, a pride in her new name.

'We're married.' Rico's hand tightened around Bella's.

Angelo gripped the edge of the table, fearing his limbs would no longer support him. Not Bella? Married? It was as if a bolt had dropped from the sky. Was God playing a joke on him? For years Angelo had longed for the little girl he adored to be his daughter-in-law, cementing what he'd shared with Jacobo since childhood. But Bella Ghione, not some Maria Cristina nonsense. And certainly not when she was already married to Michele Coen.

'This isn't a game.' His arm banged the table. They all jumped. 'They'll find you. They'll shoot you.' The vehemence of his tone, usually so kind and gentle, sounded unfamiliar, even to him.

'Don Philippe arranged it all, this afternoon. We have papers, everything...' Bella's voice wavered, her lips trembled ever so slightly.

Angelo longed to say to her: 'Be brave, little Bella, be brave. If you can't persuade me, how can you convince them?' Instead, his voice remained cold. He stood upright, filling the room with his frame. 'You're already married, Bella Coen. Remember?'

'How could the new priest have done this? He's committing a sin. In front of God, and so are you, Bella.' Santina sobbed a broken thread of sounds.

In the emptiness that followed, Angelo blamed his son. What they had, how they lived had never been enough. Rico had always wanted more. He'd wanted to study and learn, to improve himself. Angelo had always been content with his grapes, the sunshine, the smells of the earth. But not Rico, and now he had coveted another man's wife. Their lives would never be the same again.

'*Mamma*, *babbo*, you've got to remember, Bella Levi, Bella Coen, she doesn't exist. It's Maria Cristina from now on. If you call her anything else, you risk all of our lives.' Rico sought out the flickering, angry eyes of his parents, his voice pleading with them to understand. 'All over Italy people are hiding in wells, in tombs and in forests. They're changing their names,

245

converting to Catholics. Everywhere laws are being broken by us, by them and by this God of yours. We're all speaking a different language. And the problem is you're still stuck with your old one.'

'You're right, this is a different language.' Angelo sank down onto a chair, deflated as if the air had been squeezed out of him, puff by painful puff.

'Bella's a Catholic,' Rico insisted. 'She converted today. She's my wife. You must get used to calling her Maria Cristina.' There was a look of defiance in his pupils, the way he held his chin high. Yet there was a slight shakiness to his voice, that didn't escape Angelo. Underneath the big words Rico was afraid.

'Converted? Married?' Santina was shaking her finger at Bella. 'But you're already married!' She screamed so loudly Angelo wondered whether God himself would hear her. The whites of her eyes were flecked with yellow.

'To me!' Rico emphasised the words slowly, as if addressing two children. 'We're going to live here. The house documents have been changed into the name of Maria Cristina Ghione. Don Philippe arranged it all with *Avvocato* Bruscalupi. It will keep the house free of Germans, we'll all be safer that way.'

Signor Bruscalupi was the town's lawyer and a known fascist. Angelo wondered what he was doing, bending the rules and cooperating with this partisan priest who took God's law into his own hands? And for a Jewess?

Somewhere in the distance a dog barked, the crickets groaned, shaking Angelo back into the real world, away from the madness, this Gehenna where nothing made sense. The bunch of heather swayed towards him. What a poor posy it made for a bride! And her dress ragged and torn. It was all wrong.

Bella rose up on tiptoes. 'I'm your daughter-in-law,' she whispered as her lips touched his cheek. 'Finally.'

Some daughter-in-law, Angelo thought. A giant wave of disgust tumbled through him. He couldn't look at her or his son. In that moment he hated them, hated their bravery, their audacity, their secrets and their manipulations.

'No,' he shouted. He pushed Bella away from him. She let out a cry as she stumbled backwards. 'In the eyes of God, you're already married.'

'And in the eyes of the law.' Santina emphasised the words, eyes darting from one to the other.

'There is no law,' Bella replied firmly. She slid over towards Rico. Clutching the faded heather in one hand, she grasped his fingers with the other. 'Not anymore.'

Shadows, the colour of bruised aubergines, circled her eyes. Wrinkles lined her temples and the sides of her mouth. She looked like an old woman who had lived for decades. Where had they gone, the two children, the shadows of young Rico and Bella that haunted Angelo's dreams, springing at him from behind the lions in the piazza, to smell his grape-stained hands? They had vanished in the morning mist to re-emerge as the desperate adults who faced him now.

'Every law we've lived by has been broken.' Bella's lips parted into a faint smile. 'Now Rico and I live by the law of survival.'

'We'll do whatever we can to survive, save whoever we can.' Rico looked from one to the other. 'You have to help us, *babbo*, *mamma*, so we can keep as many people alive as possible.'

Angelo barely understood what either of them was saying. So many big words buzzing around him like unwanted flies; it was hard to concentrate.

'I've always loved Rico.' Bella broke another silence. 'Under the old laws, I couldn't marry him. Now we have to make our own rules.' She placed two documents on the table. 'This one is our marriage certificate, the other is the deeds of the house. They're forged but at least we'll be safe.'

'How can you be so sure?' Angelo didn't understand this way of being; Signor Bruscalupi forging documents; Rico and Bella marrying when she was already a wife; Jacobo, the Servis, Rabbi Coen all forced out of their homes. And Bella a Catholic! It was all so unfamiliar, so unnatural. He wanted to escape, rub his head in the fur of Rodeo *uno*, the one familiar friend who never changed. He wanted to escape from them all and drink a whole tumbler of wine amidst the sanctity and calm of his grapes.

Santina was still shouting at them. 'How do you know you'll be safe? People behave differently in times of trouble. How do you know you won't be betrayed?'

'Because this is Monterini.' It was Rico's turn to slam his fist down on the table. They jumped. 'We'll be protected. You'll see. Even those little children in the orphanage. They're not Catholics, you know, they're Jewish orphans. A few are the children of communists or Roma families killed by the Nazis. We've managed to keep their identity hidden. And those people hiding out in the dark, they'll be protected too.'

'May God hear your words,' Angelo said. He lifted his eyes to the ceiling, his hands forming the sign of the cross.

'What God?' Rico stared at him. 'There's nothing left of him, not in our world. We have to recreate him. Can't you see that?'

But Angelo couldn't. He placed his hands over his ears, he couldn't stomach the words his blasphemous son was saying. The life Angelo lived, that simple life, had vanished. So, this is what Don Philippe meant. Silently he wept for what they had done, for what they had all lost.

CHAPTER 4

The German army crawled through the cracks of the village and life took on the quality of a dream. SS uniforms and Teutonic sounds floated through the streets. For those who had stayed, fear pervaded Monterini with its thick, odourless stench.

Once the initial shock had settled into their bones, Angelo and Santina adapted to Bella's new name in the same way the villagers adapted to Germans living in their houses, sharing their food. So worried were they at forgetting she was no longer Bella, they simply called her *amore mio*. Not a further word was uttered about Bella's conversion or her marriage to Rico, but it lay between them like a jagged piece of glass.

The Nazis immediately requisitioned Angelo's house and the Ghiones were forced to move into Jacobo's home with Bella and Rico. A lieutenant and two of his soldiers with deep voices slept in the bedrooms in Angelo's house, ate dishes prepared by Signora Franca and Santina, and drank *vino* on the veranda.

There were too many secrets. Sometimes Bella felt her head would burst with all she had to hide. German soldiers smiled kindly and tipped their hats believing she was Maria Cristina Ghione, the Catholic wife of a *contadino*. Had they known she was hiding her Jewish heritage beneath her shawl and courteous smile, she would have been riddled with bullets. She noticed how Angelo too kept his head down, avoiding Lieutenant

Richardt when he sat in the sunshine sipping *Vino degli Angeli*, pretending not to understand when the German soldier made small talk with his smattering of Italian. 'Only dialect,' Angelo uttered, which was partly true. 'No Italian.'

The day the first tanks arrived, Bella stood with Rico in the same spot where she had witnessed her family disappear through the Arco, the arch at the entrance of Monterini. In an attempt to negotiate the narrow streets, the tanks tore through the village, decimating buildings and stone statues, spiralling pieces of rock and glass into the warm September air.

'Remember what Don Philippe said,' Rico's fingers tightened around hers and pulled her towards the maze of alleyways where no tank could penetrate. 'Stay calm and polite but keep your distance. It's a game, remember, a game of survival.'

'But now we have no protection from them.' Bella's voice was barely audible. 'Badoglio and the king have fled. Our army has been abandoned, without orders, without leaders. The Germans are in control.'

'The Allies are on their way. They'll liberate us soon. We just have to be extra vigilant until they get here.'

'You and Don Philippe always said Italy was a safer place to be for a Jew, despite our fascist regime. I never believed you. But now the army's gone I feel so frightened. Who would have thought I would feel less safe without *il Duce*?'

They were all less safe. Her family hiding God only knew where, the orphans tucked away in the villa, and all of those good souls who were trying to keep their existence hidden. Bella forced herself to accept German uniforms in the streets and cafés, but when she climbed the steps to the veranda, her heart banged against her ribs so loudly she could almost hear it. She did her best to nod at Lieutenant Richardt and his fellow soldiers, eating salami from Santina's plates and drinking wine from the same glasses her father used to use. But inside another piece of her died.

Lieutenant Richardt was tall like Angelo, with broad sloping shoulders and muscular features. His square face gave him a comical look, heightened by an irregular nose and fat lips at odds with his distinguished silver hair and soft, mournful voice. He indicated, in pidgin Italian, that he was a pianist back home in Leipzig. He had long, shapely hands with slender fingers, which he wrapped around a tumbler of wine, toasting Bella whenever she walked past him, mouthing the words *chin chin*. Bella imagined those elegant fingers closing around her slim neck, wringing, squeezing.

When Bella and Rico slept in her old bedroom in Via Meravigliosa, the room of her birth, the room where she had loved Rico and tried to love Michele, Bella would cry out loud. Rico would pull her to him, pressing his lips against hers to smother her screams, fearful she would awaken the soldiers sleeping in the house next door and give away their secret with one careless, dream-filled whisper.

Bella knew Tanaquilla visited her each night. She smelt her, sensed her, could hear the swish-swish of the white robes. There had been so many possible omens in her short life and each time she was sure this was it. Perhaps her whole life was meant to be a series of sorrows from birth till now. Perhaps she was the omen, bad luck for everyone, her mother who died in childbirth, her heartbroken father, her grieving husband Michele.

'When will it end?' she whispered into the darkness as Rico held her close.

One evening on her way back to the Fratta from a tiring day ensuring the children were well versed with the crucial task of saying *'vengo'*, *'andiamo'*, *'aspetta'* in the Monterini dialect,

Bella looked up at the dark stone walls of the cathedral and felt a strange force pulling her inside the wooden doors. Several candles blinked in the darkness, illuminating the Christ pressed to the cross, accentuating his angular features and sad eyes, his slender body. Bella stared at the crucifix, crossed herself, then sank down onto the stone floor. Angelo had insisted on teaching her the *Maria Grandine* prayer, a necessary aid in concealing her past. She recited it aloud, but inside she screamed, 'Keep them safe, keep them safe, keep them safe.'

When she left the cathedral, Bella had the sensation she was being followed. Was a German soldier checking up on her? Maybe it was Tanaquilla, shadowing her like a faithful friend. But there was no smell of sulphur in the air, no tingles racing up and down her spine. She squinted in the evening sunlight. The square in front of the cathedral was empty. Only pigeons scavenged between the cracks in the cobblestones. A cat brushed its tail against her leg, causing her to jump.

A strange yearning overwhelmed her, a mixture of loneliness and longing. She glanced around to ensure nobody was watching. Instead of making her way towards Via Meravigliosa, Bella darted down the uneven, stone steps to the right of the cathedral. She crossed Via del Ghetto and stood outside the gates of the synagogue, gripping the iron bars with her fingers. She muttered the words of the *Shema*, the prayer her grandfather had taught her as a child when she used to sit on his knee and memorise her Hebrew alphabet; the prayer he recited at dawn and dusk. The words had not passed her lips for many years but that evening, as the sun set on the gravestones of Monterini, Bella repeated them with an intensity that surprised her. It was as if she had suppressed something inside that had gained meaning and momentum by the very fact that it had been suppressed.

A hand touched her arm. She let out a jagged groan. Relief

flooded through her when she realised it was Don Philippe.

'*Padre*! What are you doing here? Were you following me?'

'Not following. Checking.' Don Philippe leaned forward to whisper in Bella's ear, his cassock brushing against her arm. 'I was in the cathedral when you were praying. I had a feeling you'd come down here.'

'I miss the synagogue, *Padre*, isn't that strange? It meant so little to me when I was growing up. In fact, I used to try and avoid going there on *Shabbat*. Now it's forbidden I feel an intense urge to visit it. Somehow, I feel closer to my family here, more so than in the house. I often wander past and stare through the railings.'

'Would you like to pray inside? I'll come with you, if you like.'

'But there's no key!'

'That's what we tell the Germans.' Don Philippe winked and slid his hand into his cassock and took out a large bunch of keys. His cheeks, usually so round and smooth, were lined with worry or age, Bella couldn't tell which. She wondered if small wrinkles had also appeared by her eyes, on her chin, brought on by the troublesome life they were leading. 'They're all here, the cathedral, the monastery and the synagogue. I've even got the keys to the palazzo, just in case.'

She laughed for what seemed like the first time in days. Don Philippe unlocked the gate, took Bella's hand and led her down the familiar steps. He reached for a second key and placed it in the lock of the large, wrought-iron door leading to the synagogue. He pulled two *kippot* from his cassock and handed her one, covering his bald head with the other.

'Meant to be for men, I know, but can't be fussy these days and still more respectful to keep your head covered, don't you think?'

'But *Padre*, how come you've saved these? What else do you have hidden away in that cassock?'

'You'd be surprised. I have secreted everything we could possibly need inside this habit! We'll say we're cleaning if any Germans pass by.'

Bella glanced round the synagogue. The light was fading fast and deep shadows stretched across the wooden benches. A thin film of dust covered the pews. It felt empty, soulless, without the vitality of the community she had taken for granted. Bella looked down the aisle leading to the *bimah*; the aisle she had walked down, her hand resting on her father's arm as he led her to meet Michele on her wedding day. Amidst the tangled memories of the recent past, it felt like centuries ago.

Don Philippe nudged her towards the stairs leading to the *bimah*. 'Pray for your family, Bella, the Jewish way.'

So, she recited the words of the *Birkat Hacohanim*, the blessing of the priests, whispering them into the musty air of the old, stone building, not sure who protected her but unwilling to take any chances: 'May the Lord bless you and keep you; may the Lord turn his face to shine upon you and be gracious unto you.'

I think I have become a willing Jewish Catholic or a Catholic Jew.' She stepped down from the *bimah* to the stone floor. 'My poor father would never forgive me.'

'You'd be surprised what forgiveness the human soul is capable of, especially at times like these.'

'Nothing surprises me any more, *Padre*. Not the good people like you or Rico are capable of, nor the bad.' She paused, then asked the question that had been gnawing at her heart. 'Do you know where my father is?'

When Don Philippe shook his head, his whole frame wobbled. 'No, *cara*, but someone is looking after him.' His eyes turned heavenwards, and Bella thought he must mean God. Then he added, 'There's an angel in the village, watching over your family.'

'We need many angels. I'm so frightened I might give myself away. Or someone else might scream out Bella Levi and Lieutenant Richardt would hear them.'

'We're lucky here; the villagers turn a blind eye. Nobody even asks questions about the orphans. Since the exodus of your people, everyone's gaze is fixed on Monterini's cobblestones.'

'We used to be a community full of gossip. Now we're a community full of secrets. My head will explode with the secrets I'm keeping, all the lies I'm telling. How do you manage it, *Padre*?'

'I follow God's path, and that path is keeping as many people alive as I can. If a secret is suspected, we have to work even harder to keep the contents safe, even if that means telling lies. He will forgive us.'

Bella listened to the priest and wondered about Angelo. Did he also have his own secret? Every few days he declared, in a loud voice, that he was going hunting. But he never took a rifle. Dottore Mazzola appeared at the door once a week with a bulging sack, for Angelo's fishing trips, he said. But Angelo never returned with any fish, and the bag was always empty.

'I think about my family every day, where they are, if they're safe, if they're someone's secret too.'

Bella raised her gaze, but Don Philippe's face remained soft and kind; secret free. She sank down onto one of the benches in the men's section of the synagogue and continued, measuring her words with care. 'I know it sounds strange but by saving the orphans I wonder if I'm saving my family.' She bit her lip. 'And myself, for what I've done.'

'You mean becoming a Catholic?'

'I mean betraying my husband, my first one. And becoming a Catholic.' She scratched the side of her neck and bit harder on her lower lip. 'Yesterday I found Michele's mother. She's hiding with Signor Gabriele in a barn near Monterini. She's safe and near Villa Sofia. I took eggs from our hens and some cheese. It's my own guilty secret from Rico.'

The priest took her hand. 'Sometimes life requires secrets, Maria Cristina. Even from those we love.'

The sound of her new name whispered along the aisles of wooden benches so familiar to her, sent shivers along her spine. She was slowly accommodating herself to the six-syllabic resonance. Yet here in the synagogue, it felt sacrilegious and at the same time powerful because it was so wrong.

'But I have a bigger secret, *Padre*. I'm pregnant. And I don't know which husband it belongs to. Because you see, I still feel as if I have two. Two of everything: two mothers, two religions, two possible fathers for my child. I'm living two lives. I feel like I'm losing my mind.' She pulled her scarf tightly around her shoulders as if for comfort, and observed the features of the priest. Would he show disgust, anger, pain? But no, his skin remained smooth, his pale blue eyes tender.

'I'm sorry to burden you.'

'It's called confession, Maria Cristina, available to you now as a Catholic. Although unusual in the Beit Israel Synagogue.'

'The *contadini* always say the two communities are joined like this.' She interlaced her fingers and stretched out her arms towards Don Philippe, laughing through tears. 'What do I do? Which baby am I carrying? A Jewish or a Catholic one?'

'A child, Maria Cristina. That's all that matters. Do you think I care about the religion of the orphans at Villa Sofia? Does the priest in Assisi who's hiding Jews in the catacombs of his church? He's never met a single Jew before, yet he's saving them.'

Bella shook her head. Waves of irritation surged through her at the simplicity of this quiet priest, this *partigiano*-cum-man of God with his own secrets and conflicting beliefs. She stared at him coldly. 'Lieutenant Richardt cares if I have a Jewish or a Catholic child. And my father certainly would care.'

'Do you care, Bella?' He whispered her real name and she was touched that he'd used it. She stood up and walked towards the wide windows at the back of the synagogue overlooking the Jewish cemetery. Night had descended on Monterini and it was impossible to see the gravestones guarded by poplar trees.

'I've always been different, *Padre*. Partly because my mother lies over there.' She nodded her head towards the cemetery. 'Partly because I was different from my Catholic friends. But also...' She hesitated, unsure whether to mention Tanaquilla. All those years ago Jacobo had called her a witch. The memory still clung to Bella like an unhealed sore. Don Philippe, despite his openmindedness, was a man of committed faith; perhaps he too would consider her a witch.

She took a deep breath. 'I see things. I have done since I was young. A presence, every time danger is around me.'

'Like a premonition from God.'

'Maybe. But a presence I feel, smell and sense, and sometimes see. I told my father once, he was furious, so I never mentioned it again.' Don Philippe's eyes appeared soulful, full of kindness. 'The thing is, I don't want to be different. I want to mould into the rock of Monterini, feel part of it, be normal. I don't want my baby to feel different.'

'Why would it feel different?'

'Because I'm not sure which side of the religious divide she will be on. Who her father is, what future she would have.'

'Why do you say she, Maria Cristina?'

Bella smiled and returned to the bench. She settled down next to the priest, her face flushed.

'Tanaquilla, that's what I call this presence, always told me to listen. So, I listen and I hear a girl growing inside me. You think I'm crazy, don't you? *Pazza*.'

Don Philippe surveyed Bella, his expression a mixture of curiosity and disbelief. He brought his fingers to his mouth, strumming the lower lip, eyes closed as if in contemplation. Then he leaned forward and planted a kiss on her forehead.

'No. Maria Cristina, I think you're brave.' He reached for her hand and together they sat in silence; the Catholic Jewish Bella and the communist priest sharing the pain of life.

CHAPTER 5

It took Angelo eight days to find Jacobo. He visited every ruin they had discovered as a child. He followed the old Etruscan *cavi*, scanned tumbledown houses, grottos, caves, praying that Jacobo and his family had found refuge amidst the fronds and bracken.

The day following the departure from Monterini, he rode out to San Colombo on Rodeo *due* to search amidst the vineyards and olive trees. He ran into the old barn at the back of the fields, turning over crates and vats hoping Jacobo would hide there until they could find a safer location. The barn was empty, the mice scuttling along the broken beams the only occupants. Angelo opened a bottle of red *Vino degli Angeli* and hunted through memory, churning over possible ruins and hiding places of their youth that Jacobo might flee to.

One afternoon he remembered La Gita. He was astride Rodeo *uno*, wandering along a forgotten path five kilometers outside Monterini, when a vision of the derelict mill rippled across his mind. La Gita was an old ruined farmhouse from the eighteenth century. Like many others in the region, it had been inherited by sheep and goats. They chewed weeds and wandered through the abandoned rooms like proud proprietors. Angelo had found it one day when hunting with his father. He had revealed the news to Jacobo and for a while the hovel became a castle for childhood fantasies. Along with Gianni Vetrulli,

Ugo Grazzi and the Zerulli brothers, the two friends spent days amidst the cobwebs and dust, hidden from civilisation by woodland and untrodden paths. They would hunt and fish and chase sheep, confident nobody knew of their whereabouts.

A memory of Jacobo leaning over a mound of broken bricks and hauling up a bucket of water flashed across his mind. Of course, there was a well. Angelo looked heavenward and crossed himself three times.

'Let it still function,' he whispered to the cloudless sky. Red kites swirled above him. In the distance an owl hooted. The mill was close to the river, there would be fish to catch, but most helpful of all, La Gita was surrounded by dense foliage; tall pine trees and thick ferns. They would be shielded from anyone searching the area.

Angelo pulled on the reins and dug his knees into Rodeo's ribs, forcing the donkey into a trot. They passed through fields of ageing sunflowers, their faces dark and dying and bent towards the soil. He turned the donkey towards a path cutting through the foliage, bending his head as he passed under branches. When he saw the ruined tiles of a russet roof peeping through the gaps in the leaves, he dismounted and tied Rodeo to a beech tree. It was mid-September and a hazy heat settled like a shroud on the ferns and shrubs. Even the olive trees appeared wilted and delicate, their leaves almost translucent.

Like a dog sniffing clues, Angelo continued along the overgrown path towards the deserted hovel. The mill loomed in front of him, kindled deep red by the late afternoon light. The front door lay on its hinges. Angelo peered through the entrance. The staircase had crumbled years ago, leaving a gaping hole. Clumps of plaster like crushed eggshells sprinkled the floor. He stepped over piles of dirt littered with mice droppings. To the right of the hallway was an arch. Angelo called Jacobo's name, softly and then more forcefully. He lowered his head and stepped into a large room draped with cobwebs. There was no sign of life. Maybe his feeling had been wrong. But he had been so sure they were hiding at La Gita. Had the crunching sound of his footsteps alerted them?

He stepped outside and paused beside a clump of purple heather. Long tufts of grass glinted in the September sunlight. The air was still, the birds silenced. Like a hawk searching for its prey, Angelo scanned the emptiness. He could almost smell Jacobo. He sniffed hard, as if forcing his nose to detect Jacobo's scent, the scent of his tears. Because tears were like grapes, alive, vibrant.

The smell of sadness was all around him, in the jagged leaves of the trees, in the crusted soil beneath his feet. Jacobo was here, Angelo was certain.

'Jacobo. Jacobo, *sono io*. Angelo.'

His voice echoed through the bracken, under clumps of fennel, over trees laden with plums. Silence followed. He drew in his breath and waited, willing Jacobo to bounce out from behind a tree. Then he started to sing the songs they had shared together as they sauntered down the aisles of grapes. Jacobo would know it could only be him. He would know, despite everything that had happened between them, that Angelo would find him.

A short distance from the mill was a stone shack, probably used to store grains or animals. Angelo moved towards it, singing the melodies of their youth. A figure appeared from behind the shack and stood underneath a peach tree laden with fruit. Like a twig in the breeze it wavered, as if unsure whether to advance.

Angelo took several long strides and gathered Jacobo in his arms. He could feel the edges of Jacobo's ribs against his belly. They held each other, without speaking. Then Angelo leaned back to look at him. A sharp pain coiled around Angelo's heart.

In eight days Jacobo had crumbled. His skin was ashen and crusted with dirt, his eyes vacant yet fearful. His nose seemed longer and more prominent. Now he resembled his father Cosimo, with milky white hair, chin studded with grey dots.

'*Lo so*,' Jacobo spoke before Angelo could gather the right sentence in his mind. 'I know, they tell me I've gone completely white, almost overnight. At least there are no mirrors here!' He inhaled deeply and squeezed Angelo's arm. 'I knew you'd find us.'

Angelo lowered his head. He feared the tears scratching his eyes would spill onto his cheeks. 'I've been looking for you for days, trailing the *cavi*, searching in disused cellars, old grottos.'

The dread of not finding Jacobo had pushed Angelo on day after day, through the heat of the endless summer. Despite everything that had happened between them, he couldn't bear the thought that Jacobo had disappeared.

'We've been hiding in this broken-down barn.'

'Is it safe?'

'Safer than the main house. It's small but the walls are thick and the roof's still standing. If the Nazis do look here, they'll search the house first. It would alert us, give us time to escape.'

Jacobo led Angelo to an oak door riddled with tiny holes. He pushed it open with the heel of his shoe, to reveal a room smaller than Angelo's kitchen in Via Meravigliosa. The floor was covered with sawdust. At the back, underneath a small window was a sink coated with rust.

'Not a palace, but it'll do,' Jacobo whispered, then in a louder voice. 'We're safe, everyone, it's Angelo. He's found us.'

Gianni Vetrulli crawled out from under a pile of large sacks, pulling his wife Rosa and son Aldo with him. Lea and the girls appeared from behind an old chest. A few minutes later, Michele slipped out from under a pile of blankets. They were watching him, all emaciated, haggard versions of their former selves. And it's only been a handful of days, Angelo thought.

'You see, Angelo. Our childhood pranks have been useful. Jacobo and I both thought of the same hiding place.' Gianni Vetrulli spoke first, holding out his arms. Angelo towered over the doctor, hugging him. Lea stood on tiptoes, placing her hands on Angelo's shoulders. She kissed him on both cheeks. Her eyes were heavy, shades of sleepless nights etched on her skin.

'*Ti ringrazio*, thank you.' Her voice cracked. 'Jacobo said you'd find us. I wasn't so sure. So much has happened between you. But he said you'd never forget us.'

Only Michele knelt on the dusty floor in silence, unable to look Angelo in the eye. He'd lost weight and his lips looked chapped and sore. He had a sunken quality, a vacuous expression, like one who'd stood at the gates of hell.

'I think we can survive, Angelo.' Jacobo turned towards him. 'As long as nobody knows we're here. But we'll need food and medicines. It's been hard these past few days, surviving on berries and fruits.'

'We've just about managed up to now, but I dread to think what will happen when the weather turns,' Lea added.

'Go to Mazzola. He'll give you what you need. Don't tell him why. He'll know,' Vetrulli suggested.

'Nobody must know,' Jacobo said. 'Not Santina, not Rico. Not even my own daughter. It could be dangerous for everyone, but particularly for you, Angelo.'

'No more dangerous than anything else,' Angelo said, averting his gaze. He thought of Bella, now Maria Cristina and wanted to weep. He searched the room, realising that Jacobo's father was missing. '*Zio* Cosimo?'

'He died the day we arrived. I was surprised he even made it here. It was a struggle; we had to carry him in the end, all through the night. Gianni and I dug a grave for him down by the river. The girls have decorated it with sprigs of lavender.

He always loved lavender, loved the smell. I sit and talk to him every day. Better he didn't live through this, better for him not to have survived…' Jacobo's voice trailed off into the distance.

Angelo's throat tightened. He thought of all the painful events heaped upon him in the past week: first the exodus from Monterini, then Bella and Rico's surprise marriage; the daily search for Jacobo fearing he lay in some ditch. And now the discovery of Cosimo's death. Staring at them all, the Levis, the Vetrullis, poor betrayed Michele, all skinny, dirty remnants of their former selves, Angelo could no longer control the tears. They slipped down his cheeks.

'She's safe,' he whispered between sobs.

'Have you seen her?'

Angelo nodded.

'She's broken Michele. I worry about him. I think he's losing his mind.'

Angelo glanced across at Michele. '*Povero*!' his heart shouted silently to the young man crouching in front of him, the man whose wife his own son had stolen.

'I think about her all the time, Angelo, all alone in Monterini.' Jacobo reached across and tugged at Angelo's shirtsleeve. '*Perdonami* Angelo. For Rico and Bella. Please forgive me.'

'There's nothing to forgive,' Angelo shouted too loudly. Inside he cried, 'It's you who must forgive us.' He longed to tell Jacobo she was safe, she was his family now, tied to him, flesh and blood.

A Catholic.

A bigamist.

But he kept his mouth shut. They were friends again. The rift between them had healed. For the moment, that was all that mattered.

CHAPTER 6

J acobo woke most mornings as grey light filtered through the dense vegetation surrounding La Gita. The floor was hard and uncomfortable despite their mattresses of straw and Angelo's best efforts to provide blankets. He inched himself up from the makeshift bed he shared with Lea and her daughters, comforted by the cadence of combined breathing; Gianni's deep snores, Elena's sharp intermittent sighs, Michele's strangled sobs. At least they were all still alive.

There was something calming about these early mornings; the silence, the wild beauty of their surroundings. It was as if he had returned to a place in his life where he was steeped in the mysteries of the universe, withdrawn from the worries of the world. The irony was not lost on Jacobo; they were withdrawn from the world because of its worries, not in spite of them.

As he stepped out of the shack, the cold morning air caressed his cheek. The damp smell of earth invaded his nostrils. The uncertainty of this existence had heightened his senses, teaching him how to feel, smell and touch all over again. The longer they remained hidden, the more sensitive he became. He could hear the rustling of a deer or rabbit long before any of the others. He could sense when Angelo was about to appear and could smell the fear and betrayal radiating from his son-in-law's skin.

It had happened to him so many times before, but then he'd tried to dampen down the sensations. With Mussolini it had been different. He'd felt the danger like a punch in the chest. No one had listened. And what difference if they had?

If he were to mention to Lea or Gianni that this prison had liberated his senses, they would gaze at him with worry. Maybe he was going mad? He had wondered the same about Michele. His behaviour had changed since their arrival at La Gita. There was a disarming look in his eyes, a mixture of torture and sorrow. He mumbled to himself, and often at night Jacobo heard him scream at the stars. He never mentioned Bella. If Luciana or Elena spoke about her, he would stare ahead, then get up and walk around in circles, panting through gritted teeth, reminding Jacobo of a caged animal. But weren't they all caged animals in their prison of broken hearts and cobwebs?

Elena spent most of the day wrapped up in a corner of the kitchen, alone with her dreams. Occasionally she got up and wandered around like a lost ghost. Luciana had become Lea's shadow, pleading with lustreless eyes if Jacobo pulled Lea away from her. They all suffered from colds and bronchitis; the damp had etched its way through their flesh to their bones. Each morning Jacobo wondered whether they would survive and each night he thanked God for the miracle.

As the sun lit up the sky, Jacobo settled himself next to the mound that marked Cosimo's grave, stroking the soft earth, scattering it with fresh lavender. Jacobo had expected to bury his father in the family plot in the cemetery overlooking the golden *tufo* of Monterini, not by the remnants of a derelict mill. He was grateful his father had been spared this perilous lifestyle, the anxious wait for Angelo's visits and the terror of being discovered.

Angelo visited them as often as he could. But it was never enough. Jacobo's intuition had become so enhanced by this nomadic existence that he sensed Angelo's arrival in the breeze. Whilst the others waited in the house, huddled together like frightened sheep, fearful that the rustling leaves marked the arrival of the enemy, Jacobo stood at the entrance of La Gita, reassured that Angelo was on his way.

Sometimes Angelo rode Rodeo *uno* but as winter approached and the paths became too treacherous, he tied Rodeo to a tree by the roadside and trudged the rest of the journey on foot, lugging sacks of vegetables, wine and cheese, medicines and bandages. He'd sold Rodeo *due*, soon after he found Jacobo hiding at La Gita. He no longer needed two donkeys, he'd said, but the way he lowered his eyes and shuffled his feet, Jacobo knew he wasn't telling the truth. There was no doubt in Jacobo's mind, Angelo had sacrificed his donkey for them.

They didn't discuss the recent past. They couldn't talk about the present. So, they talked about the things they had in common: their childhood; their love for Monterini; the games they'd played together with Vetrulli, the pranks they'd got up to; Angelo's wine, the most famous of the whole Salone province.

Once Angelo tried to mention Bella. 'She is fine, you know.'

Jacobo could barely breathe. He tried not to think about his daughter, it was easier to banish thoughts of her from his mind and concentrate on survival. If a vision of her flitted in front of his eyes, he would shake it away like an unwanted fly. If the others mentioned her, he would walk out of the shack and sit alone, comforted by the sound of birdsong, the sunlight streaming through the branches.

'She's living in the Fratta. In your house,' Angelo persisted.

'You mean, we're struggling for survival, and she's living comfortably in my home?'

'She has a false name. It's just as dangerous as this.' Angelo's hand made patterns in the air around La Gita. 'Perhaps more so, you're hidden here, you see no one.'

The muscles around Jacobo's neck ached. He couldn't bear

the thought of Bella living in his house. He wasn't even sure why. 'That's true, but we worry every day that we'll be discovered.'

'She is surrounded by the enemy.' There was an urgency to Angelo's voice that alarmed Jacobo. 'She looks at the faces around her, she wonders what they're thinking. And she wonders how long before someone betrays her.'

'But this is Monterini. We don't have to be scared of the enemy within.'

'Within and without.' Angelo's face darkened, his eyebrows, wild and bushy, formed a deep V.

'You sound like me, Angelo, a long time ago.' Jacobo sighed as he recalled those years of growing isolation as Mussolini's fame spread. He had known right from the very first encounter of Benito's beaming face splashed across *La Stampa*. Those words that had trickled through his veins, filling his heart with fear: *Pericolo, pericolo*.

'Bella can't trust a soul. You're safer here, believe me.'

'If we survive the winter, and the hunger. And the isolation.' Jacobo started to fidget. He flicked a fly away from his bare arm and stared at the silver leaves of the olive trees rustling in the breeze. 'She made the decision not to come with us, she was the stubborn one. But if we starve to death here, and she manages to survive then who knows, maybe she was right to stay.'

'I'll try to bring more food,' Angelo reassured him. 'I know it's not enough, but it's hard to hide it. Santina is not a silly woman. She knows I don't need potatoes or cheese to go hunting!' He let out a subdued chuckle. 'That's where she thinks I am, you see.'

Jacobo smiled at him. 'You're courageous to do this for us. I don't deserve it, not after all that's happened.'

'Let's not talk about it.' Angelo's sharp tone caused Jacobo to wince. Neither of them knew how to bring up what lay in the air between them.

'So much has occurred,' Jacobo tried again, shuffling large clumps of earth around with his foot. 'So many challenges to my beliefs. I struggle with them all.'

'You don't have to explain.' Angelo stared at Jacobo with a look so intense, Jacobo wasn't sure if he had forgiven him or was still wounded. Angelo opened his mouth to speak then stopped abruptly, as if he were about to reveal something, but had changed his mind.

'I don't know how to explain.' What could Jacobo say about his view on Rico? It crossed too many lines. It contravened everything he believed about treating his fellow man equally. *Ama il prossimo tuo.* Isn't that what they were all taught? Love thy neighbour?

'She married him, you know.' The words slipped from Angelo's lips. A heavy silence followed. Angelo repeated the words.

'I thought that's what you said.'

'It's wartime, remember. Anything goes. At least that's what they tell me.'

'But she's married already!'

'I was as shocked as you, at first. Everything's upside down. I have Nazis living in my house, you're hiding here and Bella's doing what she can to survive. It's as simple as that.'

'But she's married,' Jacobo repeated. 'How can you be so accepting?'

'I'm more used to it now, that's all.'

'But who would perform such an illegal ceremony?'

Angelo's skin turned strawberry red. He bit his upper lip with his teeth. 'Don Philippe, in the cathedral. Then the mayor signed the official papers.'

Feelings of fury and helplessness shifted through Jacobo, unsettling him, causing a pain so deep inside he thought he would explode. How dare they stare the law in the face and spit at it? How dare they violate every convention imaginable?

'Let's not mention her again.' Jacobo could hardly recognise his own voice threading its way through the air. 'It's better for me and it's probably safer for you.'

When Angelo left that afternoon, Jacobo hugged him deeply: 'Thank you for keeping her safe.' He wanted to add, 'and despite everything I thank him too, Rico, your son. For being brave enough to save her, for being brave enough to love her.' The words stuck in his throat. Angelo reached for Jacobo's hand and squeezed it, and Jacobo hoped Angelo could hear what his heart was saying.

They never mentioned Bella or Rico again, but every time Angelo came to visit, the couple floated between them like invisible burdens. Jacobo wasn't sure if this linked him to Angelo more closely or whether the enormity of their children's deed lay between them like a river they could not cross. All Jacobo knew for certain was that he depended on Angelo's visits as if it were the oxygen he needed to survive.

And Angelo kept coming, right until the end.

CHAPTER 7

It was December. It had rained for days and the children were feeling confined and irritable. When the rain ceased, and the wheat fields glistened, Don Philippe decided it would cheer them up to leave the villa for a while. An outing was planned to see a puppet show in the village. The priest asked Bella to choose a group of younger children and suggested that Marianne and Camilla accompany them.

At the last minute, Georges Barantova and Rico decided to join the small group. They left the villa, happy to wade through a carpet of damp leaves, inhaling the smell of burning wood. The puppets made the children giggle and, as they walked out of the theatre, Bella relaxed.

'I feel normal for the first time in months,' she whispered to Rico as he ushered the group through the Piazza del Commune.

'Better not hang around though, the area is littered with German soldiers.' Rico nodded towards a group of officials sitting on a veranda drinking grappa. They nodded as the group passed and one of them saluted.

Bella smiled back. She waved her hand through the air.

'*Ciao, ciao signori,*' two of the younger children cried out

And still Bella felt calm. Why, oh why, she wondered later that evening, did the warning come too late?

They climbed over the bridge and on to the San Gianni path towards the villa. The younger ones collected bunches of bright yellow broom from the roadside and shrivelled, russet leaves to make a collage when they returned to the villa. The two older girls chatted together. The sun slithered through blackened clouds.

A sudden chill swept over Bella. Her nose twitched, the smell of sulphur invaded her nostrils. She looked around but there was no Tanaquilla.

Then Marianne shouted out casually, playfully tapping Camilla on the arm, '*Aber quatsch, das ist nicht richtig.*'

As soon as the Teutonic words flew from Marianne's lips, Bella knew they were in trouble. She felt it, she smelt it. Like a phantom materialising out of the air, a German soldier appeared.

And behind him stood Tanaquilla, eyes closed, robes swaying.

Bella knew Georges, Rico and the other children could not see Tanaquilla. But they could all see the soldier, gun raised and pointed towards the group, eyes glinting with disbelief. Or was it satisfaction?

'*Wer ist Deutscher hier?*' The soldier spat out the words like globules of phlegm. A death sentence on them all.

They stood motionless, ice statues melting with fear. Bella pulled Marianne and Camilla towards her. Rico jumped in front of them, arms spread out like the dying Christ in the cathedral. What a blessing Georges was there, Bella thought, his German was impeccable.

'*Sie träumen,*' Georges said calmly, stepping in front of Rico. 'You must be dreaming. Nobody speaks German, apart from me. I come from Berlin. I've lived here for years. These children are orphans from Monterini. They speak only a local dialect. I'm their music teacher.'

He smiled in a relaxed manner, without a glint of fear. The gun remained at eye level. The soldier's face glistened with sweat, confusion flickered in his eyes.

'*Nicht richtig,*' he repeated over and over again, gun still pointing towards them. '*Nicht richtig.*'

'They're Italian. You need to lower your gun. Or I will have to report you.'

They were dicing with death. How they acted, what they did or said would seal the fate for all of them; the children, the teachers, all the villagers implicated in their crime.

Georges continued to talk to the soldier, placating him with his firm yet persuasive manner and perfect German. Marianne began to chat away in the Monterini dialect. The other children copied her. Soon sentences full of dialect soared through the air, drifting and dancing around the soldier.

'... *dia... dia. Dia a ca'.*'

The soldier relaxed. Though he still held the gun at shoulder height, he kept his legs slightly apart as if in the military 'at ease' position. With a delicate movement of his head, he motioned for them to move along. Rico clasped Bella's hand. She turned around and stared at the German. His chalk-coloured hair was short and neatly cut. Suspicion crossed his eyes; green just like hers. And behind him the face of the phantom was bruised with sadness.

They walked in silence, Tanaquilla floating beside them. When they turned the bend, the German soldier was no longer in sight.

'It's over.' Rico's voice cracked. 'We have two hours at the most to clear the villa. Monterini is no longer safe.'

'I hope he believed Georges.' Bella was surprised how much her voice trembled.

'He seemed to accept our explanation.' Georges nodded. 'I think he was persuaded.'

'No, he wasn't.' Rico grabbed the arms of Camilla and Marianne, urging them to walk faster. 'Soon Villa Sofia will be

273

riddled with soldiers. They'll find us and destroy us. We have to act quickly.'

'It's my fault, it's all my fault,' Marianne sobbed.

Rico turned her round to face him and with his thumb stroked her cheek. 'No, *cara*. It's nobody's fault.'

Bella and Georges led the rest of the group along the lanes towards the line of olive trees, their branches swaying like silver fans. When they reached the villa, Georges and the girls ran inside to alert Don Philippe and Mario. Rico stopped at the entrance and Bella tumbled into his open arms. He stroked her hair away from her face, hushing her as she wept uncontrollably.

'I'm scared, Rico.'

'We have to hide everyone until we can get them out of Monterini. It won't be safe for you either, even with your false papers.'

'We can't win, Rico, they're much stronger than us.' She longed to tell him what she'd seen swaying behind the soldier. But she kept her lips tightly shut.

'If we think the enemy is stronger than us, we'll give up. We must act calmly. We can save these orphans. Fight for what's right, no compromise, that's the partisan belief.'

'Rico, you're such an idealist, how can you be so sure?'

'Because that's our duty.'

'You're naive, my darling Rico, to think good can conquer all. I saw the eyes of the enemy.' She had looked back like Lot's wife, she had seen the trembling lips of the phantom. The words of the partisan song Rico whispered in her ear when they were alone floated through her mind. How real the lyrics were, how sadly pertinent:

Sta mattina mi son alzato
O bella ciao, bella ciao, bella ciao ciao ciao
Sta mattina mi son svegliato

E ho trovato l'invasor
O partigiano, portami via,
Che mi sento di morir

One morning I woke up
O bella ciao, bella ciao, bella ciao ciao ciao
One morning I woke up
And I found the invader
Partigiano take me away,
I feel I'm dying

Within a few hours, the villa lay empty, a fallow field after the harvest. Bella gazed at the empty rooms devoid of furniture and people, the closed shutters. The mansion had been a home to the orphans, providing them with shelter, safety and schooling. All that remained was the chandelier swinging from the ceiling in the hall. Shutting the wooden door, Bella blew a kiss to Villa Sofia. Would the memories of the children's laughter and their tears survive? Would she return one day and hear Tamara giggle as she tried to copy the resonance of an Italian sentence? Would she see the boys sawing wood with Angelo and little Salamone milking cows with Rico in the barn?

Rico appeared before her, his face the colour of cloudy skies. He caught her elbow and ushered her down the stone steps. He didn't even look back. Rico lived for the next moment whilst her heart followed memories, trapped by the past. That was the difference between them.

As if reading her mind, Rico bent forward, his lips touching her ear. 'Banish the villa from your mind as if it never existed.' He nodded his head towards the groups of children huddled at the entrance of the mansion. 'We need to be focused on the task in hand.'

She marvelled at his matter-of-fact way, as if this was a military manoeuvre devoid of sentimental feeling. He squeezed her waist, sending her one of his tender smiles, the smile of their childhood, their youth.

Their roles had reversed since adolescence. Then she was Rico's teacher, challenging him, encouraging him with the help of *Fontamara* and Carlo Rosselli's *Socialismo Liberale*. He had lapped up every word she'd uttered, greedily devouring the literature and anti-fascist reviews she'd suggested. Now it was Rico's turn to be her guide.

It was the week of *La Festa dell'Uva*. Every night there were festivities despite the war. Wine flowed through the village like an abundant river. Dressed in peasant costumes of past centuries, German soldiers raised their glasses and flirted with the young *signorine* of Monterini. They danced and sang, celebrating the harvest of the grapes. The streets surrounding the village were empty; the intricate alleyways silent to the muffled footsteps of the orphans and their teachers.

The surrounding farms, olive presses and labyrinth houses would open their taciturn interiors to conceal the orphans.

And nobody would know.

The children were divided into three groups. Bella and Mario Celeste were handed a group of girls and told to go silently and quickly to the monastery.

'Don Philippe will be waiting for you. Maria Cristina can cross the streets of Monterini with her eyes closed.' It always amazed Bella how easily her false name could trip off Rico's tongue.

'But are we safe? The Nazis have chased us across Europe and found us and it's all because of me and my stupid German!'

'It's not your fault.' Bella pulled Marianne to her. She remembered how skinny the girl had been when she first arrived all those months ago, her ribs jutting out like sharp blades, barely a whisper coming from her lips. Now her body had filled out, her cheeks were plump and rosy and her Italian and dialect exquisite. Bella stroked her hair, wishing she could be as confident as Rico. She had moved beyond fear to a place of numb disbelief. She searched for calming words to appease Marianne.

'This village is mine. I know every corner from Capo Bagno to the palazzo and all the twists and turns in between. We'll be safe, you'll see.'

The San Benedetto Monastery was huddled behind the cathedral. To reach it without touching the square where the Germans were celebrating, they had to crisscross the *vie* and *viccoli* like stitches in a tapestry. Bella, trailed by Mario and twenty silent shadows, darted around corners and hurtled down crooked steps. The moon soaked the stones with silver.

Tiptoeing along Via Meravigliosa, Bella glanced up at the house with grey shutters, praying Lieutenant Richardt was not sitting outside sipping Angelo's wine. The veranda was empty. She kept her eyes peeled to the cobblestones, the footsteps behind her deadened by the festivities from the piazza. When she dared to glance up, she noticed curtains twitch in the surrounding houses, faces fade from sight.

From time to time she spotted a figure hover in front of her, before evaporating into the walls of the village. Was it a Monterinese, reluctant to witness their escape? Or was it Tanaquilla, reminding her of the flight of other civilisations?

Don Philippe unbolted the wooden door of the monastery, eyes devoid of the usual twinkle.

'*Venite, venite.*' He ushered the group through the entrance.

To the distant sounds of the German song, *Die Welt gehört den Führenden,* Don Philippe, Bella and Mario secreted the children through the stone walls and down into the vaults as if they were a magician's toy disappearing within his black cape.

The touch of the *tufo* rock was cool against Bella's hand as she used it to guide her way down, instructing the children to pay attention. They stepped slowly, holding on to each other, grasping a sleeve, a waist.

'You know it's the first time we've had women here,' Don Philippe told them, leading them down through layers of rock. 'Or Jews for that matter! But I dare say it won't be the last.'

'The cathedral and the monastery were the two places in Monterini I feared the most when I was a little girl,' Bella whispered to Mario.

'I was always scared of the priests in my town,' Mario whispered back.

Bella remembered her father telling her that he too had been frightened of the priests in the village, the *fratti* who scuttled through the Fratta on their way to the monastery. She looked at Don Philippe with his potbelly, soft cheeks, kind eyes. There was nothing remotely frightening about this brave man who was risking his life for them.

She focused her attention on the vault carved out of the *tufo*, its walls pitted and pocked as if a thousand bullets had blistered its face. How strangely comforting to be hidden deep in the layers of Monterini rock. She wondered if the monks in their cells knew Don Philippe was concealing Jews in the bowels of their home. Would they betray them and their crazy, partisan priest? She sighed, a feeling of relief rinsing through her. No, of course not, this was Monterini after all.

The baby inside her kicked.

Another hidden secret.

She still hadn't summoned the courage to tell Rico about its presence, preferring to hide it beneath the folds of her skirt, just as she was hiding now beneath the folds of the village.

Marianne sidled up to her and interlaced her fingers through Bella's. Her hand felt damp.

'Will we be safe here?' Marianne's lip trembled and in those

278

dark irises Bella recognised the terror she had witnessed when the orphans first arrived in Monterini; a deep, visceral pain sifting through every cell.

The vault was much larger than Bella imagined. It was divided into several sections by natural formations of *tufo*. Some sections had a rounded arch, others a layer of rock jutting out, forming separate compartments. No doubt it had been used by Etruscans before the cathedral and monastery were founded. Bella wondered whether it had been a home or a tomb, or even a place of worship.

Don Philippe spread out blankets on the floor and pointed to pillows and bedding piled high in a corner. He had raided the monks' cells, he told Bella, grabbing hold of whatever spare items he could find. The children sat on their makeshift beds, fear seemingly forgotten as they fought over which corner of the vault to sleep in, and who would be closest to Bella.

Mario was shown to a small section at the back of the vault. He had to crouch down on all fours and slide through. Camilla and Tamara giggled as they watched his body disappear through the rock. At least they can still laugh, Bella thought. She was emboldened by the girls' excitement and wondered if their past experience in their countries had given them the resilience to deal with yet another fleeing.

When most of the children were too exhausted to stay awake, Don Philippe beckoned Mario and Bella into one of the empty sections of the vault. He motioned for them to sit down on a rug he'd spread out on the stone floor and explained how Rico and Georges had taken the boys to hide in disused barns, farmhouses and homes of trusted inhabitants. The operation known as Exit Cloud had been planned months ago with the help of Delasem, the Italian and Jewish resistance organisation. Bella remembered how this group had been instrumental in bringing the children to Monterini.

Don Philippe said, 'We couldn't tell a soul, you understand. We never knew if or when it would be necessary. Today, it became clear we had to hide you all.'

'How long will we have to stay here?' Mario asked.

'Until we can get all the orphans out of Monterini. I can't reveal too much. You have to trust me.'

Bella closed her eyes. She pictured Rico and Georges tiptoeing through the cobbled alleyways of Monterini just as she had done. She wondered whether Rico and Angelo were hiding orphan after orphan at the smallholding in San Colombo, in the old well, under haystacks, perhaps in the *cantina* of the house in the Fratta with Rodeo *uno* as a companion. The image of a small, frightened child caused her to open her eyes abruptly.

'What about Salamone Papo?' In the turmoil of packing up the villa and getting the girls safely into the monastery, she had forgotten about Rico's little shadow. Two weeks earlier, with the help of Rico and Don Philippe's contacts, they had sent Salamone to a sanatorium in the Dolomites. Tuberculosis, Dottore Mazzola had said.

'Our contacts are looking out for him. They'll do their best, but we'll have to see.' Don Philippe shook his head. 'If the Germans discover what we've been doing here, they'll find him. We must pray for Salamone Papo. We must pray for every one of them.'

He pulled himself up to a kneeling position, indicating to Bella and Mario to do the same. Making the sign of the cross he uttered the Ave Maria prayer. Bella closed her eyes and whispered the *Shema*, and the words of both prayers floated around them, entwined in harmony.

Twice a day Don Philippe unlocked the wooden door with the key he kept attached to his habit. With a smile that reminded Bella of her *nonno* Cosimo, he delivered a tray full of bread, olives, apples, steamed cabbage and very occasionally leftover rice.

'How do you manage to secrete all this food for twenty-two fugitives, *Padre*?'

'I say I'm going through a growing spurt.' Don Philippe rubbed his belly. 'And my monks simply lower their eyes and stay silent. I believe we can trust them. They don't necessarily share my political views, but they share my religious ones. We are men of God, after all.'

Don Philippe brought in exercise books and pencils, and the girls continued with their Italian lessons, encircling Bella like a fan of silent, white ghosts. How quickly their cheeks paled, their eyes dulled. Their hair became matted and unruly. After a few days she begged the priest to bring in some olive oil to use as soap and buckets so they could wash in a corner of the vault, tucked away from the ones they used for their ablutions.

During the day, Bella entertained the children with stories of her youth. She told them about Angelo's smallholding, the deep red and pale green grapes like silk that loved music and grew stronger and sweeter to the sound of Angelo's voice. She explained how Jacobo made the discovery, how she had come up with the name *Vino degli Angeli*, Wine of the Angels.

And they told her about their families, the brother left alone under a bed; the cries of their parents handcuffed, wrenched away. Days without food. Blistering pain from walking kilometers without shoes; hiding under bracken. Bella knew they could survive their days in hiding. This escape would be another story they would relate in years to come. She didn't need to reassure them, it was the calm equanimity of the orphans, their ability to contain fear that gave her hope.

The incarceration provided Bella with hours of reflection. Amidst the peaceful sounds of the girls' breaths, an image of her father floated around her, spectacles perched on the end of his nose, cheekbones jutting through his skin like needles. Sometimes *nonno* Cosimo nudged his way into her dreams, wiping her tears with the back of his deathly white hand.

But the worst was Michele.

'*Traditore*. Betrayer. You'll be punished.' He tormented her with cries and shouts, shaking his fist at her, squinting with hatred.

She woke dripping with sweat.

She lay on the stone floor, sleeping children dotted around her. She scanned the walls of rock, nose twitching for the smell of sulphur. Her eyes longed for the figure in white robes to guide her, comfort her.

But she never came.

Bella placed her hand on her belly, sensing the baby growing inside her, tying it to this world, this strange life they were living.

CHAPTER 8

It was the stillness of night.

A creaking sound woke Bella. She held her breath. With half-open eyes she saw Don Philippe ushering Rico down the ancient, monastery steps. Tamara and Marianne lay in Bella's arms, her hair a blanket of red trailing across their bodies. She gently lifted her arms from under them, taking care not to wake them. A wave of relief threaded through her. He had come back to get her.

Rico's face was leaner, there were dots of stubble on his chin and under his nose. He smiled but his expression was weary, faded as if he hadn't slept for days. He looked stale, worn out, a mere shadow of the *partigiano-contadino*. He pulled Bella towards him, wrapping his arms around her body. Bones on bones. She sucked in the smell of wood fires, chestnuts and freedom.

'I was wondering if I would ever see you again,' she breathed on his cheek, folding her fingers through his hair. He lifted her up, carrying her towards where Don Philippe was pouring tumblers of wine in a corner of the vault away from Mario and the children. 'How long have we been here?'

'Almost nine days.'

'Only nine days!' she repeated, her voice rasping. 'How long will we have to remain hidden beneath these deep folds of stone?'

'Not long.' Rico placed her on a rug covering the floor. 'You'll all be leaving soon. The soldier who saw us has gone back to Darmstadt on leave. The Italian authorities told the Germans he's imagining things. They've reassured Erich Priebke at headquarters they really are Catholic orphans.'

'And they believe them?'

'For the time being.'

'But where will you take them?'

'To the coast, south of Napoli, we have contacts there, Italian soldiers.'

'We've got false passports for every single child,' Don Philippe added. His hand was shaking, and he averted his gaze as he placed a tumbler in Bella's hand.

'That's what we've been sorting out, these past few days. Nanni Manduro has helped us forge the papers,' Rico continued.

'Nanni? But surely he's in hiding?'

'He converted, like you, and has false papers. He's living in Viterbo. He has printing contacts because of his work with your father. From Napoli we can get them on a boat for Palestine. Mario and Georges will go with them. It's not safe for Georges as a communist to stay here, although in the eyes of the Germans he is less of a worry than Mario or you. If the operation succeeds, they'll all be free.'

'What happens if it doesn't?'

'It will,' Rico said. Then he closed his eyes, took a deep breath and dashed her hopes with hurtful words. 'You're going with them.'

Bella's heart pounded so deeply against her chest, she thought it would burst through the layer of skin. She rested her gaze on the milky patches of damp adorning the walls.

'Are you crazy?'

'You have no choice. I'm not arguing with you, it's all settled.'

'But I have false papers!' The madness was kicking in, biting her, pawing her. The one she cherished was ordering her to leave. In that moment she hated him. And if she left Monterini now, for Palestine, would she ever see her family again?

Don Philippe pulled up his cassock and knelt down next to Bella. 'You're in danger. The German soldier saw you. If someone from here betrays your real identity, the Nazis will kill you. As far as they're concerned, you're still Jewish. Your conversion doesn't count.'

Rico dug deep into his jacket pocket and brought out a green booklet. He fumbled through the pages until he reached a faded photograph. Bella squinted. The wild eyes, pretty nose looked alarmingly like her.

'This is a passport in the name of Maria Cristina Ghione. You can come back as soon as the war is over.' Rico's eyes flickered in the candlelight.

'I'm staying here.' Bella fixed her gaze on the priest but addressed the words to her husband. 'Do you honestly think I'd leave you, Rico, after all we've been through?'

'If you don't leave, we may not have a future together.' Rico placed his hand under Bella's chin, forcing her to face him.

'But our future's here.' And still she could not tell him, could not reveal the heartbeats pulsing inside her.

Rico's voice was laced with irritation. 'You won't be safe if you stay. There are too many dangers.'

'My whole life I had no choice. No choice to be who I am, talk about the strange things I see, marry the man I love.' She stopped. A sensation of lightness sifted through her. 'But now I make my own decisions. And I choose to stay.'

'But what happens when the soldier returns?' Don Philippe's voice was cracking like the sound of squashed acorns in autumn.

'And your true identity is discovered?' Rico added. 'It'll be riskier once the children have left Monterini. For now, the

Germans think they are on a pilgrimage to Maratea but when they don't return, nowhere will be safe.'

'Don't you see?' Bella's eyes widened, piercing her husband with that same intense look she used to fix on Jacobo, to wear him down, to get him to agree. 'I'd rather be in danger here with you, than safe without you, in some country I don't know.'

'I'm making this decision. I'm not your father, I won't cave in. You're leaving with the orphans tonight.'

Her world was disintegrating like the colours of a beautiful painting soaked under a downpour. Moments earlier Rico had appeared smiling, full of love, now he was ordering her to leave. If she left Monterini, without him, without her family, it would be as if Bella Levi never existed.

Don Philippe took Bella's hand in his and kissed it. 'The Nazis found Salamone.'

An image flashed in front of her of little Salamone Papo forced from his bed in the Dolomites, tears sliding down his cheeks, crying out for his hero Rico. Her hand flew to her heart.

'Oh no! Where have they taken him?'

'We lost trace of him at the Austrian border.'

Rico turned his face away from her, his voice determined. 'You're in grave danger. You must leave, there's no other choice.'

The candle flickered and blew out.

Deep in the moonlit hours, Don Philippe ushered them through the heavy, wooden door. Bella and Rico guided Mario and the twenty girls along the silent alleyways, past water fountains and crevices.

The village appeared to have shrunk. The alleyways seemed alarmingly unfamiliar, the pungent smell of wood fires nauseating. Footsteps muffled by a dog howling in the distance, they sped down the steep steps of Capo Bagno, their shadows staining the *tufo* inky black. Bella fixed her eyes on closed shutters. Behind

286

them the inhabitants slept, blissfully unaware of the exodus in their midst. A flutter of a prayer escaped her lips.

At the bottom of the San Gianni path, partly hidden by tall poplars and leafy chestnuts, was a truck.

'There's a German number plate.' Bella grabbed hold of Don Philippe's arm, fear tumbling through her.

Don Philippe patted her hand. 'It belongs to the resistance organisation *Partito d'Azione*. There's a way of telling which trucks are safe.'

Dottore Mazzola and Angelo jumped out of the front seat with two men Bella did not recognise. The strangers kissed Don Philippe and Rico on both cheeks. Rico nodded, then raised his arm and beckoned into the darkness. Immediately figures popped out of the shadows, delivering boys from Rico's group. Bella recognised villagers from the Ghetto and Capo Bagno as well as Signor Boscani from Favore. There was Signor Todi, the husband of Clara the midwife, Signor Roselli and Maestra Virginia. Marlene, who used to work with Jacobo at the bookshop, was followed by Signora Petri, and Paolo and Claudio the bakers from the Fratta. They all accompanied children to the truck, holding their hands or squeezing their arms as if to reassure them. They nodded to Rico and disappeared, returning moments later with more children. The whole process lasted fifteen minutes.

Angelo and Dottore Mazzola helped the children climb into the back of the truck. Angelo lifted them effortlessly without stretching. Bella remembered how he used to lift her and Rico high into the sky to pick olives and chestnuts from the tallest branches of the trees. They had felt like they were flying back then. Soon it would be her turn to fly into the sky.

But this time forever.

She and her unborn child whisked away from the place she loved.

It was Mario and Georges' turn to climb into the truck. Rico and Don Philippe hugged them and raised their fists; a form of salute Bella had never seen before.

Rico turned to Bella and pressed his nose against her ear. 'You must get in the truck, my love, *amore mio*. I'll find you as soon as the war is over, I promise.'

Mario and Georges reached down to clasp her hands, pulling at her fingers. Marianne, Tamara and Camilla leaned forward urging her to join them. 'Come, Bella, come with us,' they whispered in unison. It reminded her of that other time when her stepsisters had tried to cajole her into leaving with them.

'Get in the truck.' Rico's voice was urgent. 'We're running out of time.'

Turning around to face Rico, Bella placed her hands on his cheeks. 'You'll have to shoot me first, Rico. Me and the baby I'm carrying.'

'Baby? You're pregnant? You chose this moment to tell me I'm a father?'

'How do you know it's yours?' There was defiance in her voice, a daring dashed immediately when she saw his cheeks collapse inwards, bones shifting with the pain of her announcement.

'Why didn't you tell me?'

'I wasn't sure how you'd react. I can't promise it's yours, but it could be.'

The hoarse noise of Rico's breath penetrated the night. He brought his face close to hers, his fingers clenched around her waist. She couldn't tell if he was worried or furious. 'Didn't you trust me enough to love you and the baby? I don't care if it's not mine. You should have told me.'

'The longer I hid it, the bigger the burden became. Whether the baby is yours or Michele's we're staying with you. I've lost my father, Lea and my stepsisters, my *nonno*. You're all I have.'

'Get in the truck,' Rico repeated, his voice low, tinged with sadness. He grasped her arm, shoved her against the edge of the vehicle. His fingers dug into her shoulders as if he were going to shake her.

She could feel heat burning her skin. 'I'm not leaving you.'

'Yes, you are. Get in.'

He stared deep into her eyes, then relaxed his hold. 'You are the most important thing in my life, and you have my word I will come and find you. You and your baby. But if you stay you may suffer the same fate as Salamone. I couldn't bear that. Please trust me and get in the truck.'

How could Rico banish her from Monterini, her childhood, her memories, her dreams? Her mother was buried in the Jewish cemetery, her father was hiding somewhere, possibly in one of the *cavi* near where they stood. She couldn't leave. But at that moment Rico's expression was as desperate and determined as her own.

'I'll never forgive you,' she said and stretched her arms towards Georges and Mario. They lifted her up. Marianne hugged her; Tamara nestled her face against Bella's neck. She heard Georges whisper, 'You've made the right choice.'

There was a hushed silence in the truck, then sighs of relief. She was joining her orphans. Bella slipped to the floor. She could almost feel the night air trembling with sadness.

There was a chugging sound; the engine began to whirr, the wheels screeched. They lurched forward as the vehicle started to move. The villagers were waving, Rico and Angelo looked like silhouettes against the trees, their expressions unreadable in the starlit night.

The truck slid down the San Gianni path leaving a trail of dust. Rico disappeared into the shadows.

They turned the corner to join the main thoroughfare

connecting Florence to Rome. Monterini rose above her, both magical and threatening. Out of the shadows she heard a voice shouting, 'Jump, jump.'

Was it Tanaquilla?

The phantom was nowhere to be seen.

Bella grasped hold of the bar at the back of the truck, her knuckles white. She lifted herself onto the ledge and with one hand flicked a kiss towards the startled faces of her orphans. She tumbled down to the grit and dirt of the road, grazing her arms and legs, bruising her shoulder against the stump of a tree. She rubbed her calves, stood up and brushed herself down.

'I'm sorry,' she shouted to the disappearing truck, hoping Georges and Mario could hear her, willing the children to forgive her.

She placed her hands on her belly.

'*Mi dispiace*,' she said, hoping her own child would forgive her too. She felt a sharp movement, almost a kick. The baby was Rico's, she had no doubt. Rico would accept her reasons for not leaving with his child. He would come round, just like her father usually did.

She climbed up to Monterini, oblivious of the nettles tearing at her shins. The streets were empty; a stray cat huddled in a doorway hissed at her as she passed. The smell of burning wood hung over Via Meravigliosa. She stopped in front of her father's house. Paint was peeling from the shutters, the tiles on the veranda were broken. It looked bleak, more fragile since she had last seen it, almost two weeks previously.

They were all fragile, she realised, hanging on to the frailty of this life with their fingertips.

As if to reassure her, the baby kicked again. It will be the lucky one, Bella thought. I shall call her Fortuna.

And then she recognised the smell of sulphur.

CHAPTER 9

The day after the orphans were spirited away, Rico and Bella were driven by Dottore Mazzola and Don Philippe to the home of a *contadino*, in the middle of the Salone hills. A slither of sunlight tore through wintry clouds. The frozen fields and stone houses reminded Bella of the previous winter in the remote mountain village of Favore. With Rico by her side, she knew she would be able to bear living in this barren wasteland. She reached for his hand, but he pulled it away, eyes fixed on the soft flakes of snow brushing the bonnet of the truck.

'This wasn't part of the plan,' he'd insisted the night before, when she arrived at the house bruised and bashed. His voice was tense, chilling her to the bone. He'd refused to look at her, refused to touch her. 'We'll have to find a safe house for you. None of us are safe anymore.'

They bumped along a dirt track, a trail of dust swirling alongside them. They passed through an area of thick woodland and stopped in front of a stone building attached to several ramshackle outhouses. Bella imagined they were used for housing pigs and cows.

The number of contacts Rico and Don Philippe conjured up never failed to surprise her. They sprouted out of the earth, in Monterini, in the surrounding fields, and beyond the borders. Rico and Don Philippe were more closely linked to the *partigiani* than she had ever realised. She had been naive at the villa, asked no questions, and even when they were all hidden in the monastery, she didn't ask with whom they were working.

When Signor Pietro opened the rickety, wooden door of his smallholding she knew he was another link in the long chain of unlikely resistance workers. His toothless mouth, pinched face, threadbare clothes made him an unexpected choice, as unlikely as Mazzola or the priest, she supposed. He was a *contadino* through and through. Poor, no doubt uneducated and quite clearly apolitical. She assumed this was why they had chosen him. His furrowed face resembled the fields they had just trundled past, his smoky grey eyes offered little warmth. Dungarees hung from him like a sheet flapping around waist and ankles. He could have been forty, Bella thought, or a hundred years old.

The cottage was small and sparsely furnished with a table and six chairs in the centre of the room. A large stove funnelled out warmth and a metal basin stood under the only window.

Signor Pietro kissed Don Philippe on both cheeks, shook Rico's hand and introduced his wife Signora Maria and their four daughters. Bella didn't recognise their dialect; she supposed it was from Elmo, the tiny hamlet Don Philippe had pointed out, lost in the folds of the hills. Just like Favore but more isolated. More difficult to find.

The women wore long, black skirts and grey shirts, faded scarves adorned their heads; a fashion reminiscent of peasant clothes from the last century she'd read about in her history books. It made Angelo and the *contadini* of Monterini seem polished and fashionable. She wondered what they thought of her and Rico. Fugitives turning up in their kitchen; disconnected fragments putting their lives at risk.

Time passed. Yellow skies. Dreamy moonlight drifting across foreign fields. Helping Signora Maria bake round loaves, cutting vegetables and picking up snippets of an unfamiliar dialect formed the framework of Bella's days.

She wondered at the simplicity of the lives of her hosts. They milked their cows, ploughed their fields, grew vegetables and stared at their guests. She didn't know if the family was paid to shelter them. She hoped they were. She knew they could be trusted, she saw it in the way Signor Pietro placed his hand on Rico's arm; the way Signora Maria forced her to eat plates of rice with vegetables and glanced at her now protruding belly, with a look of concern shading her wrinkled face.

At first the fear they would be captured occupied Bella's mind. Would they be discovered, Rico shot in front of her eyes, Signor Pietro and his family hanged in their own smallholding for harbouring traitors to the Italian cause? It was worse at night, so many bodies sleeping in one room. Rasping breath, Signor Pietro's snores and the howling of dogs on Monte Amiata. The rain splattered against the tin roof like small pebbles. Haunted faces flittered before her; her father, Michele, the orphans' eyes filled with despair. And little Salamone, arms reaching out towards her. She almost heard them cry out, 'Bella, save us.'

But she couldn't.

She longed for an appearance from Tanaquilla. The phantom left her alone. Perhaps she was safe after all in this tumbledown farm surrounded by frosted trees and bleak fields.

Safe.

She barely had the strength to utter the word.

One afternoon Don Philippe arrived at the smallholding with Mateo, Rico's younger brother. Carlo and Mateo had been serving in the army for several months. Little news of them had filtered back to Monterini. Now here he was, standing in Signor Pietro's kitchen.

'The orphans are safe,' Don Philippe announced. He pulled Rico and Bella towards him, holding them in a tight embrace. 'We did it.'

Mateo opened the bottle of *Vino degli Angeli* he'd pulled from his knapsack. They clinked their beakers of wine and shouted *auguri* in trembling voices.

It was as if Rico had stored the tension of the past few weeks into each and every cell and now it melted from him like winter snow. The breath whooshed out of his lungs. His face shifted as his flesh relaxed, his eyes seemed brighter, clearer. Bella placed her arms around him, her head resting against his chest.

It had been an arduous journey, Mateo and Don Philippe explained. The orphans had been turned back from Naples, forced to hide in the homes of Italian farmers, until the next plan of action could be agreed. Cold, hungry, they traversed the country on trains and trucks. At the Swiss border, some British soldiers came to their rescue. After several failed attempts, the soldiers helped them cross into Switzerland. They were on the final leg of their journey to Palestine.

Things had changed in Monterini, Mateo told them. Whilst they were hiding in the hills of Salone, the partisan group, Gruppi di Azione Patriottica, had planted a bomb in Via Rasella, killing twenty-eight soldiers from South Tyrol. The day after the explosion, Erich Priebke, head of the SS police force in Italy, responded by ordering a massacre in the Fosse Ardeatine.

Don Philippe recounted how 355 Italians were rounded up and murdered, amongst them seventy-five Jewish men. Lieutenant Richardt had gone, called back to Rome to deal with the fallout. He'd had to leave Angelo's house and the plentiful supply of wine to support his head of police. Herr Bauer was the new replacement. A troubled-looking man with deep-set eyes and a dark moustache, he appeared unconcerned about Villa Sofia and the orphans. The Americans were drawing closer. Slowed down by the enormous feat of crossing the Apennines, their approach towards central Italy was causing strain on Herr Bauer and his men. He had no time to concern himself with any other matter. The gossip surrounding the orphans had faded away.

Now Rico and Bella could return to Monterini.

They left that evening as the wintry light waned. Don Philipe explained how vigilant they had to be. 'The Germans are digging out partisans like crazy. Since the Fosse Ardeatine, they're searching disused railway lines, broken-down shacks. Even homes of *contadini*. The order is ten for one. All over Italy innocent men are being shot or wounded.'

'The *partigiani* are the silent enemy of the Germans. We're to be feared as much as the Allied forces approaching from the south,' Rico said.

'We believe it's safer in Monterini now. Lieutenant Richardt is in Rome and *babbo* has made a friend of Herr Bauer. He's plying him and his men with drink, carving a safe passage back for you both,' Mateo added.

'Just don't forget your Catholic name.' Don Philippe cocked his head towards Bella, his usually twinkling eyes sombre. 'You are Maria Cristina. Bella doesn't exist, remember.'

She nodded.

After the deep silence surrounding Signor Pietro's smallholding, it was difficult to readjust to the blunt resonance of the Monterini dialect, the braying of donkeys, the Teutonic sounds of the German soldiers. Bella had all but forgotten the sensation that rose from her gut to her throat at the crunching of boots on cobblestones. That twist of fear. Italy had surrendered but the enemy still lived amongst them, drinking *Vino degli Angeli*, flirting with the *signorine*.

At any moment, life for her and her child could be whisked away by an innocent betrayal.

CHAPTER 10

J acobo often imagined what the end would be like. The crisp moments of dawn, the blush of sunset provided the backdrop for these mental rehearsals. Would they be betrayed or discovered, shot or beaten? Or would they survive, with Angelo's help, until the Allies marched further and further north? The Americans and British were taking their time. As the weeks meandered into months, Jacobo prayed for allied tanks to speed through the barren fields and quiet roads of Salone, sending German soldiers scattering to their homeland.

But they never came.

The inmates of La Gita tolerated their new lifestyle in the way one gets used to an unruly mother-in-law or an arthritic joint. They became proficient fishermen, collected basil, thyme, wild garlic and oregano, tearing off the leaves and eating the herbs raw. They picked nettles and dandelion, bluey-black juniper berries and wild mint. One morning Gianni Vetrulli even caught a rabbit. They skinned and cooked it, wondering if they would be forgiven for eating non-kosher meat. They clung to each other, intent on surviving, terrified of the rustle of leaves, the arrival of sudden footsteps. Jacobo saw the relief on their faces when dawn broke and they were still alive.

Every day Jacobo prayed Angelo would appear over the brow of the hill, lugging sacks of food and bags of essentials, always with a bottle of his famous wine hidden in the folds of his coat. Like a tailor with his thread, Angelo joined gaps between visits, making sense of the scattered days, the interminable starlit nights, and Jacobo waited for Angelo's visits with the fervour of a child yearning for the festivities of *Capodanno*. Angelo was the only tangible reality in an unknown world.

Jacobo waited daily by the Etruscan fountain, carved out of the rock behind La Gita, breathing deeply, listening for the sound of footsteps, the movement of Angelo's body through bracken. Nothing else mattered. Not even the writings of the Kabbalists soothed him.

'Sometimes I feel like giving up,' he whispered to Lea one night when only a handful of stars freckled the sky. They lay in their bed of hay, cushioned by shadows.

Lea pushed herself on to her elbows. 'Is this you talking, Jacobo Levi? The scholar, the dreamer? The one who was right about Mussolini? We're safe for now, aren't we? Angelo is risking his life for us, Mazzola too. How can you talk of giving up?'

Jacobo shrugged. 'I can't make sense of this, living like scavengers, merely surviving.'

'This isn't only about surviving. It's ensuring we will have a future for our girls.'

Jacobo slumped onto the hay and pulled the blanket Angelo had delivered over his shoulders. Part of him was missing and had been since the day they left Bella on her knees in the piazza, imploring him to look back. Without her to fight for, what was left? He imagined how Michele felt. Sometimes when he watched his son-in-law, skinny and wasted, with bloodshot eyes, he wanted to take his hand and tell him he understood. He too felt the pain, the rejection.

Michele had been lost to them for some time. He sat alone in a corner of the shack, chin resting on pulled-up knees, scratching the nits on his scalp, the fleas on his flesh, shaking his arms and shouting at the air before him. Gianni tried to force him to drink cups of chamomile tea, brewed from leaves of plants surrounding La Gita. He begged Angelo to ask Mazzola to supply vitamins, medicine, anything to wipe away the onset of madness. But to no avail. Michele's lips went from flaky white to pale blue. Strips of hair fell onto the floor forming patterns of yellow. He refused food and took to running outside at night, howling into the snowy darkness. They worried he would reveal their secret hiding place to any wanderer passing by.

Only Lea could calm him, stroking his hand whilst the wind whipped their faces.

'Come back inside, Michele, my dear.'

'Why did you betray me? I loved you.'

'Nobody's betrayed you here, Michele,' Lea answered. 'You're safe with us.'

And Jacobo could only watch from the doorway.

Swirls of snowflakes; frozen rivers.

The inhabitants of La Gita deteriorated. Jacobo wondered if Angelo noticed each time he visited, but if he did, he said nothing. He always embraced Jacobo before he left, promising to bring what he could to make the winter less painful. Sometimes there was a loaf of bread and Jacobo would watch the girls and Aldo Vetrulli devour it, pulling out chunks and slugging back wine from one of Angelo's bottles. They were like scavengers, with their filthy clothes, matted hair. Bones jutted from their skin and their eyes had a blank look. Luciana had almost entirely stopped talking and spent days curled up next to her mother, her long hair trailing down her back. Even Elena, once a chubby child, was a skinny remnant of her previous self.

Ghosts, Jacobo thought, that's what they all were now.

February was as bleak and dark as Jacobo could remember.

A thick layer of snow coated the earth. The window of the hovel was frosted, icicles hung from timber. They kept warm by wrapping themselves in coats lined with newspapers, old socks and by a fire they allowed themselves the indulgence of lighting once night came and they could bear the cold no longer. Michele stood at the window, watching the sun set over the canopy of pines and poplars, blood orange.

'Come and sit with us, Michele,' Jacobo implored, reaching out towards him.

Michele shook his head. Straw-like hair hung over his eyes in strands, his cheeks were sunken, his eyebrows thick and heavy.

'I have to get out of here.'

'It's not safe.'

'I can't wait.'

'We just have to get through winter. Then we'll be free.'

'I'll never be free. I see your daughter everywhere, in the trees outside, staring at me from the window. I can't escape her.' Michele twisted his body and shook his arm free. There was a madness to the red flecks around the pupils, the hissing sound he made. 'I have to find her, make her listen.'

'No one knows where she is,' Lea said.

'You risk your life, all our lives, if you leave,' Jacobo added.

'You call this a life? My life is finished and so is yours.' His eyes softened for a moment, as if he felt sorry for Jacobo. Then he moved to his makeshift bed in the corner of the room. He unfolded the coat he used for a pillow, grabbed his shoes and headed towards the door.

They tried to stop him.

Elena and Luciana grabbed his arms. Little Aldo tugged his legs. Gianni tried to block the door. But Michele kicked Aldo out of the way and freed himself from the girls' clutches, panting heavily, eyes glinting wildly. He stood by the open door, hair ablaze with the shimmers of remaining sunlight. Then he was gone, swallowed by the approaching night.

⁂

Bella stood at the corner of Via Cavour, hands cradling her belly. Wooden planks were stacked against the door of her father's bookshop, sheets of metal boarded the window. Every few days she came to check that her one remaining tie to the past had not been burnt down. In big black letters, above the sign La Libreria Speciale, was the word *ebreo*, Jew.

She looked around to ensure nobody was watching, crossed the road and peered through the gaps. Dust and grime streaked the glass. Through the slit she saw books scattered across the floor, pages torn and ragged; chairs and a smashed table. A wave of anger surged through her. And her baby kicked.

She bent forward to pick up the basket of fennel she had placed on the ground beside her. The metal cross Angelo insisted she wore, knocked against her breast. Bella hated wearing it, but Angelo had been determined.

'*Protezione*,' he'd declared. 'Think of it as armour over your heart.'

'It feels too strange, another betrayal.'

'It belonged to my mother.'

Angelo dug his hands deep inside his trouser pocket and pulled out his mother's old rosary, broken on the day Rico and Bella were born. The beads, sparkling in the sunlight, had rolled along Via Meravigliosa and wedged like coloured jewels between the cobblestones of the street. Angelo had collected every single one and rethreaded them. He placed the rosary in Bella's hand.

Moved by the simplicity of his action, she put the silver cross around her neck and placed the beads in her pocket. Angelo believed they would protect her; an ideology so different from her own. She was a circus performer balancing on a tightrope, tiptoeing from moment to moment, never feeling safe. A sudden move could tip her off. Her only faith was in the heartbeat she was carrying; her tie to the future.

Checking nobody was watching, she blew a kiss to her father's bookshop. With the basket of fennel swinging on her arm, she walked towards the bridge joining the new town to the old. A streak of starlings performed hoops above her head.

She stopped at the top of the steps leading to the piazza and gazed at the spires of Monterini, the tiled rooftops glowing in the sunlight. Mustard-coloured fields stretched around the village, a desert surrounding an oasis. She always caught her breath at the sight of Monterini with the medieval houses, the cathedral and the synagogue perched on the golden *tufo* rock like a miniature town in a children's book of fairy tales.

A smell of sulphur.

The familiar wave of anxiety that something was about to happen.

In front of her rose the ancient, strange-looking phantom who had appeared and reappeared for as long as she could remember. Tanaquilla's mouth was twisted into an ugly smile. Bella lifted her gaze to the eyes, half silver, half blue. Tears stretched over Tanaquilla's cheeks to the jawline. Bella tried to scream but no sound escaped her lips.

Then she saw him.

The soldier was waiting for her at the bottom of the steps his gun pointing straight at her. In another time, another place, she might have found him handsome. His body was slim, aching with muscles. Thick, blonde hair parted to one side, lay smooth against his scalp. With its long nose and sculptured bones, his face reminded her of pictures she had seen of Michelangelo's David.

Steely eyes flickered with satisfaction, green like blades of grass, just like hers. When the orphans left Monterini, she'd worried he might try to hunt her down as if she were one of the deer in the woods beyond the village. As winter faded into spring and the memory of him dimmed, she thought he must have left with Lieutenant Richardt's battalion. But no. He had found her. She was his treasure, his prize.

'*Halt*,' he shrieked.

'*Ich bin Italienisch.*' She had picked up a few German words and expressions from Marianne and Camilla. Would he think she was German or Austrian, hiding in these parts just like her orphans? Trembling she dug her hand deep into her pocket and fished out the rosary, shaking it at him. 'I'm Catholic.'

'*Ne. Ne. Nicht möglich. Du bist Jude.*' He screamed the word Jew. It reverberated against the surrounding houses.

'I have papers.' She delved into her bag, searching desperately for the false documents. What could she say to persuade him to lower his gun, to make him believe her? 'This is my village. I've always lived here. My name is Maria Cristina Ghione.' She stretched out her arm, her papers flapping in the breeze. She descended the steps towards him. A twisted grin crossed his face. It reminded her of the contorted smile on Tanaquilla's lips moments ago.

She heard her name.

'Bella.'

For a split second she was confused. But it was too late, she had turned towards the familiar voice.

The soldier was beckoning someone, his voice menacing. '*Komm. Komm hier.*'

A shadow shuffled forward, a face so pale, skin hanging from bones. There was nothing left of Michele, he was a fragment of the boy who had saved her the day of the *maturità*. A dirty, broken fragment hiding nightmares in his vacant eyes.

'*Das ist sie, das ist sie?*' The rifle swayed backwards and forwards, reflections of sunlight glistening on the sleek metal. It was pointing at Bella then the shadow.

'That's her.' Michele's voice was ragged, yet sharpened with rage or fear, she wasn't sure which. He stumbled towards the soldier, dragging his feet, pointing towards her. 'That's my wife, that's Bella Levi.'

Bella's arms encircled her swollen belly; fear so strong she thought she would vomit. She reached for the iron rail.

'I'm going to die; we're going to die. Tanaquilla, where are you?'

The spectre had gone. There was only the soldier and Michele. Mad, broken Michele.

'He's not my husband, he's lying. He's the Jew. I'm not. Shoot him, shoot him.' It was as if someone else was speaking, a voice she didn't recognise, from the most desperate part of herself.

A sharp crack. Then another. A third gunshot split the air.

She was suspended in mid-air. The village swam around her, the houses bled into one another. She was tumbling, bumping her head against the stone steps, bones cracking, skin tearing. Was this what death felt like? Then the face of her mother emerged amidst the haze of pain; the face she had seen in the framed wedding photograph clinging on to her father's arm. And behind that other Bella was *nonno* Cosimo, arms outstretched.

A thud. She had landed at the feet of the soldier, crumpled, a puppet without strings. The soldier's leg shook, just like the calves she used to see on Angelo's smallholding when they were due to be slaughtered. Were her legs shaking too?

The leg of the soldier disappeared from view. She heard his boot crunching on the steps. Saliva trickled from her mouth to the paving stones. Pain swept from head to ankles. Michele was slumped next to her, his breath quiet. She tasted blood. It was everywhere, on her lips, oozing from Michele's jaw, on his chest. Her arm lay across his torso. It was drenched in blood, their blood.

'Look what you've done, Michele.' A silent thread of words.

Around her she heard shrieks and yells. Voices in German, cries in Italian. Someone held her hand.

A smell of sulphur permeated her nostrils. Tanaquilla was kneeling in front of her, face withered with centuries of sadness.

'There's a subtle magic in this town.' It seemed as if the words floated from Tanaquilla's motionless lips. 'Some like you and your father sense it. He tried to fight it. You didn't listen.'

Bella's eyes were flickering. She had fought so hard, for herself and her baby. Now she was tired. This life had beaten her.

Strong arms folded themselves around her, stroking her. Somebody was lifting her up. Hot breath stained her face. But she only saw the figure that had flown in and out of her life, warning her, protecting her.

'Who are you?'

'A piece of you.'

'There are so many pieces of me. I'm broken.'

'So come, let's put the pieces together.'

A gentle wave spread through her. Bella closed her eyes.

CHAPTER 11

The bullet had not hit Bella's heart.

Thanks to the metal cross, she was unconscious but alive. With the help of Dottore Mazzola, Angelo and Rico got her to the makeshift German hospital on the outskirts of the village. A caesarean was performed, and the baby screamed herself into the terror that was their lives. Another Levi daughter delivered to an unconscious mother; Fortuna, the lucky one, the survivor.

Immediately after the shooting, Angelo went to Herr Bauer, arms laden with bottles of wine. No one appreciated *Vino degli Angeli* more than the Germans. It was the smell of sunshine, the honeyed taste of ripe fruit, the soft fizz at the back of the throat. Placing the bottles on the table that used to be his before the house was requisitioned, Angelo begged Herr Bauer to help him. Maria Cristina Ghione his daughter-in-law had been mistaken for a Jew and shot. They feared for her life, feared for her child. Could he help them?

Herr Bauer listened to Angelo's plea with pursed lips and stern eyes. He rose from his chair, paced up and down the stone kitchen, then came over to Angelo and patted his arm. Herr Bauer searched Angelo's face as if he were looking for a hint, a hidden expression, an unexpected sign. But he must have found none. In his smattering of Italian, he whispered, 'I'll deal with it, don't worry.'

Angelo inhaled deeply. He wanted to hug Herr Bauer, for not asking questions, for accepting what he said. When he enquired whom the other dead person could possibly be, Angelo shook his head and raised his arms in surprise, hoping Herr Bauer would believe he had never set eyes on Michele before. If Herr Bauer suspected that Michele was Bella's Jewish husband, Angelo would be arrested, perhaps shot. Then what would happen to Bella? And how would Jacobo cope hidden away in La Gita without Angelo to protect him?

When Angelo arrived at the hospital, he found Rico crouched over Bella's bed, his finger curled around a lock of her hair. It struck him how peaceful Bella looked; skin creamy white, features calm despite the bandage over her shoulder where the bullet had entered.

Rico by contrast had shrivelled in the space of several hours, as if his frame had sunk inwards. Angelo stood at the back of the room twisting his hat in his hand, listening to his son tell Bella about the maroon of the sunset, the rustling of the olive branches. Angelo was certain she heard when Rico described the sounds her baby made, the touch of her hands, her eyes cornflower blue.

He noticed the way her eyelids flickered when Rico uttered the name Maria Cristina, as if she understood. They had all become accustomed to calling Bella by her Catholic name. At first it got caught between Angelo's teeth, hovering on his lips, the name Bella fighting to be heard. With time, Maria Cristina began to represent a new version of Bella, a quieter, more distant person who sat in the house knitting with Santina or patiently teaching Angelo the Italian alphabet so that he could proudly declare to the town that he was no longer *inalfabeto*. He was a *contadino* who could read.

But Angelo knew Rico's soul whispered Bella. And he knew she heard.

Rico looked up, his face aching with sadness. A flicker of defiance crossed his bloodshot eyes. 'She'll survive, *babbo*, I know she will. In the meantime, Mazzola's found a wet nurse to feed the baby. She'll come and live with you.' He walked towards the crib at the back of the room and placed Fortuna in Angelo's arms.

'Lucky to be born but unlucky to be born now,' Angelo said. He yearned to go back to his smallholding with his grapes and pigs, raise his hands to the sky and scream at God.

'There's never a right time for a child to be born,' Rico replied. 'Each generation has its own troubles.' Then he added, 'She may not be my child. Bella wasn't sure who the father was.'

Another blow. What a strange world we live in, Angelo thought.

'But we'll love her regardless,' Rico continued, face like stone. He had aged overnight. Little creases lined his lips, his skin grey in the hospital lamplight. 'She'll be ours in every way, that's what she deserves. We won't mention it again, you understand, not to anyone.'

Angelo looked down at the child in his arms, searching her face for traces of his son; the Ghione full cheeks, Santana's wide chin, his thick eyebrows. He would have even rejoiced to see his own pockmarked skin. There was nothing. A shimmer of gold peppered her rust-coloured hair, her nose was long and slim like Jacobo's, pointed at the end like Bella's. Fortuna was a Levi, there was no doubt. But with eyes the colour of Monterini summer skies, she was clearly Michele's daughter.

An overwhelming feeling of tenderness rinsed through Angelo. He didn't care who the father was, she would be his grandchild and he would love her.

A few days after the shooting, Mazzola arrived at the house in the Fratta. From the open doorway, Angelo saw him mount the steps and stop at the edge of the veranda. The doctor glanced across at the house next door, as if deciding whether it was safe to continue. He appeared thinner than Angelo remembered.

When he noticed Angelo, Mazzola reached up and removed his hat from his head revealing a small bald patch. He lowered his gaze.

'I did everything, but there was no hope. She caught an infection from the wound, I couldn't save her.'

Bella had left them.

All that remained was the tender dark.

Angelo opened his mouth to speak. No words could express the emptiness. He beckoned the doctor into the sitting room at the back of Jacobo's house. The evening sunlight from the valley cast slim shadows across the floor. The Etruscan tombs blinked inky black in the fading light.

Santina was sitting on the rocking chair holding Fortuna. Angelo took the baby from her. He placed his nose against her cheek and inhaled the sweet smell of the newborn. He felt her tiny heartbeat against his chest. Her survival was the one good thing in a world full of chaos.

'Another orphan child from a dead mother.' Santina wiped her nose with the back of her hand. 'My poor Rico, how will he manage?'

'Don Philipe's with him,' Mazzola said. 'He's reciting the vigil for the deceased. He'll deal with the funeral arrangements.'

They stared in silence at the olive trees dusting the hills. Jacobo had always loved this view. Angelo shivered at the thought of Jacobo hiding in the shack at La Gita, hungry, frightened and unaware that he had gained a grandchild, lost a daughter. A strange sensation washed through him. He could have sworn he heard Jacobo shouting at him, saying no Catholic funeral for my Bella.

Angelo walked into the kitchen and returned with a bottle of *vino* and three tumblers. With a shaky hand, he filled the glasses, passed one to Santina and one to Mazzola. He clinked their glasses.

'To our Bella. May she rest in peace. Amen.'

'To Bella. Amen.'

Angelo placed his glass on the table and indicated to the doctor to sit. He cleared his throat, trying to form sentences in his mind. He was a man of the earth, what did he know compared to this brave doctor? But of one thing he was certain, he couldn't bury Bella as a Catholic.

'I want to bury her in the Jewish cemetery.' The words flew out in one long breath.

'That's impossible. She'll be buried in the Catholic cemetery, like all Catholics.' Mazzola's eyebrows lifted into a V shape.

'She belongs in the Jewish one, with her mother.'

'But her papers state she is Catholic,' Santina interjected. 'We have to register her death at the commune.'

'Forget register, forget normal. We'll bury her where we choose. At night, alone.'

'You sound like your crazy son! *Il partigiano*.' There was a hushed silence. Santina had mouthed the forbidden word. She was staring at Angelo as if she no longer recognised him. Boldness, determination were not qualities he generally displayed.

'Say something, *dottore*.' Santina tugged at the sleeve of the doctor's jacket.

'Firstly, that word is forbidden for all our sakes.' A sweat had broken out on the doctor's brow. He turned to Angelo, his eyes pleading. 'You're an exceptional man, Signor Ghione, but you're putting yourself in grave danger. You have German soldiers living in your own house, next door. How can you keep this hidden?'

Heat rose to Angelo's neck and flooded his cheeks. He was not exceptional; he was a peasant who could barely read or write. He owed so much to Bella and Jacobo, he wanted to bury her in the way she would have wanted.

'She was teaching me to read.' Angelo's eyelids were heavy. 'She has helped me and so has her father. It's what they would want, I feel it deep in here.' He touched his chest with his fist. 'This evening, I will drown Herr Bauer and his men in wine. I'll bury her in the early hours with moonlight as my guide.'

'Jacobo would have wanted it, I suppose,' Santina squeezed her palms. 'Maria Cristina never felt comfortable as a Catholic. She always hated the mass, all that kneeling and praying.'

The doctor placed his hat on his head. 'I cannot be part of it, but I will drop round some sleeping tablets. Anyone who has these dropped into a glass of wine will be knocked out till morning.'

When he reached the door, he turned and with a strained expression told Angelo and Santina to watch out for their son. Before Mazzola had left the hospital, Rico had begged him for his hunting rifle then threatened him. He wanted to find the soldier who'd shot Bella, and Mazzola was worried for his safety. Rico had a wild look in his eyes, the doctor said.

'Don't let him be part of this funeral,' he begged. 'Rico can't be trusted. We all know what happens if one German soldier is killed, don't we?'

Angelo raised his eyes to the ceiling. Was God playing a game with him? All he needed now was for Rico to lose his mind and shoot the solider.

When Mazzola left them, Angelo paid a visit to Fernando Pratesi, previously Mario Celeste from the villa. He was living with the bakers Paolo and Claudio Zerulli. Angelo knew he had been involved in the operation Exit Cloud Rico had organised to spirit the orphans away from Monterini. Fernando was supposed to travel with them, but like Bella second thoughts had plagued him. Once the orphans and Georges were safely across the border, Fernando returned to Monterini.

When Angelo saw him in the streets, he averted his gaze. It had been the same for Maria Cristina, his Bella. People left them alone. Nobody asked questions. Gossip had died. Secrets and untruths had transformed the lives of the villagers. All that was left was a passage of fear where you trod a thin line, knowing that one foot dusting the wrong cobblestone could lead to disaster.

When Angelo knocked on the door of the bakery, he was aware of this. But his need for the help of Fernando was paramount. Paolo opened the door.

Angelo removed his hat and was kneading it in his hands. 'My daughter-in-law was shot. She died this morning.' How hard it was to utter those words; it took him several attempts to make Paolo understand. The baker nodded, put his finger to his lips and led him down a stone corridor to a room at the back of the bakery. Sacks of flour lined the walls and covered the floor. Paolo shut the door and motioned to Angelo to sit down on a wooden stool in the corner. Too agitated to obey, Angelo again tried to speak. Paolo placed his hand on Angelo's shoulder.

'*Aspetta un attimino.*'

He disappeared to return several moments later with Claudio and their lodger Fernando Pratesi. Angelo grasped Fernando's hand. It felt light and bony in his grasp.

'I need your help. I have to bury my daughter-in-law Maria Cristina Ghione.'

Even here Angelo could not say her real name. Fernando's gaze was fixed on the uneven, chalk-coloured tiles of the floor. When he finally looked up, Angelo noticed the trembling of his jaw, the mauve patches staining the skin under his lashes.

'But I want to do it properly.' Angelo's head swung backwards in the direction of the Jewish cemetery. 'With her

311

mother, in that cemetery over there, the way her father would have wanted, you understand, the way she would have wanted. Because, despite everything, she was a Jew at heart. We still had a *Seder* for the last Passover. In secret. We did it together, even though we didn't understand. She explained it all…' Angelo's voice trailed off into the distance.

Fernando shifted nervously from one foot to the other, eyelids blinking furiously.

'Please will you help me bury her? I can't let her lay in the Catholic cemetery, unknown, unwanted. It has to be over there, in the Jewish one. Or I'll tie her down with bricks and sink her in the Piccolina, God help me.'

'You mean you want to dig up her mother's grave?' Fernando spoke for the first time, his voice like a rusty lock being forced open.

'And with prayer. Your prayers.'

'Our prayers are said with ten men present, in normal times.'

'But these are not normal times. Will you help me?'

'*Sì.* I'll bury Maria Cristina. She was a fine woman, a courageous teacher. She even took me once to visit her mother's grave.'

Angelo's gaze shifted heavenwards. He made the sign of the cross, the word *grazie* formed a pattern on his lips.

'But I am a partisan. I don't believe in these prayers. I don't even know if I can remember them.'

'But you believe in history? For history's sake, let's bury her the way your religion says.'

True to his word, Mazzola returned with sleeping tablets wrapped in a linen cloth. He handed them to Angelo. Averted eyes, silent lips but the extra pressure of the doctor's hand on Angelo's arm meant more than words. The soldiers next door would sleep well, Angelo reassured himself. His wine, the Wine

312

of the Angels, together with Dottore Mazzola's pills would cast its spell.

The moon sparkled that night. It flickered through the clouds, paving the way along crumbling pathways to the Jewish cemetery. Dottore Mazzola was waiting for them on the road outside the village walls. Bella's body lay wrapped in the back of a car. Angelo thought it better not to ask to whom it belonged. Tenderly they lifted her out and laid her over Rodeo's back. As if the donkey knew his load was precious, he waited patiently without snorting or stamping his feet.

'My son, where is he?'

A crumpled expression swept across the doctor's face, a mixture of embarrassment and shame.

'With Don Philippe at the monastery. We decided it would be best to sedate him too, safer for him, for all of us.'

'Is he well, doctor?' Santina said.

'Sì, Signora Santina, he will be. But he's in shock and he's angry and it's not a good combination. We have to watch out for his safety, make sure he doesn't do anything that could endanger himself or any of us.'

Angelo's eyes narrowed as he looked at the doctor. He hadn't given anything away, but Angelo wondered, not for the first time, how involved Mazzola was in Rico's movement. A quiet player, subtly distancing himself, but clearly involved. He had appeared regularly at the orphanage to check the children. He came weekly to the house in the Fratta with medication, syringes and bandages. He never asked whom they were for. Here he was delivering them a corpse for a secret Jewish burial and, together with Don Philippe, dispensing sleeping tablets to an unpredictable member lest he lost control and betrayed them all.

Mazzola handed Angelo a small black key. 'The key to the cemetery. It's the only one we have.'

'*Grazie, dottore.*'

'Good luck to you all, go quickly, go safely.'

The doctor jumped back into the car, the fumes circling around Angelo, Santina and Fernando. Under a canopy of stars, they led Rodeo to the iron gate on the curve of the Rome–Florence thoroughfare. Monterini was sleeping. No drunken soldiers stumbled back to their lodgings. No need to explain the unusual bundle flung across Rodeo's back.

Twenty-three years after she was laid to rest, Bella Levi's grave was pummelled and pounded, the earth folded away to make room for her daughter. Fernando had metamorphosed into the Mario of a former era. A black skullcap was perched on his head. He was draped in a white prayer shawl. 'My father's,' he declared proudly to Angelo.

Into the still night he breathed the words of the Hebrew prayer: '*Yitgadal ve yitkadash sh'mei rabba.*'

Clods of earth were thrown over Bella's body. Santina blew a kiss into the air. '*Arrivederci,* Bella.'

'Goodbye,' Angelo repeated. He raised his gaze to the blue-black skies, the lavender stars and wondered which God was looking over them; the Catholic or the Jewish one?

CHAPTER 12

Nobody knew where Angelo went on his 'hunting trips'. He always took a different route to La Gita. Sometimes he meandered along the Rome–Florence road, turning inland towards Favore and cutting cross-country to join the Etruscan *cavi* down by the Piccolina. Occasionally he followed the *cavi* all the way from Monterini, snaking across the countryside on his donkey.

The days were warmer, the evenings longer. Jonquils and poppies lined the paths. Forget-me-nots sneaked out of cracks in the stones. The smell of fennel and rosemary lingered on his nostrils. Angelo guided Rodeo along the hazardous Etruscan pathways as far as the Roman sundial carved into the ground. He tied Rodeo to the trunk of a sycamore tree and ventured the remainder of the journey by foot, balancing sacks of food and medicines on his shoulders. He trod carefully and rustled the branches of the trees, the way he and Jacobo planned, so that Jacobo would know it was him.

Jacobo was usually waiting for him. Sometimes he would sit on a tree trunk, at others he would kneel by the river, running his fingers through the water. Mostly he walked as far as the Etruscan fountain at the entrance of La Gita, scouring the horizon until he spotted his friend. Then Jacobo would wave, a smile stretching across his mouth, his eyes creased with joy. Angelo knew how much Jacobo depended on his visits, that without him the two families in La Gita would shrivel and wilt like flowers deprived of sunshine.

That day Jacobo was at none of the usual spots.

At the entrance to La Gita, Angelo ducked beneath branches laden with pink buds. He placed the sacks on the ground, rubbed his shoulders then looked around. The evening air was thick with the smell of peach blossom.

Still no Jacobo.

Angelo walked towards the shack. He stopped at the entrance, breath caught in his throat. The door hung on one side, straw and pieces of old newspaper were strewn across the floor as if kicked by uncaring shoes. Cups and plates Angelo had managed to extract from the two houses in Monterini without Santina's knowledge, lay shattered over the floor.

'Jacobo,' Angelo shouted.

Only the river heard him, and the old walls filled with memories and secrets. Maybe they had changed location? He turned and ran back to the ruined mill. Here too, silence greeted him, dust and rotting beams. A sweet sickly taste filled his mouth. It had never occurred to him that Jacobo would be caught and whisked away.

'I have to find them,' he whispered to the cobwebs, the mice droppings. 'They must be here somewhere.'

He returned to the shack. Kneeling down by the fireplace he fingered the ash in the grate. It was flaky and fragile. Just like their lives.

The sun slid behind the hills, a blushing halo of crimson. The cool, evening breeze rustled the layers of dust on the kitchen floor.

'I've failed them,' Angelo whispered to the ghosts of La Gita.

When Angelo arrived home for dinner, the streets of occupied Monterini were deserted. The reminiscence of spring had dissipated into the cold night air. He fed Rodeo in the *cantina* by the San Gianni path. Rodeo munched the hay from his hand, and Angelo rubbed the animal's nose. His *asino*, his loyal donkey, had accompanied him for months up and down treacherous terrain. All in vain.

Angelo shut the stable door and walked up the steps to Capo Bagno. He passed two German officers at the entrance of a small square. They smiled at him, stamped their feet and stuck out their arms in the Roman salute.

'*Sieg Heil.*'

'*Buona sera.*'

Unaccustomed to having their salute ignored, the soldiers' eyes met. But they said nothing. They recognised Angelo. He was famous for his *Vino degli Angeli.* The oldest German patted Angelo on the back.

'*Buon vino.*' He spoke with a thick Aryan accent. Angelo wondered whether one of them had discovered Jacobo. He kept his gaze fixed on the ground as he walked away. He climbed the steps to the porch. The door to the house with grey shutters was open. Herr Bauer stood in the doorway, eyes flitting from Angelo's face to the sacks in his hand. Angelo's heart banged so fiercely in his chest, he wondered whether Herr Bauer could hear. The German's expression hardened, his hand reached up and twisted his moustache. Again, his eyes moved downwards and rested on the sacks as if trying to work out what they contained. Then he tilted his head sharply towards the house with the black shutters. 'Go inside, Herr Ghione.' And with that he turned on his heels and disappeared behind the closed door.

Angelo wiped the sweat from his upper lip. His hand was shaking. He stepped into the kitchen. Santina stood by the dresser, face flushed, fingers playing frantically with the apron strings around her waist. She looked thinner; her hair tinged with silver. This robust woman who used to load carts with hay and show off her muscles at the festivals of San Guiseppe and San Rocco, for which only the round, buxom girls were chosen, now reminded Angelo of a fragile bird.

'When did you get so thin?' he asked.

'What's the matter with you?' Santina yelled, then lowered her voice. This wasn't how you behaved these days. The shouting and clamour of the past had been replaced by a silence laced with unsaid words. 'I've been worried sick. It's late! And you're worried about my waistline! No wonder I look thin. I'm starving to death waiting for you...' Her voice trailed off into the night.

Angelo slumped onto a chair. The strain of the past few hours had robbed him of energy. He was numb through to his bones.

'What is it, Angelino? If I didn't know you better, I'd swear you've been crying.' Her eyes rested on the sacks he was clutching. 'What's this?'

When he did not reply, Santina grabbed one of the sacks from his hands. She opened it and pulled out the cough syrup and bandages, aspirins, plasters, writing paper and pens. Half a dozen eggs were wrapped individually in sackcloth. Angelo looked up at her, imploring her not to ask.

Rico walked into the kitchen carrying Fortuna. He had aged since Bella died. His cheeks were sucked in and premature grey streaked his hair. He looked at the contents on the table. A thick vein bulged at the side of his neck. His gaze met his parents; a triangle of worried eyes.

Rico placed Fortuna in Santina's arms and began to collect the contents of the sack. 'These things can't be found here. We'll put them in the baby's crib. You mustn't allow the wet nurse near it. I'll get rid of them tonight. We'll have other uses for them.'

'But they were for...' Angelo's eyes leaked tears.

'Don't say anything,' Rico interrupted, jerking his head

towards the wall separating them from the Germans next door. Then in a gentler tone. 'Don't worry, *babbo*, I'll find out where they've gone, I promise.'

'Jacobo doesn't even know about her.' Angelo reached for the baby's hand, dangling around her grandmother's waist. Rico's stare hushed him to silence. The walls had ears. The roof and the floor were new spies. Nobody was safe, not even in their own homes.

❦

Jacobo and Elena were sitting at the entrance of the shack. It was early morning. The sun had not yet penetrated through the leafy vegetation surrounding La Gita. It had been a while since Angelo's last visit. Supplies were low. Luciana could barely lift her head off her straw pillow. She was wilting like sunflowers at dusk.

They needed some aspirin for her fever. Milk, eggs. Santina's jam, fresh bread, a packet of cigarettes were delicacies Jacobo dreamt of but would never ask for. He knew how hard it was for Angelo to bring fresh supplies. Most importantly, he needed the company of the outside world. He yearned for it from the moment Angelo left until he returned. His visits gave Jacobo the strength to keep going.

There was a rustling sound in the bushes. Elena smiled. For a moment she resembled the happy, chatty child Jacobo remembered, not the wasted, ghostlike creature she'd become.

'That's him.' Her voice was low. Jacobo cocked his head to one side. It was too early for Angelo. He rarely arrived before the afternoon or early evening. He held his breath. The old, familiar sensation was churning inside him. It had been several years since he'd felt it. Jacobo sniffed the air. Blossom from the peach tree reached his nostrils.

'*Pericolo, stai attento*. It's harmful, beware.'

The same words that had warned him about Mussolini all those years ago were here once more, their presence real and tangible.

He sniffed again. Now the smell of sulphur, like a thick fog overwhelmed him. Something was wrong. He knew it. He sensed it.

Within seconds soldiers sprung through the vegetation, leaping green tigers ready to pounce, their rifled arms perched at shoulder height. They were breathing heavily, as if they had been running. Or maybe they were afraid. But their eyes betrayed no fear; they glistened with hope. The moment was suspended into a number of endless moments, a numb nightmare that replayed itself over and again.

An order was barked into the air.

There were three of them. They must have come by way of the *cavi*, along the tracks Jacobo used to take with Gianni and Angelo as children. It would have been impossible for these soldiers, with their rifles, black boots and smart green jackets to come across them by chance as they rambled through the countryside in search of a suitable hunting spot. They must have known where to find them.

The soldiers were yelling in German, fingers poised over the trigger of their rifles. Jacobo didn't understand what they were saying, but he placed his arms above his head and nodded to Elena to do the same. Jacobo could see she was holding her breath, in a huge effort to contain herself. With the butt of their guns, the soldiers indicated to Elena and Jacobo to turn around.

'That's it,' Jacobo thought. 'They're going to kill us.' He was shaking so much he could barely move. Had they not been careful enough? Was Angelo followed? An image of Angelo ambling along on Rodeo, humming to himself without any knowledge that a platoon of German soldiers was lying in wait flashed across Jacobo's mind. Perhaps Bella too was in grave danger? He squeezed his eyes shut and tried to picture his daughter. But Bella the adult had vanished. All he could conjure up was the child with grass green eyes and fiery hair staring at him with that familiar stubborn expression.

Barking incomprehensible orders into the air, one of the soldiers kicked open the door and pushed Jacobo and Elena inside. Rosa and Gianni slowly lifted their arms up to the sky and little Aldo stood between them grasping his father's shirt. Lea was staring at Jacobo with a look that combined shock and disbelief. Luciana lay on her bed of newspapers and cobwebs, feverish eyes begging Jacobo to save them all.

But he couldn't.

It seemed they walked for kilometers, huddled together like frightened goats, brushing against the thin flesh of their neighbour in search of comfort. It had been almost a year since Jacobo had ventured further than the Etruscan fountain. Spring had cloaked the area with jade, without a whisper of its arrival. A verdant carpet spread across the hills; jonquils, daffodils and crocuses sprouted out of the earth in a startling display of pinks, blues and yellows. The banks along the *cavi* were splattered with poppies.

He breathed it in. Thankfully there are flowers to remind us of colour in this dark world, he thought. A soldier stuck the butt of his rifle between Jacobo's shoulder blades, forcing him to keep moving.

They took it in turns to support Luciana. Jacobo carried her on his back. When he tired, Vetrulli took her in his arms. If the path became too rugged, too steep, Lea and Jacobo balanced her between them, supporting her small frame in the crook of their arm.

'At least they didn't shoot us,' Jacobo whispered to Lea

321

as the sun finally burst through the bracken indicating the approach to the open road.

'Maybe we'd be better off if they had. Who knows what lies ahead?'

A soldier barked an order in German.

A black rifle spun through the air and landed with a thud on Lea's skull. She crumpled to the ground, drops of her blood splattering the soldier's feet. A thick, red wave seeped from the gash in her head. A groan escaped her lips.

Jacobo was rooted to the spot. Overcome by cowardice or fear he couldn't move a muscle. Gianni lunged towards Lea, but the soldier stopped him with his rifle.

More orders in German. A gunshot, then another.

Lea's chest rose and fell. Her body quivered, then was still. Strangled sobs escaped from Elena's lips. Luciana was screaming, loudly, uncontrollably. The sun flooded through the ever-frequent gaps in the trees, highlighting their hair with streaks of amber.

A third gunshot. Luciana let out a piercing cry, her legs buckled under her at the force of the shot. Jacobo was trembling so much he thought his own limbs would fold under him. Choked by soundless sobs, he fixed his gaze on the mustard yellow path of daffodils lining the *cavi*. A soldier hitched his rifle under Jacobo's chin, forcing him to look up. His hair was dirty brown, plastered over his forehead. Lips spread into a grin; eyelids blinked rapidly. He was about the same age as Bella, a mere twenty-three. In basic Italian he barked out the words, 'Go or we kill. No looking, no looking.'

Jacobo didn't look.

He wanted to be bold, to stand up to these men who had just killed his wife and stepdaughter. He wished he could grasp the rifles from their hands, slam them in their faces. But he merely shuffled past Lea, past Luciana, sickened by his own cowardice.

An army truck was parked by the entrance to the *cavi*. An

officer in his late thirties, with a thin moustache and stubble on his chin, jumped down from the driver's seat. Polished heels clicked to attention with the grace of dancers; arms glided in front in perfect timing.

The soldiers spoke to the officer in German and pointed back towards where Jacobo's wife and stepdaughter lay. Vomit filled Jacobo's mouth. He glanced up at the others. Gianni stared at the ground, Rosa's chin wobbled, her fingers clinging to Aldo's hand. Elena squeezed her eyelids tightly shut; her teeth dug into her lower lip.

Jacobo peeled his eyes away. How fleeting a moment is, he thought, nonsensical in the normal world. Often, he had waited for moments to pass. How spoilt he was. A moment was vital, like each individual cell in the body, a tiny cog in the wheel that was their life.

It only took one moment, on that spring afternoon with the smell of green grass.

'You have enemies. Even amongst your own type.' The officer spoke in perfect Italian with a lilting accent, almost as if he were singing. Jacobo assumed he was from the Tyrol where the inhabitants considered themselves Austrian rather than Italian. He placed his lips close to Jacobo's ears and sung out the words. 'You think you're free. Only we are free.'

Jacobo detected the scent of grappa mixed with garlic on the man's breath. He averted his gaze.

'You're cowards, all of you. You can't even look me in the eye.' The officer sent a flat globule of spit flying onto the bridge of Jacobo's nose. It was warm and glue-like. It reminded Jacobo of the leeches he used to throw at Angelo when they collected them to sell to old Dottore Vetrulli, squirmy and sickening.

The globule slithered onto Jacobo's cheek. The officer nodded with satisfaction. Jacobo held his breath. Would the soldier shoot him too?

'You consider yourself Italian, do you? Only we from the Alto Adige are true to the German cause.' So, he was from South Tyrol, Jacobo had guessed correctly. 'Just get into the truck all of you. You're not worth the time of day.'

Jacobo reached for Elena's trembling hand. He placed his other palm under her elbow and helped her climb into the truck. He heard the scratchy puffs of breath she was trying so hard to control. He stroked the back of her wrist with his thumb. But still he couldn't bear to look at her.

It was spring green with dabs of yellow jonquils and blood red poppies, the day Lea and Luciana died.

CHAPTER 13

Rico moved quickly.

He had to be careful. If you are a Hebrew partisan, only declare the Hebrew part, you will be treated better by the *fascisti*. That's what they spouted in party meetings. But not beyond the borders. The stories filtering back were spattered with horror. Rico knew the Levis and Vetrullis wouldn't stand a chance once they were out of Italy.

He acted almost without thinking, wondering where his desire to save Jacobo came from. Was it a nostalgic love of his childhood memories? After all he owed him nothing, certainly not worth putting himself in danger for. But Fortuna's future was at stake. He owed it to her to deliver a grandfather, stepsisters. They had taken away her mother, they wouldn't wipe out her whole family. He had a suspicion the baby was Michele's, it was the eyes, blue like summer skies, a glint of yellow amidst the orange hue of her hair. He searched in vain for the Ghione strong chin, the charcoal eyes and olive complexion. She was Michele's child. But Michele was dead. Fortuna was Bella's and he would care for her, love her, treat her like a daughter.

He crossed the quiet streets of the Ghetto, lowering his eyes when he saw the green and grey uniforms flit past him. There were Germans in many of the houses here. He had not quite understood how his father had managed to keep Jacobo's house in the Fratta free from Monterini's guests. Perhaps because

Angelo was a famous winemaker? Rico knew he kept everyone sweet with an ample supply of bottles. Or maybe the powers that be knew where it was safe to lodge the Germans.

Don Philippe opened the door of the San Benedetto Monastery, nestling at the junction where the alleyways of Capo Bagno merged with the Fratta.

'I've been expecting you.'

'You've heard already?'

Don Philippe nodded. He scanned the street to ensure Rico had not been followed. He ushered him inside and bolted the heavy, wooden door.

'If they've crossed the border into France there's nothing we can do.'

'There has to be something within the movement.'

'It's too late.'

'We get the authorities involved, the police, local government, even go directly to the home office. They knew about the children. They knew we had the orphanage. They closed their eyes. And Jacobo has no political convictions, he has that in his favour.'

'But it's different now. The Germans are infiltrating every corner, every house. They hate them as much as the fascists hate us. Our hands are tied. Any Italian official discovered helping Jews will be executed on the spot.'

Rico shook his head. 'I'm not so sure. Look, they've retreated in the south. It's a matter of days before they're finished. The Americans are almost here.' He stroked his chin, deep in thought. 'We'll go to Grazzi,' he said after a while.

'You mean the chief of police for the Salone area? He's a committed fascist. A friend of Erich Priebke. He'll never help us, and it could be dangerous.'

'He grew up here. He was a friend of my father and Jacobo. He used to come back regularly to buy books from Jacobo's shop.'

It was the first time Rico detected an expression of anguish cross the priest's face. Even during the months at Villa Sofia, he had remained cheerful and optimistic. When the orphans were hidden in the monastery, he never betrayed tension or fear. His eyes continued to twinkle and his lips to smile.

'The Italian *fascisti* are intolerant of the priesthood, Rico.' Don Philippe fiddled with the rosary beads around his waist. 'If they feel we're acting against them, I'll be shot on the spot.'

Rico reached over and squeezed the priest's hand. 'Me too, *Padre*. And I have a daughter to look after now. We have to be clever. If we want to save Jacobo, Grazzi is our only hope.'

⁂

Angelo and Rico bumped along in the truck Don Philippe borrowed from the commune, all three of them huddled together on the front seat. It was the first time Angelo had ventured so far from Monterini.

The landscape had changed from poplars and pines to palms and cacti. Plants Angelo had never seen before painted the roadside with splashes of reds, pinks and purples. Don Philippe told him they were bougainvillea and only grew near the coast. Could this really be the province of Salone, with its long stretches of sandy beaches, unusual plants and glimpses of the sea? It was as if he were discovering a new country.

It took nearly three hours to reach the seaside town of Grosseto. They were stopped twice. They showed their papers and smiled at the group of Italian and German soldiers, listening to the sound of the two languages floating in the air.

They had nothing to hide, they were doing nothing clandestine, but each time the truck was stopped, droplets of sweat erupted on Angelo's skin. He glanced at Rico and Don Philippe from the corner of his eye. Rico always appeared calm, laughing and joking with the Italian soldiers, greeting the German ones with their traditional Roman salute. But each time they were stopped Angelo noticed how Don Philippe's hand shook on the steering wheel of the truck, his gaze directed ahead at the grey-green hills, the sun splicing through clouds.

Angelo had called earlier that morning from the post office in Monterini. It had been easier than expected to get an appointment with Grazzi. When they reached Grosseto, they asked directions to the Gestapo head office. It was located in an old building outside the main city walls, close to the beach. The crumbling structure was bleached by the sun. The air smelt of salt, Angelo could almost taste it on his tongue.

At the entrance was a jasmine with whitish-yellow flowers. Angelo inhaled. The sweet scent contrasted sharply with the saltiness on his breath, in the air around him. There was a sharp pang in his abdomen. He was unsure whether the jasmine flowers had reminded him how far away from Monterini he was, from his grapes, his smallholding. Or whether it was trepidation at the thought of what they were about to do? A peasant, a priest and a partisan begging the chief of police of the entire province to spare Jacobo.

Grazzi was waiting for them in a room on the first floor with glass windows that stretched from ceiling to floor. Angelo glimpsed the Mediterranean crashing on the browny, yellow sand. The sea was not sky blue, as he had imagined, but dirty silver with thick, white waves that glistened in the sunlight. Folders and papers were piled up on a large oak table that seemed to take up most of the space in the room.

Ugo Grazzi shook Angelo's hand warmly and kissed him on both cheeks. He seemed taller than Angelo remembered, with broad shoulders and a pregnant belly drooping over his belt. Grazzi's eyes narrowed when he saw Don Philippe, causing thick, bushy eyebrows to spread across his forehead. His nose twitched, as if he could smell the rotten odour of communist blood, all far too common within the priesthood. Angelo wondered if Grazzi thought Rico had been influenced by the priest. But it was too early to judge.

'Angelo. What a pleasure.'

'Pleasure for me too...' Angelo hesitated. In his hands he held a box of *Vino degli Angeli*. He placed it on the table next to the chief of police.

Grazzi's mouth lifted into a grin as he glanced at the bottles. 'Aha. This is the famous wine. You're quite a star amongst our German brethren.' His face darkened. 'But what exactly do you want, Angelo?'

'The Levis and Vetrullis have been taken.' Angelo cleared his throat. 'It was Rico here, my son, who thought we should come to you.'

'Can you help us find them?' Rico's voice sounded authoritative and smooth. He appeared solid, in control. It helped to stop the pounding in Angelo's chest.

Grazzi's fingers played with his moustache, as if he were moulding a piece of clay. He moved over to the window in the corner of the room and leaned against the frame. A deep inhale of breath.

'You're putting me in a very difficult situation. We know the Villa Sofia project took place in Monterini. We are not blind, you know; we simply chose to close our eyes. We know about operation Exit Cloud and the help from the British soldiers at the border. We also know your daughter-in-law was killed by a German.'

He turned away from the window and its view of the Grosseto coastline and looked directly into Rico's eyes. 'The same man has been missing for several weeks.'

Glistening beads formed a halo on Don Philippe's forehead.

With his shirtsleeve, Angelo reached up to wipe the sweat from his upper lip. Only Rico remained calm and unflustered, his olive skin smooth.

'We were hoping you would help Jacobo and Dottore Vetrulli. You were friends with them in Monterini, my father always used to talk about you. How you played the same games as Bella and me, how you used to swim in the Fiorina waterfall and skim pebbles in the Piccolina.'

'We are particularly tough with the *partigiani*,' Grazzi interrupted, spitting the words from his lips. He pronounced the word *partigiani* slowly, emphasising each syllable and with a look of disdain, as if it were venomous. 'Do you know what Priebke says, Rico? For each dead German soldier, he wants us to kill ten of ours. Partisans are best, of course, but any will do, and I have three here, right under my nose.'

Erich Preibke was the German captain in charge of the entire country, that much Angelo knew. He was aware of the sound of panting in the room. Muffled fear mingled with the cadence of breath.

'We know exactly what Priebke has done at the Fosse Ardeatine.' Rico's voice was icily calm but the muscles around his eyes and mouth twitched. 'We know about the slaughter of Roman Jews, and ordinary Italian men, not just *partigiani*. We'll use this to our advantage when the Americans and French arrive. When the war ends, they'll be the ones who'll be particularly tough with those of you on the other side.' Rico stopped abruptly as though he wanted to create a greater effect. He continued slowly, enunciating each word. 'And particularly lenient with those who make amends.'

The tension in the room pricked Angelo's skin. Rico broke the silence. 'Please remember, Signor Grazzi, Jacobo is a Jew. Not a partisan.'

Grazzi breathed out a whistle of air. His complexion had

changed from rosy pink to slate grey. 'Yes, and for us, that is a bonus. Unfortunately, not for the Germans.'

'But you are influential, Signor Grazzi,' Rico persisted; the twitching muscles had relaxed back into the fine features of his handsome face. He had the upper hand. 'And if anyone could sort it out, it would be you. I'm sure your superiors will listen to someone of such important rank. And as the Nazis retreat, we need good, strong leaders to deal with the Allied forces and to get our *Italia* back on track.'

Angelo was confounded by his son's bravery, his fearlessness. The son of a *contadino*, putting the chief of police to shame. Who would have thought it?

Grazzi stroked the badges on his uniform. There were two rows glinting on the left side of his chest. '*È vero*. I am influential, that's true.' He was like a peacock, crowned with feathers of pride. Ignoring Rico, he winked at Angelo directing the conversation towards him. 'I'll see what I can do, Angelino, but I can't promise.'

Grazzi stamped his foot, his arm stretched out in front to salute them, then marched out of the room. They could hear his hushed voice through the walls. Angelo looked across at Rico; features solid, unwavering, fists clenching and unclenching. He stared out of the window at the pounding waves, refusing to meet his father's gaze

Don Philippe collapsed on a black leather chair besides Grazzi's desk. Behind it was a large mahogany bookcase with layers of books. Angelo wondered how many came from Jacobo's bookshop. He screwed up his eyes to read the titles. But he was still slow in forming letters into words. He longed to ask Rico what he meant by the Fosse Ardeatine but was reluctant to break the silence of the room.

After what felt like hours, Grazzi reappeared, wiping his forehead with a handkerchief. 'I've just spoken to headquarters in Rome. We believe they've been sent to Fossoli di Carpi, the transit camp in Emilia-Romagna. It may be too late, but I've put in a good word.'

Grazzi perched on the edge of his desk and arched his eyebrows at Rico. 'Priebke is on the war path. He doesn't care who he kills; a Jew, a partisan or a simple postman delivering letters in Grosseto or Monterini. He'll kill us all to save his own skin.'

He slid off the desk, walked right up to Rico and pressed his nose against Rico's ear. Angelo tilted his head forward to hear what Grazzi was saying. 'What happened at the Fosse is a tragedy. And one day Erich Priebke will pay for it. But in the meantime, we'll try to save Jacobo. And in return, I expect you to vouch for me when the time comes.' He leaned back and continued in a louder voice. 'As for you, young man, be sensible, you know what I mean?'

They all knew what he meant.

Back in the truck, a combination of relief and worry overcame Angelo. The meeting had gone better than he'd expected, but it was clear Jacobo was in danger and possibly Rico too. Grazzi was right, his son had to be sensible. There was only so much Herr Bauer would do to protect them. If only the Americans would hurry up and arrive. He gazed out of the window at the waves licking the beach. 'We should have listened to Jacobo all those years ago,' he said.

'It wouldn't have changed anything,' Rico replied. 'Jacobo always sensed Mussolini was dangerous, but what could we have done?'

'This man will help us.' Don Philippe spoke for the first time, his voice faint and scratchy. 'Did you see the way he was looking at us? You frightened him, Rico.'

'He knew about Villa Sofia and operation Exit Cloud.' Rico

nodded at them, his lips spreading into a soft smile. 'He knew! But the Germans don't. And now there's the embarrassment of the Fosse. It's a disaster for the Italian Gestapo. Grazzi must be livid. I'm sure he'll do his best to help Jacobo.'

As they bumped along in the truck, slithers of light slid across the sky casting deep shadows on the roadside. They left the dusty, seaside town with its crashing waves and sped towards the hills, the slopes almost purple in the distance. The truck slowed down as it approached Monterini, then turned the sharp bend in the road. Honey-coloured houses sprung in front of them as if by magic. In the background Monte Amiata stood proud and majestic and the burble of the Fiorina waterfall reached Angelo's ears. At the sight of spires, the palazzo and the ragged outline of the village, a quiet calm descended over him.

He was back where he felt safe, with the smells of lavender and fennel, the stretches of purple grapes and silver-tinged olive trees. He reached for Rico's hand and squeezed it. 'This is a perfect place,' he said. He made the sign of the cross and together with Don Philippe uttered the Ave Maria prayer: *'Ave Maria, piena di grazia, il Signore è con te.'*

1946

The army truck stops at the entrance to the village. Two soldiers wearing American uniforms jump out and walk round to the far side. They stretch out their arms and guide an old man to the ground. He is wearing overalls tied with string and a ragged shirt, which billows in the evening breeze. His hair is as silver as the tops of the olive trees.

'Here we go, sir.' One of the soldiers reaches out to shake the man's hand. 'Once enemies, now friends. Pray for peace and take good care of yourself, sir.'

The man's bony fingers clasp the American soldier's hand. He attempts to speak, there is so much he needs to say. He'd like to explain he was never their enemy but all he manages to mutter is, '*Grazie.*'

The truck pulls away leaving a cloud of dust and gravel on the empty road. The setting sun stains the sky pink. How did he reach Monterini? Jacobo is not sure. The US army picked him up on the outskirts of Bologna, that much he recalls. He remembers the soldiers pointing out the Gothic Line, *La Linea Gottica*, and the remains of roadside battles where the Allied army liberated village after village from the Nazis. Burnt down parishes swept the countryside with churchyards full of mass graves. Rubble, debris, broken-down cottages scattered between fields of sunflowers bowing their mournful heads to the earth. Bridges blasted into the air, leaving chasms between riverbanks.

Exhausted faces staring at him from remains of ruined homes. Bumping along next to the soldiers, he was struck by a passage from the writings of the Kabbalists: 'Do not be daunted by the enormity of the world's grief. Although God feeds the universe it often appears broken.'

He watched dust settle on ruined towns and villages burnt by the Nazis or bombed by the Allies, and he remembered the words of Isaac Luria, the Kabbalist he'd read whilst sitting under the pear tree in Angelo's smallholding: 'We are all shards of broken vessels tumbling through life.'

It seemed like centuries ago, but the impact of those words spiralled through him.

He places his cheek against the golden walls of his village, wondering whether he would ever find the spark of divine energy Luria spoke of in his writings. He breathes in the familiar damp smell of the *tufo*, feels the crusty flakes peel away. Pigeons nestling in the cracks above his head peer down their beaks to inspect him. He wonders what they see; matted, dirty hair; bones jutting from skin; numbers tattooed on his arm?

He sinks down onto a bench, removes his spectacles and wipes them with a corner of his shirt. It's a miracle they survived the past weeks, sleeping in haystacks, trudging through forests, past derelict towns. He replaces them and gazes at the sandcastles of rubble dotted across the piazza. The gaps between them remind him of holes in an unfinished jigsaw.

The Allies have clearly not been kind to Monterini. The fountains still adorn the centre of the piazza, but the stone lions no longer spray water patterned with sunlight from their carved mouths. Unkempt cedars surround the square, their branches tangled, the leaves heaving with layers of brown dust.

Gone is the bank and the Zerullis' bakery. In their place are deep pits of crumbled ochre. Pieces of rock like jagged swords are all that remains of the eastern wall of the palazzo. He searches for faces he recognises, but the piazza is empty, Roberto's bar boarded up, the shops in ruins. He realises that for weeks, even months he imagined his village as it had always been; bustling, brimming with Monterinesi, alive and magical. It pains him to understand that Monterini is a fragment of its former self.

Just like him.

He takes a sharp breath, inhaling the mustiness of ancient rock, the urine of cats. At least some things remain the same. He wonders whether the monastery is in ruins too. And what about the cathedral, the synagogue? His own home in Via Meravigliosa?

Forcing himself to rise, he hobbles through the piazza and along Via Roma to the Fratta, his fingers touching the golden *tufo* walls of the houses that are still standing.

Voices arrive as if in a dream. Fleeting. Sorrowful.

'Jacobo, Jacobo.'

He senses hands flowing towards him, touching the ripped shirt, feeling the bones jut from his skin. Rabbi Coen appears before him, a pale figure, his beard milkier and longer than Jacobo remembers.

'Come to the service tonight, Jacobo. *Per favore,*' the rabbi pleads. 'We don't have any men.'

Jacobo rubs his eyes as the rabbi evaporates leaving Signora Servi clutching a stack of *challas.* 'For the Sabbath.' Her face is as flaky as the village walls.

Santina is waiting for him at the corner of Via Meravigliosa, next to her are the twins Mateo and Carlo wearing the grey-green uniform of the Italian army. Bloody bandages drape their heads, like coloured scarves. Santina twists a rosary through her fingers. It slips and falls but there is no sound of beads cascading through the cobbled streets. She places two icy hands on Jacobo's cheeks and smiles, a watery smile. Then she is gone. The twins fade into rubble.

Jacobo squeezes his eyes shut, 'Am I dreaming?' When he opens his eyes, the street is empty. Two kittens frolic under a streetlamp, tickling each other with tiny paws.

'Keep walking, *babbo*! Stay in the world of the living,' whispers a voice he recognises. As he hobbles along the cobblestones, a slender hand reaches under his elbow and guides him down the street.

The house stands in front of him, its black shutters cover the windows like a widow's veil. Dead leaves fill the flowerpots where geraniums once stood. 110 Via Meravigliosa with the view of the valley and the vineyards; the view he tried to imagine night after night but which, like a faded painting, never seemed to be as accurate as the original.

A mountain of rocks covers the house where the Ghiones once lived. Jacobo blinks but the rubble remains. He reaches out for the iron railing and pulls himself up to the veranda where a spider's web, as delicate as lace curtains, frames the entrance. He sinks onto the stone steps carpeted with crumbs of *tufo*.

Soft footsteps. A hand strokes his shoulder.

'*Bella, sei tu?*'

He clasps the hand, but it is too rough, too large with watery, purple markings. He catches the familiar aroma of wine, earth and mustiness that he always associates with Angelo.

Words scramble into the evening air. 'It's me, your Angelo. *Benvenuto* Jacobo. Welcome home, at last.'

Jacobo raises his eyes. Familiar pockmarks still stain Angelo's skin, but there are deeper groves now, around his mouth, along the bridge of his nose. And his eyes are tear filled. Jacobo reaches up to touch Angelo's cheek. He wonders if

Angelo can tell Jacobo's soul is dead. Will he notice his bleeding gums, his skin the colour of faded daffodils?

Angelo wraps his arms around Jacobo and carries him across the veranda and into the house where he was born. A child with a head of orange flames touches Jacobo's arm, near the patch of black numbers.

'It's *nonno*,' Angelo whispers.

The child backs away. An impish, heart-shaped face with startling blue eyes peeps at Jacobo from behind Angelo's legs. Jacobo reaches out to touch her hair. She lets him run his fingers through it.

'Her name is Fortuna.' Rico stands by the dresser in the kitchen. The crockery and vases balance neatly on the shelves, just as Jacobo remembers. Rico moves towards him and places his hands on Jacobo's shoulders. His touch is gentle as if he knows how delicate Jacobo is, how he might disintegrate if he presses too severely.

Rico's face is still handsome. His smooth, olive skin; the thick dark hair that sweeps across the top half of his face in a gesture of rebellion. But there is something different. The look of childish innocence and daring adolescence has mutated into something Jacobo can't quite put his finger on; a mixture of defeat, acceptance and loss all at once.

Rico wraps his arms around Jacobo. 'We've been waiting for you, *zio*. We never gave up hope.' He points towards the child. 'This is Bella's daughter.'

Angelo hands Jacobo a tumbler of wine and they drink together: the Jew, the *contadino* and the partisan.

Angelo tells Jacobo of the night the sky exploded, his house with grey shutters reduced to fragments along with Herr Bauer. Santina and Signora Franca had been employed as cleaners and were mopping the kitchen floor when crimson streaks of fire

338

engulfed them all. Carlo and Mateo are dead too, Angelo tells him sleepily, as if the act of naming the dead makes it more real; Carlo in the battle of Monte Cassino, Mateo in the battle of Anzio.

They ask about Lea, her daughters, the Vetrullis. Jacobo tries to tell them about the morning the soldiers from the Alto Adige lurched through the ferns and bracken of La Gita. He parts his lips to relate the fate of Lea and Luciana; the long, painful journey that followed. His separation from the Vetrullis at the camp; the blisteringly cold winter. The discovery that only he, Jacobo, survived. He longs to tell them how he searched fruitlessly for Elena. His tongue is leaden, his mouth a desert.

Softly, they tell him about Bella.

As the final rays of sun slice the sky, he sees her standing by the kitchen door; pale, slender, her wild hair as fiery and unruly as he remembers. His hands stretch towards her.

'*Mia Bella. Mia cara Bella.*'

Floating across the room, she beckons him to follow. His feet pad across the kitchen tiles. He steps onto the veranda with the pots of dead geraniums and broken tiles. She balances on the stone steps, arms reaching out.

'I'm here, *babbo*.'

'They told me you were gone.'

'I've been waiting for you to come back.'

'I survived, I returned to Monterini to find you. I wanted to see you, to tell you...'

Moments of silence.

'Tell me what, *babbo*?'

'I see them too,' he breathed into the Monterini sky. 'I scolded you, years ago, remember? But I was frightened, because I sense her too, I always have.'

Bella's eyes fill with ghost tears. '*Lo so babbo*. I know.'

'All I wanted whilst I was in that terrible place was to tell you I didn't know how to love you. I was always surrounded by that other Bella, your mother. I couldn't breathe. She was everywhere. There was no room for you.'

Bella reaches out her hand, it swirls above his head, wavers around his cheeks.

Then she is gone, slipped away into the golden stone of Monterini, into the wind, the river.

A woman in a long white dress hears Jacobo weep. She has watched the nature of the world repeat itself over and again. She longs to comfort this man, put her hand on his heart and tell him he could do nothing, she had read it all in the traces of the eggs. She is a haruspex, and this is the way of the world.

She stands with him as tears drip from his cheeks. He turns around, sniffs the air and stares into her eyes, as if he knew she was there; that spark of divine energy, the shards that play the strings of the universe.

Tanaquilla turns and disappears into the ancient folds of rock.

ACKNOWLEDGEMENT

This is a work of fiction, inspired by the heart-warming acts of kindness I have encountered in my research of this period. Thank you to the town of Pitigliano for providing the most beautiful setting for my novel and to my friends and neighbours for the stories that have inspired me. Thank you to Elena, Marino, Franco and Pietro. I would like to thank Julian Ingall who first told me about Villa Emma, the inspiration for the Villa Sofia story. I pay tribute to the memory of Salomone Papo, a character from that time, whose name I have borrowed. Thank you to Gill, Zena and my husband Julian for reading and rereading various drafts of this book, and to Laura for checking my Italian. Thank you to my family, Julian, Natasha and Jake, for supporting me throughout the writing of this novel and to Silvia, my sister in writing, for your constant encouragement and guidance. Thank you to both Stephanie and Gillian for your thoughts and comments and thank you to Heather my publisher at RedDoor for your support. Most importantly, thank you to all those who have fought and continue to fight against the scourge of fascism both in Italy and the world at large.

ABOUT THE AUTHOR

The Tears Of Monterini is Amanda's first novel. She studied Modern Languages at the University of East Anglia, followed by a PGCE at King's College London. She ran a company in International Advertising Sales and now teaches French and German. She lives in London with her family and spends a lot of time in Pitigliano Italy, the setting for the Monterini of the title. The book is inspired by true events in the Tuscany and Emilia-Romagna areas. She has literary representation by Curtis Brown.

in Amanda Weinberg

@amandaweinbergauthor

@amandaweinbergauthor

amandaweinberg_

amandaweinberg.co.uk

Find out more about RedDoor
Press and sign up to our
newsletter to hear about our
latest releases, **author events**,
exciting **competitions**
and more at

reddoorpress.co.uk

YOU CAN ALSO FOLLOW US:

 @RedDoorBooks

 Facebook.com/RedDoorPress

 @RedDoorBooks